SEAMON GLASS

HALF-ASSED MARINES

iUniverse, Inc.
New York   Bloomington

HALF-ASSED MARINES

iUniverse books may be ordered through booksellers or by contacting:

iUniverse
1663 Liberty Drive
Bloomington, IN 47403
www.iuniverse.com
1-800-Authors (1-800-288-4677)

Because of the dynamic nature of the Internet, any Web addresses or links contained in this book may have changed since publication and may no longer be valid. This is a work of fiction. All of the characters, names, incidents, organizations, and dialogue in this novel are either the products of the author's imagination or are used fictitiously.

ISBN: 978-1-4502-3563-1 (pbk)
ISBN: 978-1-4502-3564-8 (ebk)

Printed in the United States of America
iUniverse rev. date: 9/8/10

I dedicate these World War Two memories to Anna Glass, my wonderful departed mother. Despite maternal misgivings the harassed lady finally succumbed to persistent pressure from her contrary son. Seven months before my eighteenth birthday the loving lady reluctantly signed the document permitting my enlistment. Also, in fond memory of my stalwart father, Kadysh Glass, who passed on when I was eleven.

Appreciative accolades are due Yan, my wife. She arrived on this earth many, many years after my departure from the United States Marine Corps. While I was teaching in China, she became the bastion of my life. For seventeen years, she zealously encouraged, entreated, and literally compelled me to wrap up this novel. Completion would not have occurred without her loving prodding and assistance.

PREFACE

During eighty-four years of accumulated memories, and what I have are more than a few, among my most notable are those experienced during World War Two.

Naturally, historic recollections distort, fade, or incrassate. Thus, I ensure readers that characters in this narrative are fictional and certainly not intended to personify living or dead individuals.

Dates, locations, military happenings and incidents relevant to the tales are, to the best of my fading recollection, infused with varied validities.

I do, however, vividly recall that during World War Two, the majority of Marines and navy corpsmen encountered, as well as those not, were strong of character, sterling Americans determined to defend our beloved homeland.

Of course, I did not meet the huge majority of soldiers, sailors, coast guardsmen, and Marines who fought for our country, nobody did.

Many who survived came home broken and devastated. But the rest of us followed orders and most of us returned mentally and physically unscarred.

Countless civilians not in uniform because of age, sex, or physical infirmities also gallantly served our nation.

I judge World War Two to be our nation's last worthwhile, great, wartime challenge. Americans, I'm proud to say, met the challenge head-on and victory was ours.

CHAPTER ONE

Brian O'Bannion, Jacob Cruz, and I furtively trailed Earl Titmus through the barracks door and into the thick foliaged boondocks, as somber sounds of taps resounded across Norman, Oklahoma's Naval Air Station.

As we steathly made way through the dark woods, millions of crickets opened up. Titmus abruptly held up his hand and stopped to listen. O'Bannion braked behind him but his sudden halt caused me to come down on his heel and he snapped, "Watch where the hell you're going!"

"Your fuckin' fault!" I retorted.

"Bullshit!"

"Shut the hell up!" Titmus rasped. "You idiots want to get us caught!" He sullenly moved on and we mutely followed.

Titmus stood just over six-feet and was a compact two-hundred. He was thirty-three or thirty-four and compared to us three, and other teen-aged fuck-ups in the fuck-up barracks, he was an old salt.

Six years prior to Pearl Harbor Titmus had been a teamster navigating a two ton truck over country roads in Wyoming and neighboring states. Between hauls, according to him, he was getting drunk and laid, or laid and drunk.

After being arrested for drunken brawling, not for the first or second time, a Wyoming judge familiar with his disorderly behavior decreed, "Get your ass in the Marines or go to jail!" He chose the Corps.

Much of the time Titmus was a squared away Marine, but during his military stint he had gotten into jackpots costing him stripes, money, brig time, and blemishes in his record book.

America had been at war for little over a year and Titmus was reluctantly on his second hitch, we three had only been out of San Diego's Marine boot camp less than four months. Nevertheless, wary as we were, this escapade made us feel a touch salty; we didn't want to be ear-banging candy-assed Marines.

It was his current romantic interest, Millie Gaylord that had prompted this precarious exploit. She had recently disembarked in Oklahoma City from San Diego and Titmus was determined to see her.

We three had never met the lady, but he had ardently described her feminine virtues. He assured us that she more than likely had provocative female friends who would be more than pleased to entertain three bucko Marines.

The three of us were months into our seventeenth year. I had been in the eleventh grade struggling to make it to the twelfth when the Japs attacked. Sure, long before Pearl Harbor I was motivated to kill Nazis, but at sixteen, even at six feet three inches high and weighed in at two-hundred and two pounds, I was still too young to legally go to war.

Ten months after that December 7th "Day of Infamy" I turned seventeen, but my mother's endorsement was required in order for me to enlist.

"Go when you turn eighteen and you're called," she pleaded, "that's why they don't draft until a boy reaches a mature age."

"Lots of guys are going before they're eighteen! By the time I'm that old this war could be over. Some kids even lie before they're sixteen. I remember reading about that big thirteen-year-old kid on Guadacanal."

"Imagine his poor mother."

"Mom, I don't want to be drafted into the army, I want to be a Marine."

"Wait! Wait! Please wait! This war will keep going for a long time."

"Germans are murdering Gypsies, Jews, Americans and lots of others. It's my duty as an American and a Jew. The Japs have attacked and are killing us. We got to fight back." I repeated patriotic rites over and over.

"Only a few more months and you'll be old enough. Then you can go into the army like everyone else."

I wouldn't wait. I wouldn't listen. I was eager to fight Nazis and Japs. Poor Mother, she didn't want her irascible child to be in harm's way.

"If you won't sign, Mom, I'll go to San Pedro and ship out in the merchant marine."

"The merchant marines are bums," she sighed.

I winced. She had no idea that Jake Amato, my close friend, and I had already skipped school and tried to ship out on a merchant ship. What stopped us was the frowning dispatcher from the Sailors Union of the Pacific at Union Hall. He demanded birth certifications proving that we were eighteen. Of course, both of us were too dumb to figure out how to get a phony one.

"If I have to, Mom, I'll forge your name and lie about my age. Our country needs me. I'll do whatever it takes to do my duty!" I dramatically repeated.

"Wait!" she implored.

Like multitudes of other American teenagers I was a flag waver, but other factors added zest to my patriotic zeal. For instance, Mother didn't know how bad my school grades were. I couldn't have graduated anyway.

At the beginning of the school semester, for disciplinary reasons, I had been transferred from Alexander Hamilton High School to Venice. Several weeks into what should have been the beginning of my last school year, I stood fidgeting in Vice-Principal Slaugh's office alongside four credit-short seniors.

I was new to Venice High and only knew the other hulks by name and football reputation. I sensed that they shared similar feelings about killing Nazis and Japs.

"The colors are calling," Slaugh said, as if we didn't know, "America's at war."

Ten eyes shifted from the wall to the floor and back. Sure, I craved a crack at Nazis and Japs, but felt uneasy being prodded by this pompous administrator. "Have you stout patriots thought about answering your country's call to arms?"

After reading about Colonel Carlson's heroic 2nd Raider Battalion wreaking havoc on Makin Island and watching "*To the Shores of Tripoli*" and "*Wake Island*", I was more than eager to be a leatherneck fighting for flag and country. Day and night dreams featured battlefield heroics and beribboned medals being bestowed before admiring crowds.

"You boys can serve your country and get your diplomas," said our stalwart vice-principal, inflecting a touch of sarcasm.

We shuffled. Enlisting was as good an excuse as any to get out of school.

Motivational tidings were being spread around Venice High. Rumors were afloat that "seniors" leaving school to serve in the armed forces would, like Slaugh hinted, be awarded a diploma. An inscribed certificate ensuring that despite academic shortcomings, her son had graduated would make mother happy, especially if she didn't know the sham details regarding the gratuitous diploma.

Besides patriotic fervor I harbored other reasons which motivated me to become a Marine. Sorely lacking academic proficiency, mechanical ability or other visible skills, I did attain fair grades in creative writing classes. Thus, I envisioned becoming a writer in the mode of Mark Twain, Jack London or Ernest Hemingway. I reasoned that in order to create imaginative and meaningful prose, it would be obligatory to experience daunting adventures.

Days, weeks, and months flitted by and I kept wheedling and threatening to become involved in varied questionable endeavors in order to go to war. Five months beyond my seventeenth birthday my harassed mother sighed and signed.

She sadly watched her only child and twenty other seventeen-year old prospective warriors sworn in. She tearfully waved farewell while we boarded the bus headed for the United States Marine Corps Recruit Depot in San Diego.

Getting through boot camp was my first militaristic hurdle. Drill instructors Sergeant Lichtenberger, Corporal Downey and Private Boydstun were my three stalwart platoon leaders. They were spit-and-polish squared-away career Marines. On top of their chosen professions they were decent human beings. We boots in Platoon 183 were fortunate and we knew it.

The D.I.s in charge of neighboring 182 and 184 platoons were screaming sadists. Maybe that's why several shitbirds in those platoons didn't cut it.

I was deeply disappointed by narrowly failing to achieve "expert" status on the rifle range. However, being designated a "sharpshooter" was the next best. Sharpshooters were authorized to wear an imposing metallic cross above left chest pockets signifying marksmanship accomplishment. In addition to a buck private's fifty, sharpshooters were awarded three extra dollars per month, an appreciative sum.

By the time eight weeks of boot camp elapsed, a small group of sadsacks from other platoons, attired in outlandish checkered sportcoats, forlornly stood waiting to be shipped home. Some would become soldiers.

Anyway, boot camp seemed to take too long but youthful eagerness and exuberance in our platoon wasn't tempered because everyone in 183 made it. After completing the vigorous boot camp grind we recruits responded with appreciation by collecting a traditional cash gift for each of our drill instructors.

Shortly before the culmination of bootcamp, a placement-sergeant ordered each recruit to opt for an assignment preference. I pictured myself spiffed-up in immaculate dress blues staunchly firing a secondary gun from a cruiser. I stated my first choice, "I want to be a seagoing Marine."

"Sea School is full," said the sergeant.

Oh, well. Another gallant vision featured me harnessed to a parachute gliding through the air prior to performing daring deeds behind enemy lines. Although far from comfortably functioning in lofty quarters, I rationalized that I would enable myself to jump from an airplane. Hah!

Weighing in at two-hundred settled that option. "Too much weight for the paramarines," yawned the sergeant.

Being a rifleman in one of the elite raider battalions also sounded enticing, but again, my quest was nullified when the sergeant doefully confided, "Fifteen thousand Marines have volunteered for our three raider battalions. Their fifteen hundred quotas were filled months ago."

The sergeant was losing patience. "Choose something reasonable or you're off to Cooks and Bakers School."

That stunned me. Another attractive option suddenly loomed in my immature mind.

I envisioned soaring aloft decimating Nazis, Japs or both in man-to-man air combat. "How about if I become a fighter pilot?"

A weary smirk spread over the interviewer's face as he scribbled in his black book, "Now you're talking, Pilot."

I was recalling that despite my misgivings, several teachers had confided to me that they believed I was smarter than I acted. Of course, it wasn't until years later after I became one of them did I realize that phraseology was well worn among pedagogues.

After my stint as a pilot, I reflected, I would again opt for Sea School or the raiders.

During the recruit depot's final boot camp review, as a tearfully touched mass of relatives cheered while being pumped up by the stirring

Marine Corps Hymn, we proudly beamed with other graduating platoons strutting across the San Diego Parade Ground.

Whimsical but proud, my mother wept as she viewed the boot camp graduation ceremony. Afterwards, I promised her I'd come back in one piece, possibly with a medal or two.

"No medals!" she plaintively implored.

CHAPTER TWO

Eighteen of us teenage would-be pilots were transferred to Camp Miramar located on the outskirts of San Diego. In less than an hour we prospective flyboys cockily dismounted from olive-hued trucks. After being assigned Quonset huts we squared away our gear and lined up outside.

Platoon Sergeant Hans Olaff, an old China Hand with an evil grin, greeted us. "Another bunch of shitbird fighter pilots, eh?"

We hadn't been out of boot camp long enough to know how badly we were being snowed and shouted, "Yes, sir!"

The old fart's inflections and demeanor were far from encouraging but his next comment enlightened us, "You candy-assed fuckers sound and look dumber than the last bunch of would-be pilots!" He spat and nodded toward a mole-faced corporal who marched us to a shed and issued shovels.

"Shoulder shovels!" roared Olaff. He counted cadence in a raspy voice as he marched us to a small mountain of dirt. He pointed. "That fuckin' pile was put there by the last fuckin' candy-assed pilots. You fuckin' shitbirds move that fuckin' pile from here to there!" We gaped.

"Commence shoveling!"

We dug. "Your pilot training has begun. See, shitbirds, you pile it here, then there, and you'll be pilots. Get it?" cackled Olaff.

He wasn't funny. "Move it!"

As we shoveled, Olaff sing-songed, "*Oh, pile-it here, boys, pile-it there.*" Illusions of piloting planes quickly dissipated.

"Lighten up, fly-boys, you'll soon be flying sergeants, hah! Maybe you'll even get commissioned."

Someone had neglected to tell the old bastard that we weren't boots and should be treated with a touch of respect. Several earbangers forced a grin, not me. If collective thoughts could kill, Olaff would have been stone cold dead.

By the time daylight faded, we were physically and morally vexed, exhausted and covered with grime. Olaff merrily chanted cadence as we stumbled back to our Quonset huts where we shed our rancid fatigues and staggered to the showers. After gulping down chow at the messhall we crawled into our sacks and conked out.

Four days of dirt-digging passed before change occurred. Ladened with packs and slung rifles we galloped up and down the green hills bordering San Diego. Sergeant Olaff, like a kid on a romp, merrily jogged over the hills bellowing the "pilot-it here, pilot-there" crap.

Occasionally he slowed down to a quick-paced walk and ordered us to sing the Marine Corps Hymn. For an old beer-guzzling fart he was in good physical shape.

At first it was a sort of stimulating singing, "From the halls of Montezuma to the shores of Tripoli." But the repetition soon reduced us to wheezing and by that time the lyrics had lost their luster.

Two more weeks of digging, marching, singing and listening to Olaff's bullshit crawled by. If the opportunity had been afforded, I, along with others, would have volunteered for a suicide detail.

A fateful day finally arrived; the shit-duty eternity was over. We lined up for transfer orders. A second lieutenant holding sheets of names and designations strode down our khaki clad lines. Sergeant Olaff followed as the officer handed each buck-assed private designation orders.

The guy on my left got assigned to the parachute-rigging school in New Jersey. I was next. "Glossman, Sherman, Clerical School in San Diego." The lieutenant handed me papers. I teared a bit as I quivered in disbelief. "I didn't enlist to push a pencil, sir." I blurted.

"What!

"Sir! I just got out of high school. "

"So!"

"I enlisted to fight, not push a pencil," I strived to hold back tears as I whined.

"Says here you took a typing class."

"Before I enlisted, sir, I was in that class less than two weeks, honest to god. Got a "D" minus, would have failed, but the teacher said, "You're going off to war and will probably die so I'll give you a passing grade."

The lieutenant glared. I fought it but a tear rolled. "Honest to god, sir!"

"I don't know...."

"I can't type, sir, not even a little. My spelling ain't good either," I plaintively added. Another tear came close to rolling as I silently implored.

The lieutenant's eyes narrowed. "Well, we can use airplane mechanics."

"Yes, sir!" I shouted, relieved to be designated something other than an office pinky.

The young officer shook his head and muttered, "Glossman, Aviation Mechanic School, Norman, Oklahoma."

"Thank you, sir! Thank you!" He didn't return my snappy salute.

He called out the next private's designation, "Rifle Company, Camp Pendelton."

The guy gasped, "What the fuck, sir, I been a grease-monkey all my life."

"Watch your fuckin' language!" snarled Olaff.

"I'm into oil, sir, I bathe in it, honest to god."

"You're a Marine!" snapped the lieutenant. "Get yourself covered in oil and you'll be court-martialed for screwing up government property."

Olaff grinned.

"Sir!" whined the poor bastard.

The next guy was assigned to radio school in Jacksonville. "Sir, I've tried, really tried, but I can't tell a dot from a dash."

The lieutenant was unmoved. "Can you type?"

"Not at all, sir, I'm dumber than cat shit." As they moved on, the lieutenant's eyes narrowed in impatience and Olaff smirked.

I was elated at the chance to learn a respectable trade and decided that I was one lucky guy.

I stood among twenty-five or thirty others designated to become Airedales. That was the sobriquet for enlistees serving in Marine air squadrons. Trucks hauled us to the San Diego railroad depot where we were marched into a waiting troop train.

Hundreds of uniformed personnel from multiple military facilities were already aboard. The Miramar contingent was asigned to attend one of naval aviation's gunnery, ordinance, or mechanical schools on the Norman, Oklahoma Naval Base. Others were headed to other schools or deployments.

I happily concluded that Mother would feel better knowing I wasn't just a rifleman. After all, a mechanic, especially one with aviation know-how, is a trade that could be utilized and respected in civilian life. The more I mused about it the more I became enamored with the prospect of becoming an airplane mechanic. If determination was a factor I would inevitably become the best damn mechanic in the Corps.

Besides Oklahoma, the terminus for sailors, soldiers, and other Marines aboard the train varied. Cars were crowded with swabjockies and Marines heading to schools in Tennessee or Florida. Dogfaces on their way to East Coast camps filed aboard.

At the last moment four sallow-faced tipsy Marine noncoms staggered aboard. Their chests were adorned with Asian Pacific combat ribbons. These Guadacanal vets were in charge of Marine enlistees. They didn't seem interested in anything other than the bottles of rotgut they waved about.

The train lurched forward and we were off to adventure and a career launch. I had a window seat and complacently viewed the passing landscape while listening to the sound of steel humming over tracks.

The train made periodic stops and we were marched off to chow-down at Howard Johnson Restaurants. Meals were okay but nothing to look forward to except the opportunity to vanquish teenage hunger pains.

We were jauntily aware of the awed and curious looks directed at us during our short stays in small town eateries. Some onlookers assumed we were dauntless warriors going forth to save the nation. As we disembarked people stared and a few even applauded. Our unseasoned faces fooled most, not all.

"Marines are savages" and "cold-blooded killers" were rumors that preceded us, especially through the central states. Poor old Eleanor Roosevelt was blamed for spreading that nonsense.

At a station in Iowa, O'Bannion snarled at a couple of kids. They were impressed, but not their mother. She called O'Bannion a savage asshole.

On the train bottles of booze began to appear. I wasn't a drinker nor were most other recruits, but when a bottle passed among us, we forced the rancid stuff down.

After five tedious days the train finally pulled into Oklahoma City. We were a bedraggled bunch and stunk. As we disembarked, Mario Canelli, a guy from the Bronx who had been in my bootcamp platoon, pointed at a sign secured above one of two water fountains. "Coloreds only," it warned. Guys from the South thought nothing of it. But seeing the inscribed threat was unsettling to East and West Coast teenagers.

We climbed into waiting trucks. The gray navy vehicles hauled us directly to the Naval Aviation Station situated in Norman.

No airfield or operational aircraft were on the base. The purposes of the three schools at the huge facility were to train young navy and Marine Corps enlistees to become aircraft mechanics, aircraft metal workers or aviation ordinance personnel.

Only living quarters and classrooms were spread across the vast premises. Most of the barracks were filled with sailors. Several were designated for Marines. We were assigned cots and lockers.

The next day, after breakfast, we attended a school orientation where instructors issued dire warnings regarding military behavior and academic obligations. We were divided into small groups and marched to classes. Instructors demonstrated how to file, fit, and fasten integral parts onto airplanes. Day after day we were lectured about the ins and outs of engine functions and were required to memorize the nomenclature of aircraft engines.

In the eighth grade at Belvedere Junior High School in East Los Angeles, I had flunked auto shop. At Hamilton High School I received "Ds" in wood, metal and electric shop. At Venice High I opted out of taking any shop class. Despite my dismal mechanical abilities, sorrowful technical background and inaptitude, being designated a Marine Corps Aviation Mechanic sounded prestigious. I was motivated.

For a short span I tried, really tried. I listened, took notes, asked questions, but it was a hopeless endeavor. I was unable to fathom the complexities of airplane engines. My concentrated efforts evolved into exercises in futility.

It didn't take long for instructors to discover my technical inadequacies. On top of my lack of aptitude, I couldn't conceal my aversion to grease and oil. As realization set in that my mechanical aspirations would never be fulfilled, my interest in airplanes dissipated.

Of course, multitudes of sailors and hundreds of Marines attended aircraft mechanic, ordinance and sheet metal classes at Norman, Oklahoma's Naval Aviation School and the majority made it. Some had civilian mechanical experience, and those who possessed aptitude and relished the touch and smell of oil breezed through.

Those of us with mechanical inaptitude were billeted in the fuck-up barracks. Others were placed there for discipline reasons. Take Earl Titmus, he was mechanically inclined, but got booted out of ordinance school for insubordination, fighting and participating in other inappropriate military behavior while on liberty.

Rejects were required to constantly sweep and police our barracks. Although we were fuck-ups, we consistently surpassed Marine and navy competitors in the weekly inspections. It wasn't long before the barrack surveys became boring. We had joined up to fight Japs and Nazis not outdo swabjockies in spit and polish competitions.

CHAPTER THREE

Like Cruz and me, Brian O'Bannion had been bounced out of Norman's school and transferred to the "Fuck-up Barracks." Born and raised in Boston he appeared ganglier than his wiry six-feet. He was four months younger than me but had enlisted four days earlier. He was inclined to berate me with, "You shoulda been in the old Corps." Our aversion to oil was one of several characteristics we shared.

O'Bannion was an odd bird. He consistently babbled about Boston. According to him it was the best place in the world. Boston guys were tougher, Boston Irish girls were prettier and the city's citizens were more dependable. The hometown events, the gorgeous girls he had wooed and the guys he had fought were too numerous to enumerate.

If his tales weren't so chock full of bullshit, he'd be seventy instead of seventeen. But call him out on one of his stories and be ready to fight. He wouldn't back down and handled himself better than average. If a loudmouth was critical of the flag, muttered a derogatory remark about someone's mother or spat a negative word about Catholics, the perpetrator would have a conventional fight on his hands. However, if you bad-mouthed the Corps, you'd have to kill him.

O'Bannion and I were sidekicks but we had our differences, plenty of them. He grumbled negatively about Jews, Italians, Polacks, Protestants, soldiers, sailors, Texans and other Irishmen. He was especially verbally indicative about Irish compatriots.

15

Before meeting me he had never met a Jew. Far from being a narrow-minded bigot, O'Bannion unsparingly hated everyone equally. That made him sort of a unique liberal.

O'Bannion did love the Corps, and he respected Titmus who was tough enough to wipe the barracks up with him and two or three others at the same time. Titmus was O'Bannion's idea of how a Marine should look and act. I held similar thoughts.

Jacob Cruz, short, muscled and Mexican, weighed a solid hundred and forty-five. He and I met in Platoon 183. He was from Boyle Heights, a short distance west of my home in Belvedere so we had common topics to bullshit about. To him, being both Mexican and a Marine were parallel commitments.

When New Yorker Canelli accusingly asked him whether he had been one of those zoot suiters ganging up on service personnel in Los Angeles, he clenched his fists and retorted, "What if I was!" Canelli was spooked and sauntered off. Jacob wouldn't take shit from anybody without rank.

He surprised me by joining our AWOL venture. I knew that even more than me, he wasn't happy screwing up. He trailed close behind me and I used my elbow to keep him from wheezing on the nape of my neck.

O'Bannion ambled along like a guy accustomed to running from cops. At times he proved to be a shifty character and I was wary of him. His stark blue eyes and baby face fooled some but not me, no sir. However, to be candid, I liked O'Bannion. Outside of his constant goldbricking, bickering and twisted sense of humor he wasn't a bad guy.

Compared to us, Titmus was a salty character. Thick eyebrows tapered down to the bridge of his nose which had been flattened by overhand rights. One front tooth was missing. A replacement had filled the gap, but weeks before in the outlying town of Shawnee, prior to exchanging blows with a soldier, he had handed his single-toothed bridge to a sailor and asked him to hold it. While he and the soldier swung at each other, shore patrol bozos arrived. Titmus and his dogface opponent set aside their discord and resisted arrest. As reinforcements arrived the swabbie vanished. The melee as well as Titmus' tooth was lost.

With or without the molar Titmus was formidable looking. His countenance reflected, "One's gone and I don't give a damn if another goes." His bunk was below mine.

Millie was Titmus' fiancée and the darling of his heart. According to Titmus they first meshed when she was a waitress in a San Diego bar. It was romance at first or second sight. Ever since, they'd been preparing for a future together.

About that time the Japs bombed Pearl Harbor and their future was on hold because Titmus was stuck for the duration. Millie was the primary reason why Titmus wanted out of the Corps. I was more than a little curious to get a gander at her.

Now he hadn't exactly conned the three of us into coming, but had implied, not guaranteed, that we would down beers, connect with some ladies and return undetected.

Cruz and I had never been laid and Titmus' casual incentive was enticing. O'Bannion, of course, claimed he had been an active Lothario and bedding down with damsels was no big thing. I suspected his sexual claims to be pure bullshit.

It was O'Bannion's fault that we had gotten restricted in the first place. The four of us had been downing beer at the slopchute. Three brews and O'Bannion, as usual, was out of line. When he stumbled against a table of swabbies, beer spilled and a skinny navy guy got upset. Pushing and cursing ensued, nothing serious, but the Master at Arms, a navy guy, overseeing the slopchute ran us up for inciting a free-for-all.

Titmus, O'Bannion, Cruz, the sailors, and I got nailed with two weeks base restriction. On top of that we were ordered to stay out of the slopchute.

The slopchute wasn't that enticing but Oklahoma's three-two beer was inexpensive. To be candid, most of us didn't have enough money to traipse ashore more than a few times a month anyway.

Cool as a cucumber, Titmus furtively led us to the thick growth bordering the school. A forested area began where the pavement left off and continued to the outer perimeter fence. The thick growth of trees extended fifty yards to the northeast.

The barbed wire barrier was unlit but we could distinguish our own shadowy forms. As we approached the wire, Titmus motioned us to halt. "No guards," he whispered as he trotted to the fence.

Careful not to snag his pants he climbed over. We did the same and traipsed the length of a football field into a darkened neighborhood. We came to a stopped streetcar. As the car started to move we sprinted to its rear step-up and climbed aboard. We paid the conductor and sat.

We were the only uniforms on the rickety streetcar and stuck out like sore thumbs. I was uneasy. O'Bannion didn't seem comfortable either. Titmus didn't seem concerned and oblivious to our discomfort. Who knows what Cruz was thinking?

After a block or two on the jolting trolley we spotted a tavern and dismounted. Wooden furniture and a few cowboy decorations affirmed that we were in a typical Oklahoma City beer joint. Without asking, the bartender poured four schooners. Beer was a dime apiece. Titmus threw half-a-buck on the bar.

Our khakis were damp and streaked with chlorophyll. Cruz's uniform was the cleanest but his shoes were as caked as ours. Half-expecting the military police or a shore patrol pair to walk in my eyes nervously focused on the door. If we got nailed without passes it would mean a stint in the brig and an additional blot in my record book.

The first swallow of cold brew tasted good. I was still getting acclimated to drinking and wasn't crazy about the second but wasn't about to let on. In spite of his consistent bragging, O'Bannion wasn't much of a drinker but intently gulped down his libation.

Titmus rose, "I gotta take a leak."

"When we heading back?" I whispered.

"We just got here," snickered O'Bannion as if I didn't know.

"Why are we here!" I blurted.

"We told you."

"Tell me again."

"For the tenth time, we're gonna get laid, that's why," fumed O'Bannion.

"When? How? I don't see any girls?"

Cruz shook his head.

"It's gonna happen." O'Bannion, as usual, intimated that he had shacked up with hundreds, maybe more, lovely ladies. At times he believed his own bullshit.

Titmus returned, "The Hudson Hotel is on the corner of Grand and Robinson. We got to move."

"You sure she's not gonna mind us coming?" I said.

"Nah."

"You did say Millie's got girlfriends!" said O'Bannion.

"She's never been in Oklahoma before this morning," said Titmus.

"What about those other females you mentioned?"

"Oklahoma is full of good-looking ladies. Lots of them hang around the Hudson just waiting to meet swashbuckling Marines."

Cruz belched.

"You okay, Cruz?" said Titmus.

"I'm okay."

"Let's move."

An olive hued waitress emerged from the rear. "Look," I whispered.

"I'm lookin'. That cute little lady give me the eye," said O'Bannion.

A pasty-faced sailor commenced chatting up the waitress. Something he said provoked a chuckle.

"Maybe I should charm her," said O'Bannion.

"Brian, m'boy, that girl don't know you're alive," I said.

Titmus headed for the door and Cruz fell behind. I gave O'Bannion a sour look and followed. He grumbled, but dutifully tagged along.

We cautiously made way along side streets until we spied another rinky-dink trolley and climbed aboard. Two sleeping sailors were the only other passengers. The car clattered along until we reached the heart of the city and jumped off. We followed Titmus into *Daisy Mae's*.

It was a weekday but a semi-sizable uniformed crowd was in attendance. Several swabbies and paratroopers from Fort Sill milled about; as well as aviation cadets from Clinton. Among the shuffling patrons, sailors and Marines from our base were notably absent.

The hustling waitresses' attire were similar to Al Capp's Daisy but none looked as soft or pretty as the featured hillbilly in the cartoon strip. Nevertheless, their scanty uniforms lent an appealing touch.

A scowling waitress snapped at Cruz. "You Indian?"

"Chinese," said Titmus as Cruz stuttered, "Nah, I'm Mexican!"

"I don't give a shit what you are as long as you're not an Indian."

"Lady, China and Mexico are on our side," whispered Titmus.

"Aren't the Indians?" asked O'Bannion.

"Sure, they are," I said.

"They still don't get to drink in Oklahoma because it's against federal and state law, Buster." She set the glasses down, scooped up our money and swayed away.

"Pistol Packin' Mama", a tune played time and time again in every joint in Oklahoma, blasted from the jukebox.

Titmus gulped down his beer, "Let's move."

"I want to snow that friendly blonde," said O'Bannion.

As the waitress swished by O'Bannion grabbed her arm. "The Marines have landed!"

"Yuh all want another round?" she drawled.

"Forward to aft you're as pretty a hillbilly girl as I ever laid eyes on." O'Bannion was a guy with no class, not a bit.

"Buster, I was born and raised in Tulsa and I'm too busy to jabber with a dull Gyrene! Let go," she sighed.

"Let me tell you something, darling!"

"I got no time to listen to a load of crap."

A cocky paratrooper sauntered up, boots gleaming. "Trouble, sweet pea?"

"Nah," then she gave O'Bannion a 'I'm giving you a break' look and spun away.

The dogface and O'Bannion were eyeball to eyeball, his shiny boots were in sharp contrast to O'Bannion's caked shoes. Like most paratroopers the guy was short and compact.

"You're bothering my girl!" gritted the paratrooper.

"Screw you, Dogface!" said O'Bannion.

The trooper threw a roundhouse right and O'Bannion fell into my arms. I shoved him forward and he wildly flayed until the soldier stumbled back. Cruz was merely observing when a swabbie's arm suddenly enveloped his head with one arm and poked him in the face with the other.

Titmus belted the sailor and down he went. A general melee erupted as fists and furniture flew. Sirens sounded, impelling the four of us to stumble from Daisy Mae's and sprint down the street. Titmus led us into an alley.

We were winded and Titmus was upset. "We're AWOL and you dumb bastards got to start shit."

"The dogface started it, ask Sherman."

"Huh?" I said.

"You heard that dogface!"

"I wasn't listening."

"Tell him, Jacob," said O'Bannion. Cruz shrugged.

"I don't want to hear any more bullshit!" steamed Titmus.

We moved through and out of the alley. We almost passed Chief Jim's Saloon but Titmus abruptly barged through the door. We followed and sat around a circular table. A dark-skinned girl with high cheekbones and braided hair sidled up. "Four?" she purred.

"Yeah."

"Hold on, you look too sloppy to be Marines. Oh, well, money is money."

As she glided away, O'Bannion observed, "That squaw's stacked."

"She's an Indian," warned Cruz.

"I don't give a shit what country she comes from," snapped O'Bannion.

"Indians can't drink in Oklahoma," I said.

"She's not drinking, she's serving," enlightened O'Bannion

"Don't talk! Don't do nothin' and knock off the staring!" Titmus was pissed again and I didn't blame him.

"Hear that, Brian?" I said.

"Damned!" sighed O'Bannion and stared. We followed his gaze. An attractive Indian girl was sitting two tables away and smiling. Cruz dropped his eyes and stared into his glass.

"O'Bannion, she's not looking at you," I whispered.

"She's eyeing Cruz," he reluctantly admitted.

"Easy," warned Titmus.

To break the tension, I asked, "Titmus, you got a present for Millie?"

"Nah."

"Shouldn't you have gotten her something?" said O'Bannion, as if he were an expert or even gave a shit.

"No money, no time," said Titmus.

Cruz got up and strode to the head.

"When he gets back borrow a few bucks," advised O'Bannion.

"Shops closed by now," I said.

Conversation ceased as Titmus pointed. Cruz was sitting at the Indian girl's table.

"Didn't think Jacob had it in him," said O'Bannion.

"Damn it, I better get to him before that squaw gets his money," said Titmus.

There was a sudden crash and Cruz was stretched out on the deck. A gangly Indian adorned with a long braid knelt over and pulled him up by his field scarf.

Titmus charged from his seat and slammed an overhand right into the Indian's head. O'Bannion and I were barely out of our seats when the squaw waved a beer mug and screamed, "Mexican, I kill you!"

Titmus shoved and she spilled over the table. He pulled Cruz up and ushered him outside. The four of us raced down Reno Street.

We were soon panting and slowed to a walk.

"Loco Injun." wheezed Cruz.

"All we been doing is running," I sighed.

"Bad things happen when you fool with Injuns," said O'Bannion.

"You know a helluva lot about Indians!" I sneered.

"Shut the fuck up!"shouted O'Bannion.

I planted my feet and raised my fists.

"You assholes want to get us locked up!" snarled Titmus.

"Not me," said O'Bannion.

"Not me," I echoed.

Titmus turned crimson. "Don't want me to see Millie, do you?"

"Nothing wrong with Indians," said Cruz and glared at O'Bannion.

"No more bullshit. That's an order!" said Titmus

We sullenly traipsed along until we rounded a corner and came face to face with a four man shore patrol contingent. Both of our groups were startled.

Our mutual paralysis quickly passed and we turned and bolted. As we raced away the swabbies followed swinging their clubs.

Titmus led us around a corner into a shadowed alley. Cruz spurted ahead and O'Bannion and I, gasping for air, followed. Three of the sailors quit the chase but the fourth kept coming.

Titmus looked back. "Why we running?" he slowed to a walk. Still wheezing we did the same. As the oncoming sailor approached we halted and turned. Befuddled, the swabbie stopped and pointed to his armband. We strode toward him and he whisked around and ran.

We continued through the alley until stopped by a fence. We climbed over and still panting and perspiring reached the Hudson Hotel. "Shit, it's after one," said Titmus.

Oklahoma City's curfew for all military commenced at twelve.

"We better start back," I wistfully advised.

"I'll just say hello and goodbye," said Titmus and stumbled up to the reception desk.

A dapper attired hotel clerk with slatted eyes frowned. "Can I help you?"

"What room is Millie Gaylord in?"

"And who may I ask is inquiring?"

"Her fiancé!"

"Name please."

"What the hell is it to you!" Titmus was upset.

"Well, if it ain't Private Earl Titmus!" We turned to face two huge navy guys with S.P. bands encircling their biceps and blobs for ears.

In Oklahoma the United States Navy championed former wrestlers with cauliflower ears, put them in sailor uniforms and assigned them shore patrol duty. Most of the Oklahoma Shore Patrol personnel had never seen the ocean.

"How many fuckin' Oakie swabjockie cops they got in this fuckin' town!" growled Titmus.

"Isn't that sweet, Private Titmus got some bellhop buddies with him," chortled the other naval policeman.

"We're on liberty'," said Titmus.

"Obviously," snickered the larger of the two.

Titmus, more than a little annoyed, repeated, "More fuckin' shore patrol here than San Diego!"

"If you playboys got passes, which I doubt, you're still too damn messed up to be seen in public representing the United States Naval services," uttered the shorter of the two giants.

"Two minutes to say goodbye to my fiancée, just two, and we go quietly, you got my word," said Titmus.

"We ain't runnin' no lonely hearts club," snapped the shorter S.P.

Oh, how I longed to be back at the base swabbing the head.

"You jarheads are a disgrace to the United States Navy," said the larger sailor.

"We ain't in no fuckin' navy!" spat O'Bannion.

"The navy don't need nobody to disgrace them," I timidly offered.

"Passes!" said the shorter sailor.

Titmus suddenly leaped forward and buried a left hook in the bigger guy's belly. The hefty S.P. doubled over wheezing. Titmus didn't need much provocation to defend the honor of the Corps.

"Hold the other gorilla!" Titmus shouted as he darted into the elevator. O'Bannion jumped on the back of the hulking swabbie and I wrapped arms around his burly midsection.

As Cruz pulled the club from his hands the three of us went down in a tangled heap. Cruz rose as the other sailor made it to his feet. They warily circled each other.

Meanwhile the shaken clerk dialed and dialed again as he hysterically screamed into the phone. The first behemoth wrapped one arm around O'Bannion and held my head in a vice-like grip with the other. I was about to faint when Titmus came bounding down the stairs. "What the hell room she in!"

The clerk dropped the phone and cowered in a corner.

"Earl!" sputtered O'Bannion. Titmus charged and the sailor released his grip as the lobby door opened and the four shore patrolmen we recently eluded rushed in.

We grappled but were quickly subdued. Handcuffed, manhandled and heaved into a paddy wagon we headed back to the base. As we approached Norman, the wagon's clamorous siren accented our dismay. Our liberty jaunt was over and unsavory happenings would soon commence.

CHAPTER FOUR

Burly navy brig guards shoved us into a huge cell holding fifteen other prisoners, mostly sailors. We each appropriated one of the thin mattresses piled in a corner. Before flaking out, Titmus roundly cursed guards, fellow prisoners and the State of Oklahoma.

Unpleasant dreams stimulated sonorous sounds and grating groans from Titmus' parted lips. Other conked out brig-rats snored, farted and dispelled unsavory grinding noises. That plus O'Bannion's stuporous breathing kept me from dozing off. The thin mattress separating my aching body from the concrete deck wasn't conducive to sleep either.

Before daylight the cell door swung open and a writhing body was heaved in. For seconds the khaki-clad guy lay prone before wobbling to his feet. It was Chief Elmer Crum, an Indian who had been in my boot camp platoon. He staggered about in a circle before plopping on a vacated mattress next to mine.

While I was a recruit in Platoon 183, two platoons of Navajo Indians were also going through boot camp. They had been activated to use their unconventional language skills to deliver messages. Some wizard had deduced that enemy intelligence would have intense difficulty interpreting Indian communication. The plan worked.

Although Crum claimed to be a full-blooded Navajo, for some clandestine reason he didn't serve with his fellows. Maybe he didn't savvy the language or couldn't get along with his tribesmen, we never found out. Most likely it was just a typical big brass screwed up.

Crum lay with eyes wide open staring at the overhead. He could have been thinking about chasing rabbits or maybe a squaw across the desert.

"What'd you do, Chief?" I said.

He blinked. "Paleface son-of-a-bitch lieutenant."

"What happened?"

"Fuck you, paleface!" he spat and turned his back.

I had my own problems. "Fuck you, Chief," I mumbled and shut my eyes.

I nodded off. Two hours later a raucous banging woke me. Two guards shouted, "Rise and shine, Brig Rats! Stow your mattresses!"

Inmates painfully stood and shuffled feet. Most new arrivals, sailors and Marines, were sporting hangovers. The cell door opened and we were ordered to fall in for breakfast. Small confinement cells were opened. Every third day prisoners in solitary on piss and punk were given a conventional meal.

A potbellied guard waggled a sawed off shotgun, "Any fool tries to run I'll yell, "Drop!" When I do, you shitbirds hit the deck 'cause after one, I mean one warning, I commence spraying 30 caliber shit."

Two other guards toting shotguns positioned themselves on either side of our formation. Nobody in his right mind, I deduced, would be crazy enough to try an escape. Where could he go?

The potbellied swabbie counted cadence as we shuffled along, "One, two, three, four, one two, three, four." It was common knowledge that sailors lacked marching rhythm except when dancing.

We were steered into the mess hall and halted at two designated tables. While we stood at attention silverware was counted and issued. As ordered we sat and ate in silence. Sailors and Marines in the mess hall stared. Some sympathetically, others merely shook their heads.

We marched back to the brig. The solitary confined prisoners were ordered into their smaller individual cells down the passageway. The rest of us were issued mops and brooms and ordered to sweep and swab.

At nine an ensign arrived and inspected the cells. The smug white-uniformed officer, a pasty-faced kid, mumbled derogatory bullshit about out-of-line Marines. At ten we were ushered outside into an enclosed grassy section. For fifteen minutes we paced back and forth. The guards called it exercise. The forlorn characters relegated to solitary confinement weren't permitted to leave their cells.

Each exercising prisoner was handed a single cigarette. I wasn't a smoker so I slipped mine to Chief Crum. He stashed it in his sock. "This fuckin' place no good for Indian," he snapped.

"You think its okay for a Jew?"

He scrutinized me like I was crazier than he was but didn't say anything.

We morosely milled about for another hour before the cell door opened and a grim-faced Marine wearing an SP arm band entered and barked, "Titmus, Sherman, O'Bannion, Cruz, Crum, fall out!"

He marched us to Major Burke's office and we stood rigidly in front of Sergeant Major Larkin's desk. Larkin, an average-sized guy wearing three hash marks, had a fox-like face molded in a perpetual frowned. "You sorry bunch of shitbirds! Titmus! You've been in long enough to know better. You other playboys better learn to be Marines."

He shook his head and left us staring at the wall as he strode into Major Burke's office. None of us twitched until he reappeared.

"Attenchun!" he spat. We stood straighter.

"Forward march!" It was only steps through the door to the major's desk. Titmus was in the lead and we halted marking time. "Halt! Right face!" We turned facing the major.

Major Burke, in his early sixties, stood an inch under six-foot. His shoulder was adorned with the braided *fleur de guerre,* the regimental award earned in France during World War One by the vaunted Fifth Marines for destroying German attackers in Belleau Wood. Burke had been retired for several years but due to the war had been summoned back to serve.

The silver-haired major carried himself like a flagstaff and looked like a storybook Marine. Prior to World War One ribbons on his chest proclaimed that he had been a China Marine and had also served in Nicaraguan campaigns.

"Name and rank," snapped Larkin. Loud and clear we sounded our names. Major Burke read from papers on his desk. "Private Crum, you're accused of drunkenness, disorderly conduct, resisting arrest and disrespect to an officer. What do you have to say for yourself?"

"Don't remember it, sir." said Crum.

"Guilty as charged?"

"Probably, sir!"

"Ten-days bread and water. If it happens again, you'll do hard time."

"Yes, sir!"

"And you four are charged with drunkenness, disorderly conduct, damaging property, absent without leave and resisting arrest." Major Burke glared.

I wanted to alleviate an itch or at least shift a bit, but stoically remained motionless.

"Private Titmus, this is not the first time you've stood before me."

"Yes, sir."

"Setting a good example for these young Marines, are you?"

"No, sir."

"Thirty-days bread and water."

The major looked at me. "Private Glossman, What have you got to say?"

"Nothing, sir."

"Guilty as charged?"

"Yes, sir."

"Five-days bread and water."

Cruz and O'Bannon got the same. "Next time, you playboys won't get off so easy," snapped the major. "Get them out of here!"

"About face!" growled Larkin. We turned and he marched us to the front office. A guard stood by as Larkin expounded. "You lucky fuck-ups got off easy!"

We were aware that the major could have socked it to us, especially to Titmus. Maybe he was in a good mood. "Too easy," repeated Larkin and directed the guard to return us to the brig. In the holding cell we were issued clean fatigue pants and jackets with a large black "P" stenciled on the back.

First Class Bos'n's Mate Volker was the petty officer in charge. He was one of a complement of local wrestlers pulled into the navy and without going through boot camp were given rank. His ears were cauliflowered and his gut hung over his belt. "You playboys have been serving dead time," he gloated, "and will continue to do so until solitary cells are available." The bastard was meaner than he looked.

The former wrestler devoted time glaring at prisoners, especially Titmus, from outside the cell. He relished scraping keys along the wired mesh. "Look who's rooming with us again."

Titmus tried to ignore Volker but his lip-quiver manifested how difficult it was. "Well, if it isn't the blowhard sailor who's never been to sea," he finally quipped.

"Take heed, Titmus, I won't be as easy as these other guards."

Titmus shrugged and joined us in the corner. Cruz didn't say much and Chief Crum seldom spoke unless spoken to. O'Bannon and I had heard each other's stories more than a few times. Plenty of swabbies were in the same huge cell but we didn't mix or communicate.

The day crawled; we swabbed the deck and policed our expansive cell as well as the outside grassy patio. Besides marching to and from chow, short breaks in the monotony were afforded three times a day.

The next morning, mail-call sounded. A few sailors got letters but Titmus was the only Marine to get a one. It was from Millie. Somehow she guessed where he'd be. In a low rasp he started reading. Cruz figured it wasn't polite to listen to other people's business but O'Bannion and I surmised we were expected to.

Hudson Hotel Room 468
Oklahoma City, Oklahoma
June 15, 1943

Dear Earl,

I hope this finds you not too banged up. I learned of your visit and presume you're in the brig again so that's where I'm addressing this letter. Earl, I got all dressed up for you and was waiting. If I must say, I looked very nice. Others said so too. After all these months I was anxious to see and touch you. Naturally, I was disappointed when you failed to show up.

Of course, in the morning, I was more than a little embarrassed but not surprised when I saw the mess in the lobby caused by you and your friends.

It didn't take long for me to figure out from the clerk's descriptive rants who was responsible. The poor guy was mad at me too.

I don't know if I'll ever be able to forgive you for disappointing me so. Oh, alright, Bumpkins, I know you didn't plan it to happen, so as always, I forgive you.

Luckily, they let me keep my room. Now I got to think about returning to San Diego. Some Army Air Corps gentlemen, three of them, saw how sad I looked and invited me to lunch. They heard my woeful story and told me that it was no surprise because Marines are known to be sort of uncivilized. When I took umbrage they apologized.

To make up for it they confided that they were driving back to California. In spite of being on an important mission that couldn't be divulged, they invited me to travel with them. I know you won't be happy about it but the trip won't cost me a cent.

You don't have nothing to worry about, sweetie. These men, I mean boys, are officers and gentlemen. When I told them I was engaged to marry a Marine they were impressed, but not too favorably.

My heart is so heavy because I didn't get to see you and don't know when I will. War is a terrible thing but nothing can keep us apart forever.

Goodbye for now, bumpkins, please try to be a good boy. I'll soon be home. You can reach me at my old address in San Diego.

Love you and, as always, forgive your naughtiness.

Millie

"She's one sweet chick," murmured Titmus and might have been holding back a tear. He folded and stashed the letter. I didn't comment but O'Bannion said, "Bumpkins?"

"So!" said Titmus.

Loud banging on the cell's wire mesh interjected. "Shut the hell up in there!"

It was Petty Officer Volker in his usual nasty mood.

A young sailor yelled, "Yaaa!" Other swabbies commenced shouting derogatory remarks. We joined the chorus.

Several guards rushed into the cell. An audacious gob yelled, "Volker's a fat fag!" That did it, the crimson-faced giant charged in waving his billy club. "Which miserable brig rat said that!"

It got eerily quiet. Nobody moved. Volker grabbed a skinny sailor and started slapping.

"The kid big enough, Volker?" said Titmus.

Volker released the swabbie and his eyes narrowed. "You big enough, Titmus?"

Titmus glared at Volker like he was cow dung. "You got that right."

"Follow me, wise ass." Titmus meekly trailed him through the cell door. Another grinning guard locked the door.

Volker stepped behind Titmus and faced the guards. "Me and this mouthy Marine are going to have a counseling session. You hear noises don't disturb us, we'll be consulting."

Guards smirked. Utilizing his billy club Volker prodded Titmus into his office. The behemoth followed and shut the door. Crashes and shouts resounded. Breaking furniture and assorted bedlam noises followed. Guards grinned.

"He's killing Titmus!" shouted O'Bannion.

"Stop that shit!" I yelled. As the banging amplified the guards looked puzzled. Finally one gasped, "We don't want to be part of a murder."

Two moved toward the office and the first opened the door. Titmus shuffled out. His fatigues were spattered with blood but he was unscratched. The two guards moved into the office while a third opened the cell door for Titmus.

Volker emerged supported by the two guards but didn't look well. "Get him to sickbay!"

"We're gonna get you, Titmus!" said the third guard.

Prisoners gathered around Titmus. "Soon as he shut the door, I grabbed his fuckin' club and pounded the shit out of him."

"He fight back?" asked O'Bannion.

"He put his hands over his head and screamed bloody murder."

"Holy shit," sighed a sailor.

"They'll get you, Marine," said another.

Titmus didn't seem concerned but the swabbie was right, brig rats got no say-so. Our concern didn't last because soon after the five of us were again marched to Sergeant Major Larkin's office. We stood in front of his desk.

"Can you shitbirds stay out of trouble until tomorrow?"

None of us answered. "I'm asking a question!" said Larkin.

"Sure, Sarge," said Titmus.

"At 0800 you playboys and forty-seven other fuck-ups are being shipped to San Diego. As of now, you're prisoners at large and confined to the barracks. Get the hell out of here and pack your seabags."

We walked to our barracks unescorted. The fuck-up quarters was a cauldron of activity as Oklahoma-weary Marines folded clothes and sea-bagged belongings. The prospect of getting shot at didn't deter any in the fuck-up barracks, we all wanted out of Oklahoma. That night, sleep didn't come easily for most of us and it seemed an eternity before reveille tumbled us out of our sacks.

After breakfast we heaved seabags onto the trucks and stood shoulder to shoulder as we were driven to the train station. We rolled along shouting, cursing, whistling and waving. We were especially active when a skirted doll strolled by. After all, we were young warriors going off to war.

The train depot was bustling with whistles, steam noises and baby-faced youngsters in military garb. Cars on both tracks were heading in opposite directions. Each train window framed a stoic looking young soldier or Marine.

Second Lieutenant Foley, a tapered All-American basketball player from the University of Indiana, scanned the hectic scene and shook his head. He wondered aloud, "What the hell's going on?" He trotted away to find Captain Franks.

Jammed like cattle aboard the trucks we were damn uncomfortable. Corporal Harold Bishop, the NCO in charge of truck number one, ignored our crude bitching. As he strode from one truck to the other, Private First Class Richard Lancaster, the notorious ear banger, shouted, "Knock it off! Knock it off!"

Lancaster, Long and lean with sharp cheekbones and a concave face, was neither heeded nor respected. His threats inspired flung debris.

Captain Franks appeared, tailed by Lieutenant Foley. He wasn't as large as Foley, nobody was, but built like a tank. His jut-jawed face and crew cut was a formidable presence. If he hadn't been a captain he still would have garnered respect.

Lancaster saluted and griped but the captain ignored him. "Corporal Bishop, get these people out of the trucks!" We poured onto the pavement and stood at attention. It felt good to stretch and breathe. Franks ordered Bishop to march us up and down the station platform.

Soldiers sitting by open train windows laughed and derided, but Captain Franks' stern gaze quieted hecklers.

The coaches filled with soldiers pulled away and an empty train moved in.

"Halt!" shouted Corporal Bishop.

Lieutenant Foley stepped in front. "Attentchut!" shouted Bishop and we snapped to. Lieutenant Foley read the muster sheet. Everyone was present.

Captain Franks spoke, "Our destination is San Diego. We're going to be aboard this train for five days. Foul-ups will not be tolerated especially from prisoners at large."

Only five of us had "P's" stenciled on our backs. I was shaky but felt a touch special, as if we five were considered extra tough.

"If Lieutenant Foley or me are not in the vicinity you will take orders from Corporal Bishop and PFC Lancaster.

"Chickenshit Lancaster," some guy whispered what most of us were thinking.

"Corporal, get the troops aboard!" said Foley. Bishop barked at Lancaster and he trotted up and down the platform shouting like he was leading a charge at Guadalcanal.

We filed into railroad cars and moved into seats. I sat alongside O'Bannion. We flipped a coin. I lost which designated me to sleep in the top bunk. Titmus and Cruz were seated in front of us but didn't flip because Cruz said he didn't mind sleeping on top.

The Marines ejected from Norman occupied three cars. Cars in front of us were crammed with soldiers and those behind were filled with sailors. There were more military-filled cars behind but we were ordered not to traipse that far back.

As our train rolled west, we were permitted to walk the aisles of the car in front and back. Besides the latrines there was nothing else to view except other brooding service personnel.

"As soon as I get to San Diego I'm gonna get laid," said O'Bannion.

"Sure," I said.

"You been to Tijuana?" he sneered.

"No."

"And you live in California?"

"When at Miramar I almost crossed the border but didn't get around to it." I don't know why, but felt guilty trying to explain anything to O'Bannion.

"Maybe I'll take you there." said O'Bannion.

"Maybe I'll take you there!" I said.

"Lots of pussy there," he said.

"I know what's there," I quipped.

As the train rolled toward Diego, the gateway to the war, we were edgy.

Harold Pinsky came rushing into the car. "Crap game in the dogface car," he divulged and moved on to the next car.

O'Bannion stirred, "Got any money?"

I had one single and a fin stashed but wasn't about to part with either.

"I feel lucky," he said.

"It's a long time before payday."

"I'll double it."

"You already owe me three bucks."

"Ain't I good for it?"

"I'm keeping what I got."

His badgering finally wore me down and I handed over my two crumpled bills. I followed him to the dogface car. A suitcase was propped in the aisle and a swabbie was rolling dice against it. Assorted uniforms watched as kneeling players tossed and retrieved bills.

About twelve bucks was in the pot as the swabbie threw a phoebe. "Little Joe!" he yelled but one cube turned up a three and the other a deuce.

O'Bannion squeezed in. The sailor crapped out and a soldier threw down a fin and snatched the dice. O'Bannion covered four bucks and the sailor threw snake eyes. O'Bannion had eight bucks.

The shooter doubled his bet and O'Bannion covered half. Others covered the rest and the dice rolled. The guy crapped out and O'Bannion had ten. He covered four again and when the next guy crapped out, he waved a fistful of crumpled bills.

It was O'Bannion's turn and he smugly fingered the cubes before he threw an eleven. Much to my chagrin he let it ride. Four straight passes followed and suddenly he had two fistfuls of money. As new players squeezed in I was pushed back but O'Bannon's shout of, "Be good to papa!" resounded loud and clear.

"Aha, any part of my eight," he bellowed and was quickly covered. I tried to push through and retrieve what he owed me but the crush of bodies kept me checked. I heard, "Sweet dice, be good to Brian."

There was a soundless lull as dice bounced off the suitcase. "Phoebe," murmured several disappointed voices. The roll of dice sounded once, twice and again. Then O'Bannion stood and spat, "Shit!" It was over.

Lights suddenly went out and the car was immersed in darkness as the train streaked through a tunnel. Jostling and pushing were followed by shouts. "Quit shoving!"

"Get your hand off my cock!"

"Queer!"

"I didn't know you cared." and "Oohs!" and "Ahs" ---- all in good humor.

When the lights abruptly came on merriment ceased.

"What the fuck!"

"Where's the fuckin' money!"

"Thievin' cocksucker!"

Victims wanted to grab someone, anyone. "Nobody move!" roared a flat-nosed soldier.

"Where the fuck is that lanky Gyrene?" said a swabbie. He might have been referring to O'Bannion, but he was gone.

"Son-of-a-bitch!"

Soldiers, sailors and Marines glared at each other. It wouldn't have been healthy to avert eyes, none did. Players murmured threats as they mulled about. Most looked guilty. I suppose I did too but I sure as hell wasn't.

Two sailors strolled in unaware what had transpired. The dice lay on the floor. One threw down two crumpled singles and grasped them. "Cover that," he said.

Somebody did. "C'mon pretty dice!" whispered the shooter and the squares rolled. One cube showed four, the other a two. "Hey, hey, sweet six," the swabbie shook the cubes and rolled again. New blood elbowed in and the action continued.

I made my way back to find O'Bannion staring at the passing countryside.

"Where'd you go, O'Bannion?"

"Took a leak."

"Know what happened?"

He shrugged.

"Lights went out and the money in the pot disappeared."

"No kidding?" I had seen that 'know nothing' look before.

"Where'd you say you went!" I queried.

He handed me two tens. "You owe me five."

As I pocketed the two sawbucks I quivered with a touch of guilt but I was impressed as I reflected that O'Bannion had balls, unethical ones, but still. I shrugged and fingered the creased sawbucks before conking out.

CHAPTER FIVE

As rays of sun filtered through train windows, affable black porters attired in spotless white jackets made up our bunks and squared away the latrines.

After breakfast, crap games commenced but quickly dissipated as gambling wealth was dispensed among the few knowledgeable players. There wasn't much reading material available so bullshitting about nothing and watching the countryside whiz by were primary occupations.

About the fourth day of ennui, two swabbies reeking of booze staggered through our car. Titmus queried them regarding their source. "Talk to a porter," one advised.

Titmus cornered a beaming porter. After bantering a moment they disappeared. Titmus returned with a pint of whiskey and a bottle of 7-Up wrapped in newspaper.

He uncorked, took a swig and handed the bottle labeled *Southern Comfort* to Cruz who gulped and gasped before handing the evil stuff to me. It had a rank flavor but I choked down half a mouthful. After swallowing a mouthful, O'Bannion turned crimson and was seized with uncontrollable coughing. He and we thought he was about to die.

The porter gratuitously brought a handful of pointed paper cups, and forsook comment as he passed them around. I caught Titmus shaking his head as he viewed O'Bannion's regurgitation. I admitted, to myself of course, that the soft drink tasted better than the dubiously labeled booze.

Between gulps Titmus chanted lines of the *Raggedy-assed Marines.* O'Bannion, feeling poorly, rendered a rejectional belch and staggered off to the head.

Cruz gulped, gasped and burped before handing the booze to me. I again choked down half a mouthful and my stomach felt encased in a ball of fire. The bottle quickly emptied and I tried to look disappointed as I dispelled a noteworthy grunt. Nobody heeded my histrionics, they were wasted.

The following morning, porters ousted us from our bunks and tidied the passageway. Paperbacks and newspapers were passed around but my head still throbbed. My aching noggin made it more than difficult to concentrate.

On the fifth night of our rolling itinerary, as the overhead light faded, I was shaken awake by O'Bannion. He roused Titmus too. "The swabbies are partying."

As Titmus slipped from his bunk and pulled on his pants I groaned, but grudgingly did the same. Cruz opened his eyes but passed on our invitation. Titmus and I followed O'Bannion. On our way we bumped into the same porter who had sold us the bottle of *Southern Comfort.*

Lord, I hated that sickening perfume-smelling booze and hoped more wasn't forthcoming. When the porter informed Titmus that booze was no longer available I was relieved.

Chief Crum and two Marines, strangers to us, stood amid a bevy of white hats nibbling pretzels, potato chips and crackers. The swabbies were wary about arousing their conked out boatswain. They cautioned us to speak in whispers. All hands were in docile moods as a half-filled jug of rot gut was quietly passed around.

The gobs were on their way to San Francisco to join a newly launched submarine. "Secret stuff," confided a Seaman First Class, "We can trust you jarheads to keep a lid on secret information, can't we?"

O'Bannion didn't seem to know whether we were being complimented or insulted, neither did I. Titmus wasn't listening but some of us rendered a perfunctory chuckle. After all, we were guests.

A few imbibers got plastered or acted like they were. O'Bannion cornered a swabbie and commenced poking him in the chest. "No offense, but we belong to one rough tough fighting outfit," he lisped.

"Who gives a rat's ass!" spat the swabbie.

"At least be thankful we're on the same side."

The red faced seaman swatted O'Bannion's finger away. "Jarhead, don't talk bullshit to a submarine sailor!"

"Party's over!" announced Titmus and gripped O'Bannion's arm. I grabbed the other and we pulled him from the swabbie car and dragged him into the next. In a wavering line we three made way through the rocking train.

Almost through the last car and into our own when, lo and behold, PFC Lancaster's back loomed. We stealthily approached and heard him lambasting a wavering khaki-clad guy wearing a swabbie's hat. "Is that a sailor's hat? You're drunk and out of uniform, Buster!"

The soused captive mumbled gibberish.

"Speak up!"

The guy burped.

"You won't be so damn cocky when Captain Franks hears about this!" The guy hiccupped a muffled reply. Lancaster backed away holding his nose. "Jesus!" Sensing our presence he started to turn as Titmus snapped a short right to his head. Lancaster grunted and plopped to the floor. We gaped at Chief Crum, the guy adorned with the sailor hat.

"Paleface PFC!" he spat and burped another loud one. Without even a 'thank you,' he staggered away.

"You're welcome," yelled O'Bannion.

We left Lancaster flaked out on the floor and stumbled to our bunks. "I should have kicked Lancaster's ass," said O'Bannon.

Before I could snicker, O'Bannion plopped into his bunk and was dead to the world.

In the morning the shit hit the fan. Marines stood by bunks as Lieutenant Foley, trailed by PFC Lancaster and Corporal Bishop, strode through the cars.

Lancaster wasn't certain who or what he had encountered. Nor was he clear whether a sailor or Marine had accosted him. He was almost sure that the culprit was either a sailor in a Marine's uniform or Marine wearing a sailor's hat.

Striving to identify his assailant he surveyed each passenger. After three or four maybes or maybe nots it was obvious that he couldn't identify his assailant. At the sight of Lancaster's swollen face satisfied snickering was rendered.

"When I find those guilty of assaulting an acting noncommissioned officer, they will rue the day!" proclaimed Lieutenant Foley.

Despite the lieutenant's intimidating words it was rumored that Captain Franks told the lieutenant to forget about it and Foley wasn't reluctant to do so. The captain, lieutenant as well as Lancaster were well aware of the lack of empathy among enlistees. However, Marines and sailors were henceforth forbidden to move from car to car unless authorized by an officer or noncom. "Maybe it wasn't a 'he' who did him in but a 'she' became a moral-boosting joke.

As we pulled into San Diego, a collective sigh of relief was rendered as we filed off. Cattle trucks transported us to Camp Miramar where we were quartered in the familiar Quonset huts.

Each day Marines from East Coast bases poured in. Haircuts, shots and lectures consumed time. Camouflaged ponchos, canteens, Garands and bayonets were issued. It felt like we were finally going to war.

"I feel like a Marine," proclaimed O'Bannion.

"Hah!" I challenged as he and I drew our short bayonets and parried. "Knock off the kid bullshit before one of you lose an eye!" shouted Titmus. We immediately sheathed our weapons.

On a dark morning we were roused and marched to the mess hall for a hurried breakfast. As usual, O'Bannion was the most vocal regarding the unimaginative food. But he was right; the chow was far from being as palatable as boot camp cuisine, but far better than the navy slop in Oklahoma.

Forty minutes of calisthenics came next. Policing the area followed and we collected gunny-sacked loads of debris. "What a way to fight a war!" was the prevailing reaction.

Before lunch a sergeant and two corporals led us on a two-mile jog to Camp Elliot. We arrived and rested for ten short minutes before being ordered to run through the soggy obstacle course. After leaping over ditches and barriers we were winded and smeared with muck. We felt as dejected as we looked jogging back to Miramar.

Sweating and panting we lined up before a be-ribboned khaki-attired sergeant. As we inhaled and exhaled he lectured about gear maintenance and survival in the tropics. We heard warnings of consequences related to eating native food, drinking rotgut and screwing native women. We fidgeted as he assured us that the most dastardly vices involved ingesting native rotgut. The lecture was dull except for the part about getting laid.

O'Bannion whispered, "He's full of it. I'm not passing up a piece of tail."

"You can't get laid here, how you going to get any nooky in a place you don't speak the language?" I responded.

"Wait 'til you see O'Bannion in action," he said.

One sweltering morning four-hundred of us were divided into two groups. The Red Army marched off to defend a small airfield situated on a flat hill surrounded by thickly vegetated boondocks. The Blue army's objective was to capture the hill.

Titmus, O'Bannion, Cruz, me, and others in our Quonset hut were assigned to the Blue Army. Groups were divided into squads of nine. In my squad I was the tallest and thus first in line so I became acting squad leader. I was relieved that Titmus was assigned to a different squad because I would have felt inept trying to order him around.

Of course, my squad was a bit grumpy about my undeserved promotion, but I couldn't help being pleased at the opportunity to show leadership skills. Sure, I was a bit shaky but prideful to be in command. After exhibiting my supervising ability, I reflected, there's no telling how many other promotional accords would befall.

Major Stillman, Captain Franks and Lieutenant Foley commanded the Blue Army. We were ordered to capture the Red Army's airfield. Moral was high as our squads spread out and made way through the brush. The sun cooked and sweat poured as winged San Diego vermin swooped and stung.

Slung rifles and heavy knapsacks took their toll. We weren't cocky for long and became sullen as we crept forward to engage our entrenched opponents. Grunts and bitching prevailed.

Assuming dire battlefield conditions each squad leader was the only one permitted to carry a canteen filled with water. The rest of the squad toted empty canteens.

It was each squad leaders' responsibility to ration water from his single filled canteen. Acting squad leaders were also buck-assed privates so consequently, our hastily designated authority didn't garner much respect.

The eight others in my squad were Cruz, O'Bannion, Pinsky, and five other unhappy buck privates. Cruz was indifferent regarding my unearned promotion. However, O'Bannion and the others were a touch envious. My acting-corporal designation didn't bode well.

As we slowly progressed through wavering weeds higher than our heads, bugs stung, throats parched and my role evolved into unpleasant contention. Not long after plodding through dense underbrush my dehydrated squad members demanded water.

"Wait!" I said.

"What the fuck's the matter with you, Glossman!"

"You're worse than the fuckin' enemy!"

"You wouldn't make a pimple on a squad leader's ass!"

"I'm fuckin' dying!"

"Gimme a drink, asshole!"

"Water! Water!"

I was determined to impress the judges and resisted subordinate pressure as I steadfastly refrained from dispensing water. Other squad leaders did the same, but amid towering brush most squads lost contact. I later learned that several leaders, under peer pressure, forsook responsibility and their canteens were quickly emptied.

My squad suspected me of nefarious doings. Wary eyes concentrated on me rather than the entrenched enemy. My eight parched followers made sure I wasn't imbibing. We had an undetermined way to go and if I got caught tippling, trouble would ensue, maybe mutiny. Bone dry and craving a drink I didn't dare uncork my canteen.

O'Bannion suddenly halted. "I ain't moving 'til I get some water,"

"Me neither," groaned Pinsky.

"You're talking mutiny," I admonished.

"Give us a goddamn drink!" whined Russ Meyers.

I tried to face them down, "I'm thirsty too," I whined.

They were on the verge of mutiny. I finally acquiesced, "Okay, one gulp." I passed the canteen.

As each squad member took a hefty gulp and strove for a second, I asserted leadership by yanking back my canteen and downed the last mouthful. My parched squad glared at me with undisguised hostility.

All contact with our Blue Army compatriots had been lost but I surmised and even hoped that other Blue Army squad leaders were having similar leadership problems. As we plodded through the heavy growth my lust for command diminished. Suddenly our military objective loomed. "Crouch!" I whispered and kneeled.

From my perspective, my squad, thanks to me, had accomplished a successful maneuver. Aware that I had resolutely taken charge even O'Bannion ceased complaining. We were worn but spoiling for action. I energetically pushed onward and my squad morosely followed.

As we viewed the airfield from afar, salty as an old China hand, I snapped, "Let's capture that piece of real estate." I modestly surmised that referees viewing our strategic approach would be impressed.

When we reached the base of the plateau, I intended to emulate the legendary Sergeant Daley's inspirational, "You want to live forever!

Charge!" uttered at the battle for Bellue Wood during World War One.

I imagined my "Charge!" would galvanized my squad and be very impressive, especially if we captured the airfield.

As I crept through the phalanx of flitting insects I crouched lower. On my portside Smith inched up abreast of me. On my starboard O'Bannion also crept alongside. "Back!" I hissed.

"Fuck you!" spat O'Bannion.

"I'm in charge, assholes!"

"You're no better than the rest of us, you're a goddamn buck-assed private!" growled Smith.

Before I had a chance to retort, Borland who was behind Smith, started thrashing.

"Quiet!" grunted Smith, as if he were in charge.

"Didn't you hear!" spurted Borland.

"What?" hissed Smith.

"Rattlesnake!"

"Uh-oh, they travel in pairs," said Cruz.

"Once those goddamn things strike you're done for!" gasped O'Bannion.

"Fuck it!" shrieked Borland as he leaped to his feet and galloped away.

"Fuck the snake, this is war!" I growled, intending to calm my squad.

"Fuck you!" Shouted O'Bannion and shagged through the brush after Borland. The rest of my squad stood and sprinted after them. I was livid and bellowed, "Come back, cowards!" An unsavory underbrush rustling unnerved me, and I forsook lingering as I crashed through underbrush after my patrol.

If the Red Marine team had observed us, they couldn't help but witness our inglorious retreat. Of course, they would have no idea what prompted our hasty withdrawal. Their leaders could even have fathomed that we were engaged in a tricky maneuver.

Our fellow Blues, likewise, failed to capture the airfield. None of our compatriots got close enough for a confrontation. Much to our surprise and relief no enlisted participants, Blue or Red, were reprimanded. Hence, neither Blue squad nor Red opponents received good or bad evaluations regarding activity on the make believe battlefield.

Days later Lieutenant Foley and Captain Franks were transferred. I was disappointed because I and the others would have been pleased to continue to take orders from them.

CHAPTER SIX

About dusk on a Thursday, O'Bannion and Pinsky were sitting on the latter's bunk. Cruz and I were spit-polishing our shoes. "Payday is tomorrow and I'm heading into town. I've got to look sharp," proclaimed O'Bannion.

"Mind if I tag along?" said Pinsky.

"Uh, uh! I'm gonna bag a chick and I ain't gonna let you screw it up," said O'Bannion.

"Oh, excuse me, lover boy!" Pinsky was irritated. I didn't blame him. He was from Philadelphia, dark and a touch pudgy but not a guy to push around.

"Hah," said O'Bannion but not very aggressively.

"What you sayin?" snapped Pinsky.

"Nothin'" soothed O'Bannion.

"I'm gonna hitchhike to Santa Monica," I inserted.

"Gonna see Mom?" grinned O'Bannion.

"Yeah!"

"Anybody else you gonna visit?"

"Maybe," There was nobody, but I wasn't about to tell that to O'Bannion. He almost started another wise-ass comment but my scowl stopped him.

"Going to Boyle Heights, Jacob?" I asked.

"Got to see my mother and Lupe," he said. No one asked but we figured Lupe was his girlfriend.

"Want to meet me at Canter's for a hotdog and kosher pickle?" I said.

"Maybe," said Cruz.

Titmus strode in. "I just talked to Millie."

"She's here!" I said.

"On the phone, idiot. We gabbed for ten minutes. She's not mad at me no more. We're goin' on a date tomorrow," said Titmus sporting a shit-eatin' grin.

Borland, broad of shoulder and inches under six feet, barged in flourishing a deck of cards. "Anybody interested?"

"We play for nickels," said Titmus. "I got me a date tomorrow and I ain't goin' ashore broke."

Borland shuffled and we played until the bugle blew and lights were doused. We grumbled a bit as we hit the sack.

About three in the morning I inadvertently woke to a chorus of assorted snores. Minutes later bright lights illuminated the barracks. Sergeant Garrison strode in and roared, "Get your asses up! Pack your seabags! We're moving out!"

"What the hell!" shouted Titmus.

"We're off to the war!" said Garrison.

"I got a date!" said Titmus.

"Oh, I'll tell that to the major," said Garrison, "he'll probably hold the ship up 'til you get back from your date."

Half-clad Marines spilled from their bunks and did what had to be done in the head. Clad in fatigues we lined up in the dark and chilly dawn. Muster was called as canvas-covered trucks rolled in. Bitching was subdued as our gear was stashed and we climbed aboard.

We sat with rifles upright between our knees cursing in hushed tones as we were driven away.

Docks soon come in sight and our trucks pulled alongside the looming grey stern of the *U.S.S. Feland*, an attack transport. We dismounted and lined up. Seabags were heaved into cargo nets and hoisted aboard. Orders were executed in whispered tones.

"This is what we joined for!" ventured O'Bannion but sounded more subdued than spirited.

The first rays of daylight broke as we shouldered our Garands and filed up the steep gangway. On the midship deck, muster was called again. We were directed below decks to stow our gear.

Titmus, O'Bannion, Borland, Cruz, and I were assigned bunks one through five. Two others guys crawled into the lower bunks. We squared away our sacks, packs and rifles before stepping back up the iron stairway and pushing to the rail.

The wharf was bustle with shouting longshoremen and uniformed personnel. As additional troops arrived, noncoms directed and shouted orders. While cargo nets continued to swing back and forth depositing crates and seabags aboard, newly arrived troops filed up the gangway.

"Poor Millie is wasting another dinner," moaned Titmus.

"She'll figure out what happened," said Borland.

"Depends how smart she is," said O'Bannion.

"What?" said Titmus.

"Once she knows what's happening she'll probably invite someone else," amended O'Bannion.

"What in hell you talking about?"

O'Bannion's smugness dissipated as he tried to amend his out-of-line remark. "She's got girlfriends, doesn't she?"

It would have served the out-of-line Bostonian right if Titmus had whacked him, but he was diverted as whistles blew and black smoke belched from the smokestack. The sudden clamor probably saved O'Bannion from a short uppercut to the belly.

The tug tied alongside began moving the *U.S.S. Feland*. The ship was fifty feet from the wharf when Titmus pointed. "Millie!"

"Where?" said Borland.

We spotted a female running along the dock waving. Titmus furiously waved.

"Millie?" said O'Bannion.

"Its her!" shouted Titmus and continued to frantically swing his arms. As we pulled away she got smaller and smaller.

A sailor walked by and Borland grabbed his arm. "Where we heading?"

"Won't know 'til we get there," smirked the sailor.

"Hey, I asked a question!"

"The skipper and jarhead colonel are the only ones who know, ask them!" The swabbie swaggered away.

"Wise ass!" spat Borland.

The *U.S.S. Feland* slowly made way through San Diego's breakwater. As the shoreline faded a chilly wind kicked up. While Titmus lingered at the rail O'Bannion, Borland, Cruz and I went below to check out our new quarters.

Fifty pilots, a dozen line officers, and three hundred and fifty enlistees were crammed aboard the *Feland*. Space below the main deck was jammed with bunks, seabags and equipment. There was sparse room to move in any direction. The constant sound of wind breaking wreaked havoc on olfactory senses.

It was so stifling below that grumpy weather conditions didn't deter passengers from remaining on deck. During the first few days we swaggered around brandishing our recently issued stilettos. The long evil looking daggers intrigued the teenaged swabbies. Marines swapped knives for crap money.

Crap games and card games commenced. Off-duty sailors and Marines, those who weren't seasick, jostled and pushed, eager to donate money to one of the many games. In short time I regretfully contributed my meager share.

On the third day out, O'Bannion was in a five card stud game and he had amassed a pile of bills. Both sailors and Marines were playing on a blanket.

Titmus was writing to Millie. I was engrossed in Jack London's, *Jerry of the Isles,* about a dog's adventures in the South Pacific.

By the end of the third day most of the money had ended up in the pockets of older players. Between the usual sweeping and swabbing routines there wasn't much to keep young Marines occupied. As enlistees became bored, squabbling and bad mouthing ensued.

On the fourth day, rumors spread that a stalking Jap submarine was tailing us. In hushed tones, crew and troops were informed that it was more than just a probability. Depth charge and target practices were scheduled. Tension and combat rehearsals provided timely diversions. Navy and Marines on lookout duty kept eyes peeled.

On the fifth day out, an alarm sounded. As the ringing bell pealed, swabbie gun crews bolted to their stations loaded their heavy weapons and prepared to repel the enemy. It evolved into a practice session.

A balloon was cut loose and the order to commence firing was given. Twenties and forties opened up. The staccatos sounded ominous as the navy gun crews sought to destroy the drifting balloon. The first unscathed target drifted away and another was released. Disdainful comments from Marines unstrung the navy gunners. Critical banter was heatedly exchanged as tracer after tracer missed each soaring target.

The *Feland's* officers were livid as the sixth unscathed balloon eluded their gun crews. Negative Marine comments reaching topside didn't help.

A crisply white attired navy lieutenant stifled Marine laughter by ordering the firing to cease. The skipper of the *Feland* addressed the chortling Major Burke and challenged him to rustle up a Marine gun crew that could do better.

The majority of Airdales aboard had never handled a weapon more formidable than a rifle. Most of us couldn't identify a twenty-millimeter from a howitzer. Major Burke sent a Marine lieutenant to ferret out the few ex-line company vets. Titmus was one of the seasoned grunts. When he was seagoing he had, of course, been trained to fire secondary batteries.

The Marine challengers replaced one of the navy gun crews. They positioned their twenty-millimeter and swiveled its barrel toward the next airborne balloon. The ship plowed on as the buoyant sphere danced away. "You jarheads waiting for something?" shouted a swabbie and other swabbies chorused, "Hey! Hey! The balloon's escaping."

"Fire!"

Pow! Pow! Pow! The target disintegrated.

Another was released and another and another. Each balloon was quickly obliterated. It was a complete Marine moral victory. The deck impacted with troops gave a rousing cheer. We showered congratulations on our compatriots. Titmus and his gun mates arrogantly stepped down to the lower deck to receive a hero's welcome. They had bolstered our pride in the Corps. "I gotta write a letter to Millie," Titmus said and went below.

As a burly swabbie sauntered by, Borland chortled, "One of our distinguished swabbie sharpshooters!"

"Send my boy to the navy and teach him how to shoot!" shouted O'Bannion. The sailor was about to throw a punch, but a circle of pugnacious Marines deterred him.

CHAPTER SEVEN

Two mornings later a proclamation sounded from the loudspeaker causing general consternation. "Pollywogs! This ship will cross the equator at 1400. Lowly seafarers and Marines who have never crossed will be afforded the honor of being initiated into the solemn rites of the deep.

"By order of King Neptune and his royal court, all shellbacks, navy and Marine, report to the boat deck for further orders!"

"What the fuck's goin' on?"

"More bullshit!"

"Navy shit?"

A grinning Titmus enlightened. "Sailors and Marines who have never crossed the equator are pollywogs. To become an honored shellback you got to be initiated."

"Got to?" O'Bannion.

"Got to! The tradition goes back lots of years." Titmus stalked away.

"Where you goin'? asked O'Bannion.

"I'm a shellback!" And he haughtily shuffled off.

"You believe this shit?" asked Borland.

"They beat the crap out of you!" someone advised.

"After that they cut your hair off." another added.

"I ain't gonna let them do that to me!" proclaimed O'Bannion.

"My brother told me it's a tradition and there's no way out," said a woeful-faced Marine.

"Now hear this!" blared from the ship's loudspeaker. "It's time for lowly pollywogs to be inaugurated into the sacred mysteries of the deep. Navy pollywogs report to the starboard side of the after deck. When you get there form a single line. Marine pollywogs line up behind them. Stand at attention and keep your mouths shut. Snap to it!"

Lines were quickly formed. Nobody wanted to be labeled chickenshit and none wanted to attract attention. Pollywog sailors lined up and Marines stood in a longer line behind them. Both lines consisted of youngsters barely out of high school. The long column of pollywogs twisted and disappeared around the midship superstructure. I nervously waited behind O'Bannion and in front us was the unhappy Borland.

"Those of you who bear up will be accepted into King Neptune's kingdom. Pollywogs that go through the initiation with honor will be awarded shellback certificates. Those of you who don't will be severely punished."

More than somewhat unsettled, pollywogs warily looked about to silently curse or render a nervous chuckle. Grizzled shellbacks armed with paddles stoically waited. Bells sounded and the ceremony commenced.

On hands and knees, crawling pollywogs were mercilessly whacked as they tried to hurry through the line of eager paddle swinging shellbacks. The splat of wood against rear ends followed by grunts and yells rant the festive deck. A plethora of wise remarks accompanied victims as they proceeded.

"You can take it, can't you, Marine?"

"Want to be a shellback, do yuh?"

"Tough guys, eh?"

At the end of the line was a paunchy sailor with slitted eyes. He was the Royal Barber and with sadistic glee hacked at polliwogs' hair. His gaunt assistant anointed oncoming shorn heads with splashes of syrup.

A midshipman, draped in a white sheet and gold crown perched upon his head, presided as King Neptune. The hash-marked swabbie king assumed a haughty air as he caressed his royal belly.

As each pollywog knelt and kissed King Neptune's foot, Davy Jones, a wizened old salt, jabbed his five-foot trident into the victim's backside. Following that humiliating stab, pollywogs were prodded straight into the hose nozzle spewing a strong stream of saltwater.

A loud hubbub drew attention. A circle of indignant new shellbacks were surrounding Lancaster. "You didn't go through!" snarled a short red-faced guy.

"I did!" protested Lancaster.

"Bullshit!"

"His hair is untouched!" shouted a pissed off shellback.

"Get your skinny ass in line!" ordered O'Bannion.

"You out of your mind?" sputtered Lancaster.

"You're a sure as hell excuse for a Marine!" shouted Arnie and shoved Lancaster. He would have followed with a punch had I not grabbed his arm.

"I'm gonna run both your asses up!" spurted Lancaster.

"That did it, I'm gonna shove your shitty stripe down your throat!" spat Arnie.

"Chickenshit asshole!" snarled O'Bannion.

Lancaster pointed to his single stripe. "I got rank!" His yowl evolved into a pitiful protest as several shellbacks dragged him to the line. He was pushed to his knees and paddle wielders slammed his butt as he tried to accelerate through the enthusiastic swatters.

Lancaster proceeded to get the shit swatted out of him. Afterwards he limped to his bunk and flaked out. Two hours slipped by before he quit whimpering. Painstakingly he got up and approached Sergeant Garrison. He moaned that while carrying out obligations as acting non-commissioned officer he had been inculpably pushed in the face by Private Arnie Litman.

At the time none us, including Sergeant Garrison, knew what inculpable meant.

"You were inculpable during the initiation!" bluffed Garrison.

"Yes, sir!"

"Hmm," muttered Garrison.

Arnie had orange hair. He was a little guy with a New York accent. Sometimes when he spoke louder than he had to, he irritated listeners. How he got in the Corps was a mystery. When it came to consuming booze of all sorts, his stomach was a bottomless well. Liquored up he got brazen enough to challenge anybody to fight.

The next afternoon Arnie had to report on the bridge to Major Burke. After Arnie explained the reason he took action, Major Burke mused a second before pronouncing sentence. "Private Litman, for your infraction, you're confined to this ship for three days!"

"Yes, sir!" Arnie saluted before pivoting and climbing down the ladder. Burke's punitive decision reinforced our standing opinion about the major, he was an okay guy.

Arnie lamented that we'd have to go on liberty in the middle of the ocean without him. It got a laugh.

Word of Lancaster's candy-assed sidestepping spread and the chargined PFC was subject to grimaces and snide remarks. When he heard about Arnie's less than severe punishment he was more than unhappy. "I won't forget," he muttered. .

Scrolls and cards were dispensed with names and ranks inscribed certifying that the card bearer was a bonafide shellback. The honorable designation induced a collective show of cockiness. We swaggered about as if we finally were salty veterans who had been around a bit.

The equatorial sun beat down and sweat poured. If a guy stood still more than a few minutes the heated steel deck seared through his boondockers. When the sun dipped it cooled but the darkness became intense. The weather turned muggy and the intense blackness made it difficult to move about.

The loudspeaker finally blared out news, "Now hear this! The destination of this vessel is Tutuila, the largest island in American Samoa. In case you Marines have lost track, it's still August. Two days from now will be Friday morning. At 0600 on that day this ship will pull into Pago Pago's harbor. Gentlemen, have your gear squared away and be prepared to disembark. Marines, it was nice having you aboard. Good luck, jarheads!"

It was a welcome announcement. The rolling *U.S.S. Feland* and its below-deck stuffy confines would soon be a clouded memory.

"Where in hell is Samoa?" became a prevailing query. Except for some of the old salts most of us didn't know much about our lyrical-titled destination.

On our next to last night afloat, we were suddenly alerted to strap on life belts. They had been issued to keep us afloat in case an enemy submarine's torpedo blew us into the sea. The belts were canvas affairs and were inflated by squeezing two cartridges inserted alongside the buckle.

Most of us milled about whispering about nothing. The moonless darkness shrouded the ship. Voices eerily silenced as everyone suddenly got quiet. We uneasily stared into the portside blackness.

"What is it?" someone whispered.

"Submarine!"

"Where?"

"Shut up, asshole!"

"Just askin'!"

"They can hear you!"

"What!"

"Stupid son-of-a-bitch!"

The radar on the main mast continually turned and buzzed. Whispered prayers and curses could be heard as breathing accelerated. Sweat dripped as we apprehensively awaited the torpedo onslaught that would blow us to hell.

"Hsss," went a life belt. The inflation sound was chorused by dozens of belts being squeezed. The hissing amplified as fingers nervously squeezed cartridges and belts inflated.

A voice of authority growled, "What the hell you people doing! Don't inflate the goddamn life preservers or you'll hit the surface and bounce like a rubber ball. And you'll bust your damn necks coming down!"

The salty old bastard had stripes with two rockers came storming from aft. "Goddamn Boots! Knock off the bullshit! Ain't nothin' out there but a porpoise blowing bubbles."

"Who said so?" said a jittery voice.

"I did! Now hit your fuckin' sacks. Anybody standing around lolly gagging five minutes from now will become a volunteer for my special work party."

Most of us filed below but none felt secure enough to shed his lifebelt. Titmus was probably the only one not too jumpy to sleep.

After the sun came up, the situation looked brighter and chuckles resounded. A group lounging on the deck were shooting the shit when Eugene Kelton piped up, "They won't let me be a fighter pilot so I'm gonna transfer to a line company."

"Horseshit," said O'Bannion.

"I joined to fight and I'm going home a hero. No enlisted asshole is goin' to get medals in an Airdale outfit."

Kelton was a big buffoon with sandy hair and freckles. He was big, alright, but didn't look like a hero.

O'Bannion guffawed.

"You laughin' at me?"

"You look too funny to be heroic," snickered O'Bannion.

"Fuck you!" said Kelton.

O'Bannion got into a fighting stance. "C'mon fat boy let's see you act like a hero."

"I ain't gonna get thrown in the brig for fighting a jack-off," said Kelton.

"That's a chickenshit excuse!" O'Bannion stuck his chin out but Kelton chose not to carry it any further.

"Hero, my ass!" added O'Bannion.

Kelton was full of hot air but most of us spouted a fair share of bullshit and I thought O'Bannion was out-of-line for popping off at the pathetic sad sack.

"Anybody here ever read any Jack London?" popped Bones. He was about twenty, a tall bony kid from Minneapolis. He often sounded more or less learned. His eruditeness was probably due the year spent in college. Anyway, ever so often he fired off an educated statement.

"I read London," I said.

"His stuff about the South Pacific?" said Bones.

"Some of it." I tried not to sound like I was bragging.

"He write about native girls?" chortled Borland.

"Borland, if you see one of those hot native girls keep your pecker in your pants," said O'Bannion.

"Why?" asked Borland.

"They got some never-heard-of diseases. Our shanker mechanics don't know how to cure them," sighed O'Bannion, as if he knew what he was talking about.

"For sure?" said Borland.

"Sure as hell."

"You peckerheads sound more and more like idiots on your first cruise," spat Titmus.

On our last night at sea, I caught sentry duty along the deck and the other guard pacing back and forth near the port gun tub was Ferguson, a short squat guy. Our time in the Corps was about the same, but on or off duty he looked like he'd seen and done it all. His perpetual bored countenance didn't inspire conversation. We paced forward and aft in different directions and occasionally met midships where we shot the breeze a bit about prospects of getting laid in Samoa.

Our brief conversation was transpiring when Lancaster emerged from the dark. "You two are supposed to be walking your posts in a military manner."

"That's what we're doing, acting Corporal Lancaster," said Ferguson.

"We sure as hell are," I confirmed.

"You were talking! You can't do two things at once. Keep alert like you're supposed to or I'll run your asses up!"

"Son of a bitch!" muttered Ferguson.

"What!" stammered Lancaster.

"Nothin'," spat Ferguson.

"I didn't hear anything," I confirmed.

"We'll see about that!" spat Lancaster and glared at us as he adjusted his holster belt before striding up a starboard ladder. At the top he missed his footing, with a defined plop he hit the deck and groaned once. Silence followed, he was out.

"Fell on his ass!" chortled Ferguson.

"Should we check on him?" I said, amused but a touch concerned.

"Hell no! He ordered us to walk in a military manner and we're following his orders."

We paced off in opposite directions.

About 0330, commotion erupted near the foot of the ladder. Gaston, a salty old bastard was Sergeant of the Guard. He shouted for Ferguson and me to come on the double. We came running. We arrived and saw Lancaster sitting on a bottom rung holding his head. "What happened to PFC Lancaster?"

"Cheez! Don't know, Sarge! Is he alright?" said Ferguson.

I shrugged and tried to sound concerned. "Is he okay?"

"Corporal Brown found him all fucked up," Gaston growled.

We reiterated that we had heard nothing.

"You been drinking torpedo juice or something, Lancaster?" snapped Gaston.

"Don't drink, Sarge."

"Bullshit!" snapped Gaston.

"Honest!" whimpered Lancaster. "Especially when I'm on duty. I almost got to the top of the ladder when someone pulled me down from behind. I didn't see the guy."

"Are you sure?" I said.

"Maybe there's a Jap commando aboard," offered Ferguson.

Gaston's glare was menacing so I refrained from chortling. "My investigation is commencing. When I find out what happened there'll be shit to pay. Lancaster, you're not off the hook. You two get back to your posts!"

Ferguson and I resumed our back and forth pacing until relieved. "Watch your step," smiled Ferguson.

CHAPTER EIGHT

At 0600 on Friday, a swabbie lookout cried, "Land off the portside!" The deck erupted as troops and swabbies shouted and pointed at looming green hills on starboard, port, aft sides and forward of the bow. The *Feland's* speed was cut as she sailed between lush foliage and lofty palm trees hugging the shore.

Excitement mounted as a chugging small boat came alongside and a pilot deftly climbed hand over hand up the Jacobs ladder. He stepped aboard and made way to the bridge. Then a tug pulled alongside and deckhands tied her to our gently swaying ship.

Bones pointed at a cluster of weathered structures ashore, "Sadie Thompson could have stayed right there."

"Who?" queried Borland.

"A Somerset Maugham character."

"Who?"

"Never mind."

"Bones, you're out of your fuckin' mind!"

Bones shook his head and Borland was about to make another negative comment when O'Bannion pointed, "A dame!"

A native adorned in a white blouse with a red cloth circling her waist stood amid a group of staring natives. She was a bit hippy and her brown legs were thick, but all in all she didn't look bad. With no hint of hostility, friendliness or interest on her brown face she observed us.

"A nigger," spat some mouthy guy.

"Asshole!"

"Hey, I'd like a shot at her," said another.

"You got no class, redneck!"

"Shut the fuck up!"

"Fuck you!" and "Fuck you!" was bantered back and forth until the loudspeaker blared, "Now hear this! Marines, assemble your gear and prepare to disembark! Nice having you aboard. Good luck!"

Several bored-looking rifle-toting Marines clad in faded khaki stood watching ashore. Bare-chested natives attired in skirts called *lava lavas* strolled about.

Two more native girls in *lava lavas* appeared. The dark young things laughed and waved. They had obviously done the greeting routine before.

"Them two ain't bad," commented Arnie.

"They look good enough to eat," said O'Bannion.

The skies suddenly beclouded and torrents of rain spilled. Ashore, Marines and natives ran for shelter under lengthy thatched structures. Startled by the sudden downpour, those of us on deck were drenched.

Our soiled khakis clung like another skin. Rifles were wet and our shoulders felt bruised from pack-straps. The chilly rain continued to soak us in short bursts. All we could do was curse and groan. The dismal drenching was attributed to the lofty green mountain called "The Rainmaker".

Unkempt and unclean we plodded ashore. A *fita fita* guardsman attired in his beige *lava lava* uniform with red horizontal corporal stripes observed. More native onlookers arrived to jabber and point and laugh. They obviously were amused at our discomfort.

However, to be fair, weeks later when we became more insightful regarding Samoan mores and culture, we became aware that the jovial natives were warm-hearted people and loved to laugh which they did at almost anything, sometimes at their own misfortunes. Their actions were far from malicious.

Several of us were on the verge of erupting when a thin sergeant with a drooping mustache arrived. Three NCOs in starched khaki trailed him. People were called out, separated and marched away. Some of the departing sad sacks were destined to become brig guards in American Samoa's notorious brig. Others replaced troops finishing up their Samoan stretches and heading stateside.

Eventually thirty of us remained. Sergeant Bledsoe arrived and informed us, "You men are going to *Upolu.*"

"Where!" said Titmus, weathered enough to get away with talking up.

"*Upolu,* British Samoa. Consider yourselves lucky," said the sergeant

"What's so lucky?" asked Borland.

"Don't rain as much, mosquitoes aren't as numerous and since the island belongs to New Zealand the gooks are a damn sight less spoiled. Also, your dollars will last longer, everything is a helluva lot cheaper."

"No shit," said O'Bannion.

"How far?" said Titmus.

"Ninety-miles as the crow flies."

Another sergeant sounded off. "Right face! Forward March!" He steered us to the end of the wharf where a fifty-foot wooden patrol craft tied fore and aft to two pilings tugged with the surge. *Leoni* was inscribed on her bow. The boat looked like she could be fifty years old, maybe more.

We shuffled up her flimsy gangway and were greeted by a pleasant bearded young ensign. He bade us make ourselves at home. We dropped our gear and sprawled across the deck. Several exhausted men flaked out in the passageway.

As the *Leoni* plunged into the open sea she was broadsided by a rolling swell. One surging swell followed another. It didn't take long before passengers commenced vomiting. Splashing waves washed away smelly upheavals but didn't alleviate the groaning chorus. The dismal ten-hour rollercoaster ride featured puking, dry heaves and more puking.

It was an eternity before our new home's silhouette finally loomed. Most of us regained composure and peered about. As the boat approached we spied rust-caked remains of shipwrecks looming above the blue surface.

The sergeant, not affected by the rocky voyage said, "See those hulks, they're all that's left of British, German and American warships sunk before World War One.

"No shit." O'Bannion was impressed. We all were.

"During the early 1900's, Germany possessed Western Samoa and even then the Krauts were considered a threat. Friction between Germany, England and America was on the verge of coming to a lethal head in Apia's harbor. Warships from the three countries were off shore and their crews at battle stations when a hurricane swept in and tore into the bellicose gun ships.

"Two of the badly damaged vessels managed to limp away but others went to the bottom carrying most of their crews. See, those rusted and battered superstructures still visible. Anyway, that naval mishap postponed the start of World War One for a decade."

"Holy shit," said O'Bannion.

"One way to stop a war," philosophized Arnie.

Three green trucks stenciled with USMC were waiting. Weak and weary we climbed aboard and sat with rifles propped between our legs. As the trucks revved up, two *lava lava* clad girls accompanied by four or five kids appeared. "*Aikai, Malini,*" they shouted.

These animated ladies weren't beauties but their ebullience and animation enlivened us. While we shouted and blew kisses, our transportation roared away leaving our welcomers unamused in a cloud of dust.

"What were them kids saying?" queried O'Bannion.

The driver chuckled, "*Aikai Malini*s, means Marines eat shit!"

We were bewildered and a bit dismayed. "Not as bad as it sounds, it's sort of a traditional greeting," he said. "Most gooks speak English, some better than others. Some of you will pick up on Polynesian lingo, it ain't too tough to learn."

Only one main road used for vehicles spanned British Samoa. Our new Quonset homes were adjacent to the lone airfield and located twenty miles away. We gaped at our new surroundings flying by as our truck sped after the others toward our new home. On the seaward side calm blue water spewed gentle surf. On the inland side Mt. Alava hovered huge and green over the lush island.

We sped past villages surrounded by well coiffured greenery and dotted with thatched huts. We had been gazing at rolling grey seas for a long time and the bright colors played tricks with our eyes.

Bones Donical sat on my portside.

"Pretty, huh, Bones?" I sighed.

"Stevenson." There was his thousand-yard stare again.

"The writer?"

"Home is the sailor home from the sea, and the hunter home from the hill."

"He said that?"

"It's his epitaph, he wrote it before he died. Had it inscribed on his gravestone."

"The bastard's spent a year in college and it's screwed up his brain!" ventured O'Bannion. "Bones you're an educated idiot."

In front of the squadron's office the lead truck braked to a stop while the others lined up behind. We dismounted and formed a double line. A pale-faced captain and red-bearded sergeant sporting a thin waxed mustache glowered. Two corporals, one soft and bulky, the other long and thin, both cocky, stood behind them.

"Attentchut!" We went rigid. "I'm First Sergeant Byron Johnson. You men are now members of Marine Fighter Squadron 111."

He called out names.

"Here!"

"Here!"

"Here!" The roll call went on until all were deemed present and accounted for.

"I'm Captain Smythes. You men will be assigned duties in one of four departments. As your name is sounded step forward. Corporal Payne, Corporal Livingston and Sergeant Johnson will lead you to your quarters.

The first group was assigned to the Line Shack located near the airfield. They were destined to be trained as mechanic assistants on Wildcats. The second group was assigned to the mess hall. I breathed a sigh of relief. Doling out food, scouring pots and washing silverware was not my cup of tea, I despised it. Nobody seemed to know or care that each of us had been cashiered from one school or another. Corporal Payne led the two designated units away.

The next selected group became Ordinance Personnel. Corporal Livingston marched them away. Besides me, Titmus, Cruz, O'Bannion, Bones, Borland, Levindowski, and Pinsky remained undesignated but not for long.

"Any of you ever drive a truck?" asked the Captain.

Nobody spoke up.

"For Christ's sake, if you know how to drive a car, step forward!"

Cruz and Borland stepped forward, Levindowski followed. Titmus, Bones and I were askance since we knew Levindowski couldn't drive a car let alone a truck. He wasn't the only one. More than a few, including me, never learned how to manipulate a vehicle.

"The rest of you are assigned to Ground Defense. Johnson, show these fresh fish their quarters."

Johnson led us to our quarters. "*Fale* is Samoan for house," he said. "Move into one of these Quonset huts. It'll be your new home. Pick a bunk and square your gear away. Tomorrow you start earning your pay."

Four cots were situated on either side of the hut. Two, obviously taken, were covered with taut dark USMC green blankets and a pillow,.

We slipped out of our packs, spread blankets and squared away our sacks. After kicking off our shoes we sprawled across our new beds. We were exhausted but only Titmus conked out.

CHAPTER NINE

Before we could crap out, banging mess gear alerted us as the two occupiers of the made-up bunks staggered in.

"New pigeons," spat Cassidy, blue-eyed and black-haired, Cassidy's Irish good looks and cocky demeanor reeked of rebellion and rascality. He proceeded to mournfully inform us that he had been on this godforsaken island for six months doing nothing worth a shit. He had joined to fight Japs and Germans but was designated to dig shitholes. He was big time pissed off and pointed at the other guy, "Pop" Henderson, "this old bastard is a draftee and doesn't give a shit," snapped Cassidy.

Henderson grinned and shook his head. The former taxi driver from Chicago sported a bald head and red face. His crimson contour was creased with wrinkles and he, quite proudly, sported a small pot belly. In his early thirties and far from being in vigorous shape, looked like a guy who had never been robust and didn't give a damn about bodily contours anyway.

His beloved civilian career entailed maneuvering a cab through the hot in the summer and cold in the winter streets of Chicago. He related that after a night of driving and socializing, an official letter arrived requesting him to report to the draft board. While enduring a huge hangover he was informed by a couple of ancient draft board office ladies that he had been drafted into the Marine Corps. His protests were met with a chorus of elderly guffaws. "What the hell's use of being out of shape if they're gonna take you anyway?"

At least once an hour he'd mournfully spiel, "What the hell am I doing here? I'm too old to be a Marine. I belong in the army!"

"During World War One my dad was with the Fighting 69th," spat Cassidy. "In France my dad and his fellow fuckin' fightin' Irishmen saw more action in a week than I'll ever see in this fucked-up Corps."

"We gotta hear that again?" grinned "Pop".

"Don't talk shit, Draftee!" snapped Cassidy and went on. "Most of you new shitbirds will wind up in Ground Defense."

"Ground Defense?" said O'Bannion.

"Nobody told you?" snickered Pop.

"Sounds like we defend something."

"Ground Defense is a fancy name for Sanitary Detail, better known as the Shit Detail Unit. That's us. Our responsibility is maintaining the squadron's shithouses. We're also entrusted with other semi-skilled jobs like policing the goddamn camp and other areas too. But that ain't all. We dump garbage, not only that, we're programmed to do some killing. Yes, indeed, we spray and spray mosquitoes until they're good and dead. We also dispose of assorted bugs of varied origin.

"Believe me, there's a plenty of assorted vermin on this island that needs killing. Oh, that's not all, on occasion, when they get too sociable, we dispose of coconut crabs. "

We balefully stared at Cassidy.

"Hey, you'll find out. But don't look so upset, that's not all we do, hell no! We got other warlike duties like erecting shithouses. We keep them squared away and workable. Meantime, if the need comes up, it's our responsibility to defend them!" added Cassidy.

"Defend them! From what? From who?" quizzed O'Bannion.

"Japs, gooks, encroachers from other outfits, even our own squadron defectors. No telling who wants to defile our handiwork."

"He's right, marauders from the 22nd prefer our toilets," advised Pop.

"You're bullshitting!" said O'Bannion.

"You'll find out soon enough!" assured Cassidy.

"Is Ground Defense permanent?" I asked, hoping we were being bullshitted.

"It is. but don't be disheartened," said Cassidy, "Ground Defense does more warlike stuff too. We're also responsible for maintaining a fuckin' old fifty-caliber machine gun and a water-cooled thirty. We keep them in working order ready to repel the Japs if and when they attack British Samoa."

"Our two weapons are set up on the perimeter of the airfield. Yep, we get to clean and care for those ancient weapons. Incidentally, both are leftover relics from World War One. The Japs will be astounded when we greet them with those old guns," Chortled Pop.

"We get to fire them?" asked O'Bannion.

"Sure, we have to keep them relics in working order so once in awhile they let us shoot into the ocean," sighed Pop.

Cleaning heads and oiling obsolete machine guns were nothing to write home about. The fact that we were stuck on permanent shit-duty was disheartening. In retrospect, I sadly became conscious of the fact that as far as making a warrior-like contribution to the war effort, being an office-pinky would have been much more bellicose.

"Chow time," said Pop.

A cool breeze wafted as we grabbed mess gear and headed for the mess hall. Palm leaves rustled as tree shadows shifted before the almost impenetrable darkness shrouded us. Bones and I both agreed that British Samoa was pretty, even beautiful, but after the sun dipped, downright spooky.

"Reminds me of Panama," said Titmus, "minus the blackout."

"You been there too?" said Cassidy.

"Before the war," said Titmus.

We were about to enter the mess hall when a two-ton olive green truck came careening down the road and crashed into a coconut tree. We rushed over. The tree was damaged but the front of the truck was banged in like an accordion. Levindowski, who is happy-go-lucky, long and sinewy, climbed out of the cab. "Damn it to hell!"

"Why in hell didn't you step on the brake?" said Titmus.

"Couldn't find the fuckin' brake."

"Why you even driving?"

"That fuckin' Sergeant Laven asked who wants to be in transportation. He didn't say nothing about knowing how to drive! I figured somebody would teach me," said Levindowski, "The motor was running so I stepped on the gas and drove around the mess hall. It was easy. Nobody told me how to stop and I guess I floored the wrong peddle."

Laven, the Motor pool sergeant, cursing a blue streak, stormed up. He screamed, "Don't you know how to fuckin' drive!"

"Sure, I do, but I wasn't sure how to stop. Hey, Sarge, it's my first time."

"Why didn't you say so!"

"Nobody asked. All I heard was, 'Who wants to be in transportation?' So I raised my hand and you told me to get in and drive.

"Get the hell out of my sight!"

Levindowski joined us. "You got balls!" I said.

"Shit, it wasn't my fault. When Cruz and Borland volunteered, I did too. What the hell, I figured they'd show me. And they would have, but didn't get the chance because Laven orders me to drive around the mess hall."

Levindowski shrugged and goes into the mess hall with us and continues. "Shit no, I never drove a truck," he growled. "In fact, I never even drove a fuckin' car. If he'd a asked, I'd a told them that. Before I got behind the wheel, this Corporal Landley guy takes us to the motor pool. He shows us where jeeps and trucks are kept. He points out where they keep parts and mechanical shit. It was interesting. Landley demonstrates for a few minutes on how to care for a vehicle.

I get nervous and whispered to Cruz and Borland, "Shit, I don't even know how to drive a car, let alone a truck." Both told me to calm down and said they'd teach me.

"I figured, lots of idiots drive, it can't be too complicated. Everything would have worked out if Sergeant Laven hadn't ordered

Cruz and others to follow Corporal Landley. Off they go leaving the truck's engine running. Laven tells me to drive around the mess hall.

I stepped on the gas pedal and the truck moves. It feels good zipping around the mess hall. I go around twice. Laven waves at me to stop but I step on the gas pedal instead of the brake. It could happen to anyone. Before I know it the fuckin' truck ploughs into a fuckin' tree."

"You're in deep shit," I comforted.

"Hey, it's lucky for them I hit that tree, otherwise, I could have hurt somebody. They should give me a medal or something."

"You get away with that bullshit you'll end up being an officer," said Titmus.

Cassidy was impressed, "Yeah, maybe even a general. Anyway, if they transfer you into Ground Defense, move in with us."

Our first night on British Samoa was memorable. Most of us had been city and small town dwellers. We weren't used to jungle sounds.

Aboard the *Feland* we had become accustomed to swishing sea noises. The eerie jungle stillness was intermittently disturbed by animal noises that kept us alert and listening. Weary as we were, it took time before us island newcomers conked out.

At 0500 we were roused by Corporal Landley. After morning chow he showed us around. The enlisted men's Quonset huts were neatly situated across a lawn-like area shaded by swaying coconut trees. They were spread over a large park-like tract.

VMF's Wildcats and other aircraft were parked in revetments situated on the seaside of the runway. The length of the airfield was less than forty yards from where the ocean lapped at the shore. Blue and white breakers barely rippled as they caressed the gleaming coral sand.

At either end of the airfield, the squadron's two emplaced machine guns pointed seaward. Ground Defense was solely responsible for their maintenance. If the Japs attacked it would be Ground Defense's responsibility to repel them.

After the tour, Landry ordered us back to our Quonset hut. Our seabags had arrived and been carelessly tossed from the trucks.

We dragged our belongings into our new homes. We showered and changed into clean green dungarees with the Corps' emblem stamped on our left breast pocket.

Cassidy called our attention to a woebegone dog sprawled outside our Quonset hut. The dilapidated mongrel was about the size of an emaciated German shepherd. Neither physical nor behavioral traits betrayed a hint of his ancestry. His lineage, obviously, was a mixture of multiple breeds.

Despite occasionally being bathed by some empathetic enlistee, his sparse white and black fur remained dirty. Pink rims circled his eyes and his nose dripped. Besides being spiritless he lacked all other redeeming doggie traits.

Former Marine occupants had called him Taps, the name stuck. Even that militaristic sobriquet seemed too flattering.

If another decrepit island cur happened along to bark or gently sniff, Taps cowered into the thick foliage and remained unaccounted for until it was time to eat.

He dutifully snoozed outside our door. When one of us invited him into our hut, which was seldom, as if apologizing, he'd dolefully wag his drooping tail and refuse to enter. When someone arrived or departed he raised his begrimed head and appraised the guest.

On rare occasions, if caressed, he'd half-heartedly thump his bedraggled tail. If ordered to come, go, stand or sit, he'd do neither. As far as dogs go, he was a loser. We occupants of Quonset Hut No. 8 related to his sullen status and occasionally threw him a leftover tidbit. Other than that, we paid little heed to our bequested dweller. He paid even less attention to us.

CHAPTER TEN

Each morning Titmus, Bones, Cassidy, Pinsky, Pop, O'Bannion and I reported to the tool shack. Unskilled peons in Ground Defense were delegated to wield shovels and picks. There was nothing we could do about it except get into some kind of technical school and learn a skill. However, that wasn't likely to happen. We were stuck.

One warm tropical day we stood perspiring as Corporal Landley doled out our tools of trade. Sergeant Garland, as if we were too dull to figure it out, proceeded to instruct Ground Defense personnel on the delicate art of excavating a latrine. After his longwinded sermon pooped him out, he led us into the woods. "This is it, dig! And remember, it's for our officers! Make sure it's ten feet long, four feet wide and seven feet deep. They expect to do their business in comfort, got it!"

He marked off a perimeter with a coiled ruler and ordered us to commence digging. "I'll be back," he grunted.

O'Bannion groaned as Bones commenced chopping. While we excavated we wearily chorused, "Shit! Shit! Shit!"

"I didn't join to do this kind of crap!" Cassidy moaned.

"Hey, I didn't even join," lamented Pop.

"What about you?" Titmus pointed at me.

" I volunteered."

"You what!" Pop quizzed.

"You don't register for the draft until you're eighteen. I didn't wait."

"Hey, I didn't wait!" said O'Bannion.

"Kids!" sighed Pop. "They take a long time to learn."

"The Marines are drafting! The old Corps is really shot to hell!" ventured Titmus.

We dug for another ten minutes before Pop threw down his shovel and wheezed, "Time for a break." Nobody argued. We dropped our tools and flaked out in the shade of coconut palms. We gulped from our canteens before closing our eyes. A half hour later Pop rose to his feet and said, "Let's dig a little."

He was a buck-ass private like the rest of us. Nobody had put him in charge but Titmus didn't care, and the rest of us were used to being ordered around so we went back to digging. Anyway, Pop was mellow and none of us felt like he was playing big-shot.

After dinner we were pooped and most of us conked out before we even commenced bitching. The next morning we were back digging. The following day went the same.

When our hole was finally deep enough we carted in an oblong wood box with four ass-wide holes and situated it on our excavated ditch. I gazed at our completed handiwork with pride and felt silly being proud of a shithouse.

"Who's gonna launch it?" asked Cassidy.

"Officers' territory," warned Pop.

"We wouldn't want one of our officers to get a splinter in his ass or, worse yet, fall in," said Titmus.

"Should be tested," agreed Bones.

Titmus squatted and after awhile raised his thumb signifying, "A-Okay."

Each of us proceeded to render one or other appropriate contribution.

After the launchings Bones ceremoniously asked, "Do we find Garland?"

"So he can put us on another shit detail?" growled Cassidy.

Voices alerted us. Garland and Landley had arrived and were inspecting. "Don't look bad, Sarge."

"For a bunch of sorry shitbirds it's alright," said Garland. He seemed pleased.

"Follow me!" We tailed him to another location closer to our Quonset hut. He pointed, "Dig!" and then strode into the woods followed by Corporal Landley.

Lots of times we'd be on a detail when the roar of Wildcats zooming across the sky got our attention. Each time O'Bannion sighed, "That's what I should be doing."

I commiserated, "If you had joined the Air Corps, you'd be Lieutenant 'Ace' O'Bannion by now."

He didn't appreciate my sarcasm. "I don't want to be no flying dogface," he snapped.

Day after day was the same for us. We caught mess duty, guard duty, cleaned the two machine guns, dug and sprayed shitholes. We despised Ground Defense but were cemented in. What a way to fight a war!

After sundown lights were doused and the island became immersed in shrouds of blackness. Most nights one or more of us caught guard duty.

Sentry obligations entailed toting a slung Garand as we paced around headquarters, the mess hall, airfield or the surrounding forested area. It was difficult trotting along deep in the woods. In the midst of dense growth when the moon was obscured, sentries were unable to discern objects further than an arm's length. Wary guards pacing to and fro were frequently startled by huge bats flapping their expansive wings as they squealed overhead.

At night cattle roamed about, their bodies merging with the intense blackness. Sometimes their mournful lowing sounded. But mostly, their red fireball eyes just glowed through the blackness discomfiting nervous sentries.

It was spooky alright, and pairs of gleaming eyes never failed to scare the shit out of me. More than a few times I shouted "Halt!" at the glowing, but the eyes didn't waver. I wasn't the only one relieved when our relief guard showed up.

Those meandering cows caused more than just me, dutifully striving to perform guard duty in regulatory manner, to edge close to an embarrassing panic attack.

The raider battalion encamped nearby added to our guard duty uneasiness. Much of their commando training exercises took place long after the sun went down. Immersed in the darkness they prowled around the island intent on humiliating sailors, soldiers and fellow Marines. Those elite warriors delighted in making Airedales the butts of their training shenanigans.

After sundown one or two of us would be assigned to guard our two antique machine guns. Although we kept alert during four hour sentry stints, by morning integral parts of the weapon would be missing.

The purloined pieces, most of the time, would be dutifully and sometimes apologetically returned in the morning. Occasionally, bellicose raiders would overpower one of our pacing sentries. A telephone call would inform the officer on duty that Post Number One, or whatever, was not secure. The O.D. and Sergeant of the Guard would find the hapless hog-tied guard trussed and embarrassed. The perpetrators tried to subdue their gloating, but we knew what they thought about Airedales and it wasn't flattering.

Our C.O. angrily contacted their major who apologetically excused his men by claiming that they were restless and craved action. "After all," he apologetically added, "They're real Marines."

He also assured Major Clayson that he would order his raiders to desist from their reckless forays. However, as long as his men's antics improved their stalking ability, he didn't seem to really give a damn.

On a starless night I was on sentry duty striding the beachside of the airfield. As I trod, the murmuring surf lulled me into a semi-comatose mode. About ten yards away a jutting rock seemed to move.

I ceased moving and tried to visually penetrate the stilled blackness. There was no sound and nothing moved.

I was embarrassed but reasoned, what the hell, and bellowed, "Halt!" There was no response. "Okay," I said. "If you're Japs you're dead, If you ain't, so be it," and I raised my rifle and pulled back the bolt.

"Don't shoot!" whined a Brooklynese voice as four camouflaged Raiders stood up raised their hands and sheepishly chorused, "We're on your side."

"Get your asses out of here before I shoot the shit out of you!" They laughed but in less than seconds disappeared.

On weekends and nights if I didn't have guard duty and wasn't completely broke or wiped out, I'd saunter into a village. O'Bannion or one of the others usually came along.

We were aware that male villagers spent the days rowing, fishing, climbing coconut trees and swimming. Most were good-looking guys with sinewy bodies. Females dutifully toting loads on heads and shoulders were usually spied quietly following fathers, husbands, brothers or chiefs. The ladies seemed to be stuck doing the heavy work.

In the villages young girls and boys laughed and played. Samoans seemed perennially happy and unworried about the war or anything else. At least that's how it seemed to us.

Before World War One began, the Germans were ousted and New Zealand had taken over. A goodly number of islanders obviously had been imbued with either New Zealand or German ancestries or both. Some girls were damn attractive and as time elapsed became more so.

A number of natives were cursed with elephantitus. The horrible affliction was called *mumu*. Diseased natives were easily perceived by extremely swollen legs, forearms or both. Severely diseased males were seen carting swollen balls in wheelbarrows. Mosquitoes were responsible for inflicting the dreaded malady.

Not many Marines became afflicted, but if an American's arm, leg or nuts suddenly swelled to a disproportionate size, the poor guy would be diagnosed with elephantitus. If the swellings were dire enough, the victim would be shipped back to the states. A few, very few, didn't regret the unsightly affliction. After all, it meant going home.

Natives roamed through our camp at will. We didn't stop them. Of course, we kept eyes peeled knowing that once they spotted shirts, trousers or blankets, they had no compunctions about usurping them. According to Samoan culture, they weren't stealing. Natives just didn't fathom why an individual would or should possess more than one article of clothing while others, usually themselves, had none.

Frequently a Ground Defense buck-assed private, like me, would be ordered to take charge of a native labor detail. Long leafy fronds and stale coconuts littered the ground. Natives could earn a dollar, cans of spam, or both for gathering fallen palm fronds and coconuts.

From their point of reference, picking and piling brush served no rational or communal purpose whatsoever. They deemed our constant clean-up efforts to be a pointless American endeavor. For them, pick-up sessions became an amusing fuck-off game for which they got paid.

Natives on pick-up detail slept or disappeared until it was time to get paid. Cajoles or threats had little impact. Disciplining the happy-go-lucky people was futile. Those of us relegated to oversee work parties concluded that our designated natives had the right idea. Why knock yourself out for a pointless reason.

Native women would frequently glide into our camp hoping to do menial tasks. They would argue and barter but were happy to clean and press our green fatigues and khakis for soap or cigarettes.

The bare-bosomed laundresses soaked our uniforms in nearby ponds. They followed the dunking up by pounding our wet clothes with rocks. Afterwards they used heated rocks to press our faded fabric. The soaking and pounding whitened khaki shirts and pants and they looked worn and salty. It only cost a pack of cigarettes, a dollar bill or both to get a pile of duds laundered. We were pleased with the results.

Laundress, hustler and bootlegger, Hungry Helen was a sweetheart of an old dame. She was dark, wrinkled and knobby-kneed and her youth had dissipated a long long time ago. She didn't converse in English, but we knew she understood more than she let on. Anyway, there wasn't a need for verbal communication.

The old dame possessed a tremendous appetite. She stowed away C and K rations like each bite would be her last. When O'Bannion slipped her a can of tinned beef, more than a little grateful she presented us with a partially filled bottle of homemade gin.

The liquid tasted terrible and was officially tabooed but went down smoother than shaving lotion. The libation got Marines drunker than the proverbial inebriated skunk.

Pinsky got a kick out of touching Hungry Helen on the thigh. The old dame would squeal, laugh and flirt. She was a character alright and one of our favorite people.

When broke and unable to make into Apia we partook of another pastime. We shouldered our rifles and stalked into the jungle to shoot bats. The huge homely-looking creatures habituated towering trees. In the daytime they slept amid lofty foliage hanging upside-down. If not provoked, they kept inactive until dusk.

If we fired into trees, hanging bats would leave their daytime perches and flap about squealing eerie-sounding protests.

It was difficult to bring down the ominous looking mammals. Our bullets either passed through wing membranes or completely missed the moving target. British Samoa was an idyllic island but we were young, eager, restless and bored. We were a strapping bunch of teenagers lusting to get laid.

A month after we were ensconced on British Samoa, Binnelli, a young old timer, took Bones, Pinsky, and me to a picturesque village. Between two coconut palm trees, an old native guy sporting a rounded belly waited. He knew Binnelli, *"Talofa,"* he chuckled and led us to his thatched home.

Inside he plopped down on the dirt floor and crossed his legs. Binnelli and Bones sat. Pinsky and I followed suit.

An older man, brown, skinny, with a toothless smile and concaved-chest emerged. He set a dish of crackers and jelly before us. Our portly host plucked a cracker and smeared it with jelly prior to chomping. Binnelli and Bones likewise dabbed crackers and motioned for Pinsky and me to do the same. Far from enthused, we splotched a dab of jelly on a stale cracker.

Behind him, a heavyset mature dame followed by two girls entered. The first was short and squat, the other tall and lean. Well-worn cotton print dresses hung from the three. The young ones could have been in their twenties, neither was attractive.

Their English was halting, but they probably understood more then they let on. Binnelli knew some Samoan sentences and Bones, eager to practice Polynesian, tried. The natives seemed to appreciate his effort but giggled at his linguistic attempt. Giggling seemed to be a common Samoan reaction.

There wasn't much conversation between us that made sense, but we were careful not to say anything disparaging in either language.

The Eagle hadn't shit for three weeks, meaning payday was more than five days away, but Binnelli slipped three one dollar bills to our host. He lumbered outside and we heard him digging. He came back hugging several bottles.

The girls handed each of us well-worn cups and the old lady poured. "What the fuck is it?" muttered Pinsky.

"Shh!" warned Binnelli, "Gook beer, they have to keep it hid."

"Looks like piss, I ain't drinking this," said Pinsky.

"You insult them you'll get us killed!" snapped Binnelli,

"I gotta?"

"Shut up and drink!"

"What the hell is in it?" he rasped.

"Coconut milk, grapefruit juice, some lizard piss among other libations," said Binnelli.

"Secret stuff, good for you," confided our host and lifted his glass. We had no choice but to gulp.

It was rejectionally potent, but after a few swallows it slipped down somewhat easier.

The old guy pulled out a weathered ukulele-like instrument and commenced plucking. Binnelli impulsively staggered to his feet and swayed his arms and hips. He imagined that he was dancing and it was far from pleasant to watch.

Pinsky, looking glum, took another swig also rose and started swaying. As they twirled, the girls sweetly belted out the popular, "You are my Sunshine."

CHAPTER ELEVEN

Each Friday, if not stuck with guard duty or another mundane obligation, off-duty Marines boarded the rickety bus to Apia. Due to the warmth and humidity the starched khakis worn by Marines and soldiers on liberty quickly lost their creases. Swabbies ashore from ship or shorebases wore undress whites. Pressed or unpressed bellbottoms looked the same.

Weekend dances in Apia were held in an expansive but decrepit wooden structure. The makeshift navy and Marine musicians blared melodies of the forties.

Army, navy, and Marine contingents plus New Zealand soldiers glided, pranced, two-stepped, and bounced over the weathered deck swinging barefooted partners. As couples gyrated across the deck their sweat soaked bodies heated the room.

Early in the evening amiable moods prevailed, but as the night was whirled away, guzzled gin and home brew affected the perspiring participants, some not so amiably.

On a moonlit evening the joint was jammed. Males outnumbered females. Titmus, Bones, O'Bannion and I gave up trying to entice native girls to drink, dance or talk. After all, we conspicuously lacked stripes and were deemed low level suitors. We sullenly slipped outside and strode away from the heat, noise, smoke and congestion. Apia's streets were quiet, dark and deserted.

We were feeling down as we sipped harsh tasting gook gin from a fruit jar while aimlessly meandering through the unlit town. Outside of a bit of cursing, we trod in silence until we spotted a dull light glowing from the window of a ramshackle store. "Ahh," ventured Bones as we impulsively stepped through the open door to be greeted by a buxom lady. Her coffee complexed daughter demurely stood by her side.

The elder woman warily appraised us before gesturing for us to sit. She set three assorted cups on the table and poured *kava*. We sipped while the woman and her light-skinned offspring distrustfully observed. Of course, as expected, after paying for the sweet-tasting libation their strained smiles relaxed a bit.

The younger was a lithesome maid in her early twenties. Attractive and endowed with a trim figure; she spoke better than palatable English. She wistfully imparted that her departed grandfather and long absent father were Germans.

She ruefully imparted that when her father, without notice or fanfare, stepped aboard an outgoing vessel; she had been a mere toddler. He never returned, nor did he ever communicate. Her mother ruefully interrupted to confide that her husband's presentable looks had fooled her, but after the wedding his Nazi-like demeanor surfaced.

In her soft New Zealand lilt the younger one related that she had learned to read, write and speak English in a missionary school. A few such schools run by passel of holy people still functioned on the island.

"I like Americans," she guilelessly confided, "but I don't trust them, especially Marines."

Titmus rolled his eyes and shrugged. "Can't fault you for that." Then he indicated to Bones and me that it was time to leave.

He told our hostesses that we had better catch the last transportation back or we'd be up shit creek without a paddle. The three of us thanked the ladies for their hospitality and politely bade them *tofa*. Both smiled indulgently but weren't chagrined to see us depart.

As we jogged back to the dance hall, "I'd like to do business with that young one," I offered.

"Forget it," said Titmus, "she's out of your class."

"Way out," muttered Bones.

We got to the empty dance hall as the last conveyance, an obsolete fire truck was pulling away. We leaped aboard. The Seabee driver was half-in-the-bag. Being it was Friday night, his condition wasn't unusual. Several sailors, two Marines from the 22nd and two soldiers were already aboard as we pushed into the crowded truck bed. The driver stepped on the gas as the Seabee on the passenger side of the cab shouted, "We're on our way!"

Coconut palm leaves swayed and the shifting ocean reflected a wavy full moon. We were caressed by a warm breeze as we sped along. I closed my eyes basking in the magic of the moment when startled by O'Bannion roar. "You swabjockey son-of-a-bitch, I'll flatten your ass!"

The bed of the truck jammed with standing uniforms commenced to become a shoving, punching hullabaloo. It was next to impossible to avoid getting involved. Because of the cramped situation headlocks were more prevalent than punches.

The truck was zooming along at sixty when the driver braked to a screeching stop. The sudden lurch spilled O'Bannion, two Marines from the 22nd, two sailors and me onto the dirt road. The Seabee driver leaped from the cab "What the fuck's goin' on!"

"Get your ass back in the cab!" growled a guy from the 22nd. The driver was about to rebut but instead climbed back behind the wheel. We climbed back into the truck but the two swabbies wavering on the road declined to get back. They stood shoulder to shoulder in a cloud of coral dust watching us disappear.

"Not bad for Airdales," said one of the guys from the 22nd.

"What's that supposed to mean?" said O'Bannion.

"We're line-company," said the other.

"Yeah!" snapped the other and delivered a roundhouse right to O'Bannion's gut.

"Oh, shit!" grunted Titmus and threw a short jab at the sucker-puncher. Headlocks and grappling commenced until the truck again screeched to a stop spilling passengers.

This time the sprawled passengers on the road included Titmus, Bones, O'Bannion, two from the 22nd and me. We rolled around ineffectually whacking at each other as the driver again leaped out and whined, "Knock the shit off, will ya, I got a schedule to make. Aw fuck you crazy Gyrenes."

He got back into the cab, drove off leaving us groveling in its dusty wake. The guys remaining on the vehicle lustily waved as they sped off. I suddenly lost interest in my opponent. He too, wasn't eager to continue and we sullenly desisted our give and take shoving. O'Bannion and his combatant also ceased tussling. Our lust for battle stifled, we four and the two from the 22nd sadly viewed the truck disappearing.

The six of us sullenly trod the dusty road together until the road branched off toward our respective camps. As they went their way and we went ours, less than amiable farewells were exchanged.

The fracas on the liberty truck was too much for Bones. He refused to accompany us into town again. He found a couple of books about both Samoan Islands and their cultures and assiduously read about the natives and their islands' history. As weeks slipped by, Bones became more of a loner. Sure, he performed his share of shitty duties, but unlike us, he didn't do much complaining. At the end of the day when labors were done he was content to be by himself.

Then he began disappearing. I got wind that Bones was visiting villages and conversing with natives. When I queried him he told me that he was intrigued with the Samoan's happy-go-lucky dispositions and lazzei faire attitude toward life. He confided that he was really intrigued with the local culture and language.

A couple of days later I concluded that maybe he had something going and it might behoove me to get involved. When I confided to Bones that I was interested in that Samoan cultural stuff, he didn't seem enthused but invited me to join him on a village visit.

The elderly head-man of Vaiima knew Bones and more than cordially greeted us. *"Talofa,"* spouted Bones, and the old guy laughed and said the same. He invited us into his *fale* where we sat on the dirt deck. The old guy spoke some English and Bones chattered in Samoan. They talked and laughed and I chortled too but understood less than half of what they were saying.

His wife, a portly white-haired dame wearing a long print dress served each of us a cup of muddy-looking liquid. Soft chunks of something floated on top and the beverage was less than warm. I tried to be polite and almost was able to down the tepid stuff. Bones swallowed it as if it were a chocolate milk shake.

As I grimaced Bones whispered, "Act like you like it!"

"Hah!" I retorted."

"Manners, for god's sake, these people are sensitive!"

"I don't give a shit what they are, this stuff tastes awful!"

"Believe me, Sherman, you don't want to hurt their feelings,

I sensed he was right, so I bravely sipped a bit more. Each time I set the cup down the gaping old dame grinned and motioned for me to drink up. I felt pressured and swallowed more than half of the putrid stuff.

A broad-beamed woman in her forties came in and plopped down in front of us. Wrapped in a *lava lava* she kept staring at me. I got fidgety.

"What does she want, Bones?"

"Your body I'm guessing," said Bones.

"That old dame's not my cup of tea," I whispered.

"You're too particular," said Bones.

"You *malini*. I likee *malini*. No likee *make-male*. No likee swab jockey too," she said.

That did it, time to depart. I got to my feet and jovially directed several *tofas* to the hosts and left. Bones was far from pleased but *c'este le vive*.

It was several weeks before Bones gave me another chance to acclimate myself to the social morals of the local natives. He invited me to accompany him on a different excursion. Without asking I shrugged and went along. "You won't forget this," he said.

"Don't try to line me up again with one of your elderly gook friends," I warned.

"Too late, you blew your chance for romance."

"If I see someone interesting," I said, "I'll do my own courting, got it?"

About that time he shrugged and we got lucky. A jeep stopped and a congenial Seabee told us to hop in.

As we barreled along, Bones perused a hand-drawn map. After awhile he asked the driver to let us off. We thanked the guy and walked. He studied the map until we got to the foot of a mountain.

"We goin' up?"

"Yep."

"This mountain is pretty damn steep," I said.

Native kids were throwing a green coconut around. A twelve year old approached and pointed skyward, "You go up?"

"Grave there?" said Bones and pointed up.

"There!" and the kid pointed."

"Someone buried on the top?" I said.

"Want to see dead guy's grave?" said the kid.

"How much?"

"Two pack cigarettes."

"I give one pack for both of us." Bones gestured toward me.

"Okay."

Bones placed a pack of butts into the kid's hand. "Maybe I give another when we get to top."

Three boys got behind each of us and pushed. We were almost running as the youngsters pushed, laughed and shouted, and propelled us upward. It took close to an hour before we reached the summit and though the six kids did the work, only Bones and I were panting and sweating.

It was an elating sensation scanning the curved seascape below. Bones turned and stepped to the grave site. He seemed in a trance as he read,

Under the wide and starry sky
Dig the grave and let me lie
Glad did I live and gladly die
And I laid me down with a will
This be the verse you grave for me
Here he lies where he longed to be;
Home is the sailor home from the sea
And the hunter home from the hill

"Did you know Robert Louis Stevenson had seen much of the world before settling here?"

"Never thought about it."

"The poor guy had tuberculosis and must have figured he was nearing the end. He came to British Samoa to get cured. If he craved serenity and spectacular scenery, how can you beat this?"

I almost remarked that dead people don't enjoy beautiful views but it was too nice up there to spew wisecracks.

Birds were sounding melodious peeps when a breeze kicked up. I appreciated the view but felt it was time to go. "Bones!" I said and nodded toward the darkening horizon. He was reluctant to go but reasoned that since the gook kids had left and it was getting dark we better start down.

We tried a slow walk down but our cautious descent became a gallop as steepness impelled us to speed downward. The sides were steep as well as narrow. One precarious misstep could induce a rocky roll to the bottom.

Our gleeful urchins suddenly appeared and observed our graceless descending sprints. They expected us to stumble, but when we reached the foot of the mountain erect, they laughed and jumped about telling us that others had not reached the base in upright positions. Our chests stuck out as if we had completed a noble athletic feat.

As time went by I started spending more time in the village, not for cultural or educational reasons but because of Malia. She was slim for a Samoan, almost dainty. The brown-skinned beauty was pretty, oh, so pretty. All in all, she was nicely stacked. Despite her haughty attitude, I liked her looks and felt deeply attracted to her.

Her face and contours danced in my mind. Her image was especially vivid after I hit the sack. I really wanted to charm that girl but was too shy and uncertain of native mores to commence courting. One time, we were on the same path. As we approached each other from different directions I stammered, "*Talofa!*"

"Pardon me, please," she beamed.

Stunned by her precise English I stepped aside and she gracefully slipped by. As she sashayed down the path I focused on her swaying ass, self-consciously, of course

There were other times we met. Depending on the occasion, I'd greet her in English, other times in Polynesian. I was aware that she spoke English but decided that I could impress her if she knew I was trying to master Polynesian. I did try to engage Malia in conversation, but beyond six to eight Polynesian words I had problems expanding my Samoan vocabulary.

Anyway, I couldn't get her to exchange more than a Polynesian *talofa* and *tofa*. I sadly concluded that my romantic overtures were wasted and conceded that she was a lost cause. I abruptly ceased my futile courting efforts.

Bones didn't confide or mention Malia's name more than two or three times, but I'd occasionally spy him gawking at her. In turn, her eyes, grey because of bygone German or New Zealand ancestry, demurely appraised him with more than passing interest.

CHAPTER TWELEVE

Duty on beautiful British Samoa was far from demanding but it was dull, especially for us peons in Ground Defense.

Titmus wasn't bothered, he just wanted to get his overseas obligations over with so he could get back to Millie. Pop Henderson really missed maneuvering his taxicab along the streets of Chicago. He also missed his wife. O'Bannion, Cassidy, Pinsky and I craved action. That's why we became Marines.

One serene Sunday, while the rest of us sat around shooting the breeze about nothing and sipping distilled apricot brandy, Bones left to traipse off to a native church. He confided that he was going there to sing and pray.

After he left Cassidy solemnly announced, "Haven't you guys noticed? Bones Donigal got the thousand yard stare."

"You're full of crap!" I retorted.

"I been out here longer than you and I've seen the signs," said Cassidy.

"You ain't been in the Corps long enough to know which end is up," said O'Bannion.

"Believe me, I've seen guys go Asiatic. When I first got here there was a corporal that ..."

Titmus interrupted, "Hey, I ain't never seen a Marine that content except for a few old China Hands in Shanghai. Sure, them guys were Asiatic alright but happy too."

"A guy joins the Marines to fight," stated O'Bannion.

Only Titmus heeded his repetitive bullshit. "You're nuts, kid!"

"Bones is okay, he just ain't Marine inside," advised Pinsky.

"Who in his right mind wants to be a Marine inside or out!" snapped Pop.

Pinsky, O'Bannion, Cassidy and I glowered at Pop's outburst, but at thirty-something, he was such an old fart that we didn't redress.

"I still say Bones ain't acting right," said Cassidy.

"He'll come around," said Titmus and that was that.

Weeks slipped and Bones cleaned machine guns, policed up like he was supposed to. Unlike the rest of us constantly bitching he kept staid and performed as ordered. But as soon as the day's work was done he'd shower and be off. That is if he wasn't stuck on guard or mess duty.

We saw less and less of him. He seldom got back to camp until the early morning hours in time for muster. He didn't boast, protest, or even comment about his exploits.

On nights when he caught guard duty he seemed more agitated than normal. He walked his post in what could be regarded as less than an alert manner. In between pacing time he sat in the guard shack peering at the bulkhead.

I tried engaging him in conversation but he'd get cranky, which wasn't his usual MO.

"Hey, Bones, you got that thousand yard stare!" said Cassidy.

"Shut your oafish mouth!" snapped Bones.

Bones had never before sounded off in such a belligerent manner. His abrupt reaction astounded us, especially Cassidy who rose with clenched fists ready to go to battle stations. Titmus glared at him. "Knock it off, Cassidy or I'll tie you both in a knot!"

Cassidy almost retorted but sat down. Bones also sat but not as quickly.

Afterwards, Titmus, Pinsky and I discussed his uncharacteristic behavior. I mean, we had been aware he was kind of weird but now he was acting downright creepy.

For instance, he'd lie on his bunk and focus on the overhead. In the mess hall he'd sometimes stare at the bulkhead as if in a trance. He wouldn't move until one of us jostled him.

I tried to cheer Bones up by querying him about Samoan history and geographical stuff. Oh, when I questioned him he'd answer, but not with any enthusiasm. We invited him to join our treks to Apia, but without rending an excuse he declined. I even asked him to let me join him on another one of his village visits but he politely declined. Anyway none of our efforts to straighten him out altered his weird behavior.

One quiet Saturday, O'Bannion, Pinsky and I were getting ready to venture into town. Titmus was on his sack mulling about whether to join us or go off on his own when Bones barged in. He almost looked normal except for the shit-eating grin on his face. "Where you been?" quizzed Titmus.

"I visited Robert's resting place again."

"Home is the hunter home from the hill," I recited.

"And the sailor home from the sea," he added.

"The same kids push you up?"

"Made it up there myself. " He boasted and walked out.

"What was that all about?" said O'Bannion.

I was going to explain but thought, "Fuck it."

Bones erratic behavior concerned me but I kept my mouth shut.

A month later, with money again, O'Bannion and I were in a bar in Apia seeking feminine liaisons. We tried charm, bribery and trade but our efforts were in vain. The ladies just weren't susceptible. After several futile hours we finally acknowledged that our courting ploys were doomed and done.

We stuck out our thumbs and an uncovered truck heading in the direction of our camp screeched to a stop. On board were Marines and swabbies, the former from the 22nd. With unpleasant results we kept running into those cantankerous infantrymen. They were also in dour moods. Obviously none of our fellow hitchhikers had experienced courting success.

Before the inevitable squabble with strangers ensued, O'Bannion and I became embittered about something or other and tangled. In retrospect I'm not sure who pushed who first, but suddenly slap-bang grappling between us ensued. I had O'Bannion in a headlock and his arm was tightly wrapped around my neck. We squeezed and pulled striving to slam each other down.

Invective accompanied our tussling. Our truculent behavior annoyed our fellow travelers. "Shithead Airedales!" were among their bitter epitaphs. As our conveyance screeched to a sudden stop our grasps broke and we sprawled across the truck bed.

Three cantankerous inebriates from the 22nd pushed us from the truck. We indignantly sprawled on the road immersed in a cloud of coral dust watching our transportation gunning away.

We grudgingly got to our feet and brushed off the white dust. We didn't resume squabbling because we had forgotten what had preceded our disagreement. Still, we were not too weary to blame each other while hiking back to our camp. We trod along perspiring and grousing until we came upon the trail leading to Vaiima. Before we crossed the path leading to the village we heard sweet sounds of crooning voices backed by guitars. "Hear that!" said O'Bannion.

"I hear it."

Weary of walking but hesitant to engage in conversation we silently shuffled toward the music. As we drew nearer party sounds amplified, we came upon glistening natives gathered around a flaming pit. An enormous pig was being roasted. Tiny bubbles rose from its scorched carcass.

Shadows flickered on the oiled bodies of young girls undulating to the music of strummed guitars. Natives swayed and sang. O'Bannion dug an elbow into my ribs and pointed. I focused on an enormous half-naked regal old man, obviously a chief. At his side sat a beaming Malia looking young and radiant.

"Not him!" whispered O'Bannion and I sighted Bones Donigal sitting on the chief's other side. He too was wrapped in a *lava lava* and bare-chested. A halo of white flowers crowned his head.

Bones spotted us and beckoned. We sauntered over and Bones rattled off in Samoan what I supposed was introductions. He spoke their language like he'd been talking Polynesian all his life. Bones introduced Malia as his wife. It was a shocker, of course. The old guy motioned to us, "Sit!"

Bones spouted in Polynesian to a *teini* and a sweet looking girl sidled over and plopped down. She had a lovely teenager's smile and told me her name was Lepepa.

My envy of Bones dissipated as I again fell in love. Another attractive young *wahine* sat by O'Bannion. Her name was Vaitupa and he too was ensnared. Both girls were friendly and outgoing.

The inevitable gook gin was passed about.

"I ain't gonna drink this," said O'Bannion.

"Drink or they'll be insulted and that won't be good for any of us," whispered Bones.

O'Bannion scowled and downed his cup and held it out for more. I sipped and quickly swallowed trying to hide my frown. Lepepa giggled and filled my cup again.

O'Bannion sipped another but quietly bitched to me about it. Soon taro, breadfruit, coconuts, bananas, and other native foodstuffs were brought out.

The party lasted all night. The three of us made it back to camp before reveille. Neither O'Bannion nor I, though we tried, came close to getting anywhere with the coquettish lovelies. In the morning we were hung over but felt like it was only a matter of time before we scored with one of the pretty young damsels.

From then on, if we didn't catch guard duty or other obligation, O'Bannion and I headed for Vaiima. The villagers treated us like honored guests. Not because of us, but because of Bones. They liked him and we were his friends.

It wasn't long before Bones became a titled personage in the village, something like an honorary chief. And O'Bannion and me, by being Bones' pals, had elevated status which lent us an additional touch of respect.

I was infatuated with Lepepa and he with Vaitupa. Our courtships got no farther than mutual giggling over nothing and an occasional quick touch. It still beat getting drunk in Apia.

One evening as O'Bannion and I were leaving our *fale,* we noticed Cassidy sitting on his bunk looking glum. "Somebody die?" queried O'Bannion.

"Dear John letter," mumbled Cassidy.

"Oh, shit, one of them. Hey, come with us," said O'Bannion.

"Yeah," I said. Without a word Cassidy put on a clean shirt and without spouting his usual silly questions tagged along.

Before we reached the village outskirts, sounds of merrymaking drifted to us. We came upon a blazing fire. Natives were dining, dancing, and having a ball. Vaitupa and Lepepa approached and handed us each a bottle of gook beer. They stepped into the circle and resumed dancing. Without a word Cassidy stepped in and commenced wiggling in front of Vaitupa. She laughed and sashayed around him.

"That son-of-a-bitch," said O'Bannion.

"Relax, it's just a dance."

"I don't trust that horny bastard."

After the dance ended Cassidy strolled over. "That's my woman!" said O'Bannion.

"Sure," said Cassidy and turned and waved. Vaitupa giggled and waved back. "She likes me," said Cassidy. He sauntered toward her and she sashayed to meet him. Cassidy moved in for a kiss but she gracefully evaded. Both laughed and he tried again.

"Cut that shit out!" shouted O'Bannion. Vaitupa suddenly sat down in the circle. Cassidy dropped to his knees and made way toward her. She looked terrified and joyous at the same time. He pecked her on the cheek and she reacted with over-acted horror. Cassidy chortled and Vaitupa giggled. O'Bannon leaped forward and jerked Cassidy by the collar and both fell backwards.

Cassidy got to his feet first. "What the fuck's the matter with you?"

I moved between them. "Don't start shit!" I warned.

Cassidy fired an overhand right catching the side of my head. I reciprocated with an overhand right that bounced off his left cheek. At the time I wondered what in hell O'Bannion was doing. I caught a glimpse of him arguing with Vaitupa but was too busy trying not to get nailed by Cassidy to yell.

As a big Samoan came charging into the fray, Cassidy left me and bowled the giant over with a flying shoulder block. Two others behemoths wrestled Cassidy to the ground and fell upon him. I helped O'Bannion pull them off and we tried to make peace. But when Cassidy got to his feet and bellowed, "Goddamn savages!" and began flailing away, it was all over.

The Samoans turned on us and the three of us suddenly stood back to back fighting for our lives. There were too many. Cassidy must have sobered a bit because he abruptly broke loose and ran. O'Bannion and I galloped behind him. Rocks were thrown but, thank goodness, they didn't chase after us. A hundred yards from the village we slowed to a walk. We were still wheezing and looked like we'd been through a major engagement .

"You were trying to steal my girl," sputtered O'Bannion.

"You out yer fuckin' mind!" said Cassidy.

"You're both assholes!" I muttered.

"I ain't never inviting you to nothin' again," said O'Bannion.

"I wouldn't go if you did!" said Cassidy.

"Assholes!" I repeated.

A week slipped by before Bones informed us, "Cassidy is barred from the village for life." He added that because of his status and influence O'Bannion and I could return, but added, "Be on your best behavior or it's over for you too!"

One quiet afternoon I was entering our oil-drum shower as Bones emerged. Before he reached for his towel I spotted an array of blue tattoos etched on his body from knees to hips. Birds, caterpillars and centipedes were dyed into his skin. "What the hell!" I uttered.

"Samoan custom," he said.

"You gone nuts!"

"It's a symbol."

"Those things come off?" I gasped.

"Nope, they're on for good."

"You gone rock-happy?"

"These inscriptions mean that a boy has become a man."

"So!"

"My body, my home, my choice," and Bones strode away.

"You've gone Asiatic!" I shouted as he walked away.

Later I repeated our conversation to Titmus.

"What do we do?" I groaned.

"Wait it out, he'll come around," said Titmus.

We abruptly stopped heeding Bone's weird Polynesian babbling when exciting news distracted VMF personnel. Official orders had come through, we were moving out. Anticipation ran rampant. Action was forthcoming; VMF 111 was going to war.

Early the next morning before reveille I intercepted Bones as he sneaked in.

The rest of the guys were awake too. "Bones, are you nuts? You're gonna get your ass in a sling."

"I got obligations."

"Sure." I said with a touch of sarcasm.

"Wife's expecting."

"If the Marines wanted you to have a wife they'd have issued one!"

"Please don't hand me that stale bromide."

"You're a Marine, you know that?"

"Don't I!"

"There's a war going on and we're in it."

"I'm not mad at Japs or anyone else anymore."

"Duty, Bones, duty! You're a fuckin' American, aren't you!"

"I'm Samoan now."

"New places, new natives, we've just got here!" I said.

"My wife, my life, both are here!"

"Come back after the war," advised Titmus.

"She'll wait," said Cassidy.

"We're finally gonna get a crack at the Japs," said O'Bannion.

"I'm not mad at them anymore," said Bones.

"You've turned yellow!" said Cassidy.

"Easy," said Pinsky.

"Well, what the hell else is the matter then?"

Titmus stony glare silenced Cassidy. "Pack your seabag, Bones, we'll figure something out," he said.

"Thanks, Earl, but I'm not going."

"What!"

"I'm staying here."

"You crazy?" said O'Bannion.

"I'd be crazy if I went. My family's here. Sorry, fellows, I'm not leaving."

Titmus sighed and began stuffing Bones' seabag. Pinsky and I handed him clothes and gear from his locker as Bones warily watched his belongings being sorted and packed. "Time to go," said Titmus.

Bones staunchly stood. "Good luck, fellows, take care." Titmus spun Bones around and cracked a short right to his chin. Bones went limp.

"I didn't like doing that," sighed Titmus. We carried Bones outside to where the trucks were being loaded, heaved him onto the bed of one and climbed in. Bones groaned and tried to get up. With his foot pressing on his chest Titmus kept Bones inert as we sped toward Apia. If the driver noticed the unorthodox activity on his truck bed, he didn't let on.

In Apia's harbor a rusty old Liberty ship being held by two taut chains slowly tugged at her anchor. Banging against the decrepit dock, a landing barge awaited the restless lines of Marines. Bones opened his eyes and feebly protested as Titmus and O'Bannion each grabbed an arm and propelled him aboard.

Three or four mangy mutts that had been hanging around camp had already been deposited onto the barge. Taps stood on the dock wistfully gazing at the frenetic activity. Several guys standing on the barge yelled, "Sherman, grab Taps!"

I had never felt inclined to touch the rheumy-eyed mongrel but didn't know how to refuse so I impulsively clutched him. Fairly large for a native cur he was not used to being held and started to squirm. I was compelled to heave him onto the boat. Hands reached out to catch him but he crashed to the deck and let out a pitiful howl. He struggled to his feet and favoring a front paw limped from one side to the other.

As I jumped into the boat, half a dozen guys cursed me for hurting that damn mutt. Several spat threats and made like they wanted to carry the issue further. I was pissed and eager for action and told them all to take a flying fuck at the moon.

Then and there I decided never to touch that damn dog again.

When we got to the ship, Bones was still a little woozy. Titmus helped him up the gangway and I carried his gear up. The ensign on deck asked about Bones shaky state. Titmus told him that because of warlike exuberance he had celebrated above and beyond. For a navy officer he was a reasonable guy and smiled as we helped Bones below. We left him snoozing on a lower bunk.

As the ship started to pull away, Titmus, O'Bannion, and I stood at the rail gazing toward Apia. "I'm sure as hell glad we're finally pulling out," said O'Bannion. I felt the same.

Bones suddenly squeezed between us. He silently stared at the shore.

"Hey, Bones, don't take it personal," said Titmus.

"Yeah, don't be sore," chimed in O'Bannion.

"I'm not sore. I know you guys meant well," said Bones.

"She's a gook," said O'Bannion.

"For crying out loud!" I stammered and shot O'Bannion a withering look.

Bones winced and pulled off his field shoes.

"You're kidding?" said Titmus.

"I know what I'm doing." Without another words Bones dove over the rail.

O'Bannion and I were about to shout "man overboard!" but Titmus' finger went to his lips. We leaned over the rail and watched him cutting through the water toward Upolu.

Two guys we didn't know well sauntered up. "Did someone go overboard?" asked one.

"I heard something," said the other.

"You two been drinking joy juice?" said Titmus.

"Ha ha," guffawed O'Bannion.

"You heard a mermaid," I scoffed.

After the two grumbled and moved away, I committed Bones' field shoes to the sea and we followed Titmus below.

When morning muster was called, Bones Donigal, needless to say, wasn't around. Sergeant Byron demanded his whereabouts but nobody responded. He growled, "Absent without leave! If the simple fuck shows up, have him report to me. Maybe I can save the jerk."

Bones was listed as AWOL, and that was that.

CHAPTER THIRTEEN

The *Whistler's* ragtag crew consisted of civilian mariners, mostly foreign seamen from Estonia or Scandinavia. Compared to us, they looked old and decrepit but not nearly as ancient as their ship. Their armed U.S. Navy detail consisted of twelve disgruntled youngsters led by a seasoned old chief. Their sole duty was to man their 20 millimeter and protect the slow moving freighter. If Japs attacked by air or sea they would, of course, resist. Most of us deemed that their effort would be short and futile.

Number three and four holds had been converted into troop sleeping quarters. Rows of bunks piled to the overhead took up most of the space. It was stifling in the cramped quarters and querulous individuals occasionally exchanged blows to acquire or retain a suitable sleeping place.

At night, snoring, snarling, cursing, and sweat-soaked Marines twisted and turned below. On the congested deck it was cooler but not a helluva lot better. Each morning the round red sun rose and proceeded to broil the uncovered steel.

Chow lines formed at daybreak and again at dusk for the second meal of the day. The lines wound through the deck amid stacks of crated potatoes. It seemed to take forever before an enlistee got to the galley where he had to eat standing up.

Luke-warm sloppy eggs and cold toast was the daily breakfast fare. Enlisted personnel had to skip lunch. There were too many passengers and not enough grub or time. Dinner invariably consisted of spam and potatoes.

After a few days at sea, most of us were constantly hungry. Between our two meals we would pull raw potatoes from the crates, sprinkle a touch of salt and gnaw away.

One morning I was about twentieth in line for breakfast and another twenty were behind me as Taps limped by with his dangled tongue almost touching the deck. The bedraggled mutt had been far from gazelle-like on four legs, on three he was pathetic. There wasn't much else to look at so all eyes focused on his deck debut. His progress stopped as he detected a familiar fragrance and proceeded to move toward me.

At his limped approach, I desperately tried to silently communicate, "Move on, you dumb mutt!" He halted to uplift his woebegone face before releasing a monstrous pile of excrement.

A grumble united in its enmity erupted along the chow line. It evolved into a rumble of intimidating threats. Sergeant Byron came running and spotted Taps departing from his pile of dung. "What the fuck! Whose dog is that?"

Lancaster pointed, "His!"

"Hell it is!" I protested.

"You brought that flea-bitten mutt aboard,'" chimed another ass-kisser.

Fingers pointed and voices from those that didn't even know me chorused. "His dog! His dog!" I was infuriated but there were too many to battle.

"You bring him aboard?" queried Byron.

"He ain't mine!" I whined.

"If you brought him aboard he's your responsibility! Now clean up that goddamn mess!"

My eyes shot daggers in a vain show of defiance but Byron stared me down. "I'll be back to check," he warned as he stalked away.

I stepped from the line, found a hunk of cardboard and subject to jeering onlookers, morosely scooped Taps' load of crap and heaved it over the side. When I returned to my vacated place the guy who'd been in line behind me had moved up. "You lost your place, Mate."

"Fuck you!" I hissed and with clenched fists moved toward him. The guy swiftly stepped back.

That evening, still seething, I leaned on the portside rail trying to stare through the black night. Taps sat behind me. "Get the fuck away from me," I growled but he paid no heed.

In the morning, scuttlebutt spread. The *Whistler's* current new orders were to pull into Wallice Island, a French possession. A contingent of American medical personnel was ordered to disembark and assist French doctors. Nobody knew how long the ship would remain or whether any of us would get to go ashore, but we were hopeful.

O'Bannion and Pinsky sidled up on either side. "I'm gonna nail me a French babe," announced O'Bannion.

"Sure, you are," chortled Pinsky.

"Maybe I'll settle for a part French part Polynesian doll."

We hit the sack hopefully contemplating what lay in store for us. Awakened by the anchor spilling out early the next morning, we congregated on deck to see a beat-up chugging craft pull alongside. Mailbags were hoisted aboard and manila envelopes passed to the lieutenant JG. Sealed boxes were lowered to the barge.

Most of the beat-up potato crates were swung into the bobbing LCM. Naval officers and several corpsmen climbed down into the square-bowed vessel. As the beat-up craft pulled away they forlornly waved farewell.

We were perturbed that those lucky swabbies were getting shore leave. That is until word spread that many of the natives living on the island were cursed with leprosy.

Sergeant Byron brought attention to rows of gleaming white stones cluttering the shore. We were told they were the marked graves of leprosy victims, a devastating island disease. That dreadful malady slowly eats away at the afflicted victim's flesh. There is no cure. Lepers are transported to Wallice to die. I had read about that horrible affliction in one of Jack London's novels.

"Why would any healthy guy want to stay on that diseased rock?" said O'Bannion.

"To help people," said Cruz.

French dames or no French dames, none of us regretted not getting to step ashore on that accursed island.

Titmus got mail and waved his stained letter. It was from Millie. We weren't enthused about hearing another personal message from the love of his life, but there was no way to safely convey our displeasure. We politely listened as he read.

Dear Earl,

I don't feel well and am on my way to my job so this is a short letter. Don't worry, a longer one is coming. In the meantime, be careful and don't do anything too brave. I adore my gallant Marine. Bye for now.

Your darling,

Millie

He folded the brief note and stuffed it into his pocket.

"She must love you," said Cruz.

"Of course she does, and I love her. She got nothing to worry about, I don't intend to be a hero. Anyhow, Airdales don't get many chances to be heroes."

I wasn't happy hearing that but only asked, "You going to marry her?"

"Sure as hell intend to."

"And stay in the Corps?" said O'Bannion.

"Hell no! I'm getting out, Millie or no Millie, soon as this fuckin' war's over, maybe sooner!"

"By the time this fuckin' war's over you'll have eight years in, maybe more. That means only twelve more to get a pension," said O'Bannion.

"You nuts! The Marine Corps is no place for a married man. A guy ranked below gunnery sergeant can forget about matrimony. There ain't enough money to support a family on a buck-assed private's stipend."

"Hey, I just might stay in until I become a gunny. Maybe I'll even become an officer," said O'Bannion.

"I may sign over," murmured Cruz. That surprised me.

A stiff wind gusted from the south and the sky turned grey. The ship took a drastic roll tilting from one side to the other and back again. The response on deck was total bedlam as passengers stumbled to the rails and spilled their guts into the ocean. Many puked off the windward side. The back spray of vomit quickly affected those with steady stomachs.

The bow turned into the wind as a timely squall soaked the decks and washed away most of the spewed mess. Some afflicted passengers were able to stagger below and wait out the weather. Those too sick to give a damn grasped a stanchion or rail and stayed on deck.

As I headed for the ladder, I spotted O'Bannion, his face an ashen green. "You sure you want to be a thirty-year man?" I inquired.

Drivels of puke dripped from his pallid lips, "Fuck you," he groaned. I didn't feel well either but managed a half-hearted cackle as I made my way down the ladder.

The following morning the sea flattened and the sky turned deep blue. A sorry-looking mass of humanity huddled on deck.

The gleaming coral island of Funafuti eventually materialized. The *Whistler* slowly moved toward the narrow inhospitable looking gleaming rock. Engines were cut and the ship's rusty anchor chain rattled as it poured into the sea.

From the horizon, the flat island dotted with tall coconut trees looked hot and not the least bit enticing. As we forlornly gazed at our new home, more than a few of us pined for the lush density of lovely British Samoa. Two LCMs chugged alongside and weathered mariners deftly lashed them to our hull.

A cargo net was draped over the rail trailing down to the water level. Disgruntled troops stood shoulder to shoulder, securing helmets, adjusting packs and rifles. We stiffly clambered down the cargo net into the shoreboats. Jammed with sweating troops the lines were let go and the boats slowly chugged toward Funafuti.

As we ferried toward a narrow pier, a downpour of huge raindrops pelted. It was a short haul, but the flat-bottomed craft bobbing up and down caused more than a few to retch. A stink of sweat and puke permeated as Borland mournfully imparted, "Hear the news, Lancaster made corporal!"

"Bullshit," said Cassidy.

"It's true," said a disgruntled fellow passenger.

LCMs were tied to the pier and we stepped on the rickety pier. Trucks transported us to our new camp. Huge vacant tents were waiting and the rest of the day was spent getting settled.

That night we devoured our first decent dinner at a makeshift mess hall and wearily hit the sack. We were exhausted and slept the sleep of the dead.

CHAPTER FOURTEEN

Our canvas abode was situated more than a few dozen yards from where the sea lapped along the chalk white beach. Although a forlorn coconut tree partially shaded our tent, its interior was steamy.

During sunlit hours buzzing six-legged vermin vexed us. The green flies were joined by a colorful assortment of airborne insects fluttering in and out of our tent. Nights were worse as bloodthirsty mosquitoes awoke to stab, suck and torment. Confronting intruders day and night required unfaltering determination.

Taps chose our tent's outside perimeter for his hangout. The bedraggled mutt never tried to enter the inside of our quarters, which was fine with us. Most of his day was devoted to being flaked out under the shady side of our lone coconut tree.

Feeding and fetching water for the matted mongrel gave us something to do. We were a touch amused whenever a morsel placed in front of his snout was readily gobbled down.

When darkness approached and the hot glow slipped below the horizon, he disappeared, but never for long. None of us were curious enough to investigate his nightly meanderings. Possibly to assuage our collective lack of interest in his nightly sojourns and general welfare, we more than just tolerated the despondent animal. We considered him as a fellow loser, oh, more than that, in a peculiar way we liked him.

Early in the mornings, VMF's Wildcats roared off on training missions. Ground Defense had nothing to do with the fighter planes except at night. During four hour shifts, three privates and a corporal from Ground Defense caught guard duty. We were responsible for the safeguard of the beat-up planes. We deemed the busy work an exercise in futility. Fat chance enemy marauders would be meandering around Funafuti for any reason whatsoever.

Situated not far from our tent was a stark white building. The structure had been erected before the war by British Missionaries and used as a church and meeting center for the native population. A lengthy flagpole stood in front of the theistic structure. Both British and Japanese flags had been raised and lowered there. Of course, while the Japanese occupied Funafuti, the structure had been utilized as their military headquarters

Once the Americans invaded and the Japs were gone, the building was again being used by the natives to hold meetings and worship. The *fita fita* guard donned their issued uniforms and resumed militaristic duties. Each morning six uniformed natives marched to the front of the church and raised the Union Jack. At dusk they lowered the faded flag, folded it in militaristic manner and in unison marched off with it.

On Sundays, Melanesians, wearing their colorful *lava-lavas* and finest shell ornaments, happily filed into the cavernous white chapel to sing and worship their missionary-inspired god.

On other days, the dark-skinned locals gathered for what Samoans called a *fono*. The Melanesians, though smaller and darker than Samoans, had less material goods, but seemed to be as happy and even more trusting. Singing, praying and socializing took up much of their time.

Marines didn't attend Sunday night services but we heard their melodious voices. The spiritual sounds would get a guy reflecting about the warmth and security of home and family.

A few days after we settled in, Corporal Lancaster, rattling his mess gear and exhibiting two brand new stripes barged through our flap. "Up and at 'em! Chow down and don't dawdle! There's work to be done."

We chorused, "Lancaster, shut the fuck up!"

"Get your earbanging ass out of here!" added Cassidy.

"See these!" Lancaster pointed to his brand new stripes. "By the time I get back, you fuck-ups better be ready to turn to!" Before Titmus could knock him on his ass or any of us could retort he strutted off to the next tent.

After breakfast Lancaster prodded us to a site. "We need a four-seated officers' head built. You know size specifications by now. Don't overestimate or underestimate," he warned.

Putting on like he was a construction expert, Lancaster tried to expand his chest while glaring at us. Choice adjectives were all we could direct at him as he haughtily stalked away.

We hacked and dug at our designated project. We broke for lunch and afterwards went back to digging. By the time we finished, an oblong hole with correct specifications was ready to be utilized. At five we stowed tools and headed for our oil drum shower. "Tomorrow we'll install the seats," Titmus assured Lancaster. We wondered why Titmus was conversing civilly with a guy he could hardly tolerate.

That night, the final notes of the bugle faded and our lone light was flicked off. We lay under our nets tensely awaiting the blood-sipping mosquito invasion.

As anticipated the buzzing horde arrived. Frustrated curses and slapping sounds resounded as we fought back. It was black inside our tent but we heard Titmus pulling on his boondockers. He felt his way to the flap and stepped outside.

"Where's he going?" whispered Borland.

"He's up to something," I ventured.

"Yeah, like taking a piss," said Pinsky.

"He wouldn't put on his boondockers to piss," said O'Bannion.

"Off to barter something out of the mess hall," snapped Cassidy.

"If he wanted us to know he'd a told us," quipped Cruz.

The chorus of curses and slaps quieted and Pinsky's and Cruz's snores blended before I conked out.

I don't know how long I had been forcing a fitful sleep when O'Bannion's raspy voice startled me awake. "Where you been, Earl?"

It was still too black to see but I head, "Scouting."

"What?"

A vibrating snore was his answer.

"Hear that?" said O'Bannion.

"I heard," I said.

"He's plotting," muttered Cassidy.

"Yeah!" said O'Bannion.

"Damn it!" yelled Pinsky, "I'm trying to sleep."

The next day Titmus wielded a pick while O'Bannion and I shoveled. Cassidy and Pinsky carted off coral mounds in wheelbarrows. Cruz and Borland were assigned elsewhere digging another head.

He hadn't slept much and looked exhausted but minus his familiar streak of verbal chomping, Titmus hacked away, you'd think he was getting paid to shovel shit. After his clandestine night time excursion that wasn't easy to do.

After the bugle blew he silently slipped out again.

"He's up to something," offered Borland.

"He sure as hell is," I conceded.

"Scouting," said O'Bannion, as if he knew.

"For what?" I said.

"I got no fuckin' idea!"

"You said scouting," accused Cassidy.

"You did," seconded Borland.

"You holding back something!" I said.

"Hell no! Am I supposed to know what the hell he's scouting for?" whined O'Bannion.

"Then why say scouting?" I said.

"He told me that! For Christ's sake, don't go blabbering that you got it from me!"

"He told you scouting!" parroted Cassidy and left to relieve Cruz.

O'Bannion was about to spout off but clammed up as our tent flap parted and Titmus slipped in. He placed a finger on his lips, "Off your asses, I need help."

O'Bannion, Borland and I pulled on pants and boondockers. "Don't fuck this up!" warned Titmus. As he stepped out he beckoned us to follow. Outside he beamed his flashlight on our foxhole. Taps was flaked out on top. At our approach, the sorry looking mutt stood. Titmus missed his kick but the gloomy Taps took the hint and padded away.

Titmus stooped into our foxhole and emerged with an iron pot which he handed to me. Borland said, "What the hell's going on?"

"Clam up and watch!" warned Titmus.

"I'm bushed," whined Borland.

Titmus' glare was short and far from friendly before he stooped back into our foxhole. He came out lugging a medium-sized wooden barrel and handed it to Borland before again disappearing inside. This time he came out lugging a small gas burner, kerosene lamp, a coil of copper and a few empty bottles. He divided the stuff among us.

"Follow me," Titmus whispered and our leader led us to the silent church. He maneuvered an empty barrel under an open window. He put his finger to his lips and stepped on it wiggling through.

O'Bannion stood on the barrel and we handed him stuff to pass inside. After our burdens disappeared, Titmus gestured for Borland to stand lookout and beckoned for O'Bannion and me to climb in. It was spooky inside but up the stairs we went. Titmus approached a locked door and tried to force it open. He inserted a knife into the key hole, but it had rusted solid. Titmus pointed his forty-five at the keyhole and fired. The roar of the gun resounded like a cannon. I was sure we'd be discovered and court-martialed.

Titmus led us into a room featuring dozens of spider webs and directed us to set down the barrel and pot. Then he inserted the copper wire, lit the burner, and grinned as a small flame flickered. "A-Okay," he whispered. "Our brew barrel has been launched."

He replaced the broken lock and tiptoed below with us silently shadowing him. As we made way out through the window, Borland was on edge, "I heard a shot!"

"Killed a Jap," said Titmus.

Borland wasn't sure he was being snowed. Titmus led us back and we crawled into our sacks. Borland kept twisting and turning under his mosquito net. "Bullshit, wasn't it?" he cried, "there was no Jap in there." We were too unsettled to chuckle.

The next night, after showering and evening chow Titmus took off to reconnoiter. Cruz, O'Bannion, Borland and I bullshitted about nothing before flaking out.

Titmus got back to rouse us. "We got important shit to do."

"For Christ's sake," whined O'Bannion as he pulled on his boondockers.

"I'm pooped," griped Borland.

I wasn't happy but kept my bitching low key. Cruz, as usual, was stoic. The four of us followed Titmus as he led us in a roundabout way to the rear of the mess hall. He crouched and we did the same. Naturally, we were nervous but only rustling palm leaves quivered.

The moon hid behind a cloud and the coral shore got dark. Labored breathing and scrapes of coconut crabs moving about weren't conducive to feeling comfortable. There were also blending sounds of wind whisperings, lapping surf and our own wheezing. Noises seemed too loud and too weird. It was eerie alright and I wasn't the only one spooked.

"We're gonna get our asses in a sling," murmured Borland.

"Avast your fuckin' whining!" warned Titmus.

A lanky form emerged from around the corner scaring shit out of us. "That you, Titmus?" It was Corporal Jowlousky, the skinny cook who worked for Mess Sergeant Buell.

"Who the hell do you think it is, Tojo?"

He and Titmus huddled a bit before bills were slipped to Jowlousky who led us to a side door and inserted a key. Titmus bade us wait and he and the cook went inside.

We were nervous but kept silent. It seemed to take forever before the two emerged lugging four large cans of assorted fruit. They carefully set the booty down and went back in. They came back with a cardboard box full of assorted mess hall goodies.

Titmus and Jowlousky's exchange became a whispered squabble. Titmus called him a chickenshit money-grubber and cursed his mother before begrudgingly handing him more bills. Jowlousky pocketed the money and his shit-eating grin returned as he sidled away.

We toted the loot toward the church and our breathing stopped while a sentry shuffled by. After his crunching footsteps faded we dashed across the road. Titmus ordered O'Bannion to stand watch and climbed through the church window. We carefully lugged our stuff up to the attic.

I cut apart the bags filled with sugar, yeast, raisins and prunes. While Titmus pried open pineapple, apricots and apple juice cans. He poured the contents into a small wooden barrel. While stirring the concoction he ordered us to vacate. We left him measuring, mixing and muttering.

We cautiously made it back to the tent. Cassidy put down his book and rose from his rack. "What' goin' on?"

O'Bannion gave him a quick account. We impatiently waited for Titmus to return and tell us about tomorrow's assignment. When he finally arrived he said, "Cassidy, get us some sickbay alcohol."

"How am I supposed get it?"

"Buy it, steal it, I don't give a shit, just get it."

"Jacob, get some high octane out of transportation."

"I'll try."

Titmus' look was cold. "Get it."

Borland and I were ordered to gather coconuts.

"Red or green?" cockily asked Borland

"Both," said Titmus. Borland was sorry he asked.

Two nights later we had all fulfilled our gathering obligations. After depositing our loot in the attic, we climbed out of the window to face

Cassidy. That night it was his turn to be our jumpy guard. "What in hell took so long?"

"You're as nervous as a recruit," spat Titmus.

"You been in there pretty damn long," whined Cassidy.

"Simmer down, all is well, so far. You people got nothing more to do but wait," advised Titmus.

As we sprinted across the road toward our tent, I guess we were too excited to notice Titmus signaling us to drop. "Halt!" shouted the road guard and leveled his rifle. He was about twenty feet away, all we could see was his silhouette.

I presumed he was from another squadron because I didn't recognize his voice. We four slowly continued to move until he threatened.

"This is my second halt! After the third I got to fire." He wasn't kidding. My back was soaked with sweat as I waited for Titmus to get us out of this one.

"One more halt," the sentry assured, "then I fire."

"No spika the English," said O'Bannion.

"What?" stammered the guard.

"Banzai!" shouted Titmus.

"What the hell!" Screamed the sentry and galloped down the road shouting, "Corporal of the Guard! Corporal of the Guard!"

We sprinted back and dove into our bunks as confused shouts rent the air. Waving rifles, Marines emerged from their tents chorusing, "What the fuck's happening!"

Major Cole's frigid voice subdued the commotion. He confronted the sentry. "What the hell you blabbing about, no spika de English? You're drunk!"

"I ain't, sir," swore the gasping sentry. "I only had one brew before coming on duty."

The poor bastard wound up with a psychiatric evaluation and two days in the brig for drunkenness and dereliction of duty. Also, he was hit with a negative paragraph in his record book, but his problem wasn't ours, *"Semper Fi"*.

From that time on, after dark, when the church was empty, if Titmus didn't have guard duty, he would steal away to boil, brew and stir.

On nights he was gone a vaporous aroma gently drifted over parts of Funafuti. Dogs howled and gooney birds squawked. Mosquito slapping was minimal and deeper and more comfortable sleep ensued. It wasn't our collective imagination, fewer insects were airborne on those blessed nights and even those flitting about were uncharacteristically sluggish.

Even though I wasn't of the Faith, I didn't think it was kosher for Titmus' creation to be distilling while holy activities went on below. However my Christian tent mates didn't seem bothered so I kept my mouth shut. I knew I wasn't the only one who would be relieved when the brew was disposed of.

Needless to say, as weeks passed, O'Bannion, Cassidy, Cruz, Borland, Pinsky, and I grew impatient. It wasn't that we suspected our buddy, but within our canvas quarters we observed and tactfully quizzed him. "How's it going?"

"Almost ready."

"Really?"

"Time, takes time."

"How much more time?"

"Patience, boys, patience. Wait a minute, don't you trust me?"

"Of course, we do," we chorused.

"Anyway, I tasted a touch, it's coming along."

"Tasted? How much!"

"Half a teaspoon."

"Can we try some?"

"Didn't you hear? It ain't ready!"

Each time Titmus returned from the attic one or two of us would sidle close enough to inhale. It was a tricky maneuver and we only grew more fidgety.

Later O'Bannion whispered, "I ain't sure I trust Titmus anymore."

"Why don't you tell him?" I suggested.

"Fuck you!"

"Fuck you!"

"Why don't you two assholes shut the fuck up!" said Cassidy.

We were alerted several times before reveille to hit our foxholes. But most times air raid warnings sounded hours after the last call had darkened tents. Tempers were short and people were on edge. Bickering occurred in every tent. Everyone found something to be pissed about.

Squadron's activity increased. Our pilots were flying north to carry out two sorties a day. Something unsettling was in the air. We all felt it.

One grey tropic afternoon the heavy rain soaked the ground and left the damp foliage smelling like soiled laundry. Sergeant Goodwinch and Corporal Lancaster were nowhere in sight. Three of us were renovating a crumbling shit structure. Cruz was swabbing the wooden sides while O'Bannion and I were energetically raking. Borland was policing the perimeter. Titmus stood gazing out to sea.

"You missed a palm frond," said O'Bannion.

"If it's bothering you, pick the god damn thing up," I said.

"Hey, I outrank you!"

Because of those few days he had on me, and despite both of us being buck-assed privates, he technically outranked me. Oh, I knew he was bullshitting but I wasn't in a joking mood. "Screw you!" I growled.

"Make me!" snarled O'Bannion.

I was contemplating throwing an overhand right when Titmus quietly stated, "Tonight's the night."

"Hot dog!" said O'Bannion.

"About time," I said..

The droning of unsynchronized engines distracted us. "Listen!" said Cruz.

"Japs!" said Titmus.

"You sure?" said O'Bannion.

Before Titmus answered, ninety-millimeter aircraft guns opened up followed by the explosions of a string of bombs. As air raid sirens screamed the blasts of detonating bombs approaching from the north got louder as we raced into our foxhole. I sat with others in that dark hole and felt Taps shaking like a frond in a gusty wind against my leg. He wasn't any more unsettled than the rest of us.

"Fuckers coming this way," grunted Titmus.

"Mother of Jesus!" said Cruz.

O'Bannion mumbled a prayer.

The sound of a runaway train zooming down galvanized us to crouch and clasp our heads. A tremendous explosion rocked our foxhole. Debris rained upon our sandbagged covering. As dust sifted into our hole we coughed, wheezed and choked.

"Shit," cried O'Bannion.

"Close," gasped Titmus.

At the other end of the island, explosive sounds faded. Titmus barged out of our foxhole and we followed. Jittery people from other holes emerged pointing, gasping and conversing in subdued voices. The siren blared again signifying an all clear, the Jap planes were gone.

A gray cloud accompanied by a poignant aroma drifted from the damaged church. Drops fell dotting our dungarees. We focused on the holy edifice harboring the liquid fruits of our labor. The structure was partially obscured by smoke and dust. A crumbled white wall indicated that the stucco building had taken a partial hit. In my shocked state I visioned a distressing image of our smoky barrel.

"The fuckin' Japs fucked up our brew!" whined Cassidy.

Our conjoined outrage knew no bounds. Before we could react Lancaster trotted up, "We've been attacked, for Christ's sake! Get your asses in gear; we got to clean up the goddamn mess!"

We hurled threats and curses at him. Lancaster wisely turned and hurried off to irritate others.

Titmus had been christened by enemy fire, but this was our first taste of action. Cruz clammed up, Borland whined a bit, Cassidy and Pinsky stayed churlish while O'Bannion and I engaged in a half-hearted shoving scuffle, but he ceased tussling to smugly spout, "Hey, we just got us a star to put on our Asiatic Pacific Campaign Ribbon."

CHAPTER FIFTEEN

The recent destruction of our apparatus had plunged our tent's occupants into a melancholy state. After our creation was decimated we were left bored, bothered and bereft.

Our state of despair somewhat improved after Seabees suspended a huge white screen between two slender coconut trees. Movies were flown in and after the sun went down cowboy flicks were projected.

Invariable archaic Westerns were featured, not inspiring, but more entertaining than sipping raisin jack and focusing on our interior canvas or moaning about our sorry state of being.

On a memorable evening, minutes before floodlights dimmed and the flick commenced, a nondescript mouse, ventured out from the palm leaf cluster atop one of the trees supporting the white screen. Mesmerized onlookers ogled as he stepped onto the wire and gingerly headed toward the other tree. Precariously balancing he cautiously made way along the wire until midway between the two trees, he paused to scan his awed audience.

Shouts and huzzahs rang out as enchanted onlookers applauded the mouse's debut. His little head turned from left to right seemly acknowledging the thunderous reaction to his daring exploit. Retaining balance and composure he scampered off into the other palm tree's foliage. We named him Milton.

The next evening, the congregating audience mulled about exchanging pre-movie bullshit. Hoarded bottles of allotted ABC Beer along with homemade stuff had been brought to the outdoor theater.

Gunnery Sergeant Fisher of the 5th Defense Battalion who had been sipping torpedo juice leaped to his feet, his roar could stop a clock. Milton was making his nightly appearance. As usual our bewhiskered wire walker was punctual.

As he ventured from the fronds and trekked toward the other tree the crowd chanted, "Milton! Milton! Milton!" Fisher's welcome resounded above the crowd, "Atta boy, Milton!"

Milton paused midway to scan the audience. Show business came natural to the little rodent. His steps were calculated as he slowly progressed until he reached the other tree. He almost bowed as a round of applause accompanied his leap into the foliage.

"Fucked-up mouse!" grunted O'Bannion, but sported a wide grin.

"All this fanfare for a puny mouse," mumbled Cassidy.

Both shouted and laughed as uproarsly as the others so I dismissed their negative comments.

Milton's trek across the wire became a popular event. His ballet-like traipse across the wire was an appreciated break from our monotonous routine. The little guy was a moral booster

For what purpose, did he travel from one tree to the other? Surely, not for the accolades, he was a mouse. Nobody knew for sure, however speculation bantered about was mostly on a positive note. The majority looked forward to the mousy event.

As Milton regularly replayed his nightly passage across the wire, he seemed to savor his audience's raucous acknowledgement. Sure, elsewhere our mouse might be considered nondescript, but on Funafuti, Milton's appearances were almost religiously anticipated. Word spread and more coconut trees were felled and rolled into place to accommodate the expanding crowd.

In the front row, adorned with bars and leaves, officers reclined on folding chairs. Behind the brass perched on logs, empty ammunition boxes, oil drums, empty crates, and homemade chairs awaited the garrulous enlisted audience.

In the rear of the seated military audiences stood an assembly of half-naked natives waiting to see the magic happenings on the screen. The gook audience seemed bewildered but curious regarding Milton's acknowledged traipse across the supporting wire. However, natives were more intrigued by the magical movements on the screen.

On a Sunday night, an early crowd had gathered. Prime spaces were occupied and because my tent mates and I had arrived late we were compelled to situate ourselves in front of the standing natives. Titmus and Cassidy perched on empty oil drums and I plunked down on an ammo box. Borland, Cruz, and O'Bannion sat behind. Pinsky squeezed his apple crate between us.

That evening a minesweeper had anchored six-hundred yards offshore. A noisy gaggle of swabbies stepped ashore from an LCM shoreboat. They too, were eager to see a movie. The flick, as usual was a Western seen by most more than a few times. Still, they were luckier than their shipmates stuck on the ship with mundane duties. At least they had gotten a short respite ashore.

Their minesweeper had been patrolling the waters surrounding the Ellis and Gilbert Islands. The minesweeper rolled and pitched as it made way from here to there and back again. It was dull duty and the sea didn't pamper the dumpy little craft. Her sailors were even more bored than Marines on Funafuti.

Attired in faded blue denims, the swabbies sorely needed haircuts. They arrived pushing and playing. Some sat on logs while others stood. The dejected swabbies were ready to shell out accumulated dollars for some palatable gook gin. It was not uncommon for one or more restless young sailor to ingest native concoctions and brawl among themselves or just pass out. In the past, more than a few got escorted back to their YMS for one or another infraction.

The lights of the shimmering screen drew its usual diving, droning and stinging bugs. Slapping and swearing merged. Although the movie didn't commence until 19:45 the assorted crowd had begun congregating at 19:15.

Conversation suddenly ceased as a sudden quiet descended. Milton was due so eyes focused on the wire.

Behind us eight sailors sprawled on a log swatting at the buzzing, biting six-legged bugs. They vehemently bitched about shipboard duty.

Someone shouted, "Semper Fi, Milton!" But the wire was taut and vacant.

"He's late," muttered Cruz.

"I ain't seen that little rat but twice," lamented Titmus.

"In a minute or two he'll be here," I said. "And he isn't a rat!"

"He came last night," said O'Bannion

"Damn rights and he's coming tonight," said Borland.

"For god's sake he's a mouse. You people are nuts!" muttered Pinsky.

"Why does he go over to that tree ?" said Cruz.

"He's got a lady friend," I quipped.

"Naw, that's where he takes a leak," ventured O'Bannion.

"You guys are crude," said Borland.

"Naw, just rock-happy," said O'Bannion.

"Cracking up," I said.

"What's the difference why or what?" snapped Cassidy. "He's a diversion."

Laughter emanated from the YMS crew as they passed their clouded bottle around.

"What's on tonight, Mate?" a thin sailor asked Cassidy. Before he could utter a retort, a welcoming roar went up as Milton cautiously emerged from his palm frond. As the mouse gingerly made way across the wire the crowd reacted with shouts and applause. Even Titmus and Pinsky clapped.

"Look at that rat!" spouted a freckle-faced YMS sailor.

"That's Milton, swabbie, and he ain't no rat!" snapped Borland.

As usual, our hero made it to the center of the wire and posed. Maybe it wasn't a bow but Cassidy swore it was.

Suddenly a white chunk of coral hurled by a swabbie whizzed by Milton's ear. "Lousy shot," spat a shipmate and heaved another projectile.

Their shipmates, unaware of the stunned silence, commenced throwing coral chunks. They missed but some came close. Milton almost lost his balance as he swiftly scuttled across the wire and disappeared into the palm tree foliage.

Seconds after the barrage commenced, several swabbies became aware that something was amiss. "Avast," cautioned the bos'n. Hurling ceased and his crew peered about.

A florid-faced yeoman lowered his missile and whispered, "What the fuck's goin' on?"

Titmus grabbed the bewhiskered sailor by the throat, "You fuckin' swabjockey!"

As he gasped for air the young seaman's face reddened. An overhand right fired at Titmus by his shipmate saved him. Another flailing sailor leaped on Titmus' back. Milton's frenzied fans engulfed the outnumbered crew of the YMS 204 as scores of shore patrol giants charged into the one-sided melee and rescued the engulfed swabbies. The battered visitors were escorted to their shoreboat.

Later, within the wired perimeter surrounding Funafuti's brig, a disgruntled group flaked out in a dejected circle. Titmus' knuckles were bruised and he sported a slight blotch under one eye. "Wonder if Milton will ever show again?" he said.

O'Bannion held his throbbing head, "Bet those swabs won't."

"Who gives a rat's ass about them, I'm talkin' about Milton."

"Oh, boy, I nailed that yeoman," boasted Cassidy.

I had gotten in a lick or two but my jaw hurt and I wasn't in no mood to comment. I did visualize an image of that battered bos'n and his beat-up crew explaining Milton and the crazy Marines on Funafuti to their dubious skipper.

"Anybody cares how Milton's feeling?" muttered Cruz.

We became quietly submerged in personal thoughts regarding our affronted mouse. I imagined the little guy aloft in the coconut tree contemplating a change of venue.

Maybe he showed up the next night, maybe not. We never found out because before dawn we were released. A general, colonel or some other smart-assed officer ordered the island's nightly movie canceled. After the day's work, enlisted personnel, whether they had participated in the melee or not, were ordered to remain in their own bivouac area after dark until further orders.

For several days and nights, speculation regarding Milton's ambling future was the prime subject bandied about. Outrage and collective resentment simmered until replaced by new scuttlebutt.

VMF 111 mechanics, ordinance men, and other technicians were ordered to pack gear and file into two DC6s. Our squadron's northern movement rumor became a reality. Pilots were ordered to fly their Wildcats to a mysterious destination.

Ground Defense and other shitbirds spent long days loading bombs, guns, ammunition, and gear onto an LCM. Hours before we sailed, we were informed that movie restrictions had been canceled. *"To the Shores of Tripoli"* featuring Tyrone Power was scheduled but we were destined to miss it.

Departing from Funafuti and missing the movie didn't bother us. However, we did regret missing a farewell salute to Milton.

On the LCM we were told that our destination was Nukufetau, another island in the Ellis atoll, located sixty seaward miles away. Titmus and other old timers had never heard of the rock. Anyway, we were getting closer to the action or so we thought.

CHAPTER SIXTEEN

Fifty VMF 111 passengers boarded the landing craft. Once out to sea the temperature plunged. Shivering enlistees fecklessly strived to curl up in one of the semi-sheltered niches under the piles of lumber lashed across the deck. Despite innovative attempts, comfort wasn't attainable as the LCM's inclined bow and flat bottom battered through the rolling gray sea. Captain Plunkett, Lieutenant Greene, Sergeant Goodwinch and Corporal Lancaster were the officers and noncoms in charge. Their temporary quarters were sheltered but not much more tolerable.

Lancaster, wearing a shit-eating grin spread disquieting info that chow wouldn't be available until we reached Nukufetau. We had last chowed down on Funafuti and hours later as we ploughed toward our destination we were hungry.

Well aware that six more hours of being thrust up, down and sideways by wind and the grumpy sea would have to be endured, we couldn't stay complacent. Wet, dirty and miserable our hunger became more pronounced. Oh, there was a touch of consolation when Lancaster's state of being was observed. A pallid green hue covered his face and he was too busy puking his guts out to harass us with stupid instructions,

Goodwinch staggered by to check names. Since acquiring additional stripes, his laid back demeanor had altered. "Get squared away and start looking like Marines," he rasped as he shakily hovered over each group.

"Take a flying fuck at the moon!" snapped Titmus.

"Hey, Titmus I'm repeating the captain's orders." Despite his added stripes, Goodwinch was still in awe of Titmus.

As we bounced along, the wind accelerated and green water spewed over the bow. Cold ocean water poured across the deck and spray soaked our fatigues. Crusts of salt plastered our exposed skin. On deck not a dry patch of lumber remained.

As the sky darkened, we unrolled our dampened mattresses and spread them across the lumber. Utilizing our packs for pillows, we had no choice other than curling up and enduring the pattering wet downfall.

"Wonder if Milton showed up?" mused O'Bannion. None of us bothered to answer. We were too wretched shivering and wishing we were someplace else, anyplace, including our warm tent on Funafuti.

As ominous clouds moved across the sky and covered the stars, vocalization turned to food. "I'm starving," sighed O'Bannion.

My stomach felt queasy, still I hungered. Each time the forward hatch opened and crewmembers entered or exited, despite wind and squall, tantalizing odors wafted from the galley.

"Swabjockey fuckers are inhaling grub like kings," said Titmus, more pissed than usual.

"Did Marines take crap from swabbies in China?" asked O'Bannion.

"Course not," I said.

"How the hell would you know?" snapped O'Bannion.

Titmus got a faraway look, "Ah, duty in China was better than okay."

"Oh, yeah?" chimed in Cassidy, we all relished hearing "Old Corps" stories.

"And believe me, that dinky train that took us to Peiping rocked worse than this flat-assed boat," said Titmus.

"Cheez," I said wishing I'd been there.

"Anyway, it was good to get away from the Pogey Bait Sixth," reminisced Titmus.

"Pogey Bait Sixth?"

"Long before my time, the quartermaster of the Sixth Regiment was said to have ordered $50,000 worth of PX supplies,"

"What!"

"Forty-nine thousand, nine-hundred and ninety-five dollars was allotted to buy candy, the other five went for soap."

"For the whole damn regiment?" asked Cassidy.

"Scuttlebutt, but there could be a touch of truth to it."

Most of us chuckled, but Cassidy, a pogey bait lover, wasn't amused.

"Everyone in the Sixth Regiment was and still are entitled to wear the *fleur-de-Guerre* braid on their left shoulder," continued Titmus. "See, both the Fifth and Sixth Regiments were awarded the same citation during World War One. The braids are regimental commendations awarded to both regiments by France. Both saved French ass at the battle for Belleau Woods.

"Marines of both regiments born long after World War One also get to wear the French citation braid. The braid commemorates old time Marines who beat the shit out of the Germans at Belleau Woods.

"In China, when the girls asked about the colorful cord, buck-ass privates spread word that the dangling decoration signified that those adorned were officers. Chinese and Russian ladies were impressed. Of course, that snow job knocked those of us not in the regiment out of the running in the classy lady competition."

"Chickenshit," said O'Bannion.

"Anyway, their bullshit stopped," said Titmus.

"Yeah?" said Cruz.

"Word spread that Marines' colored braid meant the wearer was afflicted with a venereal disease. When that got around those fuckin' cords disappeared." Titmus ceased reminiscing.

His concentration was focused on the crew's quarters. The portholes were covered but ever so often a sailor would open the hatch to come or go, and for seconds a faded yellow light glowed warm and inviting.

Dark clouds continued to move across the sky hiding the stars. The cold wind gusted sheets of salt spray across the deck. Warmth and chow beckoned from behind that door but entrance, for enlisted Marines, was strictly out of bounds.

"Candy-assed swabbies," muttered Cassidy.

Titmus stepped forward beckoning me to follow. I tailed him as he snaked his way through wet huddled bodies.

We made it to the forward house, I stood behind Titmus as the door opened and a pea-coated sailor emerged. For a brief second we smelled warm coffee. The gob smirked as he banged the door shut and made way aft.

Titmus opened the door and strode in. I gasped as I breathlessly followed and quietly closed the door behind. We stood in the galley adjusting our eyes to the light. Titmus focused on the back of a denim clad sailor bent over a large box of just baked Cookies.

Titmus grabbed the back of the guy's shirt and pant's seat and I opened the hatch we had just entered. He heaved the startled sailor outside. As he rolled along the wet deck, the stunned gob never knew who or what had manhandled him. Before our victim could sound off, Titmus grabbed a huge box of cookies and we were out through the hatch stepping over the shocked sailor.

The skies opened up and rain spewed down in torrents as we headed midships and dove into our cove. Amid the thunder, wind and falling water the swabbie's cry for assistance was faint.

Titmus and I apportioned handfuls of cookies to Arnie, Pinsky, Cassidy, O'Bannion and Cruz. Observers grappled for the rest. Gobbling sweet cookies without a liquid chaser wasn't conducive to setting well with queasy stomachs but nobody complained. Titmus heaved the empty box over the side.

Bedlam broke out from the boat's quarters as an infuriated ensign trailed by a pissed-off bos'n came storming on deck. Accompanied by the shivering victim, Sergeant Goodwinch and Corporal Lancaster strode across the rollicking soaked deck. They interrogated huddled Marines asking one dumb question after another.

"Did you see any suspicious people wandering about?"

"Anybody seen a Marine eating unauthorized cookies?"

By the time the interrogators reached our lumber pile, we looked far from cooperative as we reclined on wet wood. Considering the miserable circumstances, looking pissed off and uncomfortable was not difficult.

"Attenchun," mumbled Goodwinch.

Nobody moved.

"Franklyn! Recognize any of these people?" snapped the ensign.

"Never got to see anyone, sir." whimpered Franklyn.

"Look closer!" said the ensign.

"All jarheads look alike," whined Franklyn.

"Damn it! Do as I say!" demanded the ensign.

"If you didn't see them, how do you know they were Marines?" queried Goodwinch.

"I know everybody in our crew. I would have known if it was one of our guys, sir," Franklyn was cold, wet and bruised. His heart wasn't in an identifying mode.

"I'm not a fuckin' officer, don't call me sir!" said Goodwinch. "Oh, sorry, sir, nothing personal." The ensign was wet but not too unhinged to spat a nasty anti-Marine epitaph. Trailed by the two navy bozos he departed.

"Who could have ripped off them cookies?" said Arnie. We chuckled but our mirth was lost in the wind.

Titmus spread himself out on the lumber pile and despite the downpour commenced snoring.

Cruz was compact enough to crawl into an opening at the bottom of the lumber pile. The tough little Mexican was especially uncomfortable when deprived of his three to four daily showers. He could have been the most shower-taking guy in the Corps. He was also fanatical about polishing his shoes and cleaning his gear.

The taciturn Cruz was the most squared away guy in the squadron and not a person to monkey with. When Greek, the pot-bellied mechanic, called him a "greasy spic", he charged. Cruz pummeled fast and furious. The Greek tried to quit but Cruz was steamed to kill. Two of us pulled him from his yowling target. After that nobody bothered Jacob Cruz.

About 0500 the wind subsided and the squalling ceased, but a heavy mist shrouded our up and down plodding craft. We became attentive as the LCM slowed and the anchor chain was played out. As her forward motion ceased, the LCM proceeded to drift around her anchor. We couldn't see through the thick mist but sensed that we were close to land.

Some weary shitbird commenced snoring. The harsh sounds grated but in spite of it I dozed. Faded vision of Bones Donigal dancing the Siva Siva flitted through my head. What in hell had become of him?

Sudden warmth hit my face and I opened my eyes. The mist had been burnt away by the glaring sun. Haggard fellows crowded the deck.

Nukufetau wasn't as bare or bereft of greenery as Funafuti. In fact, viewed from the sea the island seemed to be shrouded in greenery. The island was longer and much wider. Her shorelines reflected a sheer white strand of coral and clusters of coconut trees abounded. From afar, the island looked more hospitable than our Funafuti lodgment.

A flimsy wooden wharf jutted fifty yards out from shore and a ramshackle shithouse was situated close to its end. The structure marred any illusion of being on a romantic tropical island.

As we appraised our new home, the LCM quivered as engines revved up and her anchor was noisily hauled in.

"No Japs, no females, nothing. What do we do on this rock?" muttered O'Bannion.

"Build shithouses, what else?" grudgingly said Titmus.

We were relieved to be on solid ground again but sighs and misgivings rambled as we raggedy-assed shitbirds chugged toward our new home.

Come all you gents in Ground Defense,
Take shovel and pick in hand
Come get a healthy grip on them
And we'll dig into the sand.

CHAPTER SEVENTEEN

Word spread that due to the unrelenting instability of coral ground shifting on Nukufetau, army engineers had advised against building an airfield on the island. However, after the Seabee battalion had been apprised of the army's assessment, they quickly constructed, not one, but two airstrips shaped like an X. A Marine SBD Squadron eventually took control of one strip and VMF 111's Wildcats utilized the other.

Titmus, Cassidy, O'Bannion, and I, plus four shitbirds from the SBD squadron were assigned to mess duty. There were a few in most squadrons who didn't mind scrubbing pots and pans, I, like most, hated it.

Our tents and the mess hall were situated close to where the bottom angle of the airfields X was widest. Pyramidal tents were erected and we were ordered to move in, square away and prepare for the impending inspection.

Staff Sergeant Gruell, the hash marked lard-ass, was our mess sergeant. He strutted here and there bellowing unnecessary orders. His belittling practice of ordering subordinates to do dirty jobs caused us to hate him and his innocuous demands.

Corporal Jalowski, our squadron's baker, was second in command. A Polack from Michigan, he was almost as obnoxious as Gruell. His mirthless grin displayed long yellow teeth and there wasn't a hint of warmth behind his foreboding smile. Six feet tall and muscular for a cook, he was a mean conniving bastard.

Multitudes of coconut crabs inhabited Nukufetau. They sidled along day and night doing whatever crabs do. Their grating noises weren't melodious but I never heard of anyone being hurt by one of the large crustaceans. Of course, if some goofball stuck a finger between two probing pincers a painful problem would have surely evolved.

One afternoon while several of us were picking up coconut fronds in front of the mess hall, a large coconut crab came sidling by. We stopped our collecting to watch the purple hued creature slowly move along in that sideways manner peculiar to crabs.

Jalowsky noted us being entranced by the crab making way. "Where do you think he's going?" said Cassidy. Before any one answered Jalowski poured a dash of kerosene over the crab's back and touched a match to its shell. The flames spouted and smoke streamed from the crab's back as it picked up speed.

It skittered for two feet before stopping. Its projected gleaming pin eyes clouded and the burnt crustacean's pincers slowly lifted charred and fixed. We were more than a little disturbed. Jalowsky's eyes narrowed and he coldly grinned. None of us acted or commented, but we all felt a deep sense of disgust.

Corporal LeFever, another mess hall noncom, tall and sporting a wispy mustache, was another pain in the ass. He incessantly griped about mess men who had served before us and didn't endorse us either. His thick southern accent was aggravating.

Pots, according to LeFever, were never cleaned right. Before he'd inspect the kitchen apparatus and counter, he'd invariably shout, "Too much damn grease in the galley!"

LeFever scrutinized us like a hawk intent on catching one of us purloining a food delicacy or slipping an extra slice of bread to a friend. Nevertheless, despite his watchfulness, mess hall ingredients disappeared, especially canned juices and fruit. Gruell suspected everyone and plied his assortment of nefarious tricks in order to nab a purloiner.

Each day before dawn broke we were rudely roused. Sweep-downs followed by swabbing decks were the first order of business. Peeling potatoes, shelling peas or peanuts came next. By 0630 a mess boy was situated behind each oblong pot. Huge containers were filled with powdered eggs, fried potatoes, lumpy cereal, spam, shit-on-a-shingle or whatever.

As chow time commenced, a line of grumpy enlistees filed in extending iron trays. They bitched about this and that as they moved along. We slapped spoonfuls of chow on trays as another mess boy poured juice and coffee into extended canteen cups.

The chow was crappy and there was never enough, especially if canned fruit or fresh-baked bread was on the menu. Cooks, mess boys, squadron, noncoms, officers, the Corps, and lackluster chow were roundly cursed before, after and during each meal.

Officers fared better. It wasn't that their chow was so superior, but more variance was forthcoming and their tables were covered with white cloths. They also dined from dishes. Two volunteer mess boys crisply served the brass. It was easier working the officers' mess but most considered it shameful kiss-ass duty.

After each meal the mess hall had to be swept and swabbed. Scouring crusted pots and pans followed. Then the oven was cleaned. After everything that needed to be cleansed or polished was squared away, the next chore was polishing the dining and galley decks. The last chore entailed maneuvering six burdensome brimming oil drum cans outside.

It took six despondent KPs, two to each can, to maneuver each garbage container from the mess hall to the waiting truck. Four men were required to physically hoist each loaded drum onto the bed of our olive-hued truck. It was a precarious and dirty task wrestling the stinking overflowing containers.

After wrestling the containers onto the truck, four of us, occasionally three, were ordered to mount the swill-laden truck and accompany the stinking mess to the pier.

When Gruell accompanied us, he'd plump his fat ass in the cab alongside Levindowski. We sorry-assed peons rode upright in the rear doing our best to avoid being splashed by the sloshing offal.

When our smelly conveyance arrived at the flimsy wooden structure erected near the end of the pier, natives waited to transfer our stinking garbage from trucks to one of two battered scows tugging at the end of the pier. Of course, the gooks expected compensation. American dollars didn't intrigue them nearly as much as purloined cans of spam, wieners and ham. As far as dark hued islanders were concerned, what we considered rejectionable food, they considered a treat.

Gruell invariably gloated as he supervised our back-wrenching efforts but never lifted a finger to assist. He reveled in bellowing superfluous commands such as, "Watch what the fuck you're doin'!" or "Don't spill the fuckin' cargo!" After unloading our putrid cargo, we reeked of spilled slop. Gruell dramatized his disdain by pinching his nose while spewing nasal chuckles.

Other outfits on the island underwent similar garbage delivery routines. By early afternoon the narrow pier stretching seaward was jammed with cans of stinking garbage drums.

A coxswain and deckhand were assigned to each tugging LCM. Under their supervision, natives would transfer congregated cans from the pier into both scows. After each boat was loaded, gook laborers climbed aboard. Coxn's would then navigate their foul reeking craft five-hundred yards seaward so natives could dump the putrid cargos into the sea.

Screeching, splashing gulls accompanied each short trip and swooped down to partake of the dumped mishmash. An assortment of over and under-sea denizens invariably joined the banquet.

One sweltering afternoon, our stinking truck pulled up to the pier to unload. Intending to entice native laborers to unload and transfer our stinking cargo, we commenced haggling.

Sergeant Gruell swaddled out of the cab and grunted, "Avast this patronizing bullshit! No more canned food to those niggers!"

137

"Sarge, If we don't give these guys a few cans of spam, they won't unload," said Cassidy.

"Tough shit. I'm responsible for the squadron food supply and there ain't no allowances for niggers."

"You sayin' you won't let them hungry gooks enjoy cans of spam that nobody will eat anyway?" growled Titmus.

"That's what I'm saying!"

"You want us to do that backbreaking work when we don't have to? You know none of our people will touch that canned shit anyway!"

"Don't give me that! I eat it and know others who eat it too."

"Bullshit!" grunted O'Bannion.

"Hey, wise-ass, we're in a fuckin' war! A little lifting won't hurt. Besides, it's good exercise," snapped Gruell.

Not usually a speaker-upper I growled, "Slipping them poor-assed natives a few cans of that evil tasting stuff won't deprive you."

"I don't want to hear anymore fuck-off bullshit! Get moving!" snapped Gruell and he hoisted himself into the cab.

Cassidy and I climbed onto the truck bed and manhandled the drums down to Titmus, O'Bannion and an SBD guy. "Big bellied bastard!" shouted Cassidy.

Gruell bounded out of the cab. "Who said that!"

"Nobody said nothin', Sarge," said O'Bannion while our infuriated eyes glared. If looks could kill even Gruell realized he'd be dead.

"Wise asses!"

We huffed and puffed as we manhandled the last drum onto the dock. Pissed and covered with slop each of us silently plotted a nasty comeuppance for fat-ass Gruell.

On the ride back Gruell growled to Levintowski that the mess hall needed more cleaning. Our driver, of course, didn't give a shit, he wasn't on mess duty. As we pulled to a stop next to the mess hall, Gruell ordered two SBD mess men to swab the mess hall deck and polish the counter again. "We already done that," grumbled an SBD private.

"Really?" said Gruell. "Well, it don't pass my inspection, so quit fucking around and get this place squared away. The rest of you lend a hand!"

Corporal Jalowsky snickered as he meted out rags, brooms and mops. The six of us half-heartedly swept, swabbed, and polished.

An hour passed before Gruell, sporting a shit-assed grin across his pudgy face, returned. "You bozos look like you been dipped in shit. Two more hours and you'll be serving so get cleaned up! For god's sakes, when you get back, look like Marines!"

Where there's a will there's a way. Even though food supplies were regularly counted, re-checked, re-counted, inspected and mess hall workers closely watched. If one had the balls and imagination to purloin scarce goodies, satisfaction could be gleaned.

Oh, Gruell and Jalowsky kept wary eyes on food stuff going in or out so we were forced to refrain from filching more than a can or two of prized edibles at a time. Whenever an opportunity arose, O'Bannion, Cassidy, or I filched a gallon can of apricot, pineapple, peach or pears. A box or two of raisins and small bag of prunes were among our prized plunder.

Titmus had obtained a large hunk of discarded parachute. From the silk cloth he fashioned half-a-dozen silk bandannas and used red and black paint to inscribe Japanese suns and Asian-looking scrawls on each head cloth.

He accosted wide-eyed sailors strolling ashore. After his battle-featured snow job they were pleased to barter stolen sugar and sickbay alcohol for what they believed to be genuine Japanese headbands.

After dark, Titmus poured the bartered contraband into an empty vat concealed in our foxhole. Our colorful fruit and juice collection was featured in our versatile distillation efforts.

One Friday night we sat around our lone candle, sampling Titmus' current creation. It was too sweet, too sour, too bitter, and though it didn't easily slip down, the concoction had a desirable effect. We were feeling mellow until Cassidy announced. "That fat son-of-a-bitch, I'm going to kill him."

"Sure you are," I chided, a touch uneasy.

"I mean it!"

"Instead of killing him, why don't we go on strike?" blurted O'Bannion.

"What in hell you talkin' about?"

"Tomorrow, if we refuse to unload garbage cans, what can they do? That's what I'm talkin' about." snapped O'Bannion.

"Any other great ideas," I chimed.

"My brother was a longshoreman. He and his pals were pissed off because they were being screwed out of overtime so they struck. In the end, before going back to work, they got promised not only a raise in pay, but better conditions" said O'Bannion.

"Longshoremen belong to a union. They're civilians. In the military you don't strike, not unless you want to get shot for mutiny!" Titmus shook his head.

"How about this? When I lift them fuckin' garbage cans tomorrow, I'll get me a rupture," said Cassidy.

"What about the rest of us?" I said.

"For Christ's sake, think, figure something out for yourself!"

"Well, for one thing, we ain't gonna do your fuckin' work while you fake a fuckin' rupture!" said O'Bannion.

"Hells bells," I offered, "if all of us get hernias at the same time it won't look kosher."

Titmus sadly shook his head again and kept sipping.

The next morning, Lancaster roused us and ordered Cruz, Cassidy and me to report to the mess hall. We three were suffering monumental hangovers. The SBD mess guys must have had their own party because they also showed up in nasty moods.

We ladled out shit-for-chow to our bad-tempered grumblers cursing everything from the shitty food quality to the rotten mess hall service. After the diners departed we washed silverware, scrubbed pots, swept, swabbed and policed the outside area.

By the time it was time to maneuver the drums onto the truck bed, we were smeared with slop. "About time, I ain't got all day," grinned Gruell as he got into the cab.

As we sped down the coral road the six of us stood amid the garbage cans plotting vengeance. The target of our vehemence was mess duty, the Corps and Gruell.

Herman, a thin SBD guy, produced a canvas bag containing six cans of tinned beef. "What you gonna do with them?" asked Cruz.

"Give it to the gooks so they'll unload this stinkin' slop."

"Gruell won't allow it," I ventured.

"Fuck Gruell!" spat Red, a Texan from the SBD Squadron. "We got lots of canned beef. No self-respecting Marine will eat the shit anyway and the gooks love it. They'll do our unloading for a couple of cans."

"If fat-ass don't like it he can shove it," snapped Jimmy, the other SBD guy, a short stocky New Yorker.

"Gooks don't mind lifting garbage for a coupla tins," drawled Red. "What's it to that shithead poor excuse for a goddamn sergeant anyway!"

"Yeah, and why in hell should we deprive those poor natives anyway?" I added.

We got more wrathful and spouted epitaphs until our truck stopped at the end of the pier. Gruell got out and glared up at our sullen faces. "Start unloading."

"You guys with me?" said Cassidy.

"For what?" I asked.

"Strike! I'm striking. You guys in?" queried Cassidy.

"We SBD guys are with you," said Herman.

Cruz and I warily nodded assent.

Cassidy jumped off the truck and beckoned to a giant native wrapped in a *lava lava*. The muscular savage strolled over followed by four other gooks. "You unloadie, me givie," and invited the gook a peek into the bag.

"Okay dokey," said the native and grabbed the bag.

"What the hell!" said Gruell.

We dropped from the truck as the native spokesman and several others climbed into the truck bed.

"Get the hell off there!" ordered Gruell.

The natives glared at him and then us. Gruell turned beet red and yelled, "Off!"

The huge head honcho glanced at Cassidy who shrugged.

"I'll get you gooks arrested!" screamed Gruell.

The natives slipped to the coral ground. "Don't touch those cans!" growled Gruell. The muscular native clutched the sack and looked at Cassidy who was non-committal.

"Hear me!" spat Gruell. "Don't touch my garbage!"

After another quick glance at Cassidy the islander stalked off shouldering our sack of cans. His fellows grinned and followed, their bare feet slapping coral as their *lava lavas* flapped in the breeze.

Gruell faced Cassidy. "I hold you responsible for those stolen cans of government beef."

"Hah!" said Cassidy.

Gruell faced the rest of us. "Unload!"

"You lard-ass son-of-a-bitch," said Cassidy. "Do it yourself!"

I admit to being amazed at Cassidy's outburst and thinking, "The guys got balls, after all."

"Ah ha, mutiny, insubordination and stealing government vittles! Cassidy your sorry ass is in a sling!" He turned to us. "Get your asses up there!" None of us moved.

"You shitbirds backin' a mutineer? That makes you as guilty. You know what that means! General court martial for mutineers, that's what! In case you forgot, we're at war!"

Expressions of unadulterated hatred were our answer.

"I'm giving you rebels two seconds," said Gruell. We didn't stir. "Well, well," said our fat sergeant as he waddled to a field phone lashed to a pole. He dialed and sounded off loud and clear. "Lieutenant Rameron, Sergeant Gruell here. Private Cassidy is leading a mutiny!"

"Where? Oh, on the garbage truck, sir."

He held the receiver to his ear and glared. "Yes, sir! All six of them refuse to touch our garbage cans."

"I know that, sir, mutiny in a combat zone is a serious offense, sir. I'll relate the message. Yes, sir, I'll tell them it's their last chance to avoid a General Court Martial." Gruell hung up the phone and faced us. "Lieutenant Rameron told me to give you people one more chance. Refuse to unload and you'll be charged with mutiny."

"Shit," mumbled Cassidy.

"Well, what's it gonna be?"

One of the SBD guys climbed onto the truck, others followed. Cruz and I stepped in as Cassidy shrugged and braced himself to receive the first drum. We proceeded to unload the swill.

As he pulled himself into the cab, Gruell snickered, "You six will still be up on charges," We were too whipped to curse as our truck headed back.

When we pulled to a stop at our mess hall Lieutenant Rameron, soft looking for a Marine officer, was waiting. He had been a shoe salesman in civilian life, but all in all was a complacent guy. "Cassidy led the mutiny and Glossman backed him," charged Gruell.

"Mutiny during wartime is a serious offense," sighed Rameron.

"Yes, sir, I didn't like bringing it up, but mutiny is mutiny," said Gruell.

"Did they unload the garbage?" asked the lieutenant.

"Finally, sir."

"You know what happens to mutineers in the Marine Corps?" queried Lieutenant Rameron. "Or in any other service?"

Images featuring my record book, my reputation, my career in the Corps and my poor mother's reaction danced in my mind. I squirmed and others did likewise.

"The firing squad, brig time, prison sentences, I could go on," said the lieutenant. "Major Burke may even have his own idea of discipline. We're in a war and he might decide to use you men as an example. Anyway, I can assure you, his punishment won't be pleasant."

I glanced at Cassidy and Cruz, they looked as uneasy as I felt.

"There is one option," said Rameron. "Accept my punishment in lieu of a court martial, the major and your SBD CO may never learn of this troubling incident."

Cassidy's eyes locked on mine. There was a chance we wouldn't get court martialed, after all. The SBD guys, of course, had their own CO to worry about.

"We accept your punishment, sir," spouted Cassidy. Cruz and I nodded as did the SBD guys.

Our disciplinary punishments varied. I was delegated by the lieutenant to carry a loaded canister of insecticide on my back and spray the outside perimeter of the mess hall for the last full week of my mess duty stint. I was beholden to do the semi-onerous task for eight hours.

Cruz and Cassidy were issued heavy mallets and directed to pound on empty tin cans, there were lots of them. They had to be flattened so they would sink after being dumped at sea.

The three of us were ousted from regular mess hall duty to fulfill punishment obligations. The three SBD mutineers were ordered to scour the oven, sinks and garbage drums. Lieutenant Rameron sort of let us off the hook. We were grateful and even figured we owed him.

Cassidy and I labored outside. As far as we were concerned, it was better than slaving inside. Sergeant Gruell figured we got off too easy and reacted sullenly. Anyway, he wasn't too sorry to see the three of us exiled from his mess hall. However, he made a point of checking up on our exterior efforts two or three times a day. He addressed us as mutineers but that didn't bother us. In fact, we got to revel in it.

Cassidy kind of liked flattening cans. He claimed wielding the hammer was getting him in shape. The germ killing fluid in the tank strapped onto my back had to be filled with insect repellent from a fifty-gallon barrel stashed behind the mess hall. The damn load on my back got heavy after hours of toting and spraying.

I dutifully carried out my spraying responsibilities even after Corporal Jalowsky leaped out from behind the mess hall and falsely accused me of chasing the same fly around the mess hall. Lieutenant Rameron read me off but dismissed further punishment.

The inevitable came to pass. On a fateful morning the huge container containing the DDT was empty. It had either rolled from its perch or had been pushed. Refills for the burden on my back weren't available.

Of course, Gruell was incensed and angrily insisted that I finish my spraying punishment anyway. I was compelled to continue moving about toting the empty tank and aiming my empty spray gun at crawling and flying six-legged vermin around the mess hall. Anyway, our punishments eventually terminated and we returned to routine shit duty.

Titmus, who had missed our short-lived mutiny, broke out what was left of our distilled juice to toast the occasion. The thick concoction had aged a bit but its taste hadn't improved.

That night by candlelight we sipped, cursed and plotted. Sergeant Gruell, of course, was the target of our planned revenge. He and his two stooge corporals were featured in our vengeful plots.

In the morning, we reported to the Ground Defense Shack for assignments. Sergeant Goodwinch and Corporal Lancaster designated the same tiresome duties. Lancaster led Titmus, Arnie, Cassidy and me to a remote spot behind a clump of coconut trees. Two other privates, Gaston and Rosen, tagged along. "By the time you finish this head it better be the best goddamn head on Nukufetau," warned Lancaster.

"Sure," grumbled Titmus.

"I ain't joshin'!" warned Lancaster, "it's for the major himself so don't fuck it up!"

"Get your ass out of here!" said Titmus.

Lancaster almost retorted but had second thoughts and merely whispered to himself as he stalked away.

"Ear-banging asshole," said Arnie.

Titmus commenced digging. I grabbed a pick and hacked. Others did likewise. Our jackets were shed as we attacked the hard coral ground. We chopped, dug, swore and hacked away. It wasn't fun but far better than mess duty.

As we dug, the sun cooked and sweat poured. Rosen suddenly ceased cursing and picked up a fallen coconut. "Run for a pass," he snapped. Gaston dropped his shovel and galloped away. He caught the spiraling coconut and lateraled it to Arnie who ran at me and straight-armed my shoulder.

We chose sides and a touch football game commenced. Titmus observed for a few minutes before stretching out, closing his eyes and rendering loud snores.

By the time Lancaster showed up the score was forty to forty. "What the hell's going on!"

"We're taking a five minute break," panted Arnie.

Lancaster inspected our excavation. "Get the hell back to work!" He scrutinized us as we resumed digging. At 1730 we knocked off and shuffled off to chow. The football game and digging had exhausted us. After chow we showered and conked out.

The following morning we were back at work on the major's head. This time Lancaster hovered over us. It was a dreary chore but the result was imposing. If a shithouse could be labeled a work of art, the major's toilet would qualify.

We were convinced our completed efforts were satisfactory until Lancaster ordered us to redo the side sections. We again smoothed the interior and hand-packed the sides before installing the solid wooden frame.

"Major Burke will be pleased," admitted Lancaster.

"That's nice," spat Titmus.

"Yep, that's one helluva good looking shithouse," said Lancaster and posted a warning sign. "This is Major Burk's Private Facility! Keep off and out!"

CHAPTER EIGHTEEN

Torrid sun beams on Nukufetau stifled human energy and stimulated masses of green-hued flies. Most South Pacific Islands were insect infested but few could compare to the buzzing, biting six-legged denizens on Nukufetau. That was the general consensus. The irksome suckers, biters and disease bearers aimlessly flew about landing on hands, faces and other exposed body parts to bite, sting and exasperate.

After the sun dipped, the large tormenting green flies vanished leaving barely enough time for harassed service personnel to prepare for the airborne onslaught. Before Nukufetau became completely enshrouded in darkness, disturbing dronings announced the arrival of a more unsavory marauder. Gluttonous mosquitoes swarmed about satiating themselves with human blood.. The skeeters were far more irksome and repugnant than the slow moving fat flies.

Oh, we didn't apathetically await the nightly onslaught, but like other victims in neighboring tents fought back swatting, squashing and swearing. But even with our tent's dirt floor littered with dead bugs, insect tormentors multiplied.

Killing bugs expended energy and took its toll on dispositions but fighting back was our foremost release. Varied defensive measures made little impact and victims were sorely dispirited. Cursing the blood suckers and wretched island that spawned them was the best we could do.

One evening after the taps sounded and the buzzing commenced Arnie bellowed, "Shit!"

My "Fuck!" followed, Cassidy mouthed both sentiments. O'Bannion's curses were even more vehement. Cruz, as usual, sullenly endured.

Titmus wrathfully unsheathed his bayonet and swung at a consistent marauder. Before he simmered down another lengthy slit marred his tattered mosquito net. His futile response shocked but failed to amuse.

Several nights later he erupted again and fired a round at a persistent buzzer. The reverberation caused squadron consternation. Armed neighbors poured from tents rifles at the ready. The confused hubbub led to an official investigation.

Of course, we clammed up, Titmus was our tent mate. Besides, his two-hundred and ten solid pounds and close to completion of two hitches merited him some slack. We implored him to calm down and he simmered a bit but we became collectively concerned. "He's losing it," whispered O'Bannion.

A few nights later as we tensely hit our sacks he astounded us by calmly squaring away his cot and smoothing out creases in his perforated net. While he refrained from spouting even the mildest of oaths we spewed our own customary curses while he serenely hit the sack.

"Titmus, you okay?" I said.

A shit-eating grin was his response.

It was a memorable night because the blood-sipping parasites were especially active. While we cursed and slapped at the brazen probers, Titmus' colorful oaths were conspicuous by their absence. Instead, sonorous sounds emanated from his open mouth. His tranquil snores added to our discomfort.

It took forever but reveille finally sounded, but Titmus' heavy breathing continued as his tent mates wearily rose. Our banging mess gear woke him. "Morning, boys!"

We waited.

"What?"

"How come you slept?" gritted Cruz.

Titmus tapped his head.

"What the hell is that supposed to mean?" said Arnie.

"Brains," said Titmus.

"Bullshit!" said O'Bannion. Under normal circumstances none of us would have used such a belligerent tone but he was pissed, we all were. Who could blame us?

Titmus glowered as I tactfully intervened, "C'mon, Earl, we're your buddies."

A sudden movement on Titmus' cot caught our eyes. A large black lizard ensconced there slowly swished his tail. The huge reptile was six maybe seven inches long. It turned its huge head and its beady eyes leveled on each of us.

"He's big," sighed O'Bannion.

"Where'd you get him?" Asked Arnie.

"From a B-25 grease-monkey. Cost me nine bucks and a phony Jap bandana."

"Only nine?" scoffed O'Bannion.

"According to that dogface, he's got two more lizards just like him prowling his tent on the 'Canal."

"I'll be damned," said Arnie.

"Name's Gallagher."

"The doggie?"

"No, Idiot, the lizard."

Cassidy spoke. "Why didn't we think of it? Day and night millions of lizards scamper through our tent and what do they feed on? Bugs, that's what!"

We quickly shared the same thought. "Why not catch and place one or more of the local lizards in our mosquito net?" said Cassidy.

"You can't substitute quantity for size and training," advised Titmus.

Of course, none of the Nukufetau island lizards came close to Gallagher's size but it was worth a try. After we were secured from the day's shit-hole digging, we went lizard hunting. Titmus didn't join us. We each captured several scrawny reptiles and before nightfall situated them under our nets. We crawled into our sacks anticipating lovely results.

To our chagrin we suffered through another sleepless, slapping night. The little lizards failed to perform. Between sleep-induced dialogue segments featuring Millie, Titmus' grating snores and irritating mumbles added to our discomfort. At daybreak, covered with mosquito welts and nasty dispositions, we crawled from our sacks.

O'Bannion had rolled over two of his scrawny lizards and they lay colorfully pulverized. Cruz too had inadvertently squashed one of his. Cassidy's four and three of mine had escaped through holes incurred during our gook-gin revelries. We were dismayed.

Titmus commiserately shook his head, "Listen up!" He related that the dogface who sold Gallagher had confided that the big lizard had been trained by shamans on Guadalcanal. Those medicine men or whatever the hell they are, spin a protective voodoo on lizard trainees. That's what keeps them from getting squashed.

"See, Gallagher's been indoctrinated with a sense of duty. He's got pride in his snaring skills. These no-class puny lizards running here and there lack brains, breeding and training. What's worse, they got no sense of pride."

It was obvious that Gallagher was longer, smarter and had ample girth, but was he that special? I doubted it, but of course, I didn't crack my misgivings to Titmus.

A late afternoon was devoted to catching lizards. Gentle handling was required and, at first, training sessions were a welcome diversion. But trying to teach unreliable reptiles how to master a simple task was no cup of tea. Efforts, much to our chagrin, were wasted as the local lizards failed to perform.

More slapping, cursing, frustrating nights were endured. Titmus' grating snores became a constant reminder of our failed attempts.

On a sweltering Sunday as we swatted swooping greenies, Titmus impulsively reached under his net and set Gallagher on the deck. The lizard poised less than a second before darting to the top of Cruz's net and snatching a green giant of a fly.

After consuming the appetizer, he shot up a canvas wall and nabbed a yellow six-legger. After downing that one he continued to hunt and ingest.

Darting up, down and parallel, regardless of size, color or species he consumed all six-legged intruders. From then on Titmus gave Gallagher the free run of our tent.

Our lizard savior whizzed about our tent devouring the colorful mixture of creeping, crawling, winged infiltrators. His appetite wasn't appeased during daylight hours. Titmus along with the rest of us caught assorted bugs and placed them in front of Gallagher's probing snout. His darting tongue disposed of each and every gifted morsel. Our benefactor had one helluva of an appetite.

An occasional lucky mosquito, fly or unidentified six-legged intruder would zip in and out; but most ended up in his expanding gullet. Our loyal tongue-flicking savior never strayed from the inner perimeter of our canvas home. We slept like babies. As our abode became free of six-legged marauders we became jubilant, maybe a touch cocky.

All of us were fond of our savior but Titmus became deeply enamored with Gallagher. One inactive Sunday I entered our sanctum and heard him conversing. "Wait 'til you meet Millie she's one helluva girl. You two will hit it off. After she and I get spliced, don't worry, the three of us will find a nice place to live, maybe start a family."

Gallagher's bee-bee eyes glowed and his tongue flicked. I felt like an intruder and silently backed out of the tent. In a hushed voice I related what I had witnessed to the others.

Arnie thought that Titmus talking to Gallagher was funny. Cruz was a little spooked but said nothing. O'Bannion didn't give it another thought but Cassidy became a bit unhinged. I didn't comment but worriedly concluded that Titmus talking to a lizard was a touch unsettling.

As Gallagher became more of a shipmate than a lizard, we didn't tolerate infringements on his hunting grounds. Island lizards darting through our tent were scooped up and projectiled out.

Time slipped by and word of Gallagher's prowess spread. The curious and envious from all branches, including a few officers, dropped in to gaze at what had become our renowned lizard. Some brought dead flies, crumbs or other edible tidbits to place them before him. Lizard *afficianados* appreciated watching his voracious tongue snatching gifted morsels.

Six out of seven days we had military duties to perform. Soldiers, sailors and probably some Marines, if they got the chance, weren't above snatching a valuable commodity like Gallagher. While we were off doing varied shit details, don't think we didn't worry about Gallagher being kidnapped. One of us would periodically drift by our tent to check on his welfare

Visitors observed and admired, but envious distracters were evident. "How'd he get so big?" and "He's doped up, ain't he?" were a few of the callow remarks.

On special nights, Titmus would set a can of purloined peach brandy near the lone candle lighting up our makeshift table. After solemnly dipping a dead fly into a cup he'd set the sweetened corpse in front of Gallagher's probing snout. Our lizard's tongue would swiftly retrieve it and as it slipped down his gullet a facsimile of a smile would appear.

After downing a few cups, one or more of us took turns relating personal tales. Gallagher seemed to comprehend some, not all, of what was being said. After gulping several brandy-dipped flies, a benign expression would cross his face and he'd slowly swing this tail.

As Gallagher grew longer and rounder, he became more and more lethargic. Swifter insects managed to elude his flicking tongue. As time elapsed his girth kept expanding.

Our lizard's foraging ability decreased. Finally Gallagher's forward acceleration ceased altogether. It became obvious that our rotund mascot no longer relished the hunt. He preferred remaining motionless under Titmus' cot.

When we placed morsels before him; he'd blink and flick his tail before and after his tractable tongue ingested the goodies. Gallagher's inactivity distressed us so we spent more time catching marauders which wasn't difficult because they had swarmed back into our tent.

One evening while sullenly sipping raisin jack and noting our lethargic lizard Arnie said, "I got it!"

"Got what?" snapped Titmus.

"I've diagnosed Gallagher's problem."

"Sure!" grunted O'Bannion.

Arnie glowered. "He's a male lizard, ain't he? Outside of being a different species, how much different can he be from one of us?"

"What the hell you talking about?" spat O'Bannion.

"He's thinking similar thoughts," certified Arnie.

"You're out of your mind!" snapped Cassidy.

"Shut up and listen! Am I homesick, sure, who isn't? Would I like something special like a home-cooked meal?"

"Get to the point," warned Titmus.

"Gentlemen," said Arnie in his provoking manner, "we got to find Gallagher a lady friend."

"What!" roared Titmus.

"You saying Gallagher got to get laid?" chortled O'Bannion.

"Don't make it sound so crude but that's what I'm saying."

"Then he sure as hell ain't like you, Arnie, 'cause you ain't never been laid," scoffed O'Bannion.

"Shut your dumb Boston face and hear me out!" spat Arnie, his face glowing red.

"O'Bannion, you've never been laid either," went through my mind, but I didn't comment because neither had I. But like all others, I thought about it day and night, mostly at night. Hmm, maybe Arnie was on to something and Gallagher did have those thoughts.

"Arnie's could be on to something," whispered Cruz. "I get them thoughts."

Now Cruz might have had his whistle wet once or twice but he never bullshitted about it like O'Bannion.

"It's a possibility," ventured Cassidy.

"Hmm," said Titmus.

"That's what's bugging him," assured Arnie, "he needs to get laid."

"Worth a try," said Cassidy.

"Guess it wouldn't hurt," decided Titmus, a little upset because he hadn't thought of it first.

I wasn't convinced but said, "Maybe."

"Where in hell we gonna find a female lizard?" snapped O'Bannion.

"None of these trampy ones running through our tent!" bellowed Titmus.

"We got to find one with a touch of class," agreed Arnie.

"Where?"

"How?"

"We offer a reward," smugly said Arnie

The six of us chipped in and come up with twenty-four bucks. Titmus pocketed the money. That night Arnie posted our notice on the mess hall bulletin board. *"Twenty-four bucks plus a jug of apricot brandy for a suitable lady lizard. See Earl Titmus."*

Word spread that Titmus' tent were searching for a mate for their renowned lizard. We let it be known that the prospective mate would have to be superior in looks and disposition.

Several officers read the poster and figured it to be a joke. Enlisted personnel in our squadron and others from neighboring outfits became aware that we meant business.

Soldiers, sailors and Marines began bringing in what they claimed to be lady lizards. It wasn't easy, maybe impossible for the undoctrinated to tell a female from a male. Since none of us could make the scientific distinction, we had to go by gut feelings.

Cruz claimed that he had once raised tropical fish and regardless of species males always looked prettier than the female. When I was a kid, I owned a tank of fish and knew his words to be true so I seconded his assessment. Titmus said it made sense.

Lady lizards brought in by hopeful contributors were set in front of Gallagher. Some looked presentable, others not so good. Didn't matter, Gallagher wasn't interested. He spurned each and every one of them. For days Gallagher had barely stirred.

"Maybe we should ask a corpsman to check him," I ventured.

"They can't cure human beings, how in hell is they gonna cure a lizard?" said Arnie.

"A ground-up pill might help," I sheepishly replied.

"How about our good ole' doctor?" said Cassidy.

"Probably want to amputate his tail, maybe a leg," snarled Titmus.

"Good lady lizards aren't easy to find," mused O'Bannion.

A guy in Seabee blue fatigues audaciously stepped into our tent. Two burly Seabees shouldered in behind him radiating a bodyguard presence. The lanky visitor was slightly stoop-shouldered, long-legged and gaunt. One hand covered his other. "Pardon," he rasped. "Is this the home of the lonesome lizard?"

The guy had the look of an academic but thick glasses couldn't conceal that he was in the final stages of the "bulkhead stare".

The tall guy seemed oblivious to his escort as he gently cupped his hands around an enclosed object. It wasn't difficult to guess what he was concealing.

"Who wants to know?" O'Bannion tried to sound gruff.

"There are rumors that a fine specimen of male lacertilian is seeking to be joined in holy matrimony."

We scrutinized the guy to see if, because of our delicate predicament, he was putting us on. We were in no mood for joshing.

"Whud you say!" said Titmus.

"You a wise guy!" growled Cassidy.

"What you got?" said Arnie.

The guy's far off stare and warning expressions on the faces of his mates conveyed that the poor bastard had gone Asiatic. "Could happen to anyone," I silently surmised.

"I have a lady lizard."

Titmus suspected chicanery, we all did. "Let's have a look!"

With a grand flourish the guy uncupped his hand, "Gentlemen, Madam LaRue!"

Exposed on his palm was a lady lizard. Her coat was a dark purple and reddish lines ran neatly down from her head to the tip of her tail. A faint spray of goldish spots flecked across her gray head. As lizards go she was a beauty.

"If I was a lizard I'd go for her myself," of course that muse I kept to myself.

"Holy shit, we'll take her!" said Titmus waving our sheaf of bills.

"Avast, Gyrenes! I wouldn't think of selling Madam Larue," gasped the lanky Seabee.

"Then what in hell did you come here for!" snarled Titmus.

"Not for money! If Madam LaRue takes a shine to your Gallagher, it would be reward enough for me to see my little lady happy."

Titmus gently patted the tall guy's shoulder. "I like that. All lady lizards take to Gallagher but he's the particular one."

"May I please meet your Gallagher so I can ascertain if he's of suitable guise and statue to enjoin with Madam LaRue?"

Titmus, a little petulantly, pointed at Gallagher poised under the cot.

The tall guy dropped to his knees to evaluate. "He's fat."

"Fat hell!" snapped Titmus, "That's muscle."

He was pissed at the guy's attitude, we all were. If it hadn't been for his burly escorts, we'd have appropriated his lizard and heaved him out.

"You sure she's a female?" said O'Bannion.

"Indeed, she is," said the tall guy.

"How in hell do you know!" said Cassidy.

"See her dainty lines, her coloring? Anyway, before the war I was a zoology student and am well acquainted with the physical, sociological and psychological facets of lizards," said the Seabee. He glanced back at his backup and they grimly nodded.

"She don't look too healthy," spat O'Bannion.

"Look! Just look! Your horrid words and ugly lizard have made Madam LaRue ill!" the weird Seabee shouted.

Trouble might have erupted if Titmus hadn't calmly spoken. "Put her down! Gallagher probably won't pay her no heed."

Gently, very gently, the slim Seabee carefully set Madam LaRue on the deck a good six inches from Gallagher's snout. Breathing slackened as two lizard tongues flicked and two sets of lacertilian eyes scrutinized each other.

Gallagher's left foot suddenly moved forward, his first significant activity in almost two weeks. The trial step was followed by a second and third as he painstakingly crawled forward. Madam LaRue apprehensively eyed his approach.

"Holy shit," whispered O'Bannion.

"I told you so!" gasped Arnie.

"Son-of-a-bitch is in love," said O'Bannion.

"Thank the Lord," said Titmus.

Cruz crossed himself and mumbled in Spanish.

"Gallagher's gonna get laid," smirked O'Bannion.

"Hey, hey," sang Cassidy.

The long-legged Seabee obviously didn't cotton to that kind of talk and Titmus' glare wiped the smirks from O'Bannion and Cassidy's faces.

Breathing was subdued as Gallagher struggled toward Madam LaRue.

Gallagher finally made it to within a tongue's length from Madam Larues' speckled snout when she abruptly twisted. Her swished tail barely missed his probing nose as she scampered up a canvas wall.

As the lady lizard ogled Gallagher from above O'Bannion's cot, a subtle display of disdain spread across her speckled face. Gallagher, frazzled from his romantic effort, forlornly gazed up at the elusive lady.

Titmus growled, "What in hell's wrong with her!"

The tall guy shrugged. "Looks like Gallagher doesn't appeal to her."

"That slut's pretty particular!" spat Arnie.

"Lizard bitch!" hissed Cassidy.

The Seabee's face blossomed, "Avast that dirty talk!"

"I got something to say too!" I gritted.

"Look! Look! You've hurt her feelings," sputtered the Seabee.

We glared at the lady lizard seemingly oblivious to our comments.

"On behalf of Madam LaRue I demand an apology," squeaked the Seabee.

Cassidy stuck out his chin. "Hah!"

"You heard him!" growled one of the Seabees.

Titmus erupted, "Out, swabbies, before I trounce you and your lousy lizard." Titmus moved to grab Madam LaRue.

"Stand fast, Gyrene!" growled the other Seabee.

I'm not sure who threw the first punch but a melee erupted as fists, thuds and curses spewed. The tall thin guy stood aside whimpering but the other two were tough. We did have them out numbered and as O'Bannion shoved the timorous one through the flap he retreated behind his bruised buddies. Arnie grasped Madam LaRue off the tent wall and hurled her after the disgruntled trio.

As we chortled and turned to congratulate each other we noted Titmus sobbing. It couldn't have been the slight trickle from his nose; we'd seen him more battered than that.

"You okay?" Asked Cassidy.

Titmus slowly turned. Spread across the seat of his pants was the colorful remains of Gallagher. A wild punch had dropped Titmus atop our lizard. Our corpulent Gallagher had been too out of shape to steer clear.

We were chagrinned, especially Titmus. He changed trousers and we sullenly trailed him deep into the brush. Under the spread of a blooming breadfruit tree we scooped a hole and interned Gallagher and Titmus' pants.

Cruz conducted a short but despairing ceremony in Spanish. Afterwards, the six of us sadly trod back to our tent.

CHAPTER NINETEEN

Two days later as we were laboring, Corporal Lancaster, our perennial troublemaker, approached. "listen up!" he said

"More bullshit!" spat Titmus.

"Listen, I got my orders here," he whined and pulled out an official looking paper. He quickly read a code letter, file number followed by, "Two Marines from VMF's Ground Defense report for temporary duty with Boat Refuse Group One."

Titmus quickly growled, "Sherman and I will go."

"What kind of duty is Boat Refuse?" I asked, more than somewhat flattered that Titmus had chosen me to join him.

"It's a temporary transfer," shouted Lancaster. "As of now, you two are relieved from Ground Defense and temporarily attached to the navy refuse detachment."

"What kind of duty is that?" I wondered aloud.

"You'll be deckhands on a garbage scow taking orders from swabbies," gloated Lancaster.

"What!"

"Report to Ensign Piddle for further instructions. His office is in that falling down shack near the end of the pier."

"When?"

"They're expecting you as of now! And, whatever you do, don't make VMF 111 or the Corps look bad!"

Titmus walked off and I followed.

"You got less than twenty minutes to get there," shouted Lancaster. I replicated Titmus' shrug.

An amiable Seabee jockeying a two-ton truck drove us to our new place of employment and dropped us off. At the foot of the pier he pointed at the dilapidated structure perched near the seaward end. "That lovely mansion near the end is the garbage disposal unit's headquarters. I suppose you already know that."

We had seen the shack each time we rode the garbage truck to unload garbage on the pier. We were far from enthused but a touch curious as we shuffled to the door of the dilapidated shack. Titmus banged on the battered door. "Enter!" shouted a thin voice.

We stepped inside and stood before a littered desk constructed of wooden boxes. Clad in dress blues, Ensign Jonathan Piddle, the pink-faced commander of Boat Refusal Disposal Group One sat behind the desk. Displayed on his chest were South Pacific and American Theater of Operations ribbons. Dress uniforms in the tropics were unique, adorned with campaign ribbons was even more unusual.

The ensign continued thumbing through a sheaf of papers as Titmus shifted. He paid us no heed until Titmus cleared his throat for the third time. The ensign finally ceased checking papers and looked up as we properly stated our names and ranks and reason for reporting to him.

He got to his feet drawing his five-feet four inches into a ramrod stance and suspiciously scrutinized us. "I'm Ensign Piddle, your commanding officer," he squeaked "I'm in charge of Boat Refusal Group One. I run a tight ship and take no shit from anyone, especially jarheads. Boat Refuse Group One is my baby. Be warned, I run my outfit by the book, understand!"

We stared straight ahead. "Did you hear me!" snapped the ensign.

"Aye, aye, sir, we heard," said Titmus.

"Yeah," I said, wondering what kind of disastrous situation I was in.

The ensign wrathfully trembled, "Is that the way Marines talk to an officer," he screamed.

"No, sir," said Titmus.

"Uh, uh, sir," I added.

"Listen up! I'll say it only once. You Gyrenes have been assigned to Boat Refuse Group One. We're a small but a vital segment of the Asiatic Pacific Fleet.

"Each and every day, every military unit on Nukufetau truck in all kinds of offal to this wharf. It's our primary responsibility to carry the collective swill out to sea and dump it. Our responsibilities are to keep the end of this pier clear of incoming and out going debris, garbage and slop."

His impassioned delivery became screechier. "Our duties are pertinent to the health and welfare of this island. You Jarheads understand?"

"Aye, aye, sir," I snapped and Titmus nodded.

"We may not be doing the most glamorous task in the South Pacific, but our obligations are pertinent to the war effort." Ensign Piddle was apparently enamored with his rubbish responsibilities. "We have an imperative responsibility to fulfill our duties with maximum efficiency.

"And Gyrenes, don't expect public relations people to photograph your efforts. Of course, this may disappoint you glory-seeking Marines! Just remember, we got a job to do, unglamorous as it may be. We will do our duty and perform it well!"

As he paused for affect, Titmus shifted from one foot to the other.

"Didn't the navy have enough shitbirds for menial tasks?" The answer was forthcoming.

"Six of my men are down with dengue fever. That's why you two and two other Gyrenes are here. You're temporary replacements.

"We ever gonna get out of here or is he gonna talk forever?" I wondered.

"Boat Refuse Group One's objectives are clear. We keep Nukufetau garbage free. So far we've functioned in a smooth Four-O manner.

However, as in any operation there's room for improvement. Questions!"

"No, sir," we chorused.

"Two Marines are assigned to each of our two LCM to make sure that natives do what they're supposed to. Don't let them bamboozle you! Gooks are a bunch of lazy fuck-ups. However, occasionally refuse cans are too damn heavy. When they are, give them a hand.

"You two report to the *Honey Baby Two*. She's tied to the end of the pier. Seaman First Class Atkins is the cox'n and in complete charge of the *Honey Baby Two*. Understand?"

"Yes, sir," we chanted.

"One more thing, I run a tight ship! Dismissed!"

We withdrew. As we made way toward the end of the pier, "What a jerk," I muttered.

"Swabjockey asshole," added Titmus.

At the end of the pier, two corroded blunt-nosed LCMs gently tugged at mooring lines. Both were in rough shape, but the *Honey Baby Two* was even more weathered than the other. Part of the "H" on her name had peeled away and two holes gaped above her water line. The open slits were framed in rust. As we got closer we became aware of the unpleasant odor emanating from the *Honey Baby Two*. The dilapidated craft stunk.

"I don't like the looks of this," I whispered.

"You'd rather be digging officers' shithouses?" spat Titmus.

A bald-headed old sailor in dirty blue fatigues emerged from the deck hatch. His gut hung over his belt. "Fuck! Fuck! Fuck!" he snarled.

"You Atkins?" said Titmus.

"Who wants to know?" slobbered the old salt.

"Guess who we are!" growled Titmus.

"You must be the seagoin' bellhops we don't need, come aboard!"

Titmus and I jumped onto the rust-caked deck.

"We don't crave jarheads aboard but orders are orders," growled Atkins.

Suddenly Atkins scrutinized Titmus. "Jarheads all look the same, but you look familiar. Hey, weren't you seagoing on the *Maryland*?"

"Yeah, six, seven years ago," said Titmus.

"Hah! I thought so."

"But not for long."

"Long enough for you to owe me a drink."

Titmus stared. "I remember. You're the swabbie that bought a round or two in that Bubbling Well joint."

"I recall more than two."

"I'll be damned, you're right, I owe you."

"Good old days," reminisced Atkins.

"Compared to these," agreed Titmus.

Atkins and Titmus' recalls featured Russian and Chinese ladies. The elderly sailor related that he was three years shy of twenty-five but far from eager to leave the navy. "Where will I go? What the hell will I do?"

"As long as there's war goin' on, don't worry. Garbage haulers are very important to the war effort. Even if you been in for thirty they won't cut you loose," assured Titmus.

"I hope so. Anyway, this duty ain't too bad," said Atkins. "If it wasn't for Piddle, our ninety-day wonder, it would almost be good. They put the idiot here to keep him from fucking up the war effort."

"Kind of figured that," said Titmus.

Machinist 3rd Class Edgar Murson, a quiet kid from a remote Minnesota farm town hopped aboard. His faded blue fatigues were grease-stained. He shyly greeted us and began puttering about the boat's engine. It wasn't hard to conclude that he adored the *Honey Baby* and had an intimate relationship with her engines.

His demeanor concerning old Atkins was loyal and protective. The four of us made up the crew. The other battered LCM was also crewed by two sailors and two Marines. The other Marines were from the SBD Squadron. Neither Titmus nor I knew them.

Titmus and my responsibilities were to make sure our native workers followed orders and performed their loading and unloading duties.

It wasn't an easy task because the cans brimmed with smelly slop. After the LCMs were crammed fore to aft and port to starboard with drums of putrid garbage, native workers leaped aboard. Edgar let loose the lines and Atkins steered the craft out to sea.

If the *Honey Baby* wasn't loaded properly, garbage spilled from cans and she listed. The deck became a slippery mess. The rancid odors didn't seem to bother our two shipmates but Titmus and I never got accustomed to the rejectionable odors.

When our craft was half a mile from the dock our two swabbies played out the LCM's anchor and our native laborers poured the swill into the sea.

While our gook crew washed down the deck by swirling salt water around the emptied drums, seagulls squawked, swooped and squabbled as they gorged on our discarded cargo..

The offshore voyage was half-a-mile or less but I liked going out to sea. I imagined myself being an old time seafarer and recited James Mansfield's *Sea Fever,* to myself, of course.

Outside of an almost daily tirade from Ensign Piddle, our responsibilities were tolerable. We weren't designated to lift or lug cans from the incoming trucks. It didn't take long for Titmus and me to adjust to our new obligations.

Atkins was a man with connections. One of his mates ashore had a pivotal supply shack job. Consequently, on the pretense that the *Honey Baby* required it, he occasionally attained a small can of ninety-proof de-icer fluid. Titmus contributed a purloined can of grapefruit juice. Blending the two fluids created a potent concoction.

The libation didn't appeal to me. I loathed the taste, but didn't want the two old salts to think I was candy-assed so I sipped. If observed, I swallowed, if unobserved I expectorated.

Edgar had more balls. He said it tasted worse than seagull piss and after his first taste refused to touch it.

Eventually Ensign Piddle's lectures on *esprit de corps* got to the guys on the *Sweet Sal,* the other LCM. The ensign proclaimed his intention to reward the LCM crew who carried off the most garbage. The reward would include time off for Marines, perhaps even a promotion for the navy guys.

Atkins didn't believe or give a damn about Piddle's promotional promises. Edgar, too, was oblivious to the ensign's carrot. Neither Titmus nor I cared one way or the other.

The navy yokels on the *Sweet Sal* fell for Piddle's inducement. Deviating from the usual two to three garbage excursions a day, they squeezed in four dumpings.

We anchored our *Honey Baby* off shore to sample a gargle or two. We also fished a little and bullshitted a lot about things that didn't mean anything. One or two garbage trips per day was all we could manage,

As Atkins expressed it, "When representatives of two stalwart military services in conjunction with heathen people operate a common objective, diversion becomes a positive pertinent factor toward successful completion of said objectives."

I didn't comprehend all of it but was impressed by his words. Although Titmus wasn't sure about Atkins' philosophical spout, he agreed with the crux of his sentiment.

Despite Atkins' critical soundings regarding shit duty on a rusty old scow, he obviously was emotionally attached to the *Honey Baby*. Edgar too, loved the flat-nosed pile of junk. He babied her engine while Atkins vainly chipped and scraped corrode from the port and starboard sides of her battered hull.

Both tried to get Titmus and me to lend an upkeeping hand but as Titmus put it, "We ain't sailors and don't intend to do swabbies' work. Our responsibilities are with the garbage and that's where we will direct our efforts. Case closed!"

The *Sweet Sal's* swabbies and Marines worked their asses off. Sometimes they even labored past the knock-off hour. On their own time they strived to keep the pier clear of brimming drums of offal.

The two SBD Marines weren't as *Gung Ho* as the swabbies, but more inspired than Titmus and me.

One morning Ensign Piddle assembled both crews. He gave an emotional speech regarding the effort required to efficiently dispose of Nukufetau's garbage. "Do you Marines know what *Semper Fidelis* means?" he snidely asked.

"Fuck you, hurray for me," dutifully answered Titmus. Both the SBD earbangers and I chuckled.

"I'm referring to the literal Latin translation," snapped Piddle. Nobody commented. "It means Always Faithful."

There was a shrug reaction, not the response the ensign was seeking. "Alright, *Sweet Sal* crew, move out! *Honey Baby Two,* stay," he ordered. The other crew departed.

Ensign Piddle stood in a stalwart stance. "Don't think I'm not aware that the *Sweet Sal* crew has been disposing of more than twice the loads you people have carted away. I am sorely disappointed."

Titmus and I tried to look chagrinned.

"Now listen up! The *Honey Baby Second* has fallen far short of fulfilling United States Navy rubbish responsibilities. Seaman Atkins, improve your garbage dispersion or you will be replaced. Your next assignment won't be nearly as pleasant. Is that clear?"

"Aye, aye, sir."

"Dismissed!"

We endured Piddle's critical glare as he angrily returned our half-hearted salute. We sensed him glaring into our backs as we shuffled toward the *Honey Baby Two.* "Ninety-day asshole wonder," muttered Titmus.

Our gooks weren't knocking themselves out as they half-heartedly manipulated garbage cans onto The *Honey Baby.*

"What now?" moaned Edgar.

"If we don't move more garbage that prick will nail us to the cross," sighed Atkins.

"We sure as hell don't want to go back on mess duty, Titmus," I offered.

"Shit duty is shit duty," sighed Titmus.

Edgar and I tried to motivate the gooks to at least look like they were hustling. "Hubba-hubba, hurry it up!" Edgar shouted and they reacted with their usual lackluster response.

"Get moving!" I shouted. Far from being motivated, our brown-skinned natives grinned but stayed apathetic. Atkins and Titmus leaned against the gunwale and sipped from a can.

"I don't want to lose the *Honey Baby,*" said Atkins.

"I hope you don't," said Titmus, sincere sympathy in his tone.

A full load of garbage drums was manipulated onto our craft and we proceeded to chug out to sea. One mile out our uninspired natives laboriously dumped our putrid cargo into the sea. Titmus soulfully admitted, "It's not easy to get revved up about garbage."

The screech of *Sweet Sal's* irritating whistle sounded as she chugged by with her second brimming load. The sight certainly didn't bolster our sagging moral.

Late that afternoon Titmus and I were almost as despondent as Atkins and Edgar as we hitchhiked back to camp.

The next morning we showed up at the pier to be greeted by a howling wind and frothing sea. Rain swooped down in proverbial buckets. At muster, Ensign Piddle, wet and cranky, reluctantly proclaimed that it was too rough for our LCMs to venture out.

However, trucks from various Nukufetau encampments continued depositing brimming drums. Every available space on the pier was soon cluttered with swill and slop filled garbage cans.

The two native crews looked cold and glum. The mass of stinking cans haphazardly crowded the pier. The place reeked of wet rot. All hands shared negative emotions.

"Helluva blow," sighed Titmus

"I've seen worse," said Atkins.

"No kidding?" whispered Edgar.

I groaned.

As we tried to make ourselves comfortable on the leeward side of the *Honey Baby,* the rain subsided. A swabbie, one of the *Sweet Sal* deckhands, trotted up. "The ensign wants to talk crap to both crews."

"About what?" said Edgar.

"The usual bullshit, I suppose."

"Shit," echoed Atkins as he watched the swabbie jog back to the headquarter shack.

We shuffled to where Ensign Piddle stiffly waited in wet khaki. His field scarf flapped in the windy gusts as he announced, "Men of Boat Refuse Disposal Group One, a grave challenge confronts us."

Eight enlisted personnel shifted and Titmus let out a barely audible moan.

"As you can see, my pier, our pier, is overflowing with odorous offal. After this squall subsides, flies, rats and other parasitic creatures will gravitate here from god knows where.

"The well-being of all, in fact the health of every man, woman and child on Nukufetau will be in jeopardy. Colonel Jefferson advised me that it is our responsibility to rid the island of this infectious threat."

"Who's Colonel Jefferson?" whispered Atkins.

"Damned if I know," sighed Titmus.

"The quicker we rid our island of this menace the better," added Piddle. "On behalf of my boys in Boat Refuse Group One, I assured the colonel that we are up to the task.

"Men, the honor and glory of *Boat Refuse Group One* rests with you. Don't let me down, boys. Now get to it!"

There was a rousing, "Aye, aye, Sir!" from the two sailors from the other boat as they trotted toward their craft. The two SBD Marines glumly followed. The ensign cleared something from his eye. We turned to go when he shouted, "*Honey Baby* crew, Avast!"

We sort of stood at attention. "Up to now, you men have been a disgrace to Boat Refuse Disposal Group One!"

I sure as hell didn't give a damn about Group One or his navy bullshit, but I tried to show concern.

"Atkins! This is your last chance! Make a negative showing during this emergency and you will be relieved. The *Honey Baby Second* will be turned over to a worthy sailor. Understand!"

"Aye, sir," sputtered Atkins.

"Dismissed!" snapped Piddle. We saluted but not near as snappy as the one returned. We strode to our boat which was half-heartedly tugging at her fore and aft lines. Six squatting natives were waiting.

"Son-of-a-bitch is gonna give the *Honey Baby* to someone else," said Atkins.

"Chickenshit bastard," I muttered.

"No one can keep this boat running like Atkins and me," said the mournful Edgar.

"Piddle may be bullshitting," said Titmus. By now we felt a kinship with the two swabbies and appreciated what the *Honey Baby* meant to them.

Atkins poured four cups of de-icer fluid and passed them around with a can of grapefruit juice. "She just ain't as fast as the *Sweet Sal.*"

"Anything we can do to speed her up?" queried Titmus.

"I put new sparkplugs in, replaced wires, charged her battery, oiled and greased every nut and bolt, she's doing the best she can," groaned Edgar.

Atkins nodded toward the *Sweet Sal,* "Look at those ear-banging bastards," he sneered,

The other boat was a beehive of activity. Her gooks must have been spurred on by some outlandish promise. They were manhandling drums of garbage onto her deck. Her swabby crew and SBD guys were pushing and lifting too.

"We better get started," whispered Edgar.

"What for?" said Atkins.

Titmus stood. "We can't tote shit faster but we can carry a larger cargo."

"What's that supposed to mean?" said Atkins.

"Watch," said Titmus and faced our natives. "You do gooda work and me getta you some American money and more tins of beef, *sabe?*"

"More beef okay," said one.

"Much more. Hubba hubba, start loading!"

The brown-skinned six weren't overly enthused but they loved canned beef and proceeded to wrestle drums of garbage aboard. While the other LCM was almost loaded with a deckful of brimming garbage drums, Atkins poured us another round of grapefruit juice laced with de-icer fluid.

Even with a double shot of grapefruit juice, I had trouble tolerating the libation, but wasn't about to shy away while others drank.

"We're gonna save your boat!" announced Titmus. Atkins and Edgar looked doubtful but hopeful.

It wasn't too long before our head gook announced, "No more room."

He was right, our deck was crammed with a single layer of stinking garbage barrels. The *Sweet Sal* had already chugged away with her first load. "See those planks," said Titmus and pointed to a lumber pile alongside the shack. "Lay them across the garbage can and stack another layer of cans on top. *"Comprende?"*

The natives looked bewildered but when Titmus roared, they commenced lifting and loading. We helped them lift.

As the added weight of the second layer caused the *Honey Baby Second* to sink lower she began creaking. The sea sullenly lapped at her gunnels as we observed the *Sweet Sal* chugging by for another load.

"We ain't as fast but we'll be moving twice as much shit out," smugly stated Titmus.

Atkins was elated. "You saved my boat."

"Lookee!" shouted a native and pointed. Ensign Piddle was frantically waving as he jogged toward us.

"He's impressed," smirked Atkins as he downed the last of the de-icer fluid. "Cast off!"

The engine was humming as Edgar loosened our forward and after lines and hopped aboard. As we pulled away an inch of salt brine seeped over the *Honey Baby's* gunnels. By the time Piddle reached the end of the pier we were yards away. His shouted words were smothered by our engine's clatter.

"He for or against us?" whispered Edgar.

"Damned if I know," muttered Atkins.

"The little jerk is probably shouting encouragement," I ventured.

Titmus shrugged and stated that he didn't give a shit about whatever the asshole was yelling. Suddenly a grinding clamor accompanied by tearing metal sounds focused our attention. Our boat's bottom had broken loose.

With a pitiful shudder the *Honey Baby* suddenly submerged like a submarine. Amid floating garbage our native crew leisurely swam to the shore. Titmus and I treaded water and pushed away floating debris as Atkins and Edgar splashed about. A slew of big birds plummeted down about us.

Titmus and I paddled through the floating debris and climbed up the pier ladder. Atkins and Edgar came up behind us. Ensign Piddle stood agape staring in disbelief. Titmus and I smartly saluted but our commander failed to return our salutation. Instead, he ordered us to get the fuck off the pier.

Before exiting we turned and observed empty drums floating on the surface. Most of our cargo was still intact in *Honey baby Two's* deckless hull resting at the bottom of the sea.

Titmus and I hastily vacated the pier and hitched a ride back to VMF 111's compound. "Did the bottom fall out or did the weight just pull her down?" I wondered aloud.

"Who gives a shit!" said Titmus.

We dutifully reported to Sergeant Goodwinch. "I got negative reports on you two," he mumbled but didn't pursue the matter.

Needless to say, we never again heard from *Boat Refuse Group One*.

CHAPTER TWENTY

Being designated VMF 111's Ground Defense Unit didn't sound bad but our primary task was servile sanitary responsibilities. Lieutenants and above referred to us as the Sanitary Detail. Enlisted wise-asses designated mechanic and ordinance personnel referred us as "the shit-detail".

We couldn't take offense at the caption because that's what the hell we were, shitbirds. The title didn't bother Titmus or some of the others, but the shit-detail tag depressed me.

More than a few times when ignoble characters addressed me with the shithouse designation, I threw the first punch. Although I was a sizeable opponent and infuriated, I didn't always win, but lost less. Even those holding their own figured one tussle with me was enough.

For a noncom, Sergeant Goodwinch wasn't a bad sort. He wanted to get Ground Defense people to work as a team. For instance, he'd delegate Cassidy and Cruz to tote burlap bags through a trash strewed area while the rest of us speared refuse and stuck it in their large bags. As a team we gathered piles of fallen fronds, brown coconuts and scooped up other unsightly stuff.

While we performed we moaned and groaned. I suppose the perennial gripping made us feel better. Time and time again each of us attempted to see Major Burke to request a transfer to a line company. He saw each of us once, sometimes twice, and assured us that if the opportunity arose, he'd grant our wish. Months went by and nothing happened. Finally he said, "I've heard enough. The Marine Corps can't make you people do something you don't want to do. But the Corps can make you damn sorry you didn't do it." After his exasperated tirade he never tolerated another transfer interview.

Ground Defense's fifty and water-cooled thirty shielded by sandbags were entrenched on the windward side of the island. They faced the sea and were supposed to deter the Japs from pulling a Colonel Carlson type raid on Makin. We practiced firing rounds into the sea and spent two or more hours a week stripping and cleaning both weapons.

We were warned not to, but Cassidy and O'Bannion paid no heed and aimed at both porpoises rolling by and diving seabirds. As far as we could tell neither ever hit one. Anyway, firing the ancient guns was a welcome distraction from our perennial shit duty.

Lieutenant Rameron informed us that the inhabitants of Nukufetau were part Polynesian and part Melanesian. The natives weren't as statuesque or brazen as the Polynesians in Samoa.

Each morning six loin-clad natives smartly raised the Union Jack and in a snappy military manner lowered it at sunset. The Limeys paid them a stipend for that respectful ceremony.

Natives living on other islands rowed to Nukufetau each day to see what they could beg, borrow, buy or steal. Other natives, of course, were employed to handle garbage at the end of the pier.

Unemployed dark skinned groups scavenged and scrounged for food, discarded clothes and whatever else wasn't guarded or tied down. Native foraging of American food and clothes seemed to be an indigenous sort of South Pacific recreation.

One hot afternoon, O'Bannion and I dutifully finished picking up debris from the officers' compound and slipped away before Sergeant Goodwinch or Corporal Lancaster could nail us. In a remote area we found a shaded spot and flaked out under a coconut tree.

We were bullshitting about nothing when a blonde woman emerged from the brush. We were flabbergasted as the pale white lady strode across our view trailed by two loin-clothed gooks. The woman was of average height, a bit chunky and splotches marred her face. Two different colored beat-up shoes covered her feet.

"Holy shit!" cried O'Bannion.

"Damned!" We leaped to our feet.

The three heard but paid no heed and kept walking. O'Bannion cried, "Hey! Hey!" and loped after them. I was right behind him. The female and her entourage halted and turned.

She might have been anywhere from thirty-five to forty-five. She was far from attractive and probably never had been. Her eyes seemed glazed and she sure as hell didn't seem happy to see us.

O'Bannion cheerfully shouted, "*Talofa!*"

She grimaced. "You don't know English?"

"You speak English!"

"Don't all Americans?"

"You an American?" I felt stupid.

"Can't you tell!" she snapped.

"Hey, it's been a long time since we've seen an American girl," said O'Bannion.

"Ain't I a beauty though?"

"You look pretty good to me," said O'Bannion. She didn't, but I figured he was trying to make her feel good.

"Thanks! Now what the hell do you want?"

"Glad to see you," I said.

"So nice to meet both of you in the middle of nowhere," she somberly said. "See yuh around." She stepped away and the two natives followed.

"Jesus, give us a minute or two," pleaded O'Bannion. "A little talk won't hurt."

She paused. "You two knights wanna know where I came from, how I got here and how you can help me. Well, gentlemen, I come from San Francisco, and I need no help. I'm also goddamn tired of telling the same bullshit story to every pale asshole that comes along. Anything else?"

"Give us a break," said O'Bannion. "We ain't seen an American dame, uh, lady, in a helluva long time, let alone talk to one. A few minutes of your time won't hurt."

"Yeah, I bet."

"Please, lady."

"I'm an American beauty, ain't I?"

"You're alright. Sure you got some jungle rot, we all do. Clean it up and you'd be better than alright," said O'Bannion.

"I was never gorgeous but I sure as hell wasn't this bad."

"Can we do something for you?" said O'Bannion.

"Got soap?"

"In our tent."

"How much?"

"Maybe three bars between us. We can get more."

"I mean how much you gonna charge me?"

"Nothing, the soap will be our gift. Ain't that right, Sherman?"

"Of course!"

"What else you got?"

"Like what?"

"You got a knife?"

"Will a bayonet do?"

"You gonna give me one?"

"Maybe."

"How about a blanket?"

"Maybe, I got two."

"Lots of maybes."

"I can't promise," said O'Bannion. "We're not living at home."

She nodded and squatted like a native. We sat but the two natives remained standing. I thought O'Bannion was nuts. Sure, it would be interesting to hear her story, but absconding two blankets and a bayonet could get us in deep shit. With those blotches on her face I wasn't about to chance a liaison or anything else, not even a chance to hear her story.

She spouted native lingo at the two gooks. They hiked ten feet away and squatted, neither looked happy. "Before the war I lived in San Francisco. I was workin' the waterfront like always."

"Hustling?" said O'Bannion as I gulped.

"What else! I didn't have these blotches but business still wasn't good. Same customers were around but an influx of girls, younger ones, was stiff competition. The fuzz were becoming bothersome. It was that time of the year, election time, they were becoming a nuisance.

"Two different undercover flatfoots propositioned me. But I smelled copper and took no chances. Well, I'm in this bar off Market having a drink that I can't pay for when this dark lookin' guy comes in. He got wooly hair and looked like a black guy but he ain't. I got nothing against it if he was.

"Lips ain't thick and he's dressed fancy, you know, jacket, tie, clean shirt. Fact is, he looks kind of handsome in a different way. Know what I mean? He checks me out. In those days I didn't have this shit over my face. The guy doesn't talk but pulls out a wad of twenties and throws it on the bar.

"Says his name is Safua which don't make sense but is no problem to me. I've known studs with stranger monikers. He's loaded with cash and not shy about throwing it around. We hit it off like old pals. We hang together dancing, drinking and carousing for three, four days. Hell, I don't remember how many.

"Soon he throws crap at me about bein' a king on an island. In my profession I hear lots of shit so I pay no attention until the second or third day. That's when he starts spouting stuff about lookin' for a queen. Of course, I think it's a line of bullshit, different but corny. Meantime he's throwing money around like there's no tomorrow. I'm havin' a ball and hopin' it'll last awhile. He ain't a bad lover either.

"One night he tells me he's got to return home to an island. I figure it's the end, but suddenly he asks me to become his wife. I been married twice and sure as hell wasn't enthused. But I figure my life is shitty anyway and Jesus, I'm dreaming. Maybe he's on the level and I could end up being a queen. Stranger things have happened, especially to me. What in hell I got to lose?

"We find a soused up preacher and marry. We fly to Pago Pago and from there we sail to Nukufetau. When I see the grass huts, I know I'm up shit creek. Although his is the biggest, I ain't happy but I figure, 'What the hell!' And let me tell you, he's a big man in the village, especially after bringing back a yellow haired queen.

"He shows me off to his friends and other villages. I'm living it up until a couple of weeks go by. Like always, things change. I gotta wash stuff and learn how to cook strange stuff with no fancy equipment. A woman means nothin' around here, even if she is a blonde queen. If I don't do what I'm told I get the crap knocked out of me."

"That it?" said O'Bannion.

"That's not enough?"

"What's your name?"

"Moana."

Suddenly I felt a twang of sorrow. "You don't like living here even if you're a queen?"

"I ain't no more a queen than you are. This ain't England, you know. A bullshit queen that's what I am!"

"Why don't you leave?"

"How? I'm Safua's wife, legal like, I guess. He's got a reputation to think about and ain't about to let me go. Maybe if I had the moola, I'd try, but mostly they don't have much American money on Nukufetau. I stashed a few bucks, maybe forty but that sure as hell not enough. I'm gonna die in this fuckin' place and nobody will know or care." A tear or two rolled down her cheek.

She suddenly noticed her gook escorts looking uneasy and wiped her streaked face. "That's the way the cookie crumbles."

I felt sorry for the woman and perhaps O'Bannion did too. He rubbed his chin and said, "I'm gonna get you outta here."

"I'm gonna die here." She looked like she might commence weeping.

"I need money, green stuff. Dollars make things happen here like everywhere. We know that, don't we?"

"Your Royal Highness, or whatever, we're gonna make lots of cash."

O'Bannion was thinking unsavory thoughts. I didn't cotton to his creepy idea and he knew it.

"Hundreds of guys around here are craving a dame, especially a blonde." Then he looked at me. "What's with you? Can't you see we're helping the lady as well as the war effort?"

"See the scabs on my face?" she said. "They're on my body too."

"So?" said O'Bannion.

"Diseases, Buster, kinds that doctors never heard of. Besides, my old man is a chief, almost a king and got a reputation to uphold. He'd cut your heart out and that would be nothin' compared to what he'd do to me."

I hoped O'Bannion would back off but he kept on. "I'll get our corpsman to shoot you full of penicillin. That shit cures everything. You might have to do business with him afterwards but it'll be worth it."

I was uncomfortable and sure as hell didn't like the dour looks on the faces of the natives. Sweat rolled down my face and it wasn't just the heat. I knew O'Bannion was a crazy bastard but not that crazy.

"Meet us tomorrow night?" asked O'Bannion.

"Not a chance. There's half a mile of ocean from here to our village. These two do what I say but won't betray their king. And I ain't about to row here by myself, especially at night."

"We can buy these gooks off," said O'Bannion.

"With what?" asked the blonde.

"I'll take care of those details. Once you get here, we'll hide you. We'll make a pile of dough before we get you out of here. What's your name again?"

"Moana. And your's, soldier?"

"Brian O'Bannion and this is Sherman Glossman. And lady, we're not dogfaces, we're Marines."

I wanted no part of O'Bannion's scheming bullshit and hoped he wasn't expecting me to get involved.

"What about that stuff you promised?" she said.

"Follow us," said O'Bannion and we led Moana and her escorts to our tent.

"You crazy son-of-a-bitch," I whispered.

O'Bannion ignored me and collected two bars of soap, Cruz's bayonet and pulled one of Arnie's blankets off his cot. He handed them to Moana and she passed them to the gooks. They grinned but looked like they were wondering what the hell was going on.

Moana turned to go. "Tomorrow night about eight?" said O'Bannion.

"Maybe," she said.

"Same spot, Moana?"

"My American name is Florence."

"We're gonna get rich."

"Yeah," she said and stalked away followed by the two gooks. They faded into the underbrush.

"You're asking for a shit load of trouble," I said.

"Trust me, we're gonna make money," said O'Bannion.

"Not we!"

"You wanna get rich?"

"Nope."

"And you want to be a writer, hah!"

"You're a Marine for god's sake, not a pimp."

"You're scared."

"Maybe, but I'm not crazy."

"In or out?"

I shrugged.

"You, me and Florence are gonna make money, lots of it."

"Sure!" I said.

"Hey, I ain't kidding, we're gonna strike it rich on this good old island."

CHAPTER TWENTY-ONE

Arnie was highly suspect about his blanket disappearing and mumbled foul threats. He didn't waste time dwelling on the theft, but stole somebody else's olive green covering.

Cruz, too, was upset about the disappearance of his well-honed bayonet. Both suspected the same perpetrator, but when quizzed, O'Bannion became deeply affronted. Neither pushed allegations but observed him like famished hawks.

I didn't like being part of O'Bannion's charade but was destined to be his stalwart witness. I hated being untruthful to my tent-mates but still vouched to them that during the day I had seen O'Bannion in the vicinity.

I wasn't exactly looking forward to our pending rendezvous with the lady. The vigorous hacking, digging and piling of debris kept me somewhat distracted.

"You bucking for a stripe?" snapped Titmus.

"Sherman's trying to make the rest of us look bad," said Cassidy.

"Relax, will yuh?" whispered O'Bannion. I tried to temper my labor efforts but I was one nervous buck-assed private.

We knocked off earlier than usual but luckily none of the wheels noticed. After showers we chowed-down and sat musing in the tent. Titmus, Cassidy, Pinsky, and Cruz started a jawbone poker game. I declined to sit in and strolled outside and was cornered by O'Bannion.

"For Christ's sake, Sherman, you look guilty as hell. Stop worrying, we ain't done nothin' wrong yet!"

"I'm not worried."

"Well, you look and act like you are!"

"Well, I'm not!"

"Good." We stood eyeball to eyeball. "At 1930, step out to take a leak or something."

"This isn't raider bullshit so don't talk military time!" I was nervous.

"Alright, alright, take it easy. At seven-thirty go out to piss or something. Nobody'll think anything of it. After a few minutes I'll crack a reason to sashay out. Be waiting thirty yards or so behind our tent. Got it?"

"We can use help. Why don't we let the others in on it?"

"And split the loot? You crazy! Besides, Pinsky is an old lady about things like that. He won't want nothing to do with pimping."

"I ain't crazy about it either."

"And Cruz sure as hell ain't gonna go for it. Neither will Titmus. As for Cassidy and Arnie, the greedy bastards will only fuck it up".

"I don't know, Brian," I whined.

"Quit sniffling, it's you and me. We're the only ones with the balls to pull it off, so relax. We'll end up with a shitpot full of dollars. Besides, we'll be doing something real nice for a fellow American. You heard her, she's in a trap. She's up shit creek and there's nobody but us to help her. You and me can get her out of this hellhole. You can see that, can't you?"

Because I didn't have the will or guts to pull out of his dumb scheme I cursed O'Bannion and myself. I followed him back in and while he flaked out on his cot I sat on mine. The poker game was moving along.

"Call you, sucker and I raise you a quarter," said Pinsky.

"You ain't got shit," said Cassidy but he was squinting. The candle flickered as I searched faces for signs of suspicion, there were none.

The only objects getting undue attention were canteen cups as Titmus poured fermented libations into them.

Titmus was expounding about cruising down Bubbling Well in a rickshaw when O'Bannion motioned. I checked, it was seven-thirty and time to go.

I tried to stall because I wanted to hear the rest of Titmus' tale but O'Bannion's gestures couldn't be ignored. "Aw, what the hell," I excused myself and stepped outside. I pissed against a coconut tree and waited. It seemed longer than minutes before O'Bannion showed looking pretty damn nervous. "Let's go."

It was unlikely that a sentry would happen by, but we weren't about to take chances so we swiveled into a clump of banana bushes and waited. Then we made our way to the wooded area where we had met Florence and her wooly-headed entourage and nervously waited.

Half a moon cast pale reflections on the coral giving a fair view of the surrounding area.

We waited and waited. "She's not coming," I whispered, tacitly relieved.

"It's only a little past eight."

A drizzle chilled. "Shit," said O'Bannion.

"She's not coming! Let's go."

"Ten more minutes."

"I'm leaving," I whined.

"Not yet!"

"She's either changed her mind or her old man's on to her. I'm leaving."

"You're yellow!"

"What!" My heart wasn't in it, but I was about to throw a punch at O'Bannion when I was diverted by rustling brush. I looked up as Florence stumbled out of the foliage.

"Hah! You made it," said O'Bannion.

"I'm in a shitpot full of trouble," she wheezed.

"Florence, dear, you got two Marine partners and protectors, your troubles are over."

"My problems have just begun, Mr. Marine! See, I had to bribe Posena and Tu'a to row me over. It cost me my wedding ring, Safua's watch and that bayonet you gave me."

"They can be replaced," said O'Bannion.

"I ain't done. Just as we were casting off, Safua came tearing out of the woods raving like a wildman. I hit him in the face with an oar and he backed off. Posena and Tu'a tried to slip away but I told them if they didn't paddle I'd claw their eyes out and blame them for everything. As we pulled away we could hear my loving hubby howling like a banshee."

I felt like I was in a bad movie. I began to quiver as if I was in the North Pole instead of the tropics. Why in hell did I get involved in this bullshit?

"Your plans better work or I'm done for," she said. "Safua got to save face."

"Screw him! And don't worry; I got plans, plenty of plans, good ones."

"Bullshit," I murmured, to myself of course.

"We hide you out for awhile, see. I'll get some sulfuric shit or penicillin from this corpsman pal of mine. That stuff will fix you up. My pal's medical and knows how to cure all kinds of jungle rot."

I held my head but stayed silent. Anyway, neither of them was paying attention to me. O'Bannion was thinking of Bennie, one of our corpsman. The pill pusher was big and sloppy but a pretty affable guy. Much of the time he was smashed on sickbay alcohol but knew more about medical stuff than our sawbones."

"Why are you doing this for me?" Florence suddenly asked.

"Business, Honey. Oh, and you're an American, that's why. As we promised, we'll get you out of this shit hole and back to the states, and we're all gonna make a pile of dough doing what has to be done," boasted O'Bannion.

Florence looked dubious.

I felt sorry for the poor dame and was about to say something nice when I was diverted by a knife clunked into the tree trunk above O'Bannion's head.

We both froze as a bellowing brown-skinned wild man came galloping toward us. "What the hell!" grunted O'Bannion as two other gooks charged behind him. They didn't cry out but looked nasty and obviously meant business.

As Safua came abreast, O'Bannion rallied enough to bury a roundhouse punch into his flabbed stomach. He doubled up spitting and cursing in Melanese but I got the drift.

I threw an overhand right at the second guy and he stumbled back. We'd have been in trouble if not for Florence. Like a tigress she leaped into action and commenced biting and scratching. Screaming and clawing she inflicted bloody marks on the three attackers. As they backed off from her onslaught, O'Bannion and I ran for our lives.

As soon as our tent hove in sight, Taps commenced barking like a real watch dog. O'Bannion bellowed, "Attack! Attack!" And I hollered, "Help! Help!" Titmus, followed by Arnie, Cruz and Pinsky, charged out with rifles at the ready. Cassidy was passed out on his cot.

"They're after us!" we wheezed as we tumbled into the tent and got our rifles.

"What the fuck's goin' on?" said Titmus.

"A hundred gooks are coming!" gasped O'Bannion.

"Gooks? Japs? What!" queried Titmus.

"They tried to kill us!" I panted.

O'Bannion and I plus our tent mates, armed to the teeth, stared from whence we had come. Nothing moved and a foreboding silence radiated from the clumps of foliage we had emerged from. Our tent mates peered at each other and then us. "What kind of shit you idiots been drinking?" said Titmus.

Taps peered at the wooded area and barked twice. That got our attention. We stared but nobody emerged. "Gooks were after us, lots of them, honest," said O'Bannion.

"He's telling the truth, they sure as hell were," I swore. I almost hoped Florence's pursuers would make an appearance.

"Sounds like bullshit," said Pinsky.

"Hah! Where'd they go?" said Arnie.

"I got chased by a bunch of *cholos* once," said Cruz.

"Why were them gooks after you?" said Titmus.

"It's complicated," said O'Bannion.

"You got any more of whatever you been drinking?" asked Arnie

"We'll tell you all about it later," I was embarrassed.

Taps was pooped and stretched out emitting an unsynchronized snore. For a long while before filing back into our tent we warily eyed the woods.

Titmus spilled what he'd been sipping into our canteen cups. When darkness arrived we crawled into our sacks. While others snored away, O'Bannion and I kept alerted to exterior noises. Thunder rumbled and lightening flashed as bucketfuls of rain pelted our tent. We knew natives didn't relish prowling about in the rain.

O'Bannion's irritating snores abruptly vied with the thunder. I cradled my Garand and as I fought to stay awake, cursed him and Nukufetau. But it was to no avail, I finally conked out.

In the morning Corporal Lancaster roused us with his usual, "Up and at 'em, boys." He smugly informed us that immediately after breakfast, Ground Defense would commence construction on an officers' shower.

We carried lumber to a cleared area and erected solid frames to support two oil barrels. After the slats were secured, we toted buckets of saltwater and passed man to man until we filled each shower drum.

As we labored, Arnie noted that O'Bannion's and my eyes kept darting toward the thick wooded clusters. We also kept drifting toward our group's center. "Big bad gooks gonna get you?" he taunted.

"Chickenshits," added Cassidy.

"Don't stand too close to me," chided Cruz.

"If you two pissed off a couple of natives, you two are up shit creek without a paddle," said Titmus.

"Chickenshits," repeated Cassidy.

"Go fuck yourself!" I said.

"I'm gonna knock you on your skinny ass!" snapped O'Bannion and strode toward Cassidy.

"Fuck you!" spat Cassidy and defiantly raised his arms.

"Knock off the bullshit," ordered Titmus.

Cassidy, O'Bannion and I were pissed but relented after Titmus warned, "Boys! Don't get me riled."

We turned away and went back to hauling water.

New scuttlebutt began circulating. Word spread that our squadron's F4F Wildcats were obsolete. The U.S. Navy had been using the new F4U Corsairs on carriers, but due to high cockpits, lengthy fuselages and too much speed they were proving difficult to land on bobbing decks. The navy was transferring their carrier Corsairs to the Corps.

VMF 111 was to be allotted a sizable quota. That meant our pilots would have to be trained to fly the hot new aircraft. It wasn't much more than rumor. But the fidgety sensations evolve when significant change is forthcoming. Anticipation of change spread among the squadron's officers and enlisted men. After all this time, maybe our squadron was actually going to war.

Word came from the top. It wasn't a rumor anymore, VMF 111 was moving out, but not north to confront the enemy. Instead, we had been ordered back to American Samoa for retraining, refitting, reorganization and to replace our squadron's archaic Wildcats with the brand new gull-winged F4Us.

Most enlisted personnel were less than enthused about moving back to Samoa. Not that we longed to stay on Nukufetau, we loathed the place. But we did recall our short stay in rain-soaked Pago Pago. Samoa's eerily foliaged terrain and frequent downpours were a less than covetous memory.

We were well aware that *Mumu* was a dire threat on that disease infested island. Besides that, we would again be quartered farther from the action. According to island hopping reports about recent battle outcomes, the war wouldn't last forever.

"We're getting farther and farther from the action," whined Arnie.

"It's going to be over soon," sighed O'Bannion.

"Bullshit!" snapped Titmus.

"So what! Nukufetau isn't that much closer to the action," moaned Cassidy.

"Our time on this mosquito infested rock didn't help or hinder," I lamented.

"A waste of time," sighed Cruz.

"They don't give out medals on Samoa," said Cassidy.

"*Dios Mio*, they don't give medals anywhere for digging shithouses," muttered Cruz.

"Maybe we'll do something else. The navy's been on Samoa for years, even before the war. There should already be plenty of places already in place to shit," counseled Titmus.

"Hey, it can't be worse than Nukufetau," said Pinsky.

"Quit your candy-assed bitching? Any of you idiots ever think that if they keep us far from the action, we won't get our asses shot off?" Titmus was pissed about something and it had nothing to do with going back to American Samoa.

Nothing more was broached on that subject but late that afternoon O'Bannion cornered me. "We gotta find Florence."

"What the hell for?"

"I don't easily give up."

"Give up?"

"American dollars are slipping through our hands."

"Count me out."

"Scared?"

"Remember those fuckin' gooks?" I said, "they tried to kill us."

"Hah! Scared shitless, I knew it!"

"Yeah, you're right. I don't want to get killed and eaten."

"Chicken shit!"

"You're not! Hah!"

"Hey, I'm not happy, but a man's gotta take risks to help a fellow American, especially a female in distress."

"Now I got it! You're in love with that American queen of the gooks!"

"You crazy? The only one I'm in love with is me."

I believed that and emphatically restated, "Count me out."

O'Bannion wouldn't let up. Six times during the day he sounded off about rescuing Florence. "We don't know where she's at, and if we did, I wouldn't be interested," I said.

"She's a fellow American in a jackpot. What kind of a man are you?" accused O'Bannion.

"She caused her own problems! Nobody forced her to come here. Anyway, she's a Nukufetauan now, a queen, mind you."

"You heard the poor thing, she wants to go home."

"On this rock she's royalty. In Frisco she'll be a whore again and not a high achieving one. With those sores she'll wish she was back here where she's a big shot."

"You call yourself an American! I said it before, you're chickenshit!"

"Maybe if I knock you on your ass we'll see who's chickenshit!"

"Sherman, quit thinking about yourself, we got to do something."

"Hey! O'Bannion, I don't want to be carved and eaten by her kinky-haired friends. If that makes me chickenshit, so be it."

"You idiot, these gooks don't eat people."

"I know that, Sir Galahad, but if you're mutilated and dead, what difference does it make if they serve you up for dinner?"

O'Bannion spat and stomped off.

The next morning our Grummans revved up and flew off toward Samoa. A C46 crowded with mechanics, linemen and technicians followed.

Late that afternoon an LST pulled onto Nukufetau's beach. VMF's enlisted personnel manhandled our assorted equipment up her inclined ramp and into the bowels of the vessel. We stowed our two machine guns, gear, canned chow and a pile of miscellaneous equipment.

Numerous trips were made lugging stores, supplies, gear, machine guns and whatever else our squadron possessed aboard.

Titmus managed to borrow an unauthorized jeep from the SBD Squadron. He drove it up the ramp and parked it inside the LST's cavernous hull. Orders came down from Major Burke that VMF 111 should leave Nukufetau in better shape than we found it. Naturally, it was Ground Defense's responsibility to sort and discard leftover trash.

By the time the high tide rolled in we were pooped and eager to depart. As we pulled out from the beach the LST's ramp lifted. While I leaned on the starboard rail another unforeseen squall burst. Amid the shower I watched the fading shoreline. O'Bannion abruptly jabbed an elbow into my ribs. "Look!"

I followed his finger pointing at a cluster of assembling natives. They gestured toward our departing vessel. "See?" he whispered.

"What?" I squinted at the group and discerned what he was excited about. Florence was standing in the midst of the half naked assembly. I wasn't absolutely sure it was her but the light complected female had the same height and figure. Anyway, I didn't give a rat's ass if it was or wasn't Florence and said so. O'Bannion glared but kept his lips sealed.

After months on that inhospitable rock I wasn't the only one relieved to see Nukufetau drop below the horizon.

CHAPTER TWENTY-TWO

Soaring seabirds escorted our waddling vessel. They swooped down and quickly devoured garbage heaved overboard.

We were a brooding bunch of disenchanted flunkies as our yo-yo-ing carrier plunged onward. Energy was subdued and moral so low that we desisted from plotting mischief. O'Bannion kept reminding us of what most of us were thinking, "We're missing the goddamn war."

It seemed longer, much longer than expected before our conveyance finally pulled into Pago Pago's forest fringed harbor. Due to the craft's flat bottom and shallow draft we were able to pull alongside the quay. This time, neither natives, military personnel or anyone else, were on the dock to receive us.

As we shuffled down the gangway a cold drizzle spilled. One cold deluge was followed by another. Though soaked and chilled we were too beat to grumble.

Lieutenants Tamerson and Rameron, rumbled about getting drenched, but despite their yellow bars, there wasn't a damn thing they could do about it. The weather seemed to have even less respect for officers.

Canopied trucks arrived and we were hustled aboard. We pressed against each other for warmth while our transportation careened down a wet road bordered by lush greenery. Our new bivouac was situated close to the airfield.

Six of us were assigned to each wood-decked hut. Meshed screens covered most of our wall space. Three two-tiered iron bunks lent our new housing a more homelike touch than Nukufetau's canvas tents and cots.

We had arrived during the rainy season and were repeatedly doused by relentless downpours. Ever so often liquid onslaughts paused for a short time before resuming. In-between drenches the sun dried and relentlessly cooked us and the ground.

Billowing clouds swirling around Rainmaker's crest were faulted for Samoa's frequent downpours. Vapor emanated from every nook and cranny. Heat and droplets caused the lush foliage to glisten. In multiple shades of green the island's thick vegetation sprouted and spread.

The heat and dampness induced six-legged creatures to buzz, stab and suck blood from arms, legs, faces and more delicate parts. In comparison, British Samoa's mild climate and limited bug population was heavenly in contrast to our current bug-infested humid habitat.

Before our second American Samoa arrival, a two-man Nip submarine had surfaced off of Tutuila and lobbed two shells into the verdant island. One of the random fired missiles demolished the island's lone grocery store. Ironically, it was owned by the island's one and only Japanese family, not an enemy, just a migrant family trying to get along. The other detonated harmlessly in a mass of thick foliage.

Our squadron settled in and our pilots quickly adjusted to piloting the hot new gull-winged planes bequeathed by the navy. Speedier and more maneuverable than the archaic Wildcats, the transition to Corsair proved to be more complex than anticipated. Both pilots and mechanics made delicate adjustments, especially the pilots.

Ground Defense resumed its duties. American Samoa had been a U.S. naval base long before World War Two. Despite numerous established shithouses, more were required. Perhaps erecting new ones was just an excuse to keep us busy.

Taps, our undeliberate mascot, established a new hangout close to our hut and bedded down. If there had been any simple way of returning him ninety miles away to his island of birth we would have arranged it.

The chow in Samoa was better than the nasty stuff served on Funafuti and Nukufetau. Supper became an anticipated event because after dining each enlistee was issued two cans of warm beer. Some, not many, saved their sparse brew ration to later participate in a monumental drunken orgy. Most couldn't wait and swiftly consumed their two lovely cans of three-two libation.

If a guy had enough singles he could make his way to the ramshackle slopchute. A bottle of stateside brew cost fifteen cents. A few dollars worth would get imbibers feeling, well, a bit feisty.

One wet day after mail call we were reclining on our bunks perusing our sparse mail over and over when Titmus, letter in hand, sat up. He swung his knees over the edge of his bunk and said, "Listen to this!"

Of course, we were all ears.

Dear Earl,

Hope this letter finds you safe and healthy too. The Marines I met at the USO told me about the trials and tribulations endured at Guadalcanal and other terrible places. Fighting Japs is bad enough but diseases like Malaria and Mumu infecting our heroes are really horrible. Oh, I nightly pray to God that you don't get infected by one of those disgusting mosquitoes. I'd rather have you wounded or something. Not badly, of course, just a scratch or knick or ---- you know what I mean. I just want you back without disease or wound, that's all.

I ask every Marine wearing campaign ribbons if they know you. Some say they do, others say they've heard about you. One or two claimed to know you well. Of course, I know most, maybe all, are just blowing smoke.

Anyway, you know your fellow Marines better than I do, and I'm sure you're aware that it's not easy to separate fact from fiction at the USO. In spite of that, I've decided that all servicemen are basically nice guys regardless of which service they're in. I know they talk bullshit, excuse the language, but if you're a loyal American, It's something you got to accept.

Don't get me wrong I don't resent a little bullshit, excuse the language, a little of it never hurt anyone. And I like my work at the USO because I feel like doing my bit to help, even if it's just a little. .

Remember Hilton, he's that awfully young soldier boy I told you about. He's in the Signal Corps or something. Sometimes, in spite of his tender years, he sounds intelligent, but I wish he'd set his goo-goo eyes on someone more his own age. I've already told him I was too mature for him and that I got a fiancée, but he just won't go away.

Anyway, I been thinking more and more about you and me. We're not getting younger. Hah, we're not too old either, but what have we accomplished? What have we got to look forward to? I been thinking crazy thoughts like that quite a bit lately. When you get back we should have a serious talk about the future, our future. What are your thoughts on the matter? Write soon.

Love you and miss you,
Millie

Titmus smiled and carefully put the letter back in the envelope. "What a girl."

"She talkin' about getting hitched?" queried Arnie.

"She sure is," I ventured.

"Who's Hilton?" said Cassidy.

"Don't know," said Titmus looking a tad sour, "but when I get back, that doggie won't even know who he is either."

"Let's go to the slopchute," said Cruz.

Attired in presentable khaki and pith helmets we headed out. Taps loped behind us until a truck pulled to a stop to give us a lift. The screech of bad brakes scared him and he backed off. The mutt watched and wheezed. As we roared away a dust cloud obscured his forlorn face and drooping tongue.

The Seabee dropped us fifty yards from the slopchute. We walked until hailed by two teenage swabbies. "Hey," said the tallest, "Where can we buy a coconut?"

We thought he was trying to be funny and must have looked hostile because the short red-faced swabbie quickly added, "We're off a DE. Honest, we've only been ashore twenty minutes and don't know where to get anything."

"Where'd you come from?" queried Cassidy.

"Norfalk! We been through the Panama Canal and couldn't even get ashore at Balboa," said his shipmate.

"Too bad, it's a good port." commiserated Cassidy. He'd never been there. he was about to sell the youngster a fallen coconut when Cruz said, "Knock it off, Cassidy! Look, Kid, there's coconuts all over the place, just pick 'em up."

"But be careful coconuts'll give you the shits," warned Cassidy, trying to sound helpful as well as salty. Titmus couldn't be bothered with teenage swabbies and kept walking. We trotted to catch up.

The slopchute was jammed with white-clad sailors, grubby merchant seamen, and Free-French Marines off the cruiser flying the French tri-color anchored in the harbor.

A lone sailor sat at a corner table holding an almost full beer glass. He periodically sipped and stared at the wall seeing nothing. Titmus gently lifted him from his chair and propped him into a sitting position against the wall. The kid's thousand yard stare didn't waver.

We three sat while Cruz maneuvered his way to the bar and brought back four bottles of chilled ABCs. The unfavorable quinine taste was barely palatable but after the second we quit grimacing. None of us felt like talking. I suspect that Titmus was musing about Millie. We took turns going to bar and before long I wasn't the only one whose head was buzzing.

Titmus downed one bottle after the other before belching that he was ready for a third. Cassidy and Cruz were also feeling no pain. I hazily became aware that we were plastered.

"When we get back to the States Millie and me are gonna get hitched." Titmus announced and his glare warned us to be careful. Of course, we didn't comment. He added, "She's gonna have to leave the USO."

I was the first to say, "That's good, Titmus." Others added lisped congratulations.

"Everyone should get married sometime and have *ninos,* lots of them." counseled Cruz. A French Marine careened against our table almost losing his jaunty blue hat as bottles toppled. He adjusted his blue fore and aft cap and righted himself. He grinned and mumbled in French. Maybe it was an apology, maybe not. Cassidy struggled to his feet, "Froggie son-of-a-bitch!"

The French guy must not have savvied English because he just kept grinning. Cassidy swung and missed. The Frenchman suddenly executed a lofty leap flattening Cassidy with a kick. He proceeded pacing the length of Cassidy's prone body. The fracas might have ended if the Frenchman had walked away, but he delivered a short kick to Cassidy's ribs.

Titmus leaped up throwing punches. One caught the French Marine's shoulder and he tumbled against a table full of drunken merchant seamen. He quickly rose, punishing Titmus' balls and belly with swift kicks. As Titmus doubled over the Frenchman appraised his victim a second too long.

I clobbered the blue-hatted froggie from behind. Titmus recovered and the light-footed-fighter again leaped forward using his feet. Titmus sidestepped and delivered an overhand uppercut to the guy's gut. The froggie doubled up and fell backwards onto the disgruntled merchant seamen's table.

As the foot fighting Frenchman struggled to his feet, Titmus splintered a chair over his head. It was the *coup de gras*; the Frenchie was finished. His buddies cursed in their lyrical language and one burly Froggie leaped on Titmus' back. Cruz jerked him off.

By that time American merchant seamen joined the battle. Other incited slopchute patrons got involved in the banging, bashing bedlam.

In the midst of the dispute after a wild punch set me on my ass, I spied Cassidy, head down and oblivious to fists flying around him. Before I could act sirens screamed and Titmus shouted, "Out!"

We bolted outside and slipped into clumps of thick brush.

CHAPTER TWENTY-THREE

When the hullabaloo from the beer chute died down, we cautiously emerged. There weren't any streetlights in Samoa to illuminate roads, nor was there late traffic to hitch a ride. Perspiring and grumbling we walked.

"A truck could come by," advised Titmus. Lights suddenly loomed as one sped toward us. The driver ignored our thrust out thumbs and zipped right by. "That fucker saw us," I spat.

"One of those snot-nosed bastards from the 22nd," growled Titmus.

"The 22nd's on British Samoa, not here."

"Anyway, that was a Marine in the cab."

"Semper Fi!" said Cruz.

"Hey!" I said and pointed to a dim light fifty yards ahead.

"Let's look," said Titmus. We strode into a small silent village and made way between thatched *fales* scattered in a park-like field of grass. Thirty yards away we heard the sea lapping at the shore.

Despite jillions of glittering stars, we felt hemmed in by the black night. We noted a large *fale* situated in a central location. We were wavering about whether to investigate or hit the road when a white-haired guy wrapped in a *lava lava* emerged. He could have been forty plus. In those days a guy pushing those years was considered old.

His muscles glistened as he approached and sounded out an amiable "*Talofa.*"

"*Talofa,* yourself," said Titmus.

The guy grinned and beckoned. We followed him into a spacious *fale.* Three natives sitting on reed mats looked up and smiled. A *toa'ina,* old man, a *faletua,* who sits in the back of the house, better known as the chief's wife, and his pretty young daughter, *afafine* in Samoan, stood and smiled as she said, "*Talofa,* I'm Luina."

Ttapa cloths hung in three corners of the *fale* cutting off views of their sleeping quarters. As Cruz and I apprised his daughter, the older man glowered but the chief's wife smiled as she said, "*Talofa.*"

Every Marine in Samoa knew *talofa* and the three of us returned the salutation. Our accents could have been off kilter because both the chief and Luina giggled. The chief said something in Samoan we couldn't catch. The girl sprang to her feet and still chortling, strode to the rear of the *fale.*

She wore a shapeless *mumu* that didn't wholly conceal the shape of her lithesome body. We watched while she fiddled with dishes and a huge pot. "See!" said the chief diverting our attention from his daughter as he pointed to a huge world map stuck on the wall. The United States was small but discernible. "Where you live?"

Titmus pointed to Wyoming.

"Ah, cowboy place!"

"Plenty of horses," said Titmus.

Cruz pointed to California and then to himself.

"Me too!" I said as my finger went from the map to my chest.

The chief grinned, "California hot like Samoa."

"We got oranges, you got coconuts. Anyway, it may be warmer here and it's prettier," I said.

"I believe," he said and seemed pleased.

Suddenly he sat cross-legged between the *faletua* and *toa'ina* and motioned for us to do the same. Cruz and I sank and crossed our legs Samoan style. Titmus tried but his legs cramped so he sat with one foot sticking out. The natives chuckled.

Luina brought a tray loaded with the familiar stale crackers and jelly. She handed each of us different colored cups filled with warm *kava*. The crackers crumbled and were too salty while lumps of cocoa floated in the *kava*. We had learned to be sensitive and aware that it was polite to act like the taste was flavorful. Incorrect etiquette, as far as eating and drinking in a Samoan's home, could become a touchy affair.

Luina's bare feet pattered as she sashayed back across the room. She had changed into a flowered cotton dress. Her black hair glistened with coconut oil and her firm little breasts lifted the flower-printed dress above her knees. Tall and slender, she sure was a looker.

She looked less than eighteen. I was almost relieved when she sat between Cruz and Titmus.

Before she settled another girl sauntered in. This one was even younger and prettier than Luina and in a similar lilting voice pleasingly announced, "*Talofa, Malines,* I am Tulipa." She gracefully plopped down between Titmus and me. As her bare knee touched mine I tingled. "What your name?" she asked.

"Sherman," I swallowed.

"Sherman, like the General Sherman," she struggled. "Handsome name." Her tingling voice caused me to vibrate a bit.

Her long black hair was oiled like Luina's and her dress covered with printed flowers hung loose and baggy. Her small breasts pushed out against two printed blooms.

Thinner and lighter skinned than Luina, I judged her to be fifteen or sixteen. She must have sensed my uneasiness because she giggled and her pretty face reflected amusement. I inwardly squirmed as her black eyes bore into mine.

My nervousness was noted because Titmus whispered, "Easy, boy, stop acting like a recruit on his first cruise."

Scents of coconut oil emanated from both girls. Between giggling and carrying on, they conversed to each other in Samoan. Titmus produced a pack of cigarettes and held them out. The *matai* took them and extracted four before passing what remained to the others. The *toa'ina* and *faletua* each took three. The girls each took one. Luina passed the almost empty pack back to Titmus. Everyone but me puffed, I was an inveterate cigar smoker and lit up a stale stogie.

Neighbors continued to sashay in. Young guys, girls, kids and old people. The *fale* became crowded. A couple of older guys brought ukuleles; others brought eats or jars of gook gin. As before, no two bottles looked or tasted the same, but all in all the stuff smelled like the gin on British Samoa, maybe a little stronger. I began to feel as if we three were on some kind of weird display.

Titmus downed the strong concoction like he savored it, maybe he did. Cruz gulped a mouthful and I sipped, but neither he nor I were intrigued by the intense flavor.

One teenager strumming his ukulele hopped into the center of the *fale* and crooned lively lyrics while Tulipa, Luina and other girls leaped up wiggling and swirling.

They were quickly joined by dancers of all ages who shouted, sang or both. Titmus impulsively leaped in and commenced wiggling and waving. His gyrations were far from graceful, but whatever the hell he was doing the natives appreciated his whirling. More participants arrived joyfully participating in the festivity.

Gook gin was freely passed around. When the bottle got to me again I dutifully gulped. Kerosene spiked with sickbay alcohol would have been more palatable.

"Could someone have pissed in this?" gasped Cruz.

"I think it tastes worse than that," I grunted.

"If we don't drink they'll be insulted." said Titmus and gulped down a mouthful. "Tough it out!"

I had to take a leak and had no idea where the head was located. "You're not at a fancy club in California, for Christ's sake, just go outside!" said Titmus.

I wasn't comfortable about urinating on our hosts' spacious lawn and was relieved after the *matai* noticed me squirming and gestured at Tulipa who took my hand and led me outside. The heat had tempered but it was still warm and sweet smelling. She pulled me along and we trotted to the edge of the village to a clump of brush. "Do it!" she warbled.

I was uneasy but by necessity moved to the bush. She followed and fixed her eyes on my watering implement. I had misgivings but there was no stopping. After I buttoned up, I wanted to say something clever, but I was stuck. I finally uttered, "Be nice here if it wasn't for the damn mosquitoes."

"Mosquitoes live here, maybe long time before Samoans."

"I figured that."

"Next time you come bring me present, okay?"

"Huh?"

"Tomorrow you come?"

"Probably."

"Do come."

"If I don't have guard duty or some other crappy thing to do, I'll be here."

"I wait."

As she led me back to the *fale* my heart drummed.

"You okay?" said Cruz.

"Why wouldn't I be?"

"Nice looking senorita."

"She's okay, I guess." I didn't tell him that I thought she was gorgeous.

"Anything happen?"

"Yeah, I took a piss."

Titmus stood, "We gotta get back."

With wide smiles and *tofas* we parted. We silently made our way to the road and walked back to camp.

When we entered our quarters we noted Cassidy's empty bunk. "Poor bastard probably still passed out at the slopchute," said Titmus. "I just hope he's not in that Pago Pago brig."

The next morning, as usual, most of Ground Defense personnel, were designated to police up rubbish in and about plane revetments.

It didn't seem likely that so much littering crap could be on the island. But paper, beer bottles, tin cans blotched revetments and the surrounding area around the airfield. "Must be our spoil-assed pilots throwing this assorted shit around," muttered Titmus.

"Anything happen last night?" again quizzed Cruz.

"Like what?"

"For Christ's sake you know what!"

I almost lied but said, "Nah."

"You goin' back?"

"Maybe."

"I am. I kinda like that village."

"What's not to like?"

"Luina likes me," said Cruz and flushed.

"Not a bad looking dame," I said, having even more potent thoughts about Tulipa.

"I'd like to see her again, maybe tonight," said Cruz.

"Mind if I tag along?" I nonchalantly said. Cruz shrugged.

Cassidy strolled up toting a gunnysack and paper pick-up rod. "You bastards deserted me." He said for the umpteenth time.

We shrugged as he glowered and angrily peered about for debris to stab. We had already policed the area and it was clean. "We're done here," I said.

"Traitors!" Cassidy seemed contemplating whether to stab one or both of us.

"Hey," I said. "When the shit began to fly we ran. You could have come with us."

"I was out of it!"

"How were we supposed to know?" I said.

"Yeah, we figured you took off too," said Cruz.

"I almost got thrown in the fuckin' brig."

Titmus chuckled. "Too bad you weren't, Cassidy. If you had, all you would need is a dose of clap to call yourself a Marine."

"Oh, Yeah?" said Cassidy, skeptical but somewhat appeased.

"That's all you need to become a salt," assured Titmus.

A shadow of a grin crossed Cassidy's face.

The head hurting Lancaster intruded. "You fuck-offs have been ordered to pick shit up! Why in hell are you standing around jawin'! For Christ's sake, there's a war goin' on!"

Along with others I was about to blast a "Go fuck yourself!"

But Lancaster stopped me short by snarling, "A few weeks of restriction might wake you people up."

I was eager to see Tulipa so I buttoned up and quietly gathered palm fronds as if performing an solemn wartime duty.

At dusk we finally knocked off. Instead of heading to the mess hall I galloped to the shower. Afterwards, I decided, "Hell, I could eat at the village."

Cruz had the same idea "I'm off," said Cruz.

"Me too," I said.

"I gotta bring Luina something."

"Good thinking, I'll get something for Tulipa."

I wanted to wear a starched khaki shirt. Maybe I could borrow one from Arnie. Titmus came by and said, "I'm sticking around tonight."

O'Bannion was flaked out and observed with a quizzical grin as I squared away.

"Going someplace?"

"Liberty," I said.

"Really, I thought you got guard duty tonight?"

"What!"

"Just checked the roster and you got it, I don't."

My heart plopped, "You kidding?"

"Check it yourself."

"Take my duty," I pleaded. "I'll pay you back."

"Got me a date," he said.

"A date?"

"With two beers," he said.

"I'll give you my beer ration plus ten bucks and I'll owe you two guard duty shifts."

"Hah!" O'Bannion and grabbed his shaving gear and slipped out. Another "Hah!" was his exit word.

I tried to find Titmus but he was gone. Enticing others with my more than generous offer were wasted efforts. Before Cruz departed I slipped him a wrapped bar of soap. "For Tulipa! Tell her I'll try to see her tomorrow night."

Cruz nodded and walked off. There was nothing else to do but strap on my cartridge belt, shoulder my rifle and make my way to the guard shack.

CHAPTER TWENTY-FOUR

At the guard shack Corporal Bennett advised me that I had the 2000 to 2400 watch and suggested that I should hit the sack. I sprawled on a cot and tried to conk out but it was too early. Besides, an enticing vision of Tulipa cavorted in my thoughts. I wondered if she meant what she said about wanting to see me again. I considered that it could be Samoan bullshit and she had already forgotten me.

Recalling her soft breathing, delightful touch and girlish giggle made me quiver. Sexual cravings entwined with romantic images danced in my mind.

In high school and elsewhere for that matter, I'd never done well in the courting game. I gave myself a "B-" regarding last night's encounter.

Misgivings about whether Cruz would give her my soap bar gift or slip it to Luina crossed my mind. If he double crossed me my intended retribution wasn't healthy. I finally nodded off. Seldom do I remember specific dreams and didn't recall the details of this one but Tulipa was featured.

Buck-assed Private Crawford shook me. "Get your ass up!" I bolted up like I'd been shot.

On either side of the airstrip were revetments occupied by blue and white Corsairs. They were situated thirty-five yards apart.

At night the looming enshrouded palm tree trunks bordering the inland length of the airfield were impenetrable. Dense foliage and dark shadows induced imaginative possibilities featuring enemy incursions. The post I relieved entailed pacing the coral field a one hundred yard length and crossing sixty yards and return the hundred yards back.

The Jap submarine that had shelled Samoa had not been forgotten. If Jap infiltrators, at the time, had secretly landed from that submarine, they could have hidden in the thick growths pressing around the airfield. Havoc could have ensued before they'd be eliminated.

On all islands, after the sun dipped, glowing lights was a serious taboo. After dusk mantled South Pacific islands, even those far from the action, became black and spooky

The Japs had night flyers capable of dropping bombs. They purportedly flew huge distances searching for targets. Also, their probing two man submarines were another menace to be considered.

During the wet season rain clouds hid the stars on Samoa. Between downpours, droves of mosquitoes commenced sipping and supping. Helmet linings, facial nets, long socks, secured sleeve and cuff openings did little to mitigate the attacking insects. While striving to keep alert for enemy infiltrator, sentries shuffling along strived to keep alert, but constantly swatting voracious insects was distracting.

As I paced, sweat poured and lungs gasped but random thoughts kept me stimulated. "Tulipa is little more than sixteen, a high school junior in California." I reiterated over and over. "But hell, I'm only eighteen." Despite images of her small breasts and roundish after-end producing shivers, my feverish thoughts were frequently distracted by biting bugs. Perhaps that was a positive diversion. Dwelling on the unattainable is certainly less than inspiring.

Anyway, I was oddly comforted knowing nothing intense had yet happened between us. I concluded, not positively, that nothing would. I hadn't really touched her and due to a touch of guilt regarding her age, tried again and again not to think along sexual channels. Besides, pacing along with a hard-on was distracting. I was aware that I had to keep alert for enemy infiltrators.

The majority of buck-ass privates in VMF 111 were seventeen, eighteen, nineteen, some even younger. The more mature shitbirds were in their early twenties. Not many of us were emotionally mature. If we had been, we'd probably have waited to be drafted into the army. Regardless of which branch of service, countless teenagers served, I am certain most were experiencing a sex obsessed state. In VMF 111 we constantly spoke, felt and endured feminine fantasies.

Images of Cruz snowing the girls with his slight Mexican accent stoked my thoughts. "If he touches Tulipa I'll whip his ass."

I hadn't heard Corporal Aspen approach. "Yuh all walkin' your post in a military manner?" he drawled.

"What's it look like!" I said trying to sound provoked.

"Oh, you look alert," he drawled. He was a teenage noncom from Tennessee but a pretty squared away guy.

"That's because I am. I almost shot your ass off!"

"Bullshit!"

"Will it make you happy if I point my loaded rifle at you and holler halt?" I said.

"The O.D. is creeping around. If he catches yuh sleep-walking it's gonna be your ass."

"I'm wide awake." I tried to sound indignant.

"But not too alert! Sleep-walking is the same as fucking off," he snapped and stalked off.

I didn't try to eat up time bantering about nothing. Others stalled him exchanging inconsequential bullshit. I was content plying and playing with torrid fantasies. Visions of romancing Tulipa dissipated as I conjured possibilities of that sneaky O.D. trying to catch me fucking off. When Aspen sauntered back I was ready. "Halt, you sneaky son of a bitch!"

He chuckled as if I was funny. I thought about firing a round over his head.

At 2400 Pinsky relieved me and I strode back to our hut with Taps pattering behind. Cruz was the only one there.

"What the hell happened at the village?"

"Nothing."

"You see Tulipa?"

"She was there."

I was contemplating grabbing his throat when he said, "She asked about you."

"No kidding?"

"Yeah, after I gave her your bar of soap."

"That's it?"

"I think she likes you."

My face reddened. "Sure she does. How do you know?"

"Samoans are like Mexicans, that's how."

"Mexicans?"

"That's right. She kept asking about you. Wanted to know if you had a girl."

"What did you tell her?"

"The truth."

"Shit!"

"I told her you were married and had four kids."

"You bastard!"

"I'm kidding."

"Ahh, I knew that. Anyway, we only talked that one night."

"This is Samoa. These peons don't rush around much but they got their own ideas about life, love, sex, stuff like that."

"How in hell you know so much about Samoans?"

"I told you, they're like Mexicans."

"So what did you do?"

"Ate, drank, bullshitted like last time, only I came back earlier."

"You didn't make out?"

"I don't kiss and tell."

I glared. "That means you didn't do a damn thing."

"I'm gonna see Luina tonight. You coming?"

"Maybe."

I flaked out thinking thoughts about Tulipa. Sexual images prevailed, but occasionally I imagined myself in love and settling down in Samoa. Shit, I had never even had a girlfriend. And here I was wondering if love could overcome problems like race, religion, distance, environment, culture and other facets.

I finally conked out and had a disquieting dream about Bones on Upolu. In my dream he was wrapped in a *lava lava* and dancing with a crowd of happy natives. After the festivities Bones, his wife and child laughed and merrily carried on.

After long sweltering hours of labor, we were finally knocked off. After showering and shaving I joined Cruz. Decked out in starched khaki and pith helmets, we jauntily strode from camp. Between us we carried a purloined loaf of bread and gallon can of peaches. "Let's get a beer," said Cruz and we headed to the slopchute.

"One won't hurt," I figured. Cruz got the beers and we sat carefully keeping our pilfered can and loaf concealed.

"Lieutenant Tollivan and Hollering were at the village last night," whispered Cruz.

"How come?" I was uneasy knowing officers were cruising our neighborhood.

"They got girlfriends. They'd been coming before we found the place."

Tollivan and Hollering were competent pilots. Tollivan was a happy-go-lucky guy. Hollering was quiet and a touch morose. Neither pushed his gold bar or caused problems on the line.

By sundown we made it to the village and strode straight to the big *fale*. The *matai* greeted us as if we were old friends. His repeated *tolafas* made us feel welcome. He laughed as each of us handed him a chocolate bar and small can of peaches. His Samoan and inflection sounded like he really appreciated our sweet gifts.

The three of us sat native style. He again asked what city we were from. "We both from East Los Angeles in California," said Cruz.

"Ah, I know California, warm like Samoa," he repeated.

It was a familiar conversational trend. Both our vocabularies were limited.

"Yeah, but different," I said sure that we had said this before.

"Yes," he chuckled.

We shot the shit about Samoa, the Corps, the war, our homes, but his English wasn't good. Although Cruz and I knew dozens of Samoan words our conversation was simple and repetitive.

Besides, many of the Samoan words we knew weren't apropos, especially when directed at an elderly chief. As it were, we were dumber than we wanted to be and spent silent minutes just looking at each other. He grinned a lot and so did we. Cruz's had a problem grinning just for the sake of grinning. So sometimes he didn't appear especially amiable.

We tried to avoid being obvious as we nonchalantly peered around hoping to catch sight of the girls. His *faletua* showed up with three cups of *kava*. The concoction had the usual sweet and lumpy chocolate-like taste. I was weary of the damn stuff but slurped a little of the warm liquid like it was a delicious treat.

"You like?" grinned the chief.

"Good," I uttered and Cruz nodded.

We heard lilting Polynesian chattering as Tulipa and Luina swiveled in. They laughed and waved. Both shouted, "*Talofa,* Malinies, *talofa.*" Both looked sexy in their grass skirts and Marine issued tee shirts.

Tulipa twirled and swirled and gracefully pranced about. I focused on her smooth brown limbs. She looked more than somewhat lustful and I inwardly stirred as strands of her grass skirt brushed the back of my head. I yearned to run my fingers up and down her pretty brown legs.

Both girls abruptly plopped down to gab and giggle as the four of us strived to communicate in pigeon English. Despite linguistic difficulties, I sensed that they understood more than they let on. Men, boys and girls soon poured through the door. Tulipa and Luina leaped up to assist others serving bananas, poi, taro and unidentified foodstuff.

Lieutenants Tollivan and Hollering staggered in arm in arm with two laughing girls. Both second lieutenants were from the same neighborhood in Gary and had known each other when they were kids. Tollivan waved a half-filled fifth of bonded and sat. It was obvious that this wasn't their first visit.

Tollivan proceeded to talk up a storm in Samoan. He kept laughing about something and pointing at Hollering who looked dour. I wasn't offended because I knew he was a silent type of guy and knew it wasn't us that bothered him. He acted stand-offish with fellow officers too. Scuttlebutt had it that he didn't relish flying, in fact hated it.

"You boys been here before, haven't you?" asked Lieutenant Tollivan.

"Once, sir!" said Cruz.

"Me too, sir," I said.

"I thought so. And when we're off the base you can knock off the sir shit," said Hollering.

"Yes, sir," said Cruz.

"Off the base call me Tolly."

I called him Tolly once but it felt uncomfortable. Hell, he was a commissioned officer and I was a shitbird.

The lieutenant took the bottle out of Hollering's hand and passed it to Cruz who nervously took a small swig and passed it to me. I downed some. It was strong stuff and I'm not used to drinking good whiskey. As I chased it down with a swig of *kav* I coughed. Hollering grasped the bottle and took a long swig.

Someone began singing and Tollivan, gook-like, leaped up shouting, *"Siva! Siva!"*

Tollivan commenced gyrating. For a big guy he was light on his feet and pranced about. Obviously, it wasn't his first time. The lieutenants' two girls got to their feet, giggled and danced. Tulipa, Luina and others joined them.

I wished that I could gyrate but knew I was too awkward and afraid of making a fool of myself. Cruz didn't have misgivings and readily commenced dancing. He wasn't as smooth as the lieutenant but induced a Latin touch. Nobody seemed to care about what he or anybody else was doing.

I wished to be alone with Tulipa but she kept dancing, singing and laughing and having a great time. She paid little or no attention to me.

I gulped down a mouthful of gin, as usual, it tasted evil. In the midst of the revelry I felt low until Tulipa suddenly grabbed my hand and laughingly pulled me up and out the *fale*. She held my hand as we gamboled to the beach.

We stopped at the shoreline. A narrow ribbon of moonlight glimmered across the placid water. Her breathing was soft and steady but I was panting a bit. Tulipa silently tugged me along the wet sand amid the soft sound of an ebbing tide. I didn't resist but wondered what the hell she was up to.

Hopeful but wary until she suddenly stopped and pressed close. Her nipples touched my chest for a second before she stepped back and focused on my face. Jesus, I don't know why, but at that torrid moment my thoughts suddenly drifted back to Paddy Rourke, my schoolmate at Venice High. I had tried to talk him into joining up with me. "That mud and foxhole shit ain't for me," he snorted and opted for the navy. "If I'm gonna die for my country I'd rather meet the Lord from a clean ship."

If he could see me now under this starry tropical night holding a lovely girl near a gurgling sea!

"You like me?" said Tulipa.

"Sure," I stammered.

"Malini! You got sweetheart in America?"

"Nope!"

"How many years you be?"

"Eighteen."

"Me sixteen."

I didn't give a damn anymore as she gazed at me with her dark brown eyes and smiled. The wind stirred, outlining her pert breasts. Small and firm they rose and fell an inch from my chest. Timidly and awkwardly I pulled her to my chest. She lay soft and smooth against me.

I had an embarrassing hard on, and though I was desperate, I wasn't sure about what to do so I impulsively kissed her. She giggled but didn't kiss back. I noted that she didn't resist either.

We hugged and smooched again when boom, I ejaculated. She felt my release and giggled as she pointed to the sticky circle staining my khakis. I was humiliated as she hopped and hollered. I averted my eyes and thought about dying. Finally she quieted to a soft chortle and her eyes twinkled as she purred, "You love Tulipa?"

A bit wary I said, "Sure, I do."

She brushed soft fingers across my face. "Tomorrow you talk with Luina." Without further ado she sprinted away and I stomped from the beach and headed back to camp.

After I hit the sack I still lay awake feeling stupid and embarrassed. Later Cruz stumbled in and I feigned sleep. We didn't converse until morning. Hemming and hawing he told me about his activity with Luina. It wasn't as ardent a tale as mine but similar. Of course, I didn't confide all aspects of my rendezvous and I'm sure he held details back. Anyway, things were looking up.

CHAPTER TWENTY-FIVE

The day's work went on and on and on. By the time we secured for the day it was past six. Both Cruz and I had managed to get close-cut haircuts earlier. We wasted no time but showered and got squared away. We slipped into our bleached khakis, looking more than just presentable, and were eager to be off.

"You guys looking to get some tail?" queried Titmus.

"Huh?" I stuttered.

"You both look edgy."

Cruz blushed and grinned.

"C'mon now, why are you two so jumpy?"

I tried looking composed and wanted to sound salty but it wasn't easy. Hell, I might be about to get laid but didn't want to broadcast it.

Cruz and I strode from camp and bumped into Lieutenant Tollivan. He returned our snappy salutes and said, "How's it goin', boys?"

"Okay, sir," I said and Cruz nodded.

"You guys doing, okay?"

"Yes, sir," I was wary of being social with sergeants, lieutenants and above. I knew Cruz wasn't comfortable either small-talking with the brass.

"You two going courting?"

"Sort of, sir," said Cruz.

I noted distress in my buddy's inflection and hoped Tollivan hadn't caught it.

Ahh, I'm imagining a threat that's not there, I decided. "We're going to see some girls we met, Lieutenant."

Tollivan was twenty-three and, as far as we knew, an okay guy. Pilots weren't as *gung ho* as line officers and it made sense for them to be mellow with no-account enlistees. After all, their well-beings were in the hands of low ranked individuals like mechanics, ordinance people and sentries. If a disgruntled nut or idiot was negatively distracted, problems could evolve.

The lieutenant's chatter was friendly. "Lemme tell you a little about Samoan sex stuff."

"Yes, sir," said Cruz. What else could he say? We shifted and settled.

"When we're off the base talking pussy you can knock off that sir stuff," chuckled Tollivan.

"Yes, sir!" said Cruz and squirmed and altered his stance.

"Fuckin' officer!" I thought.

However, Tollivan was only curious and wanted to be helpful. Some pilots were like that, but we were eager to hit the road. Rank in the Corps was too formidable a function to ignore. Although eager to get going, I wasn't rash enough to excuse myself so I politely listened as if his advice was sanctified.

"In Samoa there are four ways to nail a dame," he confided. "After charming her like you two already have or are currently doing, arrange a secret meeting with the quarry in a secluded place. Bring a gift and then make your move.

"The Samoans call it *avaga*. We call it elopement, but not quite as permanent, and don't worry, it's not that serious. Believe me, when all is set and done, *moetotolo* is a lot more romantic much more exciting. Translated in English it means sleep-crawling; sort of like rape but in a nice way."

I just couldn't feel comfortable and suspected that Cruz was also felt funny because he suddenly growled, "I ain't gonna rape nobody!"

"Don't have to. That's not what you do," chortled Tollivan. "Not really, but then you got to get yourself a *soa*, that's an ambassador of love, and they don't come cheap."

I was piqued. "What do you do with whatever the hell you call them?"

"For a price, of course, they represent the suitor. They do the romantic talking for the suitor, in your cases, hard-up Marines. It's something like the John Alden, Priscilla courtship. You know about them?"

Cruz had no idea who Tollivan was referring too, but I remembered them from an English class. I vaguely recalled their courtship taking place in the colonies during the time of the pilgrims.

"How do we get us one of them *soas*?" I said.

"I'm not sure. It wasn't even easy for me and I can get by chatting in their lingo."

Tollivan kept throwing Polynesian words at us. "I bribed the *tuagane*, that's the brother of the girl I had my eye on. By local standards it was an expensive bribe. He acted as the *soa* for me. After he did his job, romantic deployments fell smoothly into place."

I vainly related how Tulipa had urged me to talk to Luina and how Luina had egged on Cruz to find out the courting process from Tulipa so we'd know what to do.

"You two may be in luck, that is, if you already got yourselves a couple of built in *soafines*."

Tollivan liked throwing Samoan words around. Although he couldn't carry on fluid Polynesian conversations, he flaunted his lone word facility by spouting disjointed Samoan words.

"Anyway, you got yourselves a couple of *soafines*, women ambassadors of love. Believe me, they're the best kind." I didn't catch all his Samoan bullshit and knew Cruz also was lost in a similar linguistic lock-out.

"Thanks," said Cruz and swiveled off before the lieutenant could continue. I echoed his thanks and off we went. "Hey, don't forget you guys are *papalagis*, that will pull some weight."

I should have but couldn't resist, "*Papa*—what?"

"White men, foreigners. Sometimes that'll get you privileges but be careful 'cause you'll be treading on thin ice. Remember, ice in the tropics melts quickly."

I didn't know what the hell he was referring to, and knew better than to ask another question. Neither one of us yearned for the lieutenant to keep babbling and Cruz said, "Thank you, sir, we'll be careful."

"*Tofa!*" chuckled the lieutenant, "happy hunting."

As we hit the road Cruz uttered "That guy makes me nervous."

"Tollivan sure likes to sound off in Samoan."

"I should talk Mexican to him."

"Yeah, that'll go over big."

A Seabee behind the wheel of a battered jeep gave us a lift. After a few miles he stopped alongside a flimsy shack and invited us in. It was early so we joined him. We parked our butts around a flimsy wooden table and sipped the not-so-great tasting whatever the hell it was. Cruz paid for the three small green bottles filled with a cloudy liquid.

We left with another Seabee who dropped us off near the village.

It was quiet. Most inhabitants were either away or sleeping. There were a few stoic kids being scolded by a cranky *olomatua*. They paid no heed as we sidled through village and into the big *fale*.

An ancient *olomatua* sat in one corner puffing a small pipe and chewing on a dark bark that blackened her teeth. "*Talofa,*" announced Cruz. She paid no heed so we plopped down and crossed our legs.

Thirty minutes passed before outside movement immersed with giggling broke the silence. Tulipa's smiling head popped in. We both rose but Tulipa signaled me to stay. She beckoned Cruz to join her outside.

I sat by my lonesome until Luina entered and motioned for me to exit. Yards behind I trailed her to the edge of the village. She whisked into a clump of coconut trees and waited until I caught up. "Tulipa, she my friend. She good girl and pretty, don't you think?"

Sweat dripped. "Yes."

"She love you I think."

"I think I love her."

Luina giggled. I felt awkward and felt my face redden.

"You big *Papalgi* so I talk to you."

"About what?"

"You do *moetotolo.*"

"What's that?" Then I recalled Tollivan's conversation.

"That the Samoan way. Find where she sleeps and go."

"When?"

"Sooner is better but take care."

"She wants me to come?" I asked. Luina giggled and fled.

I went back to the *fale* and sat. Images danced in my mind, most of them pleasant. Tulipa eventually noticed me and we exchanged *talofas.* After that neither girl heeded my lustful stare.

Villagers strolled in toting ukuleles. Tollivan, Hollering and two girls entered. As expected, singing, dancing, gabbing and eating ensued. Cruz caught my eye. I shrugged and he grimaced. I didn't feel comfortable, nope, not at all.

Tollivan approached, "How's it going?"

"Not sure, sir. Luina told me to *moetotolo,* whatever the hell that means."

"Then do it, you lucky bastard. And for god's sake take your clothes off before you move in."

"Off?"

"Yep, and don't make noise or attract attention. You'll be in deep shit if they nab you!"

"Jesus!"

"The local Lotharios grease themselves but you haven't got grease. Anyway, the greasy shit stinks."

"Holy shit."

"Know where she lives?"

"No." I was glad that I didn't.

"For Christ's sake find out."

"How?"

Tulipa got up and slipped through the door and Tollivan growled. "Follow her!"

It was pitch black. I couldn't see a fuckin' thing but heard rustling on the side of the *fale* and stepped toward the sound.

"*Talofa.*"

"*Talofa.*" I was one nervous Marine.

"Pretty stars." she shifted and we almost touched.

"Yes."

"I tired."

"Me too."

"I sleep now."

"Been a long night." My talk sounded stupid.

"Yes."

"Me sleep too, I got the duty tomorrow." My eyes were adjusting to the dark. I could make out shapes as my talk fell into a native-like syntax.

"I sleep there," she pointed to a *fale.* The reed woven side of the hut was rolled up and tied.

"Really?" Our strained conversation irked and I decided I wasn't going through the ritual, not this time anyway.

"*Tofa,*" Tulipa sighed and slightly touched against me as she slipped away.

I trod back to the big *fale.* A few revelers were still singing and dancing. I was relieved that both lieutenants and Cruz were gone. After a few steps inside I sighed, "Fuck!" and made my way back to Tulipa's *fale.* I sat with my back to a palm tree and stared at her home.

Twenty minutes slipped by before I said, "Aw, fuck it!" and unlaced my boondockers, shed my khaki shirt and dropped my pants. I shakily folded my clothes and placed them at the foot of a palm tree. Naked as a jaybird I was fanned by a warm breeze. Apprehensive and tingling with a hell of an erection I moved on.

The grass was soft and wet under my bare feet, I crouched as I neared the *fale.* Sleep induced sounds came from several directions. I trembled and inhaled deeply as the unsynchronized symphony emanated from the *fale.* I stood still as a statue alert and ready to take off.

Being a naked intruder in a Samoan village wasn't my concept of a fun filled adventure. I became even more uneasy creeping about with the sole intention of getting laid. I stared at her *fale.* "This is stupid, I'm gonna get myself killed," and was about to beat a hasty retreat.

"Malini," whispered a feminine voice. It sounded like it could be Tulipa.

"It's a trap, joke or worse," played in my head. Soft feminine breathing and slight rustling impelled me toward her whispered voice. I prayed that it was her as I probed through the blackness and felt her soft warm arm. I jerked closer and intrepidly ran my other hand down her smooth thigh. It was a lovely touch and when she sighed I shivered. I was in a tizzy as our bodies pressed together. The coconut salve and sweet odor of feminine sweat caused my business to re-erect. Tulipa was startled but not really frightened. She commenced punching and slapping, but lightly.

"What the hell!" I rose to retreat. She grasped my arm, "Shhh." She pulled me down. We tussled a bit and the strength of that girl astonished me. Her body heat almost drove me nuts.

All of a sudden she was on top clawing, panting and resisting my awkward grasps. As we wrestled we restrained from hurting each other. Indeed, she was strong but with redoubled effort I rolled her over and pinned her perspiring body. I couldn't part her legs and I was one pooped Marine. Suddenly her body grew slack and resistance ceased. I thrust into her and exploded.

I lay back exhausted, conscious of rolling surf sounds and her quick breathing. With my face cradled on her small breasts noises faded as I conked out.

A rumbling bassoon followed by a splattering shower awoke me. Dawn was on the verge of breaking but the downpour darkened the sky. Tulipa's luminous brown eyes bore into me. I was in sanctified territory and more than a little nervous. I moved to pull her loser but she shifted away. I surged forward wrapping my arms about her. My cock reacted to her soft wet skin. I tried to turn her over but she abruptly sat up. "Go!" she whispered.

As I pulled up my pants the sun probed through the rain. The sky continued to spill torrents as I trotted off and accelerated toward camp.

About the time I reached our Quonset hut, the watery cascade diminished into a cold drizzle. Water loudly dripped from leaves and I was drenched. As I entered I spotted Cruz on his cot staring at the overhead.

Titmus' snores drowned out the discordant sounds of the others. I shed my wet khakis and flopped on my cot hoping to get some shut eye before Lancaster stomped in.

"Where the hell you been?" snapped Arnie.

"Visiting," I sounded a bit smug.

"What!"

"Seeing a friend in a village."

"Yeah?"

"Yeah."

O'Bannion opened his eyes. "Man or woman?"

"Think I'd stick around a village to talk to a man?" I rolled over so they couldn't see my grin and shut my eyes.

"What kind of bullshit is goin' on?" asked Cassidy.

"Lover boy just dropped in."Quipped Arnie.

That was it, but I knew Arnie and O'Bannion picked up on my smug demeanor and were more than a little curious.

A few hours later clanging mess gear announced Lancaster's arrival. "Up and at 'em! There's three trucks parked behind the mess hall full of supplies. After chow you lucky people get to unload them. Move your asses!"

The usual shit-on-a-shingle was featured for breakfast and we gobbled the gooey stuff up. Three trucks stacked with crates were waiting loaded with food stuffed in cardboard boxes, bags and barrels. The drivers were asleep in their cabs.

"Maybe we can do a little borrowing," whispered Titmus.

Lancaster watched awhile and then left, leaving Sergeant Gruell and Corporal Jalowsky to keep watchful eyes on us as we toted stuff off the trucks into the mess hall.

"You'd think we were thieves," muttered Titmus.

"Who'd steal this crap anyway?" said Pinsky.

O'Bannion sneered, "Tell me about this friend you got?"

"What's to tell?"

"What she look like?" he prodded.

"Better than okay."

"She's a gook, ain't she?"

There were times, I used that derogatory sounding word myself but his tone sounded obscene. "No, she's a blonde princess outta Auckland."

"She put out?"

"She's a nice kid," I said in a low voice that suggested he lay off.

"Just asking."

"None of your damn business!"

"Nice kid, huh? Does that mean she does or don't put out?" snickered Arnie.

"I haven't got time to bullshit with you no class idiots, there's work to be done," I growled as I shouldered a bag of potatoes.

"Cheez, look whose bucking for a stripe," said O'Bannion.

"Uh, oh, he's into some serious love shit," said Arnie. I ignored them.

We spent the morning unloading the trucks. I wanted to gab with Cruz but got the feeling he was trying to avoid me. Most of the stuff was unloaded before I cornered him.

"How did it go last night?"

"Okay," he said.

"What happened?"

"Nothing."

"You got any?"

"No!"

"Why the hell not? It was arranged, for Christ's sake."

"I'm a Catholic."

"Catholics get laid, don't they?"

"I'm not into that rape business."

"*Moetotolo* isn't rape. It's how they romance here."

"Too much like rape and I ain't gonna do it."

"It's their way of doing things. They even tell you how to do it. They don't resist, maybe a little. It's a local custom. It's like a game, a local game, can't you see?"

"I ain't gonna do it."

"You coming to the village tonight?"

"I got guard duty," said Cruz.

We were knocked off at 1700 and I headed for the shower. I skipped chow again but it was dark before I got to the village. When I shyly entered the *fale*, Luina, Tulipa and the *matai* along with *toa'ina* were waiting. They sat cross-legged jawing in Samoan. "*Talofa*," they chorused. The *matai* gestured for me to sit. As my butt hit the deck a wrinkled *olomatua* handed me a cup of *kava*. I faked a sip and slowly set the cup down. She eyed me as she grinned before slipping away. "Where your dark friend?" purred Luina.

"Got guard duty."

She looked sad, maybe a little hurt.

"Nothing I could do about it."

"Much water pour from sky here," said the *matai*. "Rainmaker make it wet. Good for us. People that live on Ofu and Olesega not have it good."

I feigned interest as he went on and on about weather, the coming and going of boats and value of coconuts. His mixture of Samoan and English eluded me. Half the time I couldn't catch what the hell he was talking about. However, I nodded at what I figured to be timely pauses.

He finally wearied of talking and rose, "*Tofa*," His *faletua* and *toa'ina* followed him out. I wasn't sure how the girls felt but I was glad to see them depart. Luina giggled and stared for a short time before disappearing. Tulipa took my hand and led me outside. We strolled to the beach.

A few feet from the surf we silently walked hand in hand. The star-filled sky and gentle lapping sea made me feel like I was in a dream, a novel or movie, something surreal. From the corner of my eye I felt her observing me. I was nervous but abruptly spun her and planted a kiss. Tulipa put her arms about me and pressed and purred. Damned, she was strong for a girl. "We should start back," I said.

"Come," and she led me to a grassy clearing in the midst of coconut trees. She pulled me down on the palm strewn ground and unbuttoned my trousers. It wasn't a very romantic encounter because I visualized grass and water stains on my clean khakis. But, of course, I didn't dwell on that image and we made love.

I was pooped and slightly aware of the murmurs of the sea. Tulipa suddenly rose and without even a *tofa* slipped away. I tried to square myself away but there were stains on my shirt and pants. As I made my way back to camp, I fantasized that a coconut aroma emanated from my uniform. I kept thinking, "I'm one lucky fuckin' romantic guy."

On nights that I didn't catch guard duty I'd make way to the village to see Tulipa. There were times, of course, that I got stuck being a sentry or stuck with some other shit duty and couldn't go.

Cruz had the same problem but managed to join me most of the time. He and Luina seemed happy but when I tried to talk personal stuff he got touchy. I finally quit quizzing since it was none of my business.

We scrounged presents like purloined canned beef, spam, canned fruit, a T-shirt, soap, cigarettes, pogey bait, whatever. And we slipped stuff to other natives too. They appreciated our gifts and treated us like friends.

Once in awhile Tollivan would slip one of us a partially full fifth of whiskey. The booze mixed with native libations went over big with our Samoan hosts and their drop-in native guests. Cruz and I figured we had a better than fair deal in paradise.

It sure as hell beat our carousing, squabbling, drinking exploits in Pago Pago or Apia. Perennial hard-ons had been no fun either. Hangovers and bruised wake-ups were recalled less and less.

Tulipa and I weren't wed so our romancing had to be carried out in secret. We spent hours walking along the coral shoreline and splashing in the surf. We threw hooked lines tied to a stick and pulled in nothing more memorable than wads of seaweed but it was fun. At times she'd produce a ukulele to strum and warble lyrics in Polynesian.

I was frequently distracted by an erection which would elicit a giggle from Tulipa. Occasionally, one way or another she'd take care of my needs. Maybe she really liked me. Then again, maybe it was only a hospitable custom.

At times, I seriously contemplated staying or at least somehow come back to Samoa. Ha, bullshit! I wasn't about to pull a Bones Donigal. How could I? Besides, I wasn't nearly as smitten as Bones. And suppose I was, how would I live? My self-sufficiency talents were very limited. At eighteen, I was acutely aware but not too disturbed regarding mental, physical and creative shortcomings.

CHAPTER TWENTY-SIX

On a balmy afternoon, a soft offshore breeze fanned the island. We drifted back to work after lunch. Without a hint of forewarning, enlistees and officers commenced vomiting and defecating uncontrollably. Arnie was the first Ground Defense member to spew his guts out. Cassidy spilled next and I followed.

Toilets were jammed with defecators and pukers. Few couldn't even make it to the closest head, wholesale shitting and vomiting ensued.

O'Bannion moaned, "The fuckin' Japs have poisoned us."

"You're out of your fuckin' mind!" Between fits of defecating and heaving Cassidy gurgled, "It's the fuckin' cooks."

I was seriously afflicted and expected to meet my inglorious end. I knew I was dying. "I'll never get to confront a Jap," I moaned. "Oh, Lord, what a way to go!"

Titmus' face was a deathly gray. "I only sipped a bit of that poisoned lemonade," he lamented.

With sirens screaming, ambulances arrived from the hospital. Anxious corpsmen stacked regurgitating personnel into their rescue vehicles. Retchers outnumbered stretchers hence the afflicted were piled on top of each other.

After rescue vehicles were filled with stinking heaps of puking and shitting Marines, they headed for the base hospital. Patients being transferred continued to upchuck and defecate. The malodorous ride to salvation took forever.

At the base hospital, navy stretcher-bearers carried us pallid ill into sickbay Quonset huts and laid us on bunks. A sad faced sailor copied names, serial numbers and religions onto a pad. One of two navy doctors scanning VMF's groaning patients mournfully whispered, "Some of these poor kids aren't going to make it."

On the bunk to my right O'Bannion pitifully appealed to Jesus. On my left Cruz likewise called to *Jesus*. I entreated but was reluctant to beseech the same savior. Prayers, whines, curses, and an assortment of gastric disgorgements emanated from fellow nauseous patients.

The corpsmen were, above and beyond, tender, caring and concerned. Those young navy guys endeared themselves to us by ministering their skills as if we were family instead of hot shot Marines. Our viewpoints regarding sailors, medical or otherwise, were far from complimentary, that is, up until then.

It was a terrifying event while it lasted, but by the next morning everyone had recovered. Each of us lost pounds and felt weak. Ambulances transported us back to our camp. All former patients were advised to abide in cots for the rest of the day.

A semi-healthy lieutenant strode from hut to hut explaining the cause of our abdominal disaster. The lemonade we had consumed had been concocted in an aluminum pot. The metal had created a chemical reaction evolving lemon juice into a poison. Out of ignorance our guilty cooks had created the fateful lemon aluminum mix. They, too, had swallowed their liquid creation and been among the afflicted. We were happy to be alive and remained too grateful and drained to plot vengeance.

Titmus survived the lemonade fiasco better than most, but was again confronted with a romantic problem. A disturbing letter from Millie had arrived and as we lay recuperating he read aloud.

Dear Earl,

It's a cold and dreary morning in San Diego and I am so very lonesome. You've been gone such a long time. Sometimes I wonder if I would even recognize you if we passed on the street. I don't really mean that. It's just that I miss you so and the damp San Diego weather makes me feel blue.

Anyway, on a happier note, I got a new job. I'm now working at The Brass Bucket. It's about two blocks south of 2nd and Broadway. You've been there, I'm sure.

MacCloud, my old boss, was taking too much for granted. Not only was he getting bossier but he kept trying to get familiar. You know I won't tolerate wolfish behavior. Anyway, he was about to fire me when I beat him to it. I up and quit. As I stomped out I told him that when you got back from shooting Japs you would teach him some manners.

The old bastard, excuse me for the language, laughed some, but I could tell from his eyes that he's worried.

The tips aren't as good at The Brass Bucket but I'm pretty much on my own and that's a good thing. Oh, I forgot to tell you, it's more of a eating joint than a bar.

I'm not getting younger and been thinking a lot about you and our upcoming wedding. After the big day I intend to get into some other kind of work. I'm tired of slinging hash and serving coffee to creeps. But what else can I do?

Will this war ever end? Will we ever see each other again? I'm in a rut and, as I said, not getting any younger. You can tell I'm down, can't you? Can you blame me? Forgive me for spilling my dreary problems on you but that's what sweethearts are for, isn't it? Anyway, enough mournful stuff, you got enough troubles fighting our country's enemies.

On a merrier note I'm still with the USO but don't get to spend as much time there because of split shifts at The Brass Bucket. Most our steady customers have shipped out or been transferred to the East Coast. A lot of drunken creeps show up at night. Sorry to say, a lot of them are in uniform.

Hilton, that sweet soldier I told you about keeps coming in. You know how the streets of San Diego are at night, some what safe but bawdy. A few times he escorts me home after work. But don't fret, nothing goes on between us or ever will. I swear to that. He may not even like girls. Of course, I don't know that for sure. Anyway, I appreciate him as a friend.

Enough about me and my insignificant problems. How have you been? You've been gone over a year. Any idea about when you'll be coming home? I don't think it's fair. Maybe I'll write letters to a congressman or something. I might send one to President Roosevelt. Ha, ha, I can still laugh at my own jokes. Uh, oh, there goes my doorbell. It could be Hilton. He wants to take me to breakfast. Poor kid, I can hardly wait for you to meet him. I told him about you. When you two meet, promise not to act rough and tough. He's not that kind of guy and even though he hasn't met you, he admires you. Write soon.

Lovingly yours forever,
Millie
P.S. Once he confided that he almost wished he had joined the Marines.

Titmus folded the letter and glared around as if daring someone to come up with a smart-ass comment. None of us dared shrug. He stuffed the letter in its envelope and flaked out on his cot staring at the overhead.

Two days later a horrendous happening beset our squadron. This time it was a catastrophe on the airfield. Lieutenant Hollering was landing his F4U when a trio of natives meandered across the airfield. Gooks had been warned time and time again about runway dangers.

As the Corsair touched ground and sped toward them they hollered and ran. Two avoided the oncoming blue and white plane, but one, God knows why, darted straight into the three-bladed propeller. Blood, flesh, confusion and horror spread everywhere. His body was turned into a nasty mangle, poor bastard.

Even worse, a group of gooks stacking palm fronds at the edge of the field ran to the scene. As they pointed at the victim's torn remains they reacted like a celebration was in order. To our distress, instead of mourning the demise of their fellow, they shouted, laughed and rolled around on the ground as if they had witnessed a funny occurrence.

"Fuckin' savages!" snarled Cassidy.

"Don't judge!" said Titmus, "they're probably hurting. It could be their way of coping."

"Laughin' and jumpin' around?" said O'Bannion.

"We don't know what's going on inside their minds. They got their own ways!" counseled Titmus.

It didn't sound like Titmus but he'd been around exotic people before. He may have been on to something we were too naïve to be aware of.

"Don't judge less thou be judged," said Cruz. Ever so often he'd come up with something that sounded religious.

Later O'Bannion and I decided Titmus' assessment was probably right on. Under the grisly circumstances, laughing and hollering didn't seem right, but who were we to decide how exotic people should act?

If there ever was a prospect of our squadron moving out, the general feeling of despair could dissipate, but that wasn't happening. In our Quonset hut everyone was on edge, it was a time to tread lightly.

One sweltering noontime, both Cassidy and Arnie's pent up emotions erupted.

Cassidy, after cleaning his rifle for the fourth time put it together again and thumped the butt on the deck. "My sweetheart," he sighed.

"You'll never use your fuckin' sweetheart against anything worth shooting at!" smirked Arnie.

Arnie started stalking up and down mumbling, "Airdales, especially those stuck in Ground Defense won't shoot rifles, we only use shovels."

"What the fuck do you know?" scowled Cassidy.

Arnie didn't take the bait and stalked outside cursing under his breath.

"He's right, we're the go nowhere, do nothin' Marines," said Cassidy and slipped a round into his rifle chamber. He leveled the barrel at Arnie's pith helmet suspended from a nail and fired. The bullet passed through it leaving a neat little hole.

Titmus jerked up from his doze. "What the fuck is that!"

Cassidy's sinister grin widened as he pointed to the hole in Arnie's helmet.

"You going Asiatic, Cassidy!" snapped Titmus.

Cassidy's expression stayed spooky as he cleaned his rifle. He was acting Asiatic but not enough to give Titmus any guff.

Titmus glared at Cassidy who averted his eyes. "Knock that stupid shit off!"

Arnie barged in, "I heard a shot!" He spied the hole in his pith helmet and turned to me. "You do that?"

I was shaken but bluffed, "If I'd a done it there'd be more than two holes!"

O'Bannion's dismantled Garand lay on his bunk. He continued oiling parts as if nothing had happened. Cassidy lay back and said nothing. I leafed through a book.

Titmus was snoring again. Cruz was reading.

Arnie faced Cassidy. "You!"

"Whatcha talkin' about?"

He glanced at Titmus and Cruz before asking O'Bannion. "You?"

"Smell my barrel."

"O'Bannion's rifle's was scattered on his cot in pieces!" Arnie pointed at me, "You or Cassidy?"

"Blow it out your ass!" said Cassidy.

Arnie clenched his fists. "I'll find out and when I do!" And he stalked out. Seconds after he left another blast thundered as Cassidy fired again. The door flew open and Arnie tore in. Another hole was in his hat. O'Bannion was still wiping rifle parts as if nothing had happened. I was standing and Cassidy was stretched out on his cot. Titmus and Cruz had jerked up bewildered.

"Which one of you shit-faced cowardly son-of-a-bitches done that?" Arnie bellowed and put my rifle barrel to his nose.

"Get your clammy hands off my weapon!" I pulled it from him.

He went for Cassidy's rifle but Cassidy stood before him. "Don't touch my best friend!"

232

"I thought so!" snarled Arnie.

"You talkin' shit about my sweetheart!" snapped Cassidy. Arnie threw an overhand right that missed Cassidy's chin and bounced off his shoulder. They threw punches as Titmus leaped up and threw each of them onto their cots. "Knock the shit off!" he warned. Hate and murderous looks manifested as we glared at one another. Suddenly Corporal Lancaster barged in. "I heard shots!"

"Fuck you, Lancaster!" we chorused.

CHAPTER TWENTY-SEVEN

The slopchute in Tutuilla was a favorite hangout. After guzzling enough beers insipid situations looked a little better. Brew was available but there were always long and slow moving lines of disgruntled parched patrons.

When not stuck with some dull duty, I'd trek to the village with one or two others. I don't know how or why but it got to where I felt more comfortable hanging with the natives.

It was especially favorable when I wasn't encumbered with a Saturday day or night duty because I didn't have to report until Monday morning. If I got to the village as the sun rose, off came my shoes. And though my feet never toughened up enough to carelessly traipse around, I felt at ease while barefooted. Shorn of khakis and into lava *lava* also helped alter thoughts from shit duties.

Most of the smiling villagers were even friendlier than they looked. Sure they anticipated presents such as worn shirts, pants or edibles. Tidbits out of a ration box were okay gifts too. What we had plenty of wasn't easily attainable to the natives.

As dawn broke life in the village stirred. Flames simmered and roosters cock-a-doodle-dooed. Birds in breadfruit trees peeped. Villages were places of pleasant sounds of joy. The background of muffled surf harmonized into a kind of soothing concert.

Women happily chattered as they tended to chores. Men surged out to sea to fish. Smaller kids ate and played. Older children headed for school. Girls wove fronds into baskets. Like their masculine peers some perched themselves on the reef to fish. Young studs emerged to traipse about. They shouted, grappled, horsed around and laughed. Old men whispered and chattered as they sat, smoked and watched.

By late afternoon the sun bore down and inertia dominated. Some slept while others dawdled in the shade. As dusk shadowed, workers and horseplaying children straggled in. All seemed to be in amiable moods.

Fish were sorted, bananas hung, yams and taro readied. Roasting pig simmered or chickens boiled for special occasions and there were more than a few. Somebody always seemed to be preparing something to eat.

Most nights prayers and hymns were sung. After supper the very young ones were hustled to bed while old timers sat, smoked and bullshitted about whatever old-timers bullshit about.

Dancing or fishing by torchlight was not uncommon. It also seemed to be a motivational time for village Don Juans to lurk and prowl. After midnight, the village shut down except for lascivious activities.

Tulipa had duties during the day. One of her chores involved wading out to the reef to gather a basketful of shellfish. Sometimes, like other young girls, she'd get stuck with washing, weaving or both. She also helped her family prepare supper.

We spent less and less time together during the day. Oh, sometimes we'd splash in the ocean, but compared to her I was a lousy swimmer who could barely make way.

I was abashed when she chortled at my aquatic attempts. I tried helping her fish but sullenly flopped at that. Both skills were far beyond my expertise.

Villagers got accustomed to seeing Cruz and me wandering about. When I approached, Tulipa's girlfriends nodded and joshed. She pretended to be pissed off but enjoyed the teasing.

After dark, if she wasn't involved in some chore, we would caress under a secluded coconut tree or in the shadow of a beached canoe. I preferred the later because there was room to run, I sure as hell didn't want to get caught by her father, brother or shaman. No telling how they'd react. I was careful to be sure I had spacious room to escape.

Aware that islands were being attacked and casualties were heavy was disturbing. We also learned that the army was encountering difficulties in Europe.

Arnie got stuck on mess duty which enabled him to swipe a large box of prunes. He set the wrinkled loot on our rickety table. "Prepare yourselves for some potent prune juice nectar." Before he had a chance to further brag about his acquisition Lancaster stormed in. "Gotcha!"

"Huh?" said Arnie. Only Arnie, Cruz, Lancaster and I were in the hut.

"Stealing government property!" said Lancaster. "Arnie I'm taking you into custody!"

We three were aware that Lancaster wasn't being comical but Arnie said, "You're pretty damn funny!"

"Come with me!" snapped Lancaster.

Cruz unsheathed his bayonet and looking somewhat sinister said, "Out!" Then he moved toward the open-mouthed corporal.

As Lancaster slowly backed to the door he stammered, "You want trouble too?"

"Yeah," gritted Cruz.

"I do too," I said feeling somewhat unsettled as I, too, moved on him with clenched fists.

I don't know what we would or could have done if Lancaster hadn't bolted outside.

"Chicken shit asshole!" shouted Arnie.

"Get rid of them prunes," advised Cruz.

"Too late," said Arnie.

"His word against ours," I said.

"Who's gonna believe three buck-assed grunts against a chickenshit corporal?" sighed Arnie and stashed the prunes under his pillow.

Minutes passed before Lancaster barged back followed by First Sergeant Byron.

"Where's the prunes?" said Byron.

"Prunes?" we chorused

"They hid them," said Lancaster.

"Naw, we ate them," I volunteered.

"Break 'em out," sighed Byron, in no mood to be trifled with.

Arnie produced the box and Lancaster grabbed them. "They tried to stop me from carrying out my duty!" said Lancaster.

Byron's red mustache bristled. "So?"

"They cursed at me!"

"Any of them touch you?"

"They would have if I hadn't left."

"In the old Corps a corporal would have knocked one, two or the three of them on their ass."

"I was only doing my duty, Sarge."

"Come with me," ordered Byron and Arnie followed him out.

Lancaster looked askance as Cruz and I moved toward him. This time we meant business. He grabbed the prunes and bolted.

Arnie's office hours took place in front of Major Burke. "There's been mess hall pilfering! The stealing of food better stop or some sorry-assed thieves in this squadron will be doing serious brig time!"

It wasn't practical to tell the major that if every chow thief in the squadron was incarcerated for food theft, VMF 111 would be sorely bereft of enlisted personnel.

The brig on American Samoa was a hell hole. Arnie was handed three days of piss and punk in that unsavory place. Gunnery Sergeant Meder, a giant old China-hand was in charge. The sadistic old screwball doted on making prisoners suffer for infractions, even minor ones.

If a jailed Marine or sailor looked the least bit defiant, said the wrong thing, or didn't move fast enough when ordered, he literally got the crap beat out of him.

Most regular guards in the Pago Pago brig were sadistic pricks that had been transferred out of regular outfits. A few forlorn bastards among them had been arbitrarily assigned from incoming transports. Some tried to be okay guys but Gunnery Sergeant Meder wouldn't tolerate decency. Affable guards ended up becoming prisoners themselves.

After three days of incarceration a thinner and subdued Arnie returned. His head was shorn. "There's shit going on in that brig that's un-American," he moaned. We encouraged him to discourse but he wouldn't discuss details of his misadventure.

Christmas loomed. The United States Marine Corps has an ingrained tradition that regardless of one's religion or non-religion, it's an anticipated holiday. Regardless of location or stressful duty, Christmas meals are special. We eagerly anticipated the traditional grandiose dinner complete with turkey, pumpkin pie, trimmings and multiple delicacies.

In preparation of the timeless tradition, beer rations were stowed. Jars of strained shaving lotion were hidden. Sickbay alcohol mixed with grapefruit juice was stored. Fruit jars filled with gook gin and bottles of gook beer were concealed for the upcoming event.

On top of those liquid treasures, lively scuttlebutt regarding our squadron's upcoming move to the north kept circulating. There were collective hunches that something monumental featuring VMF 111 was about to happen.

Christmas Day arrived on a Saturday. This time our tent mates got lucky; none of us caught guard or any other kind of duty. Our inept cooks outdid themselves and concocted a feast worthy of four star chefs.

Technicians rigged up a sound system and sentimental holiday melodies wafted over the camp. A scratchy record blaring Bing Crosby's *White Christmas* was the hands down favorite. The memorable song brought tears and memories. Even Californians like me who didn't vision past green and white fringed holy holidays were affected.

On that morning, the six of us gurgled down our breakfast of beer rations. Cruz cracked open a fifth of bourbon gifted from Lieutenant Tollivan. Titmus produced the fruit jar filled with applejack. It was potent and not too palatable until after the second sip. Beset by the Christmas spirit we didn't grumble as we downed our warm-up beverages.

We were hosts to visitors and hospitably passed jugs to our guests who gratefully sampled our assorted libations. They drank, chortled, told tales and staggered off. Our booze was soon depleted. We sauntered to other tents to partake in congenial hospitality. By the end of evening chow we were down to experimenting with grapefruit juice diluted with shaving lotion.

A few late homesick drop-ins had nostalgic stories to tell but most visitors were mellow. Cruz sang a few noel songs in Spanish and didn't do too bad leading us in standard Christmas carols. He did get aggravated when Cassidy interrupted his Spanish rendition of *White Christmas* to bellow a chorus of the *Raggedy-Assed Marines*.

At midnight, holiday spirit still prevailed, all were in a jovial mood. "Merry Christmas, Fuck-ups!" shouted Titmus.

"To the fucked-up Airedales!" toasted Cassidy and gulped his last grapefruit laced lotion before falling flat on his face.

We scrutinized his prone body. "Son-of-a-bitch can't drink," accused O'Bannion before he slumped to the deck. Titmus suddenly noticed Arnie mournfully sipping. "Let's check on Lancaster to make sure he's having a nice, I mean appropriate holiday!"

"Good Christmas idea," said Arnie. He and I leaned on each other as we staggered behind Cruz and Titmus. We tried keeping pace with them as they staggered along the dark road winding through camp. Raucous singing emanated from tents and shouts of a drunken skirmish erupted from another.

Lancaster's hut was shrouded in silence. We warily peeked in, a dull bulb faintly lit the interior. Titmus pushed through the opening.

Broken glass, empty cans, spilled liquid and trash littered the deck. Two of four bunks were occupied. Sergeant Goodwinch snored in one and Lancaster, mouth agape, lay dead to the world in the other.

Titmus glowered at the disorder. "Marines, hah!"

"Drunks," slurred Arnie.

"Lancaster could use a drink," I suggested.

"Give him one," said Arnie.

Titmus lifted Lancaster and pulled his slack chin down and spilled a shot of gook gin down his throat. Lancaster gurgled and dribbled.

"Wasted good stuff!" accused Arnie.

"Hmm!" said Titmus. "Help me get this chickenshit outside."

We grabbed his legs and torso and toted the inert corporal outside. Despite trying not to bang his head against the stanchions, Lancaster's body did get bumped and twisted. We dragged him a few yards until we came upon a half empty garbage receptacle.

Titmus supervised as we placed him inside atop the trash. He was too elongated and relaxed to settle, but after a few strenuous pushes we crammed him ass first into the can. His head and feet stuck upright rendering him into a uncomfortable position. His expression remained serene as we warbled Merry Christmas and staggered away.

When we arrived at our own abode, we had a final goodnight belt and hit the sack. My last recall was Titmus, glass in hand, glaring at the bulkhead.

Later the next morning, there was still a lack of activity. Most of us slept in. Brass and stripes were too hung over to hassle those in the lower echelon.

Flights were cancelled, there was no work, no nothing and no movement of any kind. Those who had to contend with mess or guard duty did half-assed jobs. Much moaning, groaning and abstinence swearing prevailed. If the enemy had been in a position to take advantage of our general disposition, we'd have been in trouble.

Lancaster's feeble but anguished shouts brought Sergeants Goodwinch and Hertz to the rescue. It wasn't easy, they were hung over too, but with awkward effort they extricated him from the garbage barrel. The pathetic bastard couldn't recall how he had become stuck. He lamented that he couldn't remember a worse awakening.

He was advised by Doctor Baker to stay in bed for two days. However, he was too bruised and hurting to enjoy the gifted rest period anonymously bestowed upon him.

CHAPTER TWENTY-EIGHT

Besides being religious, Cruz was a moral guy. Too often those dictums don't gel together. After succumbing to Luina's feminine charms and propagating with her he was distressed. Getting laid with a girl he wasn't intending to spend the rest of his life with beset him with guilt. He didn't broadcast conscience smitten regrets but it was obvious that he was ridden with remorse.

Of course, he cared for Luina but couldn't envision settling down in Samoa. "I'm a Cholo, I can't live here," he sighed. "And Luina sure as hell wouldn't be at ease in Boyle Heights."

Rampant scuttlebutt about VMF 111 moving out kept spreading like the proverbial wildfire. Additional cartridge clips were issued. Lieutenants and sergeants inspected weapons and gear. "Maybe we're gonna be transferred to a rifle company," mused O'Bannion.

"Not a chance," sighed Titmus. "You've been candy-assed Airdales too long, you couldn't hack being a grunt."

"All Marines are basically riflemen," added Cassidy.

"Sure they are!" chortled Titmus.

"Well, we're supposed to be," I said, somewhat piqued.

"I've said it before, you people are half-assed Marines," muttered Titmus.

His debased description depressed us and we looked it.

"Hey, boys, that's still better than being a doggie or swabbie," consoled Titmus.

Throughout camp, speculation regarding our forthcoming future was bandied back and forth. Depending on whether a guy was a short timer, shaky individual, blowhard, *gung ho* type or draftee, different degrees of anticipation and misgivings ran rampant.

I swore Tulipa to secrecy. Anyway, I was certain that it was unlikely that the Japs had a spies lurking in Pago Pago or Apia. I brashly confided to her about our impending departure.

"When you go?" she purred.

"Any day."

"You will miss Tulipa?"

"You can bet your shark tooth beads I will."

"You never say about it."

I reddened. "I'm not good with words."

"I going to have baby," she sighed.

"What!"

"We do what we do, that happens,"

"Mine!"

She glared, "Who, if not yours!"

"Jesus, I didn't mean someone else's."

"Then what you mean!"

"I mean I'm sorry about the way it sounded."

"I not sorry."

"You're too young to be a mother."

"Tonight you come to *Moetotolo.*

"I'll try." I strode off feeling more than somewhat worried, maybe a touch cocky too.

As I walked into camp, Titmus stepped out heading for the shower. His towel was wrapped around his waist.

"Earl, we got to talk."

"Can't it wait?"

"Tulipa is knocked up."

"Who?"

"The gook I been shacking with."

"So?"

"I got a kid coming."

"You done it?"

"Guilty!"

"You sure?"

"She was a virgin! That's what she told me."

"Virgin!"

"What do I do now?"

"Jesus! Give me time to think, will you? Jesus!" I stepped aside as he moved into the shower. I went back and flaked out on my cot to mull the enigma over. I felt a little smug, but at the same time, mostly uneasy.

When the chowtime bugle sounded, I headed to the mess hall. The plight didn't exactly diminish my appetite but I didn't feel too placid either.

Shortly after chow I took off for the village. It was dark by the time I reached its rim so I hid in a palm grove. As the temperature dropped I became agitated. *Moetotolo* that produced a baby wasn't that much of a rarity but could become precarious when a *Malini* was responsible.

After the half-breed child was conceived, the mother would more than likely be exonerated and warmly forgiven. If the transgressor was a native, the guilty stud could be mocked and laughed at. But if the transgressor was Marine, a nerve-wracking state of affairs could evolve. The white stud could end up being beaten, stoned or both.

I had heard tales, but who really knew or could anticipate what they'd do to a *Malini?* As I crept toward the *fale,* I felt more comfortable being clothed. Uh, oh, Tulipa was waiting. As I knelt beside her, I felt a stir and began unbuttoning. "No!" she whispered. "Be ready to run!"

I got to my feet and anxiously looked around.

"Not yet," she giggled and pulled me down. I felt unsettled as I kneeled. She nestled close, causing my subdued arousal to get a second wind. I had questions but my mouth remained closed. However, my eyes and ears were alert, not a conducive approach to love making.

"Go now!" she urgently whispered as she bade, "*Tofa!*" I didn't hesitate trotting into the blackness until she screamed, "*Moetotolo!, Moetotolo!*" Then I really took off. "*Moetotolo! Moetotolo!*" rent the air. Natives emerged from *fales* shouting *Moetotolo! Moetotolo!* I wouldn't swear to it but I think they were waiting for the shout.

The uproarious bedlam blended gleeful and irate shouts. Both whoops were sprinkled with raucous laughter. Nevertheless, as villagers grasped I panicked. More women than men clutched at me. I eluded them and sprinted faster than I believed possible.

An older lady charged from the shadows latching wrinkled arms around one of my legs. As I kicked her loose she screamed bloody murder, but managed to tear off a piece of trouser with her teeth. Scared shitless, I tore through the village and huffed and puffed down the dark road until I reached our Quonset hut. Before barging in I puked.

Titmus, O'Bannion, Arnie, Cruz and Cassidy stared agape as I flopped on my cot. I palpitated heavily and sucked in air. "Holy shit," I wheezed.

My venturesome days and nights in Vailiima had been unromantically culminated. That last physical contact with Tulipa had been a harrowing happening and I felt lucky to have emerged unscathed. Of course, I was aware that when her pregnancy became obvious she needed an acceptable alibi and I was it. I couldn't fault her for that.

But she could have prepared me for that last ordeal and given me more time to elude the pursuers. I continued to shiver, imagining several nasty consequences that could have befallen if those frenzied villagers had snared me. I don't think that dusky bunch would have been reluctant to lynch, castrate or both.

Two long nerve-wracking weeks slipped by before VMF 111 was packed and ready to go. Squadron shitbirds stood in a ragged line waiting to board a rusted old Liberty rocking in Pago Pago's lush harbor. The *Princess Anjou* was weighted down to her gunnels with our trucks, jeeps and armaments plus mountains of miscellaneous equipment. Our personal gear was stowed aboard too. Pilots and a handful of mechanics were scheduled to depart at a later date.

We restlessly waited to file aboard. I stood behind Cruz and in front of him was O'Bannion. Two muscular natives wearing *lava lavas* showed up on the dock. The eldest was a weather-beaten guy and the younger about our age. Both looked vaguely familiar.

We eyed them as they beckoned to Cruz. Luckily no noncom or officer noticed Cruz breaking ranks to huddle with them. The three gabbed and gestured before they grinned and shook hands. As First Sergeant Garland strode into view, the older native clasped Cruz in a bear hug "What the hell's going on here?" said Garland.

Cruz leaped back in line. The Samoans withdrew smiling and waving. "*Tofa!*" They shouted. Garland shook his head and kept walking.

"What's going on, Cruz?" I queried.

"Luina's uncle and brother," wistfully sighed Cruz.

"What'd they want?"

"They promised to watch over Luina until I get back."

"They didn't want nothing?" Said O'Bannion.

"Nope!"

"You're never going back," I quipped.

Cruz didn't answer.

"Well, are you?"

"Don't know." Cruz looked down as we followed others up the gangway. Below decks mattresses were piled six high and each of us grabbed one, took a bunk and stowed our rifles and gear. The ship was crammed with Marines and equipment.

By midnight Samoa was astern and out of sight. Under a starless sky dolphins commenced cavorting around our bow. The *Princess Anjou* ploughed through the black sea moving along at less than nine knots. The rusted floating conveyance was in a decrepit state of disrepair. Her crew consisted of Scandinavians. They were damn good seamen and spoke better English than their South American shipmates.

Eight disenchanted American sailors made up the gun crew. Their forty-millimeter on the fantail and twenty millimeter on the boat deck would be far from able to counter a marauding Jap sub. The weapons would be even less effective against enemy aircraft.

Crates of potatoes crammed the forward and after decks. Military vehicles took up most of the space on the midship decks. Most enlisted shitbirds couldn't or wouldn't tolerate the putrid smells in the holds and opted to sleep on the deck.

Every inch of bare deck was occupied with cargo or apprehensive and querulous shitbirds. Camouflaged ponchos, knapsacks and inscribed mattresses were deemed legitimate occupational stakes.

Twice a day sloppy chow was tossed on our trays. Meals featured semi-raw vegetables, lumpy powdered eggs, oily spam and a single burnt piece of toast. Unappealing potatoes were also ladled onto trays twice a day. Several hours elapsed before those at the end of line got to eat.

Conversational topics among passengers featured fuckin' Japs, fuckin' officers, fuckin' non-coms, fuckin' war, fuckin' status of enlisted men, fuckin' Corps and prospects of getting laid plus speculation regarding our destination. The negative musing, haphazard dozing, bitching, bitching and more bitching passed the time.

On the first night out I had an eerie dream featuring Tulipa being accosted by a creepy Jap. On the second night she was being chased by a rock-happy sailor as well as being assaulted by hostile natives. I had visions of frantic battles ending up with me disarming bad guys and being hailed a hero.

Other dreams featured me in front of our own *fale* strumming a ukulele. Tulipa would be engaged in wifely business while our striking son and his lovely sister played nearby. Even though I'm musically inept and tone deaf, those dreams featured an image of me happily singing and strumming.

I was almost determined to keep in touch with my native sweetie and even started to write a letter but suddenly wondered, "Can Tulipa read English?" Damn it! I had neglected to find out.

The *Princess Anjou* slowly pushed her way north. Most every night was squally. There was no comfortable place to keep dry. Throughout the night we stayed miserably wet. Although it was dry in the hold the stink was unbearable and even more dismal.

As the morning sun rose it scorched. There were too many guys on board to get assigned to work details at the same time. We didn't crave busy work but anything would be better than just sitting, waiting and bitching.

Titmus was glum, Arnie was seriously seasick and others became afflicted with the bulkhead stare. We craved distraction to vent our frustrations. We needed to know that we were going somewhere to do something worthwhile. For god sakes, we were Marines. Ahh, war is hell.

Cassidy snooped around seeking something to steal whether it was needed or not. Out of boredom Cruz went along. The two of them eyed the four armed guard personnel sprawled around the twenty-millimeter. The husky blonde-bearded bos'n glared at them and snapped, "What in hell you bellhops looking at?"

"Only belle I ever hopped was your sister," cracked Cassidy. Blonde-beard leaped from his post and fired an overhand right catching Cassidy above his left eye. Cassidy flailed back and Cruz joined him. Two swabbies joined the fray.

The Lieutenant J.G. in charge happened upon the fracas. He was a jutting jawed guy. "Attention!" His authoritive roar stopped the squabble before harm could be done. Cruz snapped to, but Cassidy threw a roundhouse left just missing the bos'n.

The J.G. ordered everyone except the perpetrators and gun crew to make themselves scarce. Captain Plunkett, Lieutenant Rameron and Sergeant Byron arrived.

"Clear the boat deck!" said Captain Plunkett.

"Clear the boat deck!" echoed Lieutenant Rameron.

"Get your asses the hell off this deck!" roared Sergeant Byron.

"Off the boat deck!" mimicked Corporal Lancaster.

"You too, Lancaster, move it!" said Byron.

In seconds the boat deck was clear of sight seeing enlistees. Cassidy, Cruz, the four gun crew sailors, Byron, and the officers remained.

On the lower deck we waited for what seemed like a helluva long time. Cruz and Cassidy finally climbed down the ladder. "Holy *Madre de Maria*, there were bad things said, especially to Cassidy," disclosed Cruz.

"In front of them damn swabbies Captain Plunkett announced that we were a disgrace to the Corps." Cassidy was simmering.

"Made us apologize," said Cruz. "And it was them that started it!"

"That blonde swabbie J.G. got a kick out of us being humiliated," spat Cassidy.

"The old Corps is shot to hell," muttered Arnie and looked at Titmus for approval.

"Hey, fuck-ups, no brig time, no shit detail and being buck-assed privates you can't get busted. So forget it!" said Titmus.

While we hovered about, O'Bannion grunted, "The honor of the Corps has been trifled with."

CHAPTER TWENTY-NINE

Bickering ceased as the doldrums took over. We became a shipload of sleepwalkers. Not Titmus, he kept busy stashing secretive odds and ends.

"The old guy's flipped his lid," noted O'Bannion and I grimly agreed.

On the morning of February 2nd, an edgy voice came over the loudspeaker. "Now hear this! The destination of this vessel is the Japanese occupied Island of Roi-Namur. Roi-Namur consists of two small connecting islands joined by a coral walk-away. They are a part of the Kwajalein Atoll and are included in the formation of the Marshall Islands.

Elements of the Fourth Marine Division have landed and are engaging Jap defenders as I speak. This vessel's ETA will be three days from now at 0800. That's this coming Saturday. Have your weapons and gear ready and be prepared to disembark. Good luck, Marines!"

Disinterest and depression immediately disintegrated. We quickly became a ship full of speculating warriors spouting blustery bullshit.

"The candy-assed Marines are finally gonna see action!" announced O'Bannion. "We're going to war."

"Think they'll actually send us in to fight?"

"You're kidding? We're Airdales, we'd only get in the way."

"For Christ's sake! Every Marine is basically a rifleman."

"Shit, I ain't fired mine since boot camp."

"You forget how?"

"Nah, you're just chickenshit!"

"Fuck you!"

"My rifle ain't been sighted in for months."

"Use your bayonet, asshole."

"They won't use us Airedales until everyone else is dead."

"Of course not, we're technicians."

"We dig shitholes."

"I'm not talkin' about us per se. What about our mechanics and ordinance people?"

"Stop whining. You enlisted to fight fuckin' Japs, didn't you?"

"You bet! And I'm finally gonna get a crack at them."

"Your heart'd stop if you saw one."

"You callin' me yellow?"

"Nah, just chickenshit."

"Well, fuck you!"

"Fuck you!"

"I gotta get me a souvenir, something to show my kids."

"You ain't got kids."

"Fuck you too!"

"Me?"

"You!"

"You'll get your souvenir, a pretty hunk of lead in your ass."

Dialogue exchanges kept going non-stop, some bitter, some funny, some crazy. Some babbled more than others.

In our circle O'Bannion, Arnie, and I uttered the most nonsense. I admit that I kept spouting dumb things to calm my nerves.

Titmus kept contemplations to himself. In a way he seemed indifferent. The only thing he offered regarding our prospective engagement with the enemy was a shrug as he repeated, "They tell you to go, you go, that's it."

As darkness fell we congregated around Titmus' potato crate. "You really think we'll see some action?" droned Arnie for the fifteenth time.

"We got other things to think about," said Titmus and pointed at the shadowy gun tub on the boat deck.

"Huh?" whispered Arnie.

"Revenge! When it gets darker we'll wake up those smart-ass swabbies."

Titmus pulled out a coiled length of wire stashed between potato crates but didn't explain. "Got to get more wire." He gave stern orders. Arnie was dispatched to steal two life jackets. Cassidy's assignment was to bring back more wire; Cruz was sent to swipe a pair of pants; O'Bannion's responsibility was to collect a helmet or helmet liner. Me, I was told to snatch a flashlight.

"What's all this shit for?" said Arnie.

"Move out!" snapped Titmus and we scattered.

I climbed down the hot, stuffy hold. Only a few depressed characters were flaked out. I nonchalantly meandered through the narrow aisles while eyeing gear hanging from cots. I couldn't sight a flashlight.

Lots of life jackets and helmets were dangling from bunks and it would have been easy to walk away with two, three or more. Swiping a jacket and pants seemed to be a minor problem compared to purloining a flashlight.

Arnie and O'Bannion got off easy, I thought and was about to quit and go topside when I spotted a snub-nosed black flashlight in the hands of a coughing Marine.

The pallid grunt sat on an upper bunk staring at the bulkhead. He seemingly was in a semi-trance. I noted his thousand-yard stare and contemplated easing the flashlight out of his hand. Perhaps my scrutinizing penetrated his stupor because he suddenly set down the flashlight and snapped, "Looking for somethin' to steal, Mate!"

"I'm trying to find someone," I stuttered.

"He ain't here!"

"Guy's name is Arnie, he's from my home town."

"Bullshit!"

"Hey, I told you I'm looking for him."

"Ain't nobody by that name here so keep moving!"

"Fuck you!" I spat and was ready to finish whatever the asshole wanted to start.

"Get your fuckin' hands off my lifejacket!" sounded a steamed voice from the other side of the hold.

"This fuckin' lifejacket is mine and been mine for a fuckin' long time!"

"The hell you say!"

Scuffling and a few fuck you and fuck you back followed. Two flaked out sweating Marines left their bunks and pushed toward the action. "Coming Dennis!" yelled the flashlight owner and leaped from his perch and stumbled toward the commotion leaving his flashlight. I swooped it up from his blanket and stumbled up the ladder.

O'Bannion was standing by with a purloined helmet and though he didn't remark, I could tell he was impressed by my acquisition. Cruz arrived with a beat-up pair of pants rolled up under his jacket. Cassidy pushed in with a coil of wire. Arnie was the only one unaccounted for. I didn't mention the verbal exchange I had heard because Titmus might have asked why I hadn't stood by and assisted him.

Arnie showed up dragging a single jacket and looking bedraggled. About that time a dark cloud half covered the moon. When the cloud moved away we spotted his bruised cheek.

"Trouble," he muttered, "but I took care of it."

Titmus nodded approval and said, "One will do." He then directed us to stuff the jacket and pants with rotten potatoes and lash them together. We created a dummy and secured the helmet on its makeshift head. Slats pried from crates supported our facsimile of a man. We approvingly viewed our creation. From ten feet away, obscured by darkness, the dummy easily passed for a human being.

"Not bad," crowed Titmus.

"What's next?" queried O'Bannion.

"The touchy part," he whispered as he tied one end of the coiled wire to the dummy. Cassidy, Cruz, and Arnie dangled our make believe man over the rail. Titmus, O'Bannion and I unobtrusively moved under the gun tub. As we progressed we uncoiled wire. A cluster of Marines watched but none questioned.

It wasn't hard to figure something dramatic was about to happen. What was going down was against regulations but that wasn't anything to get upset about. As we manipulated under the gun tub, sweat poured and I was certain that we were about to get caught. I again regretted being involved in one of Titmus' asinine escapades. Would I ever learn?

Titmus waved two fingers and gestured for O'Bannion to alert Cassidy. Then he paused another moment before tugging at the line and swinging his own end over the side. Those at the other end pitched our dummy over the side where it slapped against the hull. "Light him up!" spat Titmus. I directed the flashlight beam on the fake figure four feet dangling above the lapping sea.

"Japs on the starboard side!" roared Titmus.

"Where! Where!" All hell broke loose as the forties opened up followed by twenties and the three-incher on the fantail. I dropped the flashlight into the sea.

Shouts, commands, screams of bedlam resounded. "Japs!"

"Stations!"

"Where the hell are they!"

"Over here!"

"No! Over there!"

"Periscope abaft!"

"They're comin'!"

"Holy shit!"

"Mother-of-God!"

We retreated back to our places amid the potato crates. Titmus lounged and grinned and seemed unperturbed. The bedlam soon subsided but we were too shaky to laugh. The suspicious bos'n fingered the wire attached to the handrail, but most of the tattered dummy had dropped into the sea.

Sailors swore they had seen Japanese frogmen trying to climb aboard. "They came from a submarine!" claimed one hysterical witness.

Rampant speculation and bullshit continued to be bandied back and forth. Vigil was increased, especially at night.

Two more days went by before swabbies and Marines ceased pointing and calling each other idiots, assholes, stupid bastards and much less flattering names.

The swabbies in the gun tub were constantly beset by questions. "What'd they look like?"

"Did you see Japs?"

Those bastards in the gun tub, much to our chagrin, began acting like heroes, especially the blonde-bearded guy. Ridiculous renditions regarding reasons for firing were bandied about. Eventually most bullshit was discounted. I, for one, was relieved. Court-martials for that shenanigan would have been severe and repercussions nasty.

CHAPTER THIRTY

As Roi-Namur hove into sight, the relevancy of the dummy episode faded. We viewed the flat unattractive rocks from the slow moving *Princess Anjou*. As she dropped anchor a hundred yards from the shore an audible sigh of relief sounded. Nobody regretted the ending of thirty miserable days aboard the bucket of rust.

The loudspeaker blared, "Now hear this! Yesterday at 1400 the twin islands of Roi-Namur were secured. Elements of the 4th Marines raised the stars and stripes on both. Gentlemen, the islands are ours."

The authoritive voice went on to inform us that not a tree was left standing on Roi and only a few shell-shredded coconut trees remained on Namur. A narrow coral road rising several feet above the sea connected the two rocks. As Marines raced across both islands, they devastated the defenders. Before both rocks had been secured, over one-hundred and ninety Marines had been killed. After four combat days the Stars and Stripes were raised.

Roi measured about 1,250 yards north and south and 1,200 yards east and west and Namur was even smaller. "Less than the combined length of several dozen football fields," speculated Titmus.

Those area limitations didn't dampen the anticipation of troops eager to set foot on stationary ground. LCMs piloted by cocky sailors banged alongside the *Anjou's* rusty side. Arnie dug his elbow into my ribs and pointed at Taps pensively observing me with jaundiced eyes.

"Your dog is waiting!" said Arnie.

"Bullshit!"

"You brought him aboard!"

"I hereby disown him," I snapped.

Blonde-beard and a short swabbie walked by. "Hey, that's your mascot, ain't it?" said Shorty.

"Nope!"

"Ugly creature," mumbled blonde-beard.

"Any mascot in a pinch," said the little guy and reached for Taps.

"Hands off," I snarled. The startled swabbie backed off. I grabbed Taps, secured a line around his flea-bitten body and lowered his skeletal form into the rocking barge below. Hand-over-hand, Arnie and I climbed down the net and stood on either side of Taps.

We were adorned like warriors as we ferried toward Roi. For some undecipherable reason the order to fix bayonets was sounded. We were well aware that action against the entrenched Japs had abated but commands had to be obeyed. Bristling with weapons, we drew closer, seeing shell-stripped trees, battered ramparts and blackened fortifications.

Twenty yards from shore our LCMs hove to and ramps were lowered. "Everybody out!" a cox'n shouted and we jumped into three feet of swirling water. Rifles were held at high port as we splashed ashore.

As we stepped from the surf to the beach, the acrid stench of rotting bodies hit us. Not all the Jap dead had been buried. Decomposing enemy bodies were still scattered about. The smell was nauseous and several of us didn't react well.

Weathered line company onlookers didn't conceal their contempt by shouts of, "The Airedales are here!"

"We're saved!"

"Noncombatant sons-of-bitches!"

"My god, they're dressed like real Marines!"

"They're Airdales playing Marine, imagine that!"

"Hey, a day late and they're gonna get a campaign ribbon."

A Jap airfield pockmarked by shell holes, bomb craters, and debris stretched across Roi. Seabees were vigorously clearing the mess. We shuffled across the field to set up living quarters. Three neat lines of pup tents were soon situated. Two men were assigned to each shelter. O'Bannion and I bunked together

Flat as a pancake, Roi's white coral rose several feet above the lapping sea. The smell of death emanated from the decaying bodies of unburied Japs. More than a few were still sprawled about. Mean looking glutted rats ran in and out of crevices and jauntily glared at us.

Sluggish green flies slowly swarmed about, lighting on food and bodies, dead or alive. It was a necessary but disgusting exercise killing them. If a green fly landed on a K ration cheese or chocolate, appetite faded, well, almost. We were too hungry to discard the tainted morsel.

On the leeward side of Roi-Namur several warships tugged at anchor chains. War ships drafted by one battlewagon were anchored offshore. Twenty or more merchant ships bobbed in the offing. Visible was the impressive *U.S.S. North Carolina* looming above the dwarfed ships surrounding her. Her huge guns pointing forward as she tugged at her anchor. Circling shoreboats moved in and out loading and unloading.

"Two shitty little islands and we're stuck here for the duration," lamented O'Bannion.

"Maybe the Japs will come back just to make you happy," sighed Titmus.

"I hope they do," said O'Bannion.

"Think they might?" queried Cruz.

"They haven't contacted me," chortled Titmus.

"Why in hell would they want this rock?" sneered Cassidy. No answer was forthcoming.

Our new twin island home was not far from the equator, maybe two or more degrees, but our first night ashore was far from warm. In fact, the temperature was comfortably brisk. The cool nights were ideal for sleeping because after dark, sea breezes blew mosquitoes away, but sleep didn't come easily surrounded by the stink of rotting bodies.

Cruz and I shot the shit for awhile. We discussed Luina and Tulipa, but agreed that we could never do what Bones Donical did. From any angle you looked at it, Bones, our buddy, was a fuckin' deserter.

About two in the morning the air raid siren wailed. Pup tents emptied and we nervously stood in the cool air staring up and cursing at the sky. There was nothing to do and no place to go. Thirty minutes later the "All clear" sounded and we shuffled back into our warm bedrolls.

Before daybreak most of us managed to nod off. Hours later we were aroused for a K-Ration breakfast and assigned to various work details.

Cassidy and I got stuck unloading cargo from incoming vessels. Day and night, trucks hauled stuff brought ashore from incoming ships.

Three shitbirds from another outfit joined our work detail. Their sergeant eventually came and led them away for noon chow. Lancaster neglected coming to relieve us.

"The hell with this shit," said Cassidy and stalked off. I joined him.

Raggedy-assed individuals were meandering everywhere. Nobody paid attention to them or us. We approached the remains of a Jap gun emplacement. The huge battered gun had been appropriated by the Japanese after they vanquished the British in Singapore.

Our navy's big guns and bombs from carrier planes had blasted the former Limey coastal weapon into gnarled metal.

We moved on to observe a Seabee manipulating his bulldozer's blade to push piles of Jap stiffs into a wide shallow hole. He covered the hole with a layer of coral. Another weathered Seabee stuck a "Tough Shit" sign atop the mound.

Each of those decaying stiffs had family members and friends waiting, wondering and possibly praying somewhere in Japan.

Blackened pillboxes had been bombed and engulfed by flame-throwers. They still stood empty and useless. Cassidy and I entered one. The stink of roasted rotted flesh permeated the pillbox. "I'm gonna get some souvenirs," wheezed Cassidy

Cassidy stooped and picked up four discarded Japanese coins. I spotted a photo album. "Cheez," I said as I turned pages. Family snapshots of older Japanese, women, children and uniformed relatives proudly posed on page after page. As we browsed we were touched by the similarity to our own family albums.

I followed Cassidy, carrying the album as he headed toward the door. He impulsively kicked a sizable lump of black substance protruding among the debris and the burnt mass fell apart exposing what had once been a Japanese defender. His thorax split apart revealing red colored flesh and spine. The poor bastard had been roasted alive by a flame-thrower. We puked as we staggered out of the pillbox.

"What in hell was that?" sputtered Cassidy but he knew, we both did.

"That guy's body was burnt black and his insides were cooked red. That poor guy" I gasped.

"My God!" he added. Then he tried to followed with a nonchalant, "Just a dead Jap." It didn't work.

Both of us felt horrible as we sullenly headed for camp. We were too late for chow but neither of us was in any mood to eat. I sat outside my tent leafing through the photo album.

The first page featured an elderly woman and her wrinkled husband. On the second, somewhat younger folks solemnly stared at the camera. There were snapshots of young men in army and navy uniforms posed next to little tykes. Only a few little ones smiled. Most solemnly gazed at the camera.

On one page a sweet young girl pouted. On the next another smiled, her winsome expression reflected pride and concern. She looked like the type most guys wished they had waiting for them. Of course, at the time, we weren't longing for Japanese female liaisons.

Snapshots of little girls with straight bangs and little boys decked out in student uniforms stared from other pages. Some seemed to have been laboring to keep from squirming.

There were also shots of a Japanese family gathered at a picnic. None of the photos reflected a sneaky enemy.

There was no way of knowing which photo depicted the owner of the album. Most likely, he was one of the charred soldiers rotting in the pillbox.

I felt deeply relieved that I wasn't responsible for that mess of cooked humanity viewed in the pillbox.

CHAPTER THIRTY-ONE

After two hours of hacking and shoveling, O'Bannion and I agreed we had filled more than enough sandbags so we slipped away. We strode purposely along a narrow coral road figuring our bravado attitudes would keep us from being discovered. We stumbled over a dead Jap sprawled on his back. He lay with outstretched arms. His open eyes stared at the sky.

One of the corpse's legs angled straight out, the other oddly askew, was bent at the knee. He was bloated but the dead Jap must have been a giant. His faded green fatigues were as filthy as ours. The guy's wide shoulders and prominent chest manifested that he had most likely been an Imperial Marine. If it wasn't for his puffed-up Oriental face he could have passed for one of us.

"Why didn't somebody bury the poor bastard?" snapped O'Bannion.

"They haven't got to this one yet."

As O'Bannion moved in and bent to get a closer look, a swarm of buzzing flies lifted from the deceased's face to hover a second before descending. They covered most of the dead Jap's face. I imagined that his relatives looked like those in the album and were probably wondering about him.

"Don't think he's got something we can sell to a swabby, his pockets have already been turned out." O'Bannion looked disappointed.

"What would you do if you came face to face with one of these guys?" I said.

"Kick his ass like this!" O'Bannion stepped forward and thrust his foot into the dead guy's ribs. The insect swarm rose and buzzed as the Jap's outstretched leg jerked backward. The corpse sat up and his outstretched arms swung across his chest startling us. O'Bannion crossed himself and called on Jesus to save him.

The stiffened body poised less than a second before toppling back. As we scurried away insects again swarmed over the dead man's face.

"Sneaky son-of-a-bitch!" snarled O'Bannion.

"Boy, did you scoot!" I smirked as if I wasn't just as scared.

"You sure as hell didn't look so fucking brave either!"

Our conversation would have gotten heated if an ensign hadn't hailed us. The officer was in his early twenties and looked like he had never shaved. "Got a Jap rifle you want to sell?"

"Jap rifle?" said O'Bannion.

"If not, a Garand or carbine will do."

"Don't you think we need our weapon? We ain't stationed on a ship, you know."

"I know that. There must be a few not being used and I figured you Gyrenes could use a few extra bucks."

"You want to shoot someone on your ship?" said O'Bannion.

"I'm a hunter and I want an exotic weapon to take home."

"A rifle is a Marine's best friend," I spurted realizing too late how corny I sounded.

"How much will you pay for an M1?" said O'Bannion.

"If it's in fair shape I'll give you fifty."

"Nobody would give up his rifle for that measly amount!" I said.

"One-hundred!" said O'Bannion.

"That's steep!"

"Take it or leave it!" Bluffed O'Bannion.

"Okay," said the ensign.

O'Bannion told the guy to wait and we hurried back to our pup tent to retrieve O'Bannion's rifle.

"You crazy? A Marine can't sell his rifle." I said.

"Be nice to have a few bucks," he said.

"You're nuts!"

"I'll borrow one."

"You're gonna steal some poor bastard's rifle?"

"Not exactly," he said.

"You're a poor fuckin' excuse for a Marine! You're on your own!" As I stalked out I said, "touch my rifle, I'll kill you."

Twenty minutes later I returned to find O'Bannion disconsolately sitting on his cot. "Change your mind?" I queried.

"Yeah."

"Did you go back and tell the ensign"

"Nah."

"That poor guy is probably still waiting."

"Fuck him!" said O'Bannion ending our conversation.

When the tide was low, LSTs rammed their bows onto the beach and Marines became stevedores loading or unloading burdened vessels. As soon as one was emptied another would move in. Work parties never ceased.

Loading, unloading, and carting off equipment to be dispensed among several outfits went on day and night. Bombs for aircraft scheduled to land as soon as the field was in shape, conventional ammunition, crates of rations, construction equipment, and varied wartime crap were stacked along the runway waiting to be dispersed.

A Seabee battalion was deployed to get Roi-Namur's newly conquered airfield squared away. Those weathered old construction workers paid little or no heed to rules. Most were too old to get drafted but they knew how to work. Their officers, former construction bosses, were even more scornful of military decorum. Despite advanced years exempting them from military service they had volunteered to serve. Most had been either retired or had left civilian construction jobs to serve the country. The Seabee motto was "Can Do" and the slogan was well-chosen

After wading ashore, their traditional self-chosen chore was to construct a still. Fermenting assorted juice collections followed. Then they proceeded to build whatever the hell else was needed.

Ground Defense's ten hour labor stints were no picnic when two or three flat bottomed vessels awaited their turn to unload.

Thievery was precarious, but few of my sidekicks could or would resist stealing. Anything from gear to canned fruit was purloined to be traded, consumed or sold.

At 0400 on February 22, George Washington's Birthday, Lancaster harshly rousted O'Bannion and me. Others were also awakened. "You Ground Defense warriors are gonna have the distinguished job of unloading an LST," he gloated.

"That's all we've been doing," said O'Bannion.

"It's a patriotic holiday," I moaned.

"Washington's Birthday, for God's sake!" groaned O'Bannion.

"Gentlemen! Listen up, we're at war." Lancaster's sarcasm was interrupted by a screaming siren. "Another damn drill!" he snapped and sauntered off.

"Shit!" said O'Bannion and I echoed his sentiment. We pulled on our boondockers and slowly dropped into our hole. "Can't these goddamn phony drills cease for awhile?"

"You'd rather be longshoring under Lancaster's evil eye?" I goaded.

Pup tents emptied as bitching, cursing and whining commenced. "Bullshit drills!" spouted Arnie.

Most irate risers, not called for work party duty, didn't bother putting on boondockers. A few didn't even bother getting up. Very few toted rifles into the shallow foxholes. We had endured more than a few practice alerts since settling in on Roi-Namur. The holes were shallow because if dug deeply water would seep in.

Huge searchlights ensconced on each of the four-corners of Roi and probed the sky. Their narrow beams crossed as handlers swung their huge lights to and fro. The probing beams outlined the island.

If Japs were up there searching for targets, our own defenders were making it easy for them.

The unsteady rumbles of Japanese engines roared. Unlike the hums of American engines those above were unsynchronized. O'Bannion's breathing amplified.

From a foxhole Titmus shouted, "Japs!"

We hugged the ground as the huge cannons situated on each corner of the island, opened up. They were joined by a hodgepodge of smaller weapons. Ack-ack bursts were obliterated by down-coming whishings. "Incoming!" someone shouted.

As descending "choo-choo-choo" noises amplified, I clawed the coral bottom of our foxhole. "This is it!" I cried.

There wasn't time to think, pray, change position or be petrified. A blinding light followed by a thundering explosion hit as the first bomb quivered the island. O'Bannion and I were propelled upward and plopped down with a thud. I doubled up as if I'd been punched in the gut. We lay gasping while hot shrapnel fell about us. I grasped the top of my helmet and howled as metal scorched my hands. Flames lit the airfield while I tumbled back into our shallow hole. Explosions continued rumbling as I clawed into the coral trying to dig deeper. O'Bannion was doing the same.

Dropped bombs ignited stacked missiles and munitions piled along the airfield. One after another, strings of exploding detonations rocked the island. Hot metal and coral chunks rained upon us. Flames raced across the airfield.

"Head for the beach!" shouted a high pitched voice. Unsynchronized engine noises faded as the enemy aircraft zoomed away.

Our pup tents and weapons had been disintegrated. All of our personal possessions had been dissolved. As enlistees scurried in all directions to find places to hide, officers were conspicuously absent. Maybe they were dead. If anyone in charge was alive and knew what the fuck was going on he wasn't in our area.

Another string of bombs exploded along the offshore reef. O'Bannion sped away disappearing into the frantic mob heading for the shoreline. In the midst of the panicked crowd I galloped along gasping for breath. Their second round of bombs missed the island and exploded in the sea.

Big gun crews kept firing into the sky. Panicked troops, including me, helter skittered in all directions. Imaginations ran amuck, none of us knew where to go or what was going on.

Like others, I felt like a sitting duck and craved a weapon, anything to fire back. When I spotted a large sandbagged structure I sprinted for the opening. The mouth of a twenty-millimeter barrel swiveled into my chest. "Don't come in here, Mate!"

"What the fuck!"

"This is a gun emplacement."

"You think I'm a Jap!"

"Get the fuck out of here!"

I spat and moved away as a hysterical voice shouted, "They're making another bomb run!"

"Japs have landed!" shrilled a voice.

"We're gonna get slaughtered!"

"Where in fuck's a rifle!"

"Where the hell are the fuckin' officers?

"They been evacuated!"

"Hell, no, they're hiding!"

Fires raged along the airfield, clumps of stacked munitions ignited and a nerve wracking series of intense detonations shook the island. The crackling of small arm explosives and thundering blasts of ignited bombs caused stooping people to aimlessly dart about. Disorder reigned unabated.

Clouds that had obscured the moon slowly slipped by, illuminating bent human forms knee deep in the placid sea. They appeared to be crouched Japs moving toward the shore. Their shadowed forms were eerily visible.

"The fuckers are comin'!" someone shouted. Others took up the cry.

I was regretting like others that I had stupidly left my weapon to melt with my tent. What a dumb un-Marine thing to do! I cursed myself and wasn't the only dope feeling helplessly unarmed.

We were sure the enemy was landing and without weapons we couldn't fight back. If I was going to die, I sure as hell wanted to take one or more of the enemy with me.

Very few scurrying Marines possessed a rifle. Those few belly-flopped aiming their Garands toward the sea. I plopped alongside one pointing his at the incoming silhouettes. If he died his rifle was mine.

Titmus loomed. "Those are our people! For God sakes what the hell's the matter with you people!"

"Whut in hell are they doing out there!"

"Being stupid like you assholes!"

"They look like Japs."

"The jerks ran out there to get away from the bombs. They're our people, dumb ones, but on our side!"

"Lucky you didn't shoot," I said to the guy with the rifle.

"I couldn't shoot, got no cartridges," he confided.

The stooped shadows splashed ashore and took off in different directions. If Titmus hadn't come on the scene some of our own would have been shot. I tried to tag after him but he disappeared. Mobs of disoriented Marines ran by. I didn't know what else to do so I fell in with a group.

All of a sudden my bowels reacted and I dropped my pants to dump in the nick of time. Then I continued running and before long dropped my pants again. It would have been a humiliating function if others hadn't been doing the same. The archaic platitude, "So scared he shit!" came to mind.

Marines flopped on the beach and commenced digging shallow holes. I fell to my knees and scooped coral. My hole was inches deep before I remembered to shovel with my helmet. I vigorously dug and threw coral. My shallow hole quickly got deep enough for sea water to seep in. As the sky became lighter we realized the enemy planes were gone. We weren't being invaded.

I ceased digging and peered about. Guys were on their knees beseeching Jesus to look after them. Flames kept racing along the runway while bombs and smaller ammunition continued to detonate.

Lieutenant Rameron looking bewildered staggered into view. "Lieutenant!" I shouted. He didn't hear but saw me.

"Where the hell is everybody?"

"Don't know, sir. Haven't seen anybody but Titmus, but he disappeared."

"Can't hear, eardrums gone!" He looked like he was going to cry. Rameron moved away and I rose to follow. I needed someone to lead and he was better than nobody but he disappeared. Again I was bewildered among lost strangers.

CHAPTER THIRTY-TWO

As dawn broke, a disoriented mob aimlessly plodded about. More than a few were dazed, some more than others. Seabees were billeted closest to the airfield so their battalion suffered the brunt of the hit and casualties were numerous. Several from our squadron, more than a few laboring enlistees from the 22nd and those toiling on either field or LSTs were among the torn up. Scuttlebutt spread that dead or wounded on Roi-Namur numbered 1,500. The more seriously wounded were transported to the hospital ship.

That 1,500 number, if authentic, meant that next to Hawaii, bombs dropped by aircraft emblazed with the Rising Sun caused the second largest number of casualties in the South Pacific Theater. Twice as many dead and wounded were counted after the infamous Pearl Harbor attack.

My blistered hand hurt so I shuffled into the huge tent that had been converted into a field hospital.

Blood and exposed wounds were everywhere. Bleeding and groaning people, sprawled on cots and ground, were tended by harassed doctors and corpsmen. Rameron barged in and put his hand on a corpsman's shoulder. "My ears are gone!"

"I'm busy, sir," said the corpsman.

"Can't hear!" Yelled Rameron.

"Then you won't hear this. Go fuck yourself!

"What!"

"We got wounded to attend to!" said the corpsman and moved away. As Rameron grabbed his arm the sailor might have flattened him, but our squadron's corpsman, Benny, stepped between them. "Sir!"

"My eardrums are broken," whined Rameron. Benny looked into his ear and shrugged.

"What about you, Sherman?"

"Can't hear too good but I'm okay."

"Lemme look at that hand."

With all the groaning and blood in that giant hospital tent my laceration seemed insignificant. I felt guilty diverting attention. "I'm okay," I sighed and stepped outside.

The morning progressed as I poked along hoping to find someone I knew. As luck would have it, I spied Ferguson waving a huge revolver. The gun had been his grandfather's. "Ferguson!" I shouted. He swung around and waved his giant weapon.

"Watch out, idiot, I'm not a Jap!"

His eyes were glazed. "Huh?"

"You okay, Ferguson?"

"Japs!"

"What?"

"They been following me, two of them!"

"Ain't no live Japs left on the island."

"I seen them." He pointed. "There they are! Those two in black! Don't let them sneaky bastards fool you." Ferguson cocked his pistol and took off. He galloped over the dunes firing and shouting, "Fuck with Marines, ahhh!"

Cassidy staggered alongside. "See Ferguson?" I said.

"That him shooting?"

"Poor bastard," I mumbled.

"Poor bastard, my ass, he's pushing to get a section eight."

"If it's an act, it's a damn good job."

"Saw the shitbird perform before."

271

I wasn't in the mood to discourse. We meandered back to our destroyed campsite. Tents were blackened into ash piles. Spiraled smoke wafted from sizzling belongings and smoldering rifle barrels.

Small groups of former occupants clustered amid the smoking mess. More bewildered people kept drifting in. We were still too baffled to act. There was nothing we could do but wait. We needed an authorative figure to command, any order would do.

Major Burke appeared trailed by several pilots to view what was left of our headquarters tent. While they conferred, forlorn enlistees kicked through smoking ash piles.

"A hot shrapnel hunk the size of a half dollar burnt a hole in Arnie's left bicep." Announced Titmus.

"Bad?" said Cruz.

"Million dollar wound," said O'Bannion.

"It'll get him a purple heart," said Cassidy.

"Where's he at?"

"At the field hospital being tended to by a gorgeous nurse with a mustache."

Lancaster, helped by Goodwinch limped up, a dirty rag was wrapped around his left foot.

"Stepped on a broken beer bottle," said Goodwinch.

"Lousy luck," moaned Lancaster.

Gunnery Sergeant Byron climbed on the hood of a battered jeep. "Gather around!" he yelled. We surrounded him. Orders, any kind, would be a welcome diversion.

"Tents and personal gear are gone. Nothing we can do about it, understand? Supplies will come in shortly and so will orders. In the meantime we're up shit creek without a paddle."

"What about rifles?"

"We don't need them. No Jap can get through the fleet. Our navy got these islands surrounded. Anyway, we got more important things to worry about."

"There's Japs out there!" someone shouted.

"They'll be coming back!"

"Bullshit, ain't no live Japs anywhere near here except for a couple of prisoners. And those few are probably Korean laborers."

"You sure?"

"Those lucky slant-eyed bastards hit our ammo dump with a couple of wild-assed drops and that's it. Ain't nobody out there but the U.S. Navy."

We weren't convinced.

"We got nothing to defend ourselves with," someone whined.

"You listening, asshole, ain't no Japs around!"

An airplane engine roared overhead.

"They're back!" screamed someone. We looked up and began to disperse. "Avast! It's one of ours!" roared Byron. The silent crowd hesitated. "Listen, Idiots, those engines you hear are synchronized!"

"Ours!" said Titmus.

"VMF 111 is moving to Namur. Get yourselves over there and find a place to sleep. We'll muster tomorrow morning. They are feeding on Roi. Find out where and eat something to tide you over. You're on your own until tomorrow. Find out where we assemble and be there promptly at 0600 or your ass is mud. Dismissed!"

Munitions on the field continued detonating as we tensely crossed the narrow white connecting road. Namur was about the same size as Roi but its trees had been deprived of foliage and height shortened by the pre-landing barrages. O'Bannion, Cruz and I found a partially destroyed pill box surrounded by burnt palm tree stumps. We dug, cleaned and rolled a few rotting logs over the top.

Titmus meandered over. "Get those logs off that hole," he said. "If a bomb drops nearby, the logs will crush your tender bodies."

We groaned but proceeded to lift and roll the logs away. We didn't bother topping our foxhole. Arnie drifted in wearing a dirty bandage over his lacerated left arm. "Shrapnel."

"That could get you a purple heart," said O'Bannion.

"It's infected," whined Arnie.

We were too filthy and hungry to envy or sympathize. Goodwinch showed up to bark that rations were available. We meandered over to the blockhouse and retrieved the boxed handouts. The biscuits were stale and tasteless, but we were starving refugees and gulped the unappealing rations along with the faded orange cheese clumps.

Afterwards, we waited in a long line for a blue issue navy-work shirt, mess gear, C Rations and a new canteen.

"They expect me to wear this navy shit?" snarled O'Bannion.

"It's something to cover your shivering body!" Advised Titmus.

We shuffled back to our new hole and slithered in. Although the sun still shone we conked out and slept like dead men.

As dawn broke the chilled wind roused us and we dazedly peered about. Titmus and Cassidy were nowhere around. "We're one or two degrees from the equator," said Cruz. "How come it's so damn cold?"

None of us answered because none of us knew.

"There gotta be some chow somewhere," said O'Bannion and moved outside.

Arnie, Cruz, and I followed though we were sure he didn't know where the hell to go.

"Anyway, we finally saw action," said Arnie.

"We ain't seen nothing," muttered O'Bannion.

"Will the Japs try to take this rock back?" I wondered.

"Hell's fire, they could take this fuckin' shithole back with no trouble; we ain't got nothing to fight with," said Arnie.

"Someone sure as shit better get us some rifles!" said O'Bannion.

"Or what?" said Arnie.

"We're up shit creek without a paddle," said Cruz.

"You heard Byron, the whole American fleet's out there," I said.

"Just hope that the bastards don't come back before we get weapons," said Cruz.

A single blanket was issued and it was all we had besides pants and a shirt to keep from freezing. We crammed together and the mutual body warmth helped. On our second night of exhaustion a smallish stinking wet body landed in our midst. We kicked, cursed and lashed out. "Simmer down, its Taps," cried Arnie. We hadn't seen or thought about the dog since the bombing.

"Son-of-a-bitch scared shit out of me!" cursed Arnie.

"Fuckin' mutt!" snapped O'Bannion.

"That dog stinks!" I added.

"If I still had my rifle we wouldn't have to worry about him!" snarled Arnie.

Curses and kicks impelled Taps to patter off. Yards away he curled up and pitifully whimpered. His plaintive sounds didn't set well with us. Fortunately for him none of us were armed.

As the wind kicked up and the temperature dropped, sleep didn't come easy because periodic sentry shouts or rifle shots roused us. We rose on elbows to curse before nodding off. Despite disconcerting sounds we dozed for short periods. We were up before dawn hoping there was something to do, anything. O'Bannion still snored but we roused him.

The next cool morning we meandered near a wrecked blockhouse trailed by Taps. We joined other VMF personnel congregated around a coral mound. Other raggedy-assed people kept drifting in. Major Burke wasn't around but Captain Plunkett stood stolidly before us. "Listen up!" shouted the gunny.

Captain Plunkett read from an official notice, "From this moment on fresh water will be used for drinking only, got it! Saltwater showers will now be utilized. And listen closely, a mess hall for troops has been constructed on Roi. Until this rock gets squared away, all hands will be limited to one hot meal per day! Ration cartons are available for other meals, got it!"

We expected the captain to follow up with a conventional pep talk but he snapped, "Fuck it!" and strode off trailed by Lieutenant Foley.

"Dismissed!" roared the gunnery sergeant and trotted after them.

Titmus beckoned and we followed him across the coral span connecting the islands. We crossed over to Roi. "Fuckin' brass doesn't know shit from shinola," he announced. "We're on our own, got it, on our own!"

"Somebody must be in charge." Said Arnie.

"The captain don't know shit, it's every man for himself!" Said O'Bannion..

"Plunkett's got his head up his ass," said Titmus.

That seditious statement unnerved me. "What do we do?"

"Fend for ourselves," said Titmus.

We shuffled back to battered Roi. The little island looked devastated. A corpsman affirmed what we had heard, fifteen hundred had been torn up, most of them wounded by shrapnel from our own exploding ammunition. He didn't know how many had bought the farm. Every man in Ground Defense had been accounted for, a few of them had been evacuated but none from our immediate group.

Lieutenant Rameron came stumbling by. His hearing had gotten somewhat better. He related that Ferguson had gone off his rocker, was secured in a straight jacket and transported to an offshore hospital ship. He disclosed that fourteen from our squadron, mostly pilots, had shrapnel wounds serious enough to merit transfer to the hospital ship. "The good news," he said, "My ears are better, I can hear."

Seabees bivouacked closest to the airfield had suffered the most casualties. Marines from the 22nd took the second most drubbing. In comparison VMF 111 got off easy; busted eardrums, minor shrapnel wounds, lots of bruises but best of all, no fatalities.

At 1400 we fell into a winding chow line that writhed across the Roi like a snake. As the line inched onward the raggedy-assed troops spread morale sucking scuttlebutt. Ceaseless rumors were bantered about, most of it ridiculous bullshit.

After slopping down soggy shit-on-a-shingle, the six of us meandered back to Namur to strip and splash into the sea. We scrubbed and scrubbed, but without conventional lather or saltwater soap it was wasted effort. No matter how hard we tried salt water didn't wash grime away. Bathing in salt water was better than nothing but not by much.

"I hope we're out of here before the Japs come back," said Cassidy. "Tokyo Rose keeps spouting that these two islands are saturated with mines. She also swears hidden snappers are waiting to blow us to hell."

"Banzai fanatics could be hiding in one of the island's drainage pipes," I merrily volunteered.

"The Japs installed them and got no qualms about launching suicide attacks," agreed O'Bannion.

"Hah," spat Titmus. "Both you and Miss Tokyo are out of your fuckin' minds! There's no place to hide on these barren rocks."

Guard duty was a shaky affair especially at night. Sentries were unnerved enough to shoot first and yell halt afterwards. It was downright menacing to move about or even stand erect after dark.

Weeks and months at sea took a toll on navy personnel. Sailors ferried ashore from anchored or incoming vessels craved recreation, souvenirs, anything. But both islands being barren, their short time on dry land was far from fulfilling.

Many carried canteens or foul weather jackets as well as accumulated dollars. Those working as ship stewards sneaked canned edibles ashore to trade. The swabbies craved souvenirs, who could blame them? Like any healthy American, they sought to prove to hometown girls and kin that they had been someplace, seen something and done memorable deeds.

An Imperial Marine's head-bandanna could fetch a five-gallon can of peaches. Other bandanas featuring rising sun, Jap flags, rifles, pictures, coins, uniform buttons were desirable items. Jap swords and side arms were the most marketable. Combat infantrymen had them, but not many others, especially Airdales.

When bartering, it was expedient to provide titillating bullshit to accompany the phony plunder. Of course like any healthy American, the souvenir hunters wanted their hometown audience to envision them doing heroic deeds against the foe.

Titmus, Arnie and I were strolling along the north side of Namur looking for potential patrons. Each of us carried a weathered Japanese flag recently fashioned from a discarded parachute. As on Nukufetau, we utilized sickbay mercurochrome to draw circular orange suns audaciously rising on tattered parachute flags.

A noisy group milling about a "Stay Away!" ammo dump stocked with discarded enemy ammunition mounds caught our attention. We got to the hubbub as an ambulance screeched to a stop.

The crowd's attention was on a distraught young sailor. Tears gushed as the kid held up his blood-shredded hand and bawled for his mother. His shipmate groaned that his buddy picked up a discarded Japanese hand grenade and it detonated destroying his hand.

Two blue fatigued corpsmen emerged from the ambulance. "Ain't you fuckin' people been told a hundred times to stay away from fuckin' Japanese shit!" shrieked one of the disgruntled corpsman.

The guy with the bloodied hand wept.

"What's it take for you fuckin' kids to learn!"

"It's too late for a sermon so shut the fuck up and tend to the kid's hand!" snarled Titmus.

The sweating corpsman grimaced at Titmus but started administering and wrapping. The weeping kid was hustled into the ambulance and with siren shrieking it sped away.

"Think they can save the fingers?" I asked.

"Looked like a skeleton's paw," said Arnie.

"The kid's hand is gone," said Titmus.

A cold wind kicked up and our motivation to peddle homemade flags dissipated. "Let's get back," Titmus muttered,

Soon after the sun dipped we hit the sack. As Titmus snored away I fell into a depressed doze. Suddenly I felt a sharp elbow jab my ribs. It was O'Bannion. "What the fuck!"

"Shh!" he cautioned. I saw Arnie crouching and listening. None of us had a stiletto, bayonet or any other weapon. How I missed my sweetheart, my rifle.

Titmus slipped in among us, he was armed with a purloined '03 Springfield. Cassidy and Cruz crowded behind him, both weaponless.

"Whut's goin' on?" gasped Arnie.

"People movin' toward the beach," whispered Titmus.

"People?" panted Cassidy.

"Shh!" said Titmus.

"What they doing?" gasped Arnie.

"Japs?" said Cruz.

"I got a fucked up arm," whined Arnie.

"Shhh!" said Titmus.

"Why didn't the fuckers evacuate me?" whimpered Arnie.

"You're too fuckin' heroically important to be evacuated," snapped O'Bannion.

"We're sitting ducks," said Arnie.

"What do we do?" I was shaking.

"The whole fuckin' fleet's out there and nobody's fired a shot. How in hell could it be Japs?" gritted Titmus.

American voices sounded from the shoreline. The sky was clear, the coral beach white and shimmering surf unobstructed. Titmus led us toward the bustle to push in among jumpy Marines staring right, left and seaward.

Perturbed whispers hushed as click-click-click sounds in the surf continued.

"What the hell!"

"Burrowing Japs!" said an unhinged voice.

"They're digging," another sobbed.

"I knew it! The bastards are going to blow us to hell," groaned another.

"The slant-eyed bastards will explode too," whined Arnie.

"They don't give a fuck as long as they blow us up too," encouraged O'Bannion. "Suicide's part of their culture."

"That's how they expect to get to their happy hunting grounds," said Cassidy.

The clicking stopped for seconds before starting again. As the crowd's uneasiness spread the eerie staccato seemed louder.

"What the fuck!" said O'Bannion.

"I've heard that tick tick sound before," said Titmus,

"Japs laying mines?" I contributed.

"You're nuts!" spat Titmus.

"Well, what the hell is it?" said O'Bannion.

Speculating ceased as two lieutenants and a captain showed up as the mysterious sounds subdued a bit. A cold wind kicked up, the captain signaled for quiet. As the officers stared at each other someone whimpered, "Goddam Corps don't know or give a shit."

"Semper Fi!"

"Fuck you, hurray for me!" voiced another.

Clicking sounds again amplified as a grizzled warrant officer shouldered in. The gunnery's face cocked sideways attuning to the "Click-click-click."

"Gooney birds!" he chuckled. "Heard 'em on Wake, heard 'em on Midway. Thems goddamn birds making that fuckin' noise."

"You sure, Gunny?" said the captain.

"Hell, yes, I'm sure!" Grunted the old salt and with no further ado disdainfully waddled back from whence he had come.

CHAPTER THIRTY-THREE

We weren't starving but we were frequently hungry and always on the lookout for edibles. As our C and K ration diet plus manual labor tasks pealed away excess fat we became lean, brown and looked like field Marines were supposed to look, or so we imagined.

Hard-eyed line company sentries warily watched roving Marines. Those hard-assed sentries wouldn't tolerate thievery from those they didn't know. They were especially motivated to nab or shoot Airedales, swabbies or Seabees.

"We need some decent chow," whined Arnie for the third or fourth time.

"The fuckin' brass and stripes are getting theirs," muttered O'Bannion.

"Forget it, we're low life peons," I grunted.

"I've seen nothing worth stealing but canned fruit, canned juices, canned vegetables, canned soup. All canned shit," said Cassidy.

"It's still better than the stale crap in ration boxes," I ventured.

"A hot tamale and pile of beans would make me happy," said Cruz.

O'Bannion asked, "Titmus, got any ideas?"

"Too risky. Those nervous guards want to shoot and ask questions later. They're especially jumpy after dark."

"A guy be taking a piss could get his ass shot off."

"There's got to be a way," said Arnie.

"There's a password being used. If we find out what it is...." I volunteered.

"Those kids will shoot first and ask for the password after," said Titmus. "Lemme think."

We tried sleeping but it was another fitful night. Challenges rent the air, "Who goes there!" Unrecognized shouts roared, "Shut the fuck up!" was a chorused retort.

It seemed to take forever for daybreak and though dead tired, we were relieved to rise and look about. We didn't notice that Titmus was gone until he came shuffling over a knoll. He beckoned, turned and headed for the road that led to Roi.

Arnie, O'Bannion, Cruz, Cassidy, and I tailed him to a two-ton Marine green truck parked next to a burnt out pillbox. The engine was humming with Chief sitting at the wheel and Titmus pointed, "Get aboard!"

We climbed in the back and Titmus said, "Go!" Chief shifted and pulled out.

"How'd you get this?" said Arnie.

"It was unattended," said Titmus.

"Who does it belong to?"

"What the fuck's the difference?"

Chief drove straight to a food dump and screeched to a stop before backing up. A pasty-faced guard scrutinized us but seemed too detached to challenge. He must have deduced that we looked official and didn't unsling his rifle.

Titmus got out of the cab and heaved a crate of canned fruit onto the truck's bed and commenced barking orders like a sergeant. "Move; I ain't doing your work!"

Looking like a legitimate work party we heaved crates onto the truck.

The sentrie's eyes abruptly narrowed and he shuffled towards us. The truck was less than half loaded as Titmus bellowed, "We're through here, mount up!"

Chief gunned the motor and stepped on the gas. We congenially waved as the sentry unslung his rifle. He reciprocated by waving his middle finger. We sped across the coral embankment to our area where Chief screeched to a stop. We toted our pilfered goodies to respective dugouts.

Chief drove off but returned afoot with two friends to claim his pillage share and slip away.

Enough loot was left to trade and swap with a ninety-millimeter gun crew. They took acquired canned fruit and gifted us with a cloudy bottle of Japanese rice whisky.

The night was spent gorging on canned fruit and chasing the sweets down with Jap booze. If some dames had been around it would have concluded a lovely evening.

The following day a fox-faced lieutenant followed by two buck-assed grunts from the 22nd came snooping. One was the pasty-faced guy who was about to challenge us as we zoomed from the dump in our stolen truck. Titmus stayed relaxed but Cruz, O'Bannion and I were disquieted as the lieutenant snapped, "Walgrove, these people look familiar?"

Walgrove recognized us but said, "Can't tell, sir, all Airdales look alike."

"You people know anything about a stolen truck?" said the lieutenant.

"Sir!" barked Titmus, "why in hell would someone steal a truck? There's no place to go and you can't sell the damn thing." The rest of us shrugged and looked as innocent as babes in the woods.

"When we catch the fuckin' thieves we'll hang their sorry butts out to dry," muttered the lieutenant and stalked off followed by the two disconsolate privates.

As they departed the skinny one who had saved our asses mouthed, "You owe me!"

"We do," whispered O'Bannion.

Before the chance to compensate the guy, VMF 111 received orders to pack possessions and stow remnants aboard a waiting LST. Twenty stateside replacements joined our depleted outfit before we sailed.

"Bet some of us are goin' home," predicted Cassidy.

"We ain't never going home," whined Arnie.

"What you think these replacements are for?"

"To dig more shit holes, what else?"

The LST sailed for Kwajeline. It took less than a day and a half before the nearby glistening coral island hove into sight. It was larger but just another shitty coral rock situated sixty miles from Roi-Namur.

An eighth of a mile from the shore another LST and repair ship were lashed together. Our LST was tied to the repair ship. Anchors from the three kept us fairly motionless.

From the deck we could clearly see Kwajeline. Most of the island's trees had been shorn and stripped by shells and aerial bombs. It was another flat rock.

The army division commanded by an army general had attacked Kwajeline. Soldiers waiting behind a classic artillery bombardment had become bogged down. After their advance faltered, General "Howling Mad" Smith and his 22nd Marines finished the operation. Marines stormed past the entrenched doggies and engaged the tenacious enemy. They took casualties but wasted no time in dispatching Jap defenders. The island was quickly secured. Anyway, that's what we were told.

Several of us on deck were staring toward the island as Corporal Lancaster swaggered up. "O'Bannion, you and Glossman get on that other LST and carry those potato sacks from there to here."

Lancaster wanted to impress the new replacements and he did have two stripes. I might have heeded if O'Bannion hadn't spat, "Fuck you, Lancaster, you ear-banging office-pinky!"

Lancaster's pasty face whitened and he gasped. "Move those potatoes!" We glared as he squeaked, "Privates! Get moving!"

"You want them moved, move 'em yourself!" snapped O'Bannion.

"You office pinky asshole," I added.

Replacements were wide-eyed while fellow short-timers cackled. He stepped back and his eyes bored into mine. "Insubordination!" he spat.

With enthusiasm I said, "Shove off, asshole, or I'll dump you over the side."

Laughter erupted as Lancaster's pale face bleached whiter. I almost regretted my response but the damage had been done. I cogitated my military career dissipating as Lancaster hurried away.

Brave talk ensued amid congratulations until he strode back with Captain Plunkett. "These two, sir," said Lancaster and pointed at O'Bannion and me.

"Insubordination and refusing an order in a combat zone," snapped Captain Plunkett. "That's serious stuff!"

As O'Bannion and I stood rigidly an aggravating itch plagued my privates but I was too petrified to scratch.

"O'Bannion and Glossman, you two been talking mutiny! Got something to say?"

O'Bannion breathed deeply and blurted. "Lancaster's an asshole, sir."

Captain Plunkett blinked. "You got something to add, Glossman!"

"He's that, sir." I gulped.

Plunket's jaw tensed, he was unnerved. There was a general feeling that he agreed with the asshole part but said, "You two got two seconds, one each, to apologize to Corporal Lancaster."

We both fidgeted and O'Bannion blurted, "But, sir, why should we, he is one."

I didn't speak but sadly assented.

"That's it!" said Plunkett. "Refusing an order in a combat zone plus mutinous behavior! You two insubordinators will stand office hours. Incidentally, both of you are up for promotion. If I were CO you'd be saying goodbye to that stripe. Now get your butts over to that work party."

Plunkett eyeballed us as we climbed onto the other LST and started muscling crates into the cargo net. Minutes later he stalked off followed by Lancaster sporting a shit-eating grin.

Other shitbirds did view us with a touch of awe. The outfit, in general, disapproved of Lancaster, he was a pariah. Some of the old timers nodded approval.

A more momentous problem came up. Jacob Cruz was missing. He hadn't answered the last muster and nobody remembered seeing him on board since we pulled away from Roi-Namur. O'Bannion, Arnie, Cassidy, Titmus and I flaked out on the fantail discussing his disappearance. "I'm almost sure he came aboard," said O'Bannion.

"I didn't see him," said Arnie.

"That's 'cause he didn't come aboard," said Titmus.

"Where the hell is he?" said Arnie.

"Maybe he fell overboard," offered Cassidy.

'Bullshit!" said Titmus.

"Maybe he did what Bones did," I said.

"They ain't no dames on Roi-Namur," said Titmus.

"How the hell could he go AWOL on Roi-Namur?" queried Arnie.

"He did say something to me before he disappeared," said Titmus. We waited. "Told me was sick of digging shit holes. He said he joined to fight Japs."

"Didn't we all?" said O'Bannion.

"So where'd he go and why?" asked Cassidy.

Titmus enlightened us. "The 22nd lost over two-hundred on Roi-Namur and a few on Eniwetok. Cruz talked to a line lieutenant who told him that if he happened by, he'd see to it that he'd get a rifle and put in a squad needing replacements."

"The lucky son of a bitch got himself into a line company?" said O'Bannion.

"I'll be damned," said Arnie.

"He could get his ass shot off." said Cassidy.

"I should have thought about that," mumbled Arnie.

"This Airedale shit softens a man," said Titmus. "You're half-assed Marines. If you guys had brains you'd shut your traps and thank your lucky stars."

CHAPTER THIRTY-FOUR

Sergeant Goodwinch was standing by the starboard rail surrounded by an audience. We pushed in. "The captain let it slip after he chewed your asses out, Makin Island is our next island."

"Makin?"

"I've heard that name before."

"Where in hell is it?"

"In the Gilberts."

"Where?"

"Another atoll, asshole."

"That's the fuckin' island where Carlson and the 2nd Raider battalion landed." sighed Titmus.

"Now I got it!"

"Sure you do!"

"Came in two submarines and wiped out the Jap garrison," said Titmus. "Happened over a year ago."

"The way to fight a fuckin' war!"

"They left nine men behind."

"Why?"

"Could have been a mistake," said Titmus.

"Jimmy Roosevelt, got wounded there."

"Right!"

"The 27th Army Division invaded Makin while the 2nd Marine Division took Tarawa. Ain't nothing but dogfaces on Makin now."

"We'll be sitting on our asses, as usual, doing nothing gathering coconuts and fronds."

"They'll keep us busy doing the usual shit duty."

"Bet your ass on that."

"Thank your lucky stars."

"I shoulda gone with Cruz," mused O'Bannion.

"What do yuh think, Earl?" said Arnie.

"One rock's not much different from the other," he said and stalked away.

Two more days of smooth sailing before the Makin Islands hove into view. Both had been possessed by the British before the Japs took over.

In 1943 while the 6th Marine Regiment was involved in the murderous invasion of Tarawa, the 27th Army Infantry Division attacked Makin. The Japanese defenders on Makin proved to be a less costly campaign.

The loudspeaker informed us that the larger island was Makin and the other one was Little Makin, our destination. Unlike Roi-Namur, neither was coral based. They consisted of earth partially covered by coral.

Nearing the shore we spied a tipped and ripped up Japanese flying boat mired in Makin's shallow bay. A Rising Sun was painted on each wing. The downed plane's metal fuselage was ripped ragged. Strips of the silver painted metal had been torn. They had been bent into souvenir bracelets by American soldiers.

We disembarked and personnel proceeded to erect pyramid tents on the former army campground close to the airfield.

Titmus, O'Bannion, Cassidy, Arnie, and I situated ourselves and inventoried our brand new equipment. New canteens, mess gear, folding cots, and rifles had been issued. We still needed mattresses and olive green blankets. We followed Titmus and retrieved our dumped seabags.

Bedrolls, blankets, seabags and clean new mattresses belonging to the replacements were scattered about. The new guys assembled elsewhere for an incoming briefing. We shouldered our seabags, grabbed five mattresses and blankets and sped back to our new home.

"We're stealing?" Cassidy smirked.

"Semper Fi!" uttered O'Bannion.

Titmus announced, "Possession is nine tenths of the law."

Identification inscriptions were eradicated and we inked our own names over previous owners scribbled identities. We squared everything away before flaking out on our brand new cots.

Sergeant Goodwinch strode in. "Off your asses and on your feet!" Coming from him the order didn't rile because a touch of levity vibrated in his inflection. We followed him to a clearing where he told us to collect coconut fronds. "Same shitty job," I grunted.

"What else does a Ground Defense Airedale do?" moaned O'Bannion.

Others mouthed similar sentiments. "Fuck the Corps, fuck the fronds and fuck all sergeants!" By that time, Goodwinch was out of sight and sound.

Days later a promotion list was posted in the mess hall. It was a blanket squadron promotion, not unusual in aviation units. Every enlisted man in the squadron except for new guys was gifted an additional stripe, in some cases a rocker. Promotions became effective eight days ago. Former buck-assed privates were now making fifty plus an additional four per month. At the time, nothing to sneeze about.

O'Bannion and I were conferring about what we were going to do with the four extra bucks and playfully pulling rank on each other when Herb Swiller, a new office pinky, timidly stepped into our tent. He relayed that O'Bannion and I were wanted in the headquarters tent.

"What the hell for?" snapped O'Bannion.

"I been told to tell you, that's all I know!" whined Swiller and he withdrew.

"I bet it's something about Lancaster," sighed O'Bannion as we strolled to the headquarter tent.

"Ear-banging bastard!" I muttered.

We were at attention in front of Major Burke's desk when Captain Plunkett and Lancaster entered and stood behind us. Lancaster's sleeves was adorned with three new sergeant stripes.

"Privates Glossman and O'Bannion, you are charged with insubordination, refusing orders and showing contempt to a noncommissioned officer. Serious offenses, what do you have to say for yourselves!" said the major.

We shuffled.

"Guilty or not guilty!" snapped the major.

"Sir," said O'Bannion.

"Guilty or not?"

"Guilty, sir," said O'Bannion.

"Guilty, sir," I echoed.

"You're both reduced to the rank of Buck Private and confined to the base for thirty days. Dismissed!"

"About face!" shouted Captain Plunkett.

"And hear this, I don't want to put up with anymore bullshit coming from either of you."

"Yes, sir!" we chorused.

"Forward march!"

We stomped out, trailed by Plunkett and Lancaster.

"Get back to your quarters! Believe this, next time you won't get off so light," said Plunkett.

I wanted to punch Lancaster's smug face and knew O'Bannion had the same urge. We meekly strode toward our tent.

"Private First Class for eight days," muttered O'Bannion. "Shit!"

"I'm going to write a letter to my Mother with PFC on the return address. It'll make her proud for a short time. At least until she gets the second letter," I reflected.

I was depressed. After all, I had been overseas almost a year and my militaristic accomplishments had been nil.

A list of guys scheduled to go back to the states was posted.

"I'm going home!" announced Arnie.

"Hell, that's why the replacements are here, I'm on the list too," beamed Cassidy.

"You and me aren't going," groaned O'Bannion, as if it was my fault.

"We haven't been overseas long enough," I reminded.

"They won't keep us here too much longer," he said. "When more replacements come, we'll be on the next batch heading home."

"They can't keep us overseas more than a couple more months, can they?"

"They do whatever they want, boys. You should know by now that your ass belongs to the Corps." grunted Titmus.

"They can't keep us longer than fourteen months," protested O'Bannion.

"They can and they will, shitbirds! The fuckin' Corps does whatever it fuckin' well pleases. You two been in long enough to know that!" snapped Titmus.

We pouted.

"Shit, I learned that before I was out of boot camp," snapped Titmus and stomped away.

Major Burke and most of the pilots as well as other non-flying officers were heading stateside. Sergeant Goodwinch was among the enlisted going home. That would make Buck Sergeant Lancaster ranking NCO in Ground Defense and that didn't bode well.

For the second time Rameron failed to be promoted and was put in direct command of Ground Defense. Officers considered the Ground Defense assignment to be degrading. The poor fucking lieutenant was easy going and presentable looking, but in an un-marine way which didn't set well with commissioned brothers in arms.

The laid back nonconforming guy had graduated from some unrecognized midwestern college and his civilian job had been selling shoes. Despite of his colorless background, he manifested a standoffish aura that irritated fellow officers. The officer outcast spent more than allotted time reclining in his sack.

Major Burke despised him and scorned officers who didn't ignore him. It was a sad situation. On Makin Island, fellow officers rendered him the silent treatment.

Since he couldn't converse with officers, he spent time with Ground Defense rejects. He especially avoided commissioned fellows when they were poker playing, engrossed in drinking sessions or both. Occasionally he would present a bottle of stateside booze or beer to share. Some of us felt sorry for the ostracized lieutenant. After all, he frequently acted as a buffer between us and Lancaster. But in spite of friendliness it wasn't easy to relax around him. Lieutenant bars were too formidable a barrier. Enlisted fuck-ups and commissioned are a twain that seldom meets.

He didn't pay much heed to our bullshit sessions. After all, most of us hadn't graduated from high school and our blah-blah sessions were limited to dames, booze and creative ways to fuckoff. He obviously was interested in more erudite topics.

We restrained from discussing creative pilfering angles or ways to shaft Lancaster in front of him. Being an officer, we couldn't trust him.

Our pilots had their work cut out. Bomb racks had been installed on the Corsair bellies so planes could be used as dive bombers. Ordinance guys wheeled in 500-pound bombs and secured them to the fighter underbellies.

Our pilots flew north soaring over Wotje and Jaluit, two isolated Jap held islands. They'd swoop down and drop explosives on airfields and troops before continuing north to Majuro. After refueling and being loaded with huge bombs, they'll drop the bombs on the return flight to Makin.

Despite the daily double bomb-pounding, enemy anti-aircraft guns continue to fire at our attacking Corsairs. Planes returned with wings and fuselages dotted with holes. The Japanese defenders were far from subdued. None of our Corsairs were downed but pilots became more and more apprehensive. That sooner or later one or more of our pilots was bound to become a casualty became a silent but gloomy assumption.

One overcast day, Corsairs returned to Makin at dusk. Eight had flown out but only six landed and their distraught pilots dismounted. Morose ground crews silently pushed the planes into revetments. The six disconsolately strode into a single tent where whisky was passed around.

Word spread. Captain Black, a newly arrived pilot and Second Lieutenant Tollivan while preparing to land on Majuro suffered a miscalculation. After circling before landing, wings collided and both Corsairs plunged into the sea.

Lieutenant Tollivan had been a pleasant, good-humored well liked guy. None of us had a chance to know Captain Black but he had seemed to be a happy-go-lucky okay guy. The two young officers' deaths put a dismal cloud of gloom over the squadron.

CHAPTER THIRTY-FIVE

About that time Titmus received a letter.

San Diego, California
Dear Earl,
I was overjoyed to get your letter and learn that you were still in one piece. As newspaper columns tell about more islands being fought over and casualty lists getting longer, I really worry. I know that the mail situation isn't good but I do wish you'd write more often. If you can't, I understand.
You may think this kind of silly, and it is, but it's got to be kind of a status thing at the USO to have a boyfriend overseas. We girls all know about each others' sweethearts and husbands. We worry for each other. Gossip is traded about what's in each others' letters. It's all girl stuff and you probably won't worry about what I'm babbling about.
By the way, I'm doing real well at my job. Tips have been good and I'm saving money. Of course, I use most of my spare energy at the USO where I feel I'm doing my part for the troops. Just a little patriotic stuff from a female compared to men and boys giving their all, but every little bit helps.
I'm sure I helped by dancing and just jawing a bit. I know I've made lots of young kids a little less lonely. I don't mean to brag, but I do have a way with homesick service guys.

Hilton, the soldier with the thick glasses I told you about, believe it or not, he's a sergeant now and almost in charge of a big office. Imagine a kid like that a sergeant. I don't think he could even make it as a buck private in the Marines. Poor kid thinks he's in love with me.

I haven't encouraged him, honest. I treat him like I'm his sister. Gosh, I'm ten, well, maybe eight years older. Besides, he isn't my type. Believe it or not he respects you and our relationship so there's nothing to worry about. He feels that he's heard so much about you that it's like he knows you. He told me that he is looking forward to meeting you and telling you how lucky you are. Isn't that sweet?

I was very touched by your last letter. I do want to marry you but we've got to be practical too. There aren't many jobs you could qualify for in civilian life. And if you want to learn a trade you'd have to start from the bottom.

Even though I wouldn't mind being married to a career Marine, I know you don't want to stay in the good ole' USMC. Anyway, I wouldn't want to be married to a Marine who's still a buck private. I did notice that one of your letters said Private First Class on the return address, but then on the next letter it said buck private again. Also, remember the time when you made corporal, I was so proud.

Anyway, if we're going to get wed, and believe me I want you to be my husband, you're going to have get some stripes. I don't expect you to become a general (ha, ha). If you really love me, you'll try. I know you can do it.

Well, goodbye for now. Love and kisses, darling, I miss you.

Semper Fi forever,
Millie

"What about that stuff she said about stripes?" said Arnie.

"Don't mean nothing, I don't think." sighed Titmus.

"Sounds like she might mean it," said O'Bannion.

"Don't matter! I sure as hell ain't staying in the Corps. Anyway, no more fucking around. From now on I'm gonna be an ear-banging candy-assed Marine."

"You're gonna be a what?" said Cassidy.

"Gotta get me some stripes. Maybe two, maybe three. You know, come to think of it, wouldn't be a bad idea if you guys did the same."

The idea of being a perennial buck private was far from inflating. At least, I had lots of company.

I soon tuned out the 'how do I get promoted' brooding and concentrated on the letter from Tulipa.

Pago Pago, American Samoa
Dear Handsome Strong Marine,

You much in my mind. I think of you and good times we had. We don't know each much long but I think we have much fun together. Don't you? I don't know you ever come back. Many Marines say be back but I don't know. Many friends say Marines lie. Maybe you have American girl with yellow hair and she very pretty or maybe you killed by Jap.

Anyway, we have baby boy you happy that to know you are a father. He look like you but dark like Samoa and handsome boy. He cries some but laugh too. He very good baby. I hope he stay that way. I name him Malini Corps.

Please take care and don't get to brave. Maybe I see you again, if no, I understand. I will tell baby nice things. Tofa, my malini.

Tulipa

P.S. Luina send love to Jacob. She also got baby but little girl get sick and die. Everybody sad. Luina say tell Jacob she sorry.

I folded the letter, opened it, and read it again and again. As others bullshitted about stripes and careers in the military, I closed my eyes. Assorted images flitted around my jumbled mind.

Bones Donigal surviving in the green hills of British Samoa, Jacob Cruz moving out with the 22nd, Tulipa nursing a baby, maybe mine. I even contemplated going back to *Upolu* after the war but not too adamantly. I conjured up images of residing in Samoa's steaming wet jungle, inhaling poignant smells, swatting mosquitoes and reclining in a *fale*. Uh, uh, I concluded that life on the island wasn't my cup of tea. Nope, I knew I couldn't fit in. No more than Tulipa with her calloused bare feet and half naked ways could be at ease in Venice, California.

Major Payton got a letter from the CO of a 22nd rifle company that dampened spirits even lower. The major's office pinky spread the word. Cruz had landed with the 22nd on Guam and stumbled in front of a bazooka fired by one of his squad members. He lost his head and that was that.

"Poor little bastard," muttered Titmus.

"Never got off the beach," sighed O'Bannion.

A shitty atmosphere prevailed as we sourly continued doing our routine shit duty.

We'd been digging shit holes, toting garbage and gathering debris for six straight days. On a fading, sweltering Sunday afternoon, Ground Defense had the day off. Occupants of our tent were disposed to, well, relax. Of course, we kicked back other times, but on this day we didn't have to look around to see who was snooping about trying to catch us.

It was late afternoon, too early for the sun to hide behind the horizon, when Cassidy, Arnie, O'Bannion, and I headed to the shower. We intended to wash off sweat and grime before the blood sipping mosquitoes replaced the flies.

Clean and alert we hit the mess hall to chomp down portions of dull fare before meandering back to our tent. As we approached we heard squawks coming from our tent. The weird sounds transfixed us and we shuddered in unison. Shrill discordant continued.

"What the hell?" sputtered Cassidy.

O'Bannion crossed himself.

If I only had my Garand I would not have been so inclined to run.

The grievous squawk resounded.

"Jesus! It ain't human!" mumbled Cassidy.

"They got Titmus!" bellowed O'Bannion and charged through the flap. Cassidy, Arnie, and I scrambled after him. We halted as we confronted Titmus. Perched on his leg was a species of the poultry persuasion. Titmus was conversing with the bedraggled fowl.

"Titmus has lost it," whispered Arnie. The pathetic chicken was vested with a disarray of off-white plumage and a sprinkle of mottled feathers, a faded orange crest topped his head.

A dirty string tethered to his leg was lashed to Titmus' cot. The creature focused malevolent yellow eyes on O'Bannion and then ogled each of us with an unnerving glare.

"What the hell is that?" said O'Bannion.

"Don't they have chickens in Boston?" spat Titmus. "Oh, I forgot, you slickers were brought up in cities. Only chicken you've ever seen was hanging in butcher shops or cooking in pots."

"That supposed to be funny?" grumbled O'Bannion.

"Somewhat humorous," guffawed Titmus.

"That's one queer looking chicken," remarked Arnie.

"I wouldn't eat a thing like that," said O'Bannion.

"Can't taste worse than the shit we been gettin," said Cassidy.

"Listen up, wise asses! Any galoot lays a glove on this guy will be one sorry jarhead," cackled Titmus.

"Where'd you get him?" said Arnie, more to break the tension than curiosity.

"Bought him! Well, kind of, I traded canned goods for him."

"Why?" I queried.

"We need a mascot."

"Why?" said O'Bannion.

"For a moral booster, dummy, that's why."

"We got Taps," I ventured.

"Hah!" retorted Titmus. "By the way this bird's name is Smedley Butler,"

"What!" said O'Bannion.

"Next to Gunnery Sergeant Daniel Daley, General Smedley Butler was the fightingest Marine that ever lived," announced Titmus.

"You should have called him Daniel or Daley."

"Daniel Daley was a helluva Marine but he was only a Master Sergeant. Smedley Butler was a famous general. As you can see this bird has a touch of officer quality."

"We gonna eat him?" I asked.

"Pay attention!" Titmus snarled. "Don't even think about him and dinner in the same thought!"

We weren't sure if Titmus was serious or snowing us, he wasn't that easy to read.

"Where you gonna keep him?" asked O'Bannion, as if he didn't know.

"Where do you think?" said Titmus.

"Not in our tent!" bravely stated Arnie.

"Why not! He sure as hell ain't gonna take up too much room, is he?"

"He's makes clucking noises," stated O'Bannion.

I came up with, "He'll shit where he roosts!"

"Roosters crow early, real early in the morning," said Arnie.

"Ease up! After I train him he won't be no trouble. When he gets to know you and you get to know him, everyone will get along. Until that time, nobody fucks with him! Get it!"

No further comments were forthcoming. Days later Titmus untied Smedley's leg string rendering him the freedom to investigate our tent's interior. The creature crowed, crapped and strutted about like a vain peacock.

When the sun dropped the mottled thing roosted on one of our mosquito nets. He seldom spent two sequential nights atop the same cot. Nor did he opt to perch above Titmus.

Before reveille he crowed and his raucous screech never failed to startle. The horrible bird sensed that we loathed him. He did retain a soft spot for his owner, at least, Titmus thought so. But it was easy to discern his distaste for the rest of us.

He had a disturbing habit of toadying up to Titmus by presenting him with bugs or lizards. Titmus thought it was cute and in turn gifted Smedley with assorted tidbits from the mess hall.

Our rifles, mess gear, cots and seabags became tainted by odorous chicken deposits. When Titmus was not around we subjected the nasty creature to caustic remarks. He became a prime target for projectiles. But our wrathful intents were unfruitful.

It flustered us because Titmus was usually squared away. We couldn't comprehend why or how he could tolerate his tacky bird. We tried to reason with him, subtly at first and later bluntly, but our reasoning went unheeded.

We could do little more than endure hoping he and Smedley would clash. In the meantime, our tent reeked with the stench of chicken shit.

Smedley's talons tore additional rips in our mosquito nets. Added holes encouraged winged tormentors to venture in to sample our blood. As if we didn't have enough critical distractions, droppings had to be disposed of before weekly inspections.

Poor Taps was one of Smedley's targets. During the day, our apathetic dog searched for a shady nook to nap. While the sun baked, Smedley left our tent to persecute Taps. The docile dog endured continuous chicken squawks and pecks.

Our persecuted hound became so weary that his night roaming became limited. Only after dark while Smedley was inactive could the bedraggled dog rest. Instead of gadding about in the dark, as dogs are wont to do, he slept.

The lack of daylight rest and recuperation took a heavy toll on our spiritless mutt.

One hot day Arnie came stomping into the tent. He had been reamed out by Lancaster and reacted as upset as I'd ever beheld him.

"If I ever catch that prick on a street in San Diego, I'll knock him on his sorry ass and to hell with the consequences!"

At that moment Smedley uttered a spiteful crow. Arnie's foot impulsively booted the chicken's rear and the awful rooster was propelled screeching through the air. Titmus entered as squawking indignantly Smedley floated down amid flying feathers. Without a word Titmus drew his bayonet from its scabbard and lunged. In the nick of time Arnie sprinted from the tent with Titmus close behind. Twenty yards were covered before Titmus became winded and quit.

Later, much later, a subdued Arnie entered our tent and appeased Titmus by apologizing to Smedley. The rest of us, though annoyed, refrained from voicing criticisms.

Perhaps Smedley sensed our submission because droppings intensified and his strutting became more brazen. He was a helluva disgusting entity.

On a sweltering afternoon Arnie, O'Bannion, Cassidy and I convened. "We gotta do something," whispered Arnie

"We sure as hell do," agreed O'Bannion.

"I hate that bird," I spat.

"Who doesn't!" snapped Cassidy.

"Titmus doesn't," muttered O'Bannion.

In Titmus' absence we strived to induce the rejectionable creature to fly away. Spitting, kicking and throwing objects at the miserable creature merely affected outrageous squawks. The dirty fowl thwarted us at every turn leaving us angry and distraught. Our efforts were in vain. Oh, sometimes we succeeded to get the rooster to vacate for hours but it consistently reappeared.

After lengthy but animated conversation we concluded that Smedley's awful presence was, indeed, reincarnated evil and a detriment to health, happiness and the war effort.

None of us were crazy enough to induce Titmus' wrath by sending Smedley to a bird afterlife but we were desperate, enough was enough. We pondered more than a bit before unanimously agreeing. The demise of our feathered nemesis had become a dire necessity.

On the momentous evening, a cowboy flick was scheduled but Titmus failed to note that only he from our abode would be attending. "Smedley, behave yourself," he cautioned and left.

By the time Titmus meandered in from the movie his tent mates were feigning sleep. He kicked off this boondockers and shed his clothes. "Where's Smedley?"

A few of makeshift snores vibrated but none of us answered. Titmus lifted Arnie's mosquito net. "Where the hell's Smedley?"

"Ain't he here?" yawned Arnie.

"You know goddamn well he ain't!"

"I didn't notice, honest."

Titmus lit a candle and stomped from one cot to another shaking each of us. "I thought he was with you," whined O'Bannion.

"I didn't know he was gone," I said. "I swear!"

"Damned if I know where he's at," said Cassidy.

"He was here when I left and you wise-asses know it. I'm going looking and believe me, I better find him."

"Hey, I'll help," said O'Bannion. We all volunteered to search. Pulling on pants and shoes we joined Titmus and spread out. We called out for Smedley and devoted one energetic hour poking through brush and likely locations. We quizzed neighbors, those on guard duty and several bewildered gooks. None of them had heard, seen or knew the bird's whereabouts.

"Chickens sleep at night, don't they?" volunteered Arnie.

"Yeah, but something ain't right," growled Titmus. "Keep looking!"

The sergeant of the guard backed by two sentries appeared. "If you idiots keep prowling you're gonna get your asses shot off."

"We're looking for Smedley," explained Titmus.

"Get back into your fuckin' tent!"

In our abode Titmus suspiciously viewed each of us. He roughly grabbed Arnie by the throat. "You didn't like Smedley, did you?"

"I had nothing against him, honest!"

"Arnie was with us all night," I said.

"If he had gone someplace or done something we'd a spotted him," advised Cassidy.

"Maybe the bird got kidnapped?" offered O'Bannion.

Titmus released Arnie. I was as shaky as the others.

"Why would somebody kidnap a beat up rooster?" snarled Titmus.

"To eat!" discreetly said Cassidy.

"Yeah, some guys really like to eat chicken," I volunteered.

"Wait, that could be it! Gooks will eat anything," said Arnie.

"Why not offer a reward?" suggested O'Bannion.

"Hey, let's face it. Some of us had differences about Smedley," admitted Arnie, "but after awhile we got used to him, sort of."

"I miss him," I added, "Somewhat."

"You're all full of shit, each and every one of you!" snapped Titmus. "I'll get to the bottom of this, and when I do, something's gonna fly and it won't be feathers."

The next morning was Sunday. Arnie and I were eager to assist but we both got a case of the runs and barely made it to the head. Cassidy and O'Bannion begged off and both went to church. I silently speculated what they'd be praying about.

Titmus searched and quizzed. Before the sun set, he stumbled upon the smoldering remains in a wooded area. A few scraggled feathers and charred bones were amid the ashes. He mournfully deduced that the remains belonged to Smedley.

"Gooks!" growled O'Bannion.

We were jolted to realize how much Smedley meant to Titmus and heartfully commiserated. He skeptically eyed us and told us to shut our yaps. Of course, we clammed up. Order to our tent was restored and for a period of time all but Titmus slept well.

CHAPTER THIRTY-SIX

Titmus would neither forget nor forgive. He continued confronting us separately and interrogating. "When was the last time you saw Smedley?"

"Don't bullshit, I know you know something!"

In a mean mood he'd snarl, "Happy he's gone, ain't you?"

Occasionally he'd grit his teeth and snap, "You neither seen nor heard nothing! Hah! You're lying!"

Of course, we weren't disturbed because Smedley was gone, but we'd bask in delight after that abominable creature faded from his memory.

Three mornings later, Titmus' grieving dissipated after Lieutenant Hollering entered our tent. It was his first visit since Tollivan bought the farm. "You guys okay?" he asked and self-consciously peered about before producing a fifth of stateside whiskey.

It's seldom easy for officers and enlisted personnel to be sociable in each other's company. I speculate even less so in line companies. The lieutenant self-consciously set the bonded bottle on our table. We shifted a bit as he stuttered an apology for barging in, "This is from b-both of us," he whispered and left.

"Hmm," sighed Arnie.

"I'll be damned," said O'Bannion.

"Someone's coming," whispered Titmus and slid the bottle under his mattress.

Sergeant Lancaster barged in shouting, "Attentchut!"

Major Burke, Captain Plunkett, Lieutenant Fields and Sergeant Major Byron pushed in behind him.

Byron held a pencil and small black book. Disapproval reflected on the major's face as his eyes probed each corner of our tent.

Our quarters were in better than fair shape and our rifle barrels were clean and oiled. Rips in mosquito nets and tent punctures were beyond our control. We had diligently prepared for the squadron's field day inspection.

Frequent downpours had muddied our deck but that wasn't unusual. Other tents had suffered similar damages. Mementos of Smedley's unsavory presence remained.

Major Burke counted perforations on our canvas walls. He also sounded off on domicile imperfections including askewed pillows, wrinkled blankets and our semi-soppy deck. Byron copied each criticism into his black book.

Burke ranted, "The holes in this goddamn tent are the most numerous in the squadron!"

We stood rigid as Byron echoed the major's rant, "You fuck-ups are not only a disgrace to the Corps but you're a detriment to VMF 111 and whatever----," he stuttered while scribbling.

Lancaster sagely nodded.

The major moved his face inches from Titmus' nose. "Private Titmus, you been in long enough to know better!"

"Yes, sir!" said Titmus.

The major checked his watch. "Get this tent squared away and I mean, now!"

"Yes, sir," snapped Titmus as the sky opened up and rain spilled. The major groaned before striding out as rivulets streamed across our earthen deck.

Above the noisy downpour, we heard our Corsairs roar into the air and zoom away. "I wish I was flying one," wistfully mumbled Arnie.

The major's demeanor didn't upset me for long. I had become inured to doing things wrong and being held accountable.

Thunder exploded over Makin and torrents cascaded. We listened to the huge drops pounding our shelter. A muddy stream sloshed through our tent.

Titmus opened Hollering's bottle, taking a long swig before passing it to me. It tasted mellower than Titmus' green-tinged raisin jack. After Hollering's gift emptied we went back to sampling Titmus' evil tasting concoction.

"Ear-banging bastard."

"Ass-hole!"

"Kiss ass!"

"Prick!"

Haranguing Lancaster kept us focused. "Please pass the canteen cup," said O'Bannion.

"You're fucked up," I lisped.

"Like hell I am," snapped O'Bannion.

"You wouldn't say please if you weren't," I goaded

"You mean I got no manners?"

"I didn't say it but it's true."

O'Bannion made like he was going to get up until Titmus announced, "I've decided to kill Lancaster!"

"What?" said Arnie.

Titmus staggered to our rifle rack and pulled out his Garand. He shoved a clip into the breech.

"Easy Earl," said Arnie.

"The slippery ear-banging bastard is out to get us!" said Titmus and slid. We held our breath as he splatted in the mud. He struggled up and tripped to the flap. "Don't leave!" "You're drunk!" "We'll get him later!" "At least wait until it stops raining!" were our imprecations..

"Rain will cover my tracks," said Titmus as he lurched outside. Darkness had descended as slanted water fell in proverbial buckets.

"He's gonna kill Lancaster," sighed Arnie.

"We better stop him!"

"How can anybody stop Titmus!"

"He's drunk!"

"We're all drunk."

"We gotta get him!"

"Let's go!"

We moved outside and were engulfed by torrents. Cold and drenched we crowded back to our tent. Suddenly shots sounded. O'Bannion counted four as screams commenced. We were still aghast when Titmus, drenched and dripping, barged in.

He swung his rifle onto the rack, pulled off shoes and clothes and slipped under his mosquito net. Still cold and wet his eyes closed. "Get in your sacks," he rasped. A series of phony snores gushed.

We were in various stages of undress as Sergeant Major Byron tailed by Corporal Jones and PFC Martin burst in wet and armed.

Cassidy gaped and muttered, "What's up, Sarge?".

"You don't know?" snapped the Sergeant Major.

We looked perplexed. Titmus peeked out from under his net. "We being attacked?"

"Sons of bitches tried to kill Lancaster!"

"Did the Japs get him?" I said.

"The assassin missed."

"Too bad," muttered Arnie.

"That's bad!" corrected O'Bannion.

"Wounded?" queried Cassidy striving to smother a hopeful inflection.

"Holes in his tent!" spouted Martin.

"Poor bastard could get wet," said Titmus.

"Who could have done such a crazy thing?" said Arnie.

"It wasn't Japs," said Byron. "Any of you leave this tent tonight!" He searched for telltale footprints but our deck was too muddy.

"I'll get to the bottom of this bullshit!" snapped Byron and stalked out trailed by Jones and Martin.

"How about that?" said Arnie.

"Byron didn't check our rifles," said O'Bannion.

"No, he didn't," and Titmus grinned as he slipped under his mosquito net.

Rain continued until late the next morning. After it tapered off, the ground was still too wet and muddy to dig and collect debris.

Bad weather kept planes from leaving Majuro so they remained there for three days. On the fourth, the downpour slackened to a drizzle and our pilots flew toward Makin. On the way back they bomb dropped Jaluit.

By that time thunder again exploded over Makin and deluges fell. Our squadron came in from their return run. One by one they dropped out of the blackened sky. Seven landed through the driving rain. One was unaccounted for.

Squadron pilots and ground crew gathered at the radio shack. Lieutenant Hollering was piloting the missing F4U. We heard his broken but legible message. "Too much static I can barely read you," he rasped.

"Where are you?" implored Sergeant Blue, our radio operator.

"Don't have a clue," answered Hollering.

"What about your compass?"

"Ain't working."

"Can you see anything?"

"Nothing, too soupy and I'm running on empty." His voice was calm. Drawn faces paled and breathing was labored.

"Into the drink," calmly said Hollering as if heading for the slopchute. "Maybe I'll meet my buddy."

"Shit!" said Major Burke and stamped into the outside deluge. Tearful pilots withdrew while we grimly drifted back to our sodden quarters.

CHAPTER THIRTY-SEVEN

Little Makin, our new home base, was two hundred miles from Tarawa, another coral island in the Gilbert chain.

A guy could drown, get devoured by a shark, bashed in by falling trees or picked off by prowling Jap survivors. Posted warnings directed personnel to be especially cautious regarding falling coconuts.

Those unforeseen threats seldom occurred, but the archaic British Marine saying, 'Tell it to the Marines!' was still in vogue.

After our squadron had settled, explored and investigated, there was little to do and or look forward to until a lively announcement stirred things up.

Jack Benny and his U.S.O. entourage, including Carole Lombard and Martha Tilton were scheduled to arrive.

We joyfully anticipated seeing and hearing the renowned beauty. 'Liltin' Martha's coveted 8x10 was displayed above Arnie's cot and her winsome photo adorned other tents too. Oh, yes, Makin's varied military personnel eagerly awaited the renowned troup's arrival.

On the big night the stage area was jammed. The suspenseful audience was too numerous, many were unable to sit. Those compelled to stand did so without complaining. When the festive troupe stepped on the stage a spirited roar welcomed them.

After Jack Benny delighted his audience with jokes, beautiful Carole Lombard and lovely Martha warbled popular songs. During the show, the vivacious ladies exchanged delightful quips with wise-cracking Jack Benny while he soberly strummed his violin.

The accomplished violinist and world renowned funnyman was a class act. As he and his entourage entertained, the indomitable actresses were attacked by the island's voracious insects. As the unsavory assortment of six-legged swoopers dove about them, those gutsy ladies manifested feminine courage. We were delighted as they reacted with feigned terror.

Their audience appreciated show-biz's "The show must go on!" tradition with gleeful cheers as the ensemble gallantly continued.

The show lasted two hours but ended too soon. After the finale clamorous applause was showered by the appreciative audience. The delighted audience had been thoroughly entertained.

The following morning the repertoire departed for other isolated posts to bring home and hearth memories to other bedraggled troops. After they left, we fondly discussed their spirit-lifting visit. But as days slipped by ennui's disheartening cloud returned and we again were enshrouded with listlessness, languor and futile lust.

Weeks went by before word spread that Bob Hope, accompanied by a bevy of entertainers and lovely ladies, would soon be landing. All hands anticipated another appreciative break from our repetitious bullshit work.

The day Bob Hope's troupe landed, Ground Defense was still squaring away the interiors of our tents. We didn't want to give Lancaster or any other authoritive demon an excuse to keep us from attending.

Speculations ran amok. Who could foresee what Francis Langford, Hopes' accompanying songstress might pull. Some lucky buck-ass private could be pulled out of the audience for a courtesy kiss, dance or whatever. Our tent's occupants did harbor concerns. After all, a few poor bastards would be obligated to perform guard duty and miss the show. We could be among the unlucky scapegoats.

Like a bird of doom, Lancaster stepped into our abode. We sullenly dared him to find something wrong. He scanned our quarters. "Hmm, hard to believe! This tent is actually squared away. You people must be expecting visitors."

"You're irritating us, Lancaster?" snarled Titmus.

"Now Titmus, that ain't no way to talk to a sergeant!" whined Lancaster. "You been a Marine long enough to know that!"

"You wouldn't make a pimple on a real Marine sergeant's ass!" snapped Titmus.

"Well, since I'm not bearing good news, I'll let that pass."

"Uh, oh," said O'Bannion.

"I'm sure you people are aware that Bob Hope is putting on his show tonight."

Titmus squinted.

"You realize that most personnel will be attending. I mean everybody in every outfit on this godforsaken rock."

"So!" said Titmus.

"Now the Nips know it too. You've heard Tokyo Rose, she seems to know about everything we do. The colonel has ordered us to stay alert in case the Japs try to pull a Carlson type raid. They haven't forgot what he did."

"He wants reliable people to guard against possible enemy forays. Guess who are chosen for this precarious duty?" Lancaster grinned like the cat that ate the rat.

"Pulling your usual bullshit, eh, Lancaster?" spat Titmus.

"Wasn't my idea," grinned Lancaster.

"Who picked us!" said Arnie.

"Captain Plunkett! He said something about you people always being involved in shady shit. Guess he figures you can use some quiet time to think over misdeeds. Those are his words, not mine."

Titmus moved like he was about to snatch Lancaster's throat.

"You'll be acting sergeant of the guard, Titmus!" blurted Lancaster.

"Bullshit!" snapped Titmus clenching his fists.

"Captain Plunkett's order!" cried Lancaster. "Not mine!"

"Shit!" snapped O'Bannion.

"He'll have someone checking on you people so I advise you walk posts in a military manner."

Arnie called out, "Suckass!" as Lancaster withdrew.

The hours flitted by until banter and laughter spilled as people vacated tents to move toward the show place. Before 1800, a disgruntled Corporal Hayden arrived and ordered us to follow. Titmus, Arnie, O'Bannion, Cassidy and I filled canteens, grabbed rifles and apathetically followed him. Taps, as usual, forlornly trailed us to the guard shack. He sprawled outside and chewed on his thigh.

Four shitbirds from the SBD squadron were also stuck with the depressive duty. We were a morose collection of losers.

As Arnie, O'Bannion, and two fuck-ups from the other group walked posts on first shift, the rest of us crapped out on the guard shack cots. We silently awaited our turns to walk our post to guard against nothing.

We tensed as thundering machinery suddenly shook the guard tent. The cacophony diminished to a low rumble as Taps yelped and was heard pattering off. "What the fuck!" said Titmus.

Foul curses preceded the stumbling entry of a broad-shouldered buck sergeant. The aged noncom was attired in faded fatigues. Each sleeve on his tapered shirt was adorned with three stripes. Short and solid, his battered nose, jutting jaw and bull-neck proclaimed problems.

"Is a sorry looking poor excuse fuck-up called Earl Titmus here?" he roared.

Titmus leaped out from under the mosquito net. "Demolition" Hogan, you son of a bitch I thought you was dead."

Grins spread as they leaned on each other pumping hands and pounding backs. When the greetings subsided Titmus turned. "Demolition" Hogan is my old shipmate from the Fourth. We done duty together in Shanghai before you fuck-ups were out of grammar school. Hell, Hogan, I thought you were trapped with the Fourth on Corregidor."

"A month before Pearl they sent me to Lejune to learn about armored shit."

"Lucky bastard."

"Got transferred into tanks. Screw that walking shit."

"Lot of good guys gone," said Titmus.

"Biggy" Johnson, "Slim" Halloway, "Bug-eye" Bernstein – all of them."

"Didn't you go seagoing, Earl? Thought you'd be deep-sixed by now."

"Had enough seagoing spit and polish bullshit. I'm an Airdale now."

"Never figured you to become a candy-assed Airdale."

"Wasn't my choice but it ain't bad duty, Hogan."

"Ran into Byron at the sorry-assed noncom club. He told me you were here. He's a fuckin' Airdale too."

"He's still hard assed."

"Same squared away bullshit, eh!"

Cassidy and I were stunned. We hadn't known Byron and Titmus had served together.

Titmus eyed the stripes on Hogan's sleeve. "That shirt borrowed or you've been banging ears!"

"Earl, I'm a technician now. Technical bars ain't as prestigious as rockers but the stripes pay the same."

"I'll be damned," muttered Titmus.

"Come on, I'll show you my darling."

He led us to a small coral dust covered tank parked near our shower. A short compact guy was hosing down the small tank. "This is Emily, the most sensitive lady among baby tanks. And this wetwasher is Johnny Carson, my second in command. We even get a third crewman; he'll take orders from Johnny."

Carson was impassive, but when Hogan nodded, he broke out a jar of liquid that looked and smelled like de-icer fluid. They accompanied us back to the guard tent. "I ain't surprised you got something stashed," said Titmus.

Hogan diluted the evil looking stuff with water and poured some into each of our extended cups. Titmus pried open a gallon can of peaches he pulled out of nowhere and plunked half a peach into each cup. It looked better than it tasted but nobody complained.

"How long you been in tanks?" queried Titmus.

"Oriented me into them when I got to Lejune."

"I'll be damned."

"It's a helluva change."

"I bet."

"I ain't complainin'."

"I can see that."

"Now how'd in hell did you get to be an Airdale?" asked Hogan.

"I ain't sure, but you know how it is, the right way or the Corps' way. You sure as hell won't die from excitement, but it ain't bad duty."

"Well, what do you do, Earl, fly? No you don't do that! Do you?"

"Hell, no! My MO is Ground Defense."

"Anti-aircraft shit?"

"Not even close!"

"What kind of shit you into?"

"Shit details, that's what! Yeah, that's what we do."

Hogan thought Titmus might be kidding. "If you're inclined, old buddy, I could get you transferred into my outfit."

"I ain't interested in squeezing into tanks or any other military shit."

"These tin cans grow on you."

"Don't interest me even a little. You see, I got plans, Hogan. As soon as I get back I'm getting hitched. As soon as this war's over I'm through with uniforms."

"Ahh, you couldn't fit into a tank anyway."

While Hogan and Titmus sipped they reminisced about the sashaying dames along Nanking and Bubbling Well Roads. We had heard the tales before but lurid modifications piqued our interest.

"This camp deserted?" asked Johnny, "Where in hell is the rest of your outfit?"

"Bob Hope is giving a one night show," mumbled Cassidy. "We got stuck with guard duty."

Titmus spat details featuring Lancaster and Plunkett's nasty doings. Cassidy and I added unpleasant accounts about our hostile superiors.

Hogan and Johnny got the picture. "The old Corps is shot to hell," whispered Hogan and huffed his way to his feet. "C'mon, Earl, I'll take you guys for a ride."

"We can't fit in that can," said Titmus.

"Leave the technical shit to me," slurred Hogan.

Cassidy's eyes were wide open but he was in no condition to move. It wouldn't be long before he'd be relieving Arnie. "I'd better pass," he sighed.

Johnny filled his glass with a shot of jungle juice as Titmus and I followed Hogan outside. He tried to simplify tank workings for us but I couldn't fathom whatever he was trying to convey.

Titmus heeded Hogan's foot to shoulder directions of how the turret man directs the unseeing driver. Titmus was too bulky to squeeze himself into the tank's cockpit. Hogan and I pushed, pulled and pressed until we managed to get him jammed in. Hogan positioned himself atop him. I boarded and clung.

Hogan's verbal foot directions to Titmus somehow got the metal thing moving. Emily ploughed through the bush and clanged onto the road. We rumbled past Arnie dispiritly trudging along. His rifle hung listlessly from his shoulder and he paid little heed as we clanged by.

We roared through our deserted encampment, worming between and around empty tents. At the edge of the officers' compound Hogan brought the tank to a grinding stop.

"Captain Plunkett's tent," I pointed.

"Where is he?" said Hogan.

"At the show," I said.

"Hold on!" said Hogan. As the tank moved Titmus adjusted his cumbersome bulk. I prayed to be somewhere else. The tank picked up speed and I hollered. I was ready to drop off but the armored missile kept barreling along.

As we rolled toward Plunkett's quarters my heart pounded. While the tank rolled over the captain's tent I shut my eyes. When I looked back and saw the captain's flattened tent, I became nauseated. Hogan guided us back to the guard tent.

We had trouble ejecting Titmus. Hogan and I struggled as we pushed and pulled. The three of us were panting and soaked in sweat before Titmus was extracted.

"That should give your chickenshit captain something to think about," said Hogan.

Titmus almost looked composed but I was scared shitless. Johnny came out and greeted us. He was more than half in the bag but managed to position himself in the tank.

"We're moving out tomorrow," said Hogan. "Earl, take care."

"You too," said Titmus. "Thanks for the ride."

We half-heartedly waved as Hogan and Johnny rattled off in a cloud of coral dust.

It was after pitch black by the time the Bob Hope show ended. While we trod our posts, we heard Captain Plunkett thrashing about trying to find his tent. When he discovered its remnants a terrible commotion erupted. Flashlights probed the tank tracks. Flattened debris told the story.

Of course, tank tracks told the story and officer and noncom investigators strived to solve the enigma. All sentries unanimously agreed that rumbling noises were heard but there were no witnesses. Arnie and those of us on guard duty were continuously quizzed but unable to shed enlightenment. We were as nonplussed as the rest regarding the disaster that had befallen our captain's quarters.

For not walking his post in an alert manner, Arnie was again sentenced to three days of hard-time in Makin's army stockade. Other problems abruptly beset VMF 111, causing the ongoing investigation to be shelved.

Audience members who had witnessed both performances assured us that Bob Hope's show had been a rollicking affair, but not nearly as roisterously entertaining as Jack Benny's joyful ensemble.

CHAPTER THIRTY-EIGHT

Chilly droplets drenched mortals, dogs, tents, planes, and all else as the monsoon season burst upon us. While liquid torrents pelted, discomfort was somewhat mollified because watery deluges lessened fly and mosquito action.

During cloudbursts, Corsair forays ceased. There was nothing for anybody to do but guzzle home brew and grouse about whomever or whatever.

"What a fuckin' way to fight a war!" spat Cassidy.

"You're still snowing yourself that you're one helluva warrior!" I smirked.

Cassidy leaped to his feet. "You wanna test me, wise ass!"

Spoiling to settle differences, I leaped up, raised fists and danced about as Cassidy warily circled me. We lounged toward each other but stopped short when Titmus said, "Set your dumb asses down!"

We sat.

We were still pouting when Arnie, water pouring from his poncho, shouldered into the tent. He looked like a drowned rat. He shed his soaked clothes and sat. "The promotion list is posted," he sighed.

"So you ain't on it," smirked Cassidy.

"Neither are you," stated Arnie.

"You shittin' me!" Cassidy snapped and glared as if it was Arnie's fault.

"That Lancaster fucked me again?" Although Cassidy sensed the disconcerting news was true he jogged through the downpour to see for himself. The rest of us, sure we weren't on the list, stayed put.

Cassidy returned and shed his wet clothes. Without an utterance he crawled into his sack. He may have laid there all night staring up and seeing nothing.

In the morning, rain subsided and Ground Defense had much to do. The ground was littered with coconuts and palm fronds. Ground Defense was ordered to gather up and erect nice neat piles of debris. "Shit duty! Shit duty and more shit duty!" proclaimed Cassidy.

Days later an LST pulled into Makin's shallow harbor. Supplies along with a passel of shiny-faced replacements were ferried ashore. We were hoping, no, praying that the new guys were our relief.

No information was posted, nothing official, but a frenzied feeling spread that barring some kind of invasion we old timers would be going home. Scuttlebutt was rampantly bandied about.

Most of the newcomers were eager seventeen and eighteen year youngsters eager to enter the fray. But there were also apprehensive draftees among the starched and squared away arrivals.

We didn't have the spirit to welcome them with the traditional but over-used, "You'll be sorry!"

The foul weather tapered and the tropical sun toasted. While we hopefully awaited venue change, Staff Sergeant Lancaster barged into our tent with a new straight bar under his sergeant stripes.

He limped from the forgotten beer bottle laceration acquired on Roi. "A one-star general named Pierce is gonna inspect VFM 111. The squadron's gonna parade in review. We're gonna be inspected and graded.

"Look sharp and don't fuck up or you'll rue this day. The general is gonna give a speech and pass out medals, purple hearts, flying commendations, the whole shebang. That's straight from Major Burke. Dress khakis and clean boon-dockers will be the uniform of the day.

"Be at the airfield by 1400 looking like Marines! By the way, some of us are gonna get Purple Hearts for Roi-Namur." He purred.

"Are you serious?" said Arnie.

"Medals! Citations! We've been in action, remember?" quipped Lancaster.

"That half-assed bombing wasn't action!" scoffed Titmus.

"Some of us got wounded," simpered Lancaster.

"Hah!" retorted Titmus.

"The general wants to hand out citations. You want to argue with him! The major is edgy so Ground Defense fuck-ups better act and look sharp. Don't say I didn't warn you!"

As Lancaster headed out Arnie said, "Why you limping?"

"While you guys were hiding on Roi-Namur, I caught a hunk of shrapnel in my ankle."

"Before or after you stepped on the broken beer bottle?"

"Fuck you!" snapped Lancaster and slipped away.

Like everyone else in the squadron we got squared away. Shortimers couldn't afford to take chances. A minor fuck-up could give some hard-ass officer an excuse to keep a guy from heading home when his overseas time was up.

We stood decked out for the first legitimate formation called for in a long time. Major Burke, Captain Plunkett and Brigadier General Pierce, a stout figure attired in starched khaki stood beaming flanked by the major and captain. He tried to suck in his stomach but his belly still protruded over his shiny brass buckle. The buckle glow matched the shiny star pinned on each starched collar.

Officers observed as Sergeant Major Byron sounded cadence. Attired in half-pressed khaki, VMF 111's enlisted privates and noncoms almost looked sharp marching up along the airfield. We were maneuvered into two lines behind a double row of pilots and line officers. All hands fought to refrain from fidgeting as we stood at half-assed attention.

Major Burke droned on about exceptional duty for Corps and country expected and fulfilled at Roi-Namur. General Pierce gave the final speak. "Like Marines in the past, you men have done your duty.

You're a credit to the Corps, the flag and country. This squadron has lived up to the tradition of the Corps. You have done your duty well." He continued on and on about honor, tradition and sacrifice. "Blah blah blah."

As Sergeant Major Byron sounded off names, individuals stepped forward, stood, saluted and remained rigid while purple hearts were pinned. Each salute was returned by the captain and the recipient about-faced, smartly stepped back into the ranks. Arnie stared impassively into space as a medal was pinned on his shirt.

Lancaster's name was called and a bitter rumble rose while he limped forward. The major's scowl didn't quell disquieting mumbles.

"Broken-beer bottle, son-of-a- bitch," murmured Cassidy.

Muffled chortles reverberated. Corporal Martin heard but couldn't or wouldn't pinpoint the source. Chilly drizzles dropped and we were dismissed and made for our tents.

We took turns fingering Arnie's Purple Heart. We were a touch envious, at least I was. Shit, I reflected, I should have taken Corpsman Benny's offer. A Purple Heart looked impressive, somewhat heroic. Of course, I kept my misgivings to myself. Arnie's indifference to our exaggerated hullabaloo was disquieting. His moods were becoming more vexing and irksome.

"What's eatin' you, Arnie?" blurted Titmus.

A sorrowful grimace spread across his face. "Nothin'," he grunted.

"Well, you sure as hell been doin' a lot of moping," said Cassidy.

"Ain't gonna make it," quietly stated Arnie.

"Bullshit," said Titmus, "we're going home."

"Soon," added Cassidy.

"I won't be goin'," said Arnie.

"Sure you will, we'll see to it!" said O'Bannion

Arnie sadly shook his head. "I don't want to go."

His constant look of despair exasperated us. His negative attitude got to be a pain. Despite our concern and scorn regarding his downed attitude, we sensed something was deeply amiss. We shied off demanding that he participate in squaring away our tent.

Even Lieutenant Rameron spotted something amiss in Arnie's behavior and advised Lancaster to lay off him. The rest of us commenced dividing his clean-up responsibilities.

As our departure day neared we became more edgy. The rain finally ceased and we were blessed with a sunny day.

Titmus got our attention as he reminisced about when the *U.S.S. Yorktown* was in New York Harbor receiving guests. The huge carrier was being inspected by Mrs. Vanderbilt and a Mrs. Astor. Both ladies were blue bloods. Both wealthy ladies were impressed by the ship and crew. They related their mutual admiration of the giant ship and crew to Admiral Halsey.

"I think everything about this great ship is simply marvelous," gushed Mrs. Vanderbilt. "But I was really impressed by those Marines and would like to invite those handsome boys to my mansion for a tea party."

"The entire Marine contingent?" queried the dubious admiral.

"Of course," smiled Mrs. Vanderbilt.

"I'll convey your invitation."

"Captain O'Merlin was senior officer of the Marine detail and implicitly instructed grizzled Gunnery Sergeant Hamber to caution his seagoing Marine detail to watch their manners and décor during the forthcoming soirée."

Sergeant Hamber cautioned, "Don't do or say anything that will discredit the Corps!"

"Aye, aye, Sergeant!" was the spirited response.

"It was a grand affair. Young Marines attired in dress blues conversed and sipped tea with attractive debutantes. All was going well and Mrs. Vanderbilt was more than a little pleased until she spotted Gunnery Sergeant Hamber gingerly balancing his teacup. She approached and said, "Sergeant, would you like a crumpet?"

"Oh, no thank you, Madam, I don't eat that shit!" he grunted.

Vanderbilt moved off but stopped. "Did that man actually say what I think?" she murmured, to herself, of course. "No, he couldn't have." She had to make sure and converged on Hamber. "Sergeant, sir. Would you like a crumpet?"

"Madam, I told you I don't eat that shit."

Vanderbilt indignantly strode to the captain who was regaling a ring of admiring debutantes about responsibilities aboard the *Yorktown*.

"Captain, could I have a word?" said the distraught Mrs. Vanderbilt.

"Excuse me ladies," and the captain joined her.

"Your Marines have been perfect gentlemen," she simpered, "but that older one, oh my," and she pointed.

"What did he say?" said the captain and stared at the gunnery sergeant.

Mrs. Vanderbilt blushed and tearfully sighed, "That horrid man said, I don't eat that shit!"

The captain turned crimson.

"I had merely asked him if he'd like a crumpet," wept Mrs. Vanderbilt.

"Fuck him, madam!" snapped Captain O'Merlin, "let him starve!"

We cackled and whooped it up but not a chortle came out of Arnie.

Titmus broke out a can of distilled Prune juice. Arnie sipped but didn't react, not even a belch. Because of his solemn attitude none of us were enthused. We tried to ease Arnie's dilemma by getting him pissed at us. We placed an evil looking coconut crab under his blanket and short-sheeted his cot. We chided him about his fucked-up attitude. He merely shuffled about looking like death warmed over. Nothing worked.

"I've seen that thousand-yard stare before, it ain't a good sign," said Titmus.

"We should do something," said O'Bannion.

"He'll come around," said Cassidy.

CHAPTER THIRTY-NINE

It was squally but not bad until Lancaster sporting his usual smirk stepped into our domicile. He smugly stipulated that personnel in our tent were designated to decommission a deteriorating officers' head.

"That glory hole has outlived its usefulness and you eager beavers have the honor of dismantling it. After that challenging task is completed, Captain Plunkett has entrusted you specialized shit house rejuvenators to fix up a less derailed shithouse."

His sardonic instructions included prying off a splintery wooden covering and igniting piled dung beneath. Afterwards we were designated to cover the wreaking waste.

As ordered we tore off worn planks and tossed them into the brush as falling rain lessened to a paltry drizzle. By the time we finished dismantling the outmoded toilet the weather cleared and the sun baked.

As we shoveled powdered coral over the odorous crevice the nasty odor attracted clouds of flies. The indignity of our task dismayed us.

"Dig, cover, dig," moaned Cassidy. "What do I tell them back home?"

"Tell them you served your country with honor by bravely digging shitholes," advised O'Bannion.

Arnie sighed, Titmus grunted and the rest of us stood staring. Our morale was far below zero.

Possibly from frustration, O'Bannion jostled me and I shoved back. We pushed and pulled each other. It was grimmer horseplay than the usual. Somehow Arnie, not paying attention, was unintentionally shoved. He lost his balance and before our horrified eyes slid into the gaping hole. His heart wrenching howl stabbed at our hearts as he plopped on the shit pile.

We didn't chortle but sadly waited while he struggled up and out. We abashedly followed him to our shower and stood at a respectable distance while he soaped, soaked and scrubbed. He showered three times satisfying neither us or himself. He finally emerged and we took our turn.

That night while Arnie was out of sight doing a guard duty stint we unanimously agreed that he was burdened with heavy problems. We agreed to attempt uplifting his downtrodden demeanor. Oh, yeah, we were determined to cheer him up.

Before our good intentions could be materialized, the stateside transfer notification was posted. All residents of our tent made the list. We would be on our way back to the good ole' USA in less than a week.

Excitement flared among the short timers. Even the forlorn looks of those remaining didn't dampen our homeward bound spirits. We hustled, bustled, and squared away gear and personal belongings. Promises to contact relatives and friends were made. Debts were paid and petty disagreements dispelled.

Arnie, tailed by Taps looking as forlorn as the man he trailed, took long walks in the woods and along the shoreline. Titmus advised us to let him sort things out by himself and we did.

Cassidy finagled a fourth of a raggedy parachute and cut the silken cloth into head band shapes. He again used his limited artistic ability to stain mercurochromed circles etched in red. His criss crossed markings could be taken for Japanese inscriptions. He modestly displayed his phony raggedy head banners to ambulating swabbies. Dog faces assigned to radar or meteorological tasks were also willing patrons. They weren't particular regarding souvenirs. The soldiers were technically smart, but Cassidy's snow job about phony Japanese head bands satisfied them. They eagerly exchanged booze, smokes and money for his creative bandanas.

"How can you live with yourself?" said O'Bannion.

"What you talkin' about?" snapped Cassidy.

"You're peddling bullshit, that's what!" O'Bannion was ready to go to battle stations.

"Hold it! I'm doing these kids a favor by saving them from spending money on gook booze. That poison will eat a guy's guts out. Remember those poor guys that went blind in Samoa. Nobody gets sick or hurt showing phony parachute bandanas. Because of me they get to go home heroic like."

"I don't believe it!" uttered O'Bannion.

"Well, what have you got to show for our time out here?"

"A campaign ribbon!"

"Big deal! Everyone's got one or more of them. You can buy them!"

"Yeah, and you'll end up in the brig or getting' the shit beat out of you!"

"Okay, tell the girls back home that you dug shitholes, that'll impress them." While Cassidy shook his head O'Bannion stalked out of the tent.

Titmus got a letter from Millie but didn't take time to read it. "I don't want to read about that dogface. First thing I do when I get back is straighten him out." Titmus looked concerned but assured us that he'd take care of the problem. His marriage was still on.

"Titmus, those corporal stripes look impressive," I said.

"Sixty-six bucks is nothing to sneeze at," added O'Bannion.

Titmus' thoughts were elsewhere. The wind abruptly kicked up and the skies spilled buckets. As rain pounded our tent we peeked out to see trees bending and coconuts thudding into the ground.

Fallon, one of our new replacement neighbors, opened our tent flap. "The world's coming to an end and I don't want to…." A coconut thudded off the back of his head and he plopped into our midst. He lay stunned but before we could act he sat up.

"What the fuck?" he groaned.

As we helped him into a cot he whimpered, "What happened?"

"A coconut tree got you," I said.

Still woozy Fallon rose and staggered back to his own tent.

Shortly afterwards another calamity evolved. The following day while the deluge worsened, Taps padded in front of a jeep and got hit. The driver had been slowly moving through the downpour. When he saw the bedraggled pooch cross in front he stomped his brake but his vehicle slid. Taps froze as the uncontrollable jeep glided toward him. The woeful mutt bounced off the bumper and lay inert amid the downpour.

Arnie gently scooped up the wet creature and carried the wounded canine to our tent and laid him down. We gathered around and moodily watched as Taps soulfully gazed up at Arnie. The pathetic animal throated a soulful whimper and expired.

Those of us scheduled to be relieved became leery. Chances of becoming a freak casualty before departure became more than somewhat conceivable.

The big day arrived before any more horrid happenings. On the morrow we'd sail to Majuro, another captured island of the Marshall Island chain. From there we'd head home. It sounded too good to be true.

Titmus finagled a can of green liquid. It wasn't great but not too bad. Arnie sipped with us but didn't converse. Taps untimely demise disturbed him.

"Relax, Arnie, we're going stateside," quipped Cassidy.

"I ain't going," said Arnie.

"Being Asiatic is worse than a fever. Snap out of it before it consumes you," warned Titmus.

At the chow hall we indulged in the familiar shit-on-a-shingle but not one complained. We were practically on our way home and would be eating edible food.

In our tent as we lounged about nursing what was left of Titmus' green jungle juice, our usual bitching was put on hold. "We have been to war and saw action, you know, kinda." said O'Bannion.

"Not much, but some," said Cassidy.

"Next to nothing," Titmus guffawed.

"Bombing raids are more than nothing," I said, somewhat put out. "There were casualties, remember!"

"It was no picnic!" said O'Bannion.

"Who cares? When the lovelies see my ribbons and hear about my action against the enemy, they'll swoon," said Cassidy.

"You gonna flash some phony ribbons too?" I said.

"If Lancaster can get a Purple Heart for stepping on a broken beer bottle, I guess I can spread a little bullshit too."

"It ain't kosher," I said feeling kind of stupid.

"Hey, Cassidy, you're not gonna wear phony medals or fancy Crosses, are you?" snapped O'Bannion.

"I'm still thinking," said Cassidy.

"I don't know about you two," I said as I swiveled to face Titmus for reinforcement.

"Who gives a shit!" he muttered, "don't make no difference to anyone except family and friends, maybe not even them."

"Cruz wanted to be a hero and look how he ended up," said O'Bannion.

"He was a fuckin' good Marine," said Cassidy.

"Yeah, I coulda been too if I'd been a pilot, rifleman or something besides a head digger," said O'Bannion.

"Sure," said Cassidy.

"If a guy does something heroic, lucky, dumb or whatever and gets a medal, good. If he don't, so what! Do your time, do what they tell you and try to stay alive." After his explosive tirade Titmus looked pissed.

We were feeling no pain as we sipped and bullshitted until midnight and were ready to call it quits when Titmus said to O'Bannion, "You really wanted to fly?"

"I do," said O'Bannion, "I do!"

"You're gonna get a shot at it."

"He can't drive a car let alone fly," I laughed.

"Let's find out if O'Bannion got what it takes," lisped Titmus and signaled to us to join him. Fairly tanked we followed Titmus outside. Only Arnie stayed put. Drizzles fell on as Titmus led us to the airstrip.

Allanby, a new replacement, was supposed to be guarding the strip but was no where in sight. We assumed he was hiding under a wing keeping dry.

Titmus led us to a revetment where one of the SNJ Dive bombers were parked. He motioned for O'Bannion to climb in. O'Bannion belched, stepped on the wing, pulled back the canopy and plopped into the front cockpit.

We watched as Titmus inserted a cartridge and spun the prop. The engine grunted and the propeller moved. The engine's cough came close to sobering us up.

"Shit! Let's get out of here," advised Titmus.

O'Bannion reluctantly scrambled out of the cockpit as Allanby came hot footing down the runway. "Who the fuck goes there!" he shouted and fired a round over our heads as we sprinted into the brush.

The wind kicked up and heavy rain fell. We were drenched by the time our haven hove in sight. We were ten feet from our canvas home when a huge coconut tree fell crumbling our tent.

From its interior we heard Arnie's scream. Marines emerged from neighboring tents. They helped us drag back the downed canvas. The tree trunk lay across Arnie's leg. He hollered bloody murder while a mob of us pulled the fallen trunk off his leg. Our corpsman drove up and we lifted Arnie into his jeep and drove him to sickbay.

In the excitement's aftermath, Allenby's disjointed report of intruders on the airfield was forgotten. Since Allenby had obviously not been doing what he was supposed to be, he didn't press the subject.

The next day before the mishap was sorted out homeward bound troops were ordered to board an LST heading for Majuro. We didn't even have time to visit Arnie at the army hospital.

"He'll be okay," said Titmus.

"Arnie will think he's in heaven tucked between clean sheets," observed Cassidy.

"Poor Arnie being pampered by cute army nurses while we're on our way Stateside," portended Titmus.

"Lucky bastard," said O'Bannion.

"Would you take his place if you could?" I snidely asked.

"Not for a million bucks," sighed O'Bannion.

"Shit, I'd do it for a million," said Cassidy.

CHAPTER FORTY

The LST pulled away from Makin Island after thirty homeward bound short timers boarded her. The short trip back to the Marshall Islands was subdued and uneventful. Majuro, our immediate destination, was wooded with green foliage and much larger than Roi-Namur. To us, it was just another rock wrested from the Japs, but it was a stepping-stone toward the U.S.A. and that kept us spirited.

We were scooted ashore and quartered into one of the island's haphazardly erected tented compounds. Scores of Marines from line company outfits were billeted in adjoining transient tents. They also were impatiently awaiting stateside transportation

Titmus, O'Bannion, Cassidy, and I found a semi-isolated pyramid tent and moved in. Tents occupied by transient troops were erected above slightly warped wooden decks, a luxurious addition.

After Roi-Namur and Kwajalien had been taken, a less furious skirmish against Japanese technical troops ensconced on Majuro had been taken by a contingent of the 22nd. Scuttlebutt still ran rampant that some desperate enemy holdouts still lurked in Majuro's scraggly forest.

Line-company Marines hadn't spied them, but stateside-bound transients stayed wary. We were on our way home and it would be exceedingly untimely to get shot before our long awaited homeland reentry.

Despite downpours, there was a shortage of purified drinking and bathing water. Skivvies, khaki trousers and single bars of saltwater soap were issued. Personnel who had already been ensconced long before our arrival had built oil drum showers. Those still around could luxuriate in freshwater cleansing.

Transient troops had to make do with ocean bathing. Saltwater soap didn't lather, so after emerging from saltwater sea baths skin felt far from refreshed.

"My pores are plugged," moaned Cassidy.

"You expected purification?" said O'Bannion.

"By the time we leave this shithole, we'll be decorated with colorful new jungle rot afflictions," I predicted.

Each morning, along with other short-timers, we policed the surrounding area. Rumors regarding hidden Japs ran rampant. We were skeptical, after all, alarming bullshit among leathernecks was far from a rarity. But being new to the island and not knowing our way around, we weren't about to take chances. We stayed wary, none of us fancied being clobbered by a holdout Jap.

Two days of interminal waiting and scuttlebutt that we maybe spending weeks waiting for transportation home inspired Titmus to procure an empty gasoline drum. It was a grubby can caked with rust but usable.

O'Bannion and I staged a shouting, shoving match about whether California was better than Massachusetts to distract Seabee carpenters. The elderly construction workers, anticipating a fight, focused on us while Titmus and Cassidy purloined several planks from their lumber pile.

Titmus borrowed a hammer and stole some nails and we commenced constructing. There wasn't a carpenter among us but we managed to drill a hole in our battered barrel and mounted it.

A short distance from our canvas domicile was a semi-freshwater lake continually being replenished by rain water. The expanse held semi-clear water.

With minimal bitching we devoted hours to wearily shuffling back and forth from lake to oil drum toting brimming helmets filled with water.

By mid-morning our drum was brimming. We drew cards to see who would go first, second, third and so on. O'Bannion hit the launching jackpot. Stripped and impatient we stood behind for our turn.

Draped with towels Titmus, Cassidy, and I observed O'Bannion gingerly stepping onto the planking. As he shivered while soaping we shouted at him to hurry. He finally yanked the shower cord and sighed with pleasure while lovely liquid cascaded over him.

We were shouting at him to hurry when the unmistakable sound of a carbine pinged as it struck the makeshift shower. As the bullet penetrated two streams gushed out from both sides of our oil drum shower. We all crouched and watched Titmus sprinting to our tent.

He emerged with his Garand at high port and told us to move. While he scanned the woods the rest of us retrieved our rifles and tried visualize the sniper.

O'Bannion claimed there was movement in the wooded area and fired.

"Avast!" roared Titmus as a grizzled old line company gunnery sergeant waddled up.

"What the hells goin'on!" he roared.

"Somebody took a potshot at us," said Titmus.

"Jap?" said the sergeant.

"We don't know," said Cassidy.

"Has to be!" spat O'Bannion.

"The phantom sniper," sighed the gunner.

"What?" said O'Bannion.

"Some bastard's been taking indiscriminate potshots. He's been at it for a couple of days."

"Jap?"

"If it is, he's got an American carbine."

"Hit anybody?" asked Titmus.

"Not yet."

"The fucker don't shoot good! If he's a Jap he lost his glasses," said the gunner.

"Maybe he don't want to hit." I offered.

"He's came damn close," growled Titmus.

"He almost got one of our corporals at headquarters. We been tryin' to track the slippery bastard."

"Shit, the fucker ruined my shower. I'm going after him," said O'Bannion.

"Don't do nothin' stupid! I'll report this to the right people. Keep your eyes peeled," cautioned the gunner and took off.

As we scrutinized the foliage clump from afar, suggestive shadows played havoc with our imaginations. We became a bunch of unsettled trigger-happy boots. Only Titmus' curt admonishments kept us from haphazardly shooting at the clump of trees. After darkness enshrouded the island, it was impossible to detect a realistic target,

In the morning, we patched the two holes and hauled more water. By four we were exhausted but our drum brimmed. It was time for our cleansing rituals.

This time Titmus was first. He draped his towel over a protruding nail before stepping in.

Cassidy was next. O'Bannion and I, armed and alert, scanned the area while Titmus reached for the shower cord. As water poured, a single shot ricocheted off the top rim of the barrel. We crouched and scrutinized the mass of trees.

"In them trees again!" said Titmus.

We couldn't penetrate the thick growth. The wind was still and nothing moved. Labored breathing and buzzing insects were the only sounds. At Titmus' signal we cautiously backed into our tent.

"Jap holdouts?" said O'Bannion.

"Maybe, but it could be some asshole thinking he's funny," offered Cassidy.

"Let's lay a trap," said Titmus.

"How?"

"Whatever or whoever it is, a Jap or one of our own is playing a stupid game, he got to pay," gritted Titmus.

The next morning in kneeling and prone positions, our rifles at the ready, we waited.

"Should we fire?" queried O'Bannion.

"At what!" spat Titmus.

"I thought something moved."

"Bullshit!"

"Let's show the cocksucker we mean business," said O'Bannion.

The gunnery Sergeant from the 22nd lumbered up. "Now what's goin' on?"

"He's out there again," said Titmus.

"Stow that bullshit, the asshole was nabbed this morning."

"What!" said O'Bannion.

"How?"

"Where?"

"Jap?"

"Nope, just a crazy Airdale staff sergeant. Name's Lancaster, ring a bell?"

"Holy shit!"

"Nuttier than a fruit cake."

"You sure?"

"Flipped his lid. We found him under a bush whining and babbling that there were people out there worse than the Japs. Then he tried beating his brains out with his rifle stock, the guy went bananas." The gunner looked chagrinned. "I've seen guys go rock-happy before but not that bad."

"Lancaster off his rocker," chortled Cassidy.

"What a shame," snickered O'Bannion.

We refrained from chuckling as we set aside weapons, and stripped. It was time to shower again. Cassidy picked the lucky slip and stepped under the spigot. He pulled the cord and water cascaded over him, we cheered until the corroded circular base of the barrel precipiticously unhinged and its metal bottom plummeted down brushing his head. As blood spurted from his mangled scalp he screamed bloody murder. We got him to the sickbay where the corpsman on duty bandaged him up.

Three mornings passed before the *U.S.S. Britton,* a baby aircraft carrier, dropped anchor in the offing. She had come to transport homebound troops to Pearl Harbor. Cassidy was in no shape to travel and sat on his cot looking despondent. We signed our names on his huge head bandage and tried to comfort him as we bade goodbye.

"Hey, Cassidy, you might even get a medal for getting wounded by a shower barrel," offered O'Bannion.

"You think so?"

"Why not?" encouraged Titmus.

"A Purple heart is a Purple heart," I added.

"I bet you do get that Purple Heart," grunted Titmus and thought he was being amusing, but he was the only one thinking it's funny. Of course, Cassidy bravely tried to grin, but the only thing that somewhat cheered him was when O'Bannion assured him that Lancaster was going home in a straitjacket.

None of us knew for sure, but Titmus assured Cassidy that in the fucking new Corps anything could happen. "All hands could wind up with a medal," he said. We left Cassidy despondent but hopefully musing about decorative possibilities.

CHAPTER FORTY-ONE

The wide-decked ship was crammed with troops. The freshly-painted gray vessel was designated to transport several hundred overseas veterans, most of them from different air squadrons to Hawaii.

The picturesque island of Ohau was to be our last port-of-call before resuming our final stateward bound journey. VMF 111 veterans and jubilant passengers from other outfits were finally going home. Nothing could derail us, or so we thought, we were on our way.

Incapacitated jeeps and trucks destined to be repaired were lashed on the top deck. Bunks were stacked below. Each narrow bunk was occupied by a homeward bound Marine.

We sat, paced and gazed seaward. The decks above and below were crowded with restless young people. Many were adorned with stripes, Airedale personnel were promoted more frequently than line company troops. Because of the ship's cleanliness and crew congestion, there were few shit duties to perform.

The second day out I scrutinized a poker game played on the hangar deck. I fingered four hundred accumulated bucks stashed in my pocket and observed the five players engrossed in the game. They looked normal.

I had seldom done well gambling, I wasn't smart or lucky enough excepted for one unusual streak in a dice game on Makin when I won three hundred dollars. Five other twenties in my pocket constituted what was left of three months back pay. After fourteen months in the South and Central Pacific I was elated to be going home with a wad of bills. My luck had finally changed I concluded.

The lone Marine and swabbie dealer invited me to join. I committed a blunder by buying one-hundred dollars worth of chips. The dealer shuffled as if he was playing a musical instrument. I didn't heed that subtle warning

The other players were as deft and I quickly lost my first hundred. Soon another hundred went and then another. When dealt credible hands I raised but to no avail, I kept losing.

Finally, I won one hand but later sadly surmised it had been an accident. Poorer and somewhat wiser, I meekly surrendered my seat and departed. I was aware that I had been taken for the proverbial sucker ride. It was a deflating experience and I concluded that Japanese and Germans weren't the only enemies.

As we pulled into Pearl Harbor, we were greeted by two tugs. They towed and shoved our looming vessel between the battered wrecks of the December 7th American disaster. It was a sobering sensation to witness remains and reminders of America's dastardly defeat.

Many scars from the disastrous debacle were gone, but more than a few still taunted. The *U.S.S. Arizona's* looming superstructure was the most salient reminder of the despicable carnage against our flag and country.

The *Britton* slowed and her progress almost ceased, anchors spilled, splashed and sunk. LCMs pulled alongside and eager Marines trod down the gangway to crowd into them. They ferried us ashore where we were jammed into the familiar olive green trucks and transported to *Eha,* the renowned U.S. Marine Corps Air Station.

Barracks in Hawaii were clean and comfortable. We were issued crisp new khakis and served lovely stateside chow. The grub was better than good and positive feelings pervaded. We basked in comforting stateside showers before hitting the sack. After adjusting to non-rocking land-locked bunks we conked out like dead men.

After morning reveille sounded, we ate our first stateside breakfast. Afterwards, jauntily wearing our newly issued khakis topped by new piss-cutters, Titmus, O'Bannion and I caught a bus into Honolulu.

The city's streets were overflowing with soldiers, sailors and Marines. Most uniformed gapers were recently arrived wide-eyed kids from the mainland.

Bars up and down Hotel Street were crammed with sitting, standing and jostling uniforms. In front of every saloon, lines of drink craving uniformed personnel waited in lengthy lines for customers to vacate. Patrons in each saloon were allowed three watered-down drinks before being hustled out to make room for the next thirsty customer.

Titmus led us to Reno Street where numerous whorehouses had recently prevailed. Because pious religious leaders and holier-than-thou citizens had mustered up sacrosanct outcries, the discredited establishments had been shut down. We had missed the bawdy and comforting harlotry by a few weeks.

"Just our fuckin' luck!" I moaned.

Titmus voiced his philosophical slant. "Whore houses are necessary; they give a guy the chance to relieve the pressure on his spine."

On the jammed bus to Waikiki, uniformed passengers, indifferent civilians and sanctimonious stuffed shirts ignored each other.

Famed Waikiki Beach was small, congested and unimpressive. A sun-soaked mass of burnt bathers obscured the sand. The pink Royal Hawaiian Hotel looked enticing but lower echelon enlisted personnel were discouraged from entering. Oh, if a lowly seaman or private was able to flash an impressive wad, he would be tolerated. A three striped noncom or petty officer displaying a roll of greenbacks would be indulged, sort of.

"What we got to lose?" said O'Bannion, "let's go in and order a drink.

"Officers' country," admonished Titmus.

"They won't take our money?"

"We won't get past the door," assured Titmus.

We disconsolately moved to a side street until we espied a scruffy little bar, our kind of hangout. The unkempt joint was eight blocks from the beach. Depressed by our low social status we swilled beer after beer. Other low level enlistees wandered in and out. Not a single female graced the establishment, not even an unattractive one.

By midnight we were low on funds and started back. As we shuffled down busy Hotel Street we came across a tattoo shop. A sailor was paying for a blue anchor perforated on his bicep. Titmus took his vacated place. The bored tattoo artist carefully inscribed *"Millie"* beneath his faded globe and anchor.

O'Bannion opted for the illustrated head of an English bulldog topped with a World War One helmet. *U.S.M.C.* was inscribed beneath. I was hesitant but they goaded me into getting a grass-skirted hulu dancer with an etched *U.S. Marines* on my forearm. After finishing his artistic renditions the tattooist smeared Vaseline on his creations. We paid, absorbed his post tattoo instructions and departed.

Ethnic Hawaiian blends produced enchanting feminine lovelies. Polynesian, Chinese, Korean, Japanese, and Pilipino or Portuguese mixtures were gorgeous. We'd spy gorgeous young things on and off the base, but for us they were untouchable. Viewing them from a respectable distance was all we could do.

Weeks passed and we were finally summoned to join a thousand passengers boarding the *U.S.S. E.T. Collins,* a charted army transport. The huge vessel bristled with armament and had many decks. Most people aboard were uniformed personnel.

The troop ship was destined to dock in San Francisco. As she pulled away from majestic Pearl Harbor, I didn't catch one regretful comment regarding our departure.

Soldiers, sailors, coastguardsmen, construction workers, Marines and sixty discharged prostitutes were among those heading home. Chipping paint, sweeping, swabbing, cleaning the head, endless chow lines, and guard duty took up the civilian crew's time.

O'Bannion fell in love, sort of. We spotted him on his twelve-to-four passageway watch conversing with a prostitute. He informed us that he was more than somewhat interested in the pleasant looking whore. "She's in her late twenties and really a nice girl."

"So?"

"Okay, she told me she's working in the same cathouse for three years."

"So?"

"She averaged twenty to thirty tricks six days a week."

"That's a lot of fucking!" I gasped.

"Marines, swabbies, dogfaces doled out five bucks a crack. She got to keep three and they never stopped coming."

"Cheez!"

"She paid rent but not much. She didn't need a lot of clothes and food expenses were reasonable. She confided to me that she got over twenty-thousand smackeroos in the bank."

"She's still a whore."

"Not any more! She's got plenty of money now. She plans to settle in some little town in Iowa or Nebraska. You know, one of them small hick places where nobody knows her. She'll marry a respectable guy with a house and small business. After that they'll have a slew of kids."

"What if a former customer passes through?" I queried.

"A thousand to one shot," assured O'Bannion. "Besides, who remembers what a whore looks like?"

"You never know!"

"Haven't you heard?"

"Heard what!"

"Whores make the best wives!"

"Who spread that bullshit, other whores!"

"You're so damn righteous! They've been around. They've seen and done it all. By the time they meet a guy they really like, they're ready to put that sordid stuff behind and settle down."

"You wouldn't worry?" I said.

"Because she's an ex-whore?"

"Right."

"Not more or less than if she was a phony goody-good dame."

"O'Bannion, you're out of your mind."

"Not so fast! If she became a Catholic it would change her. In that case I'd hitch up with her," said O'Bannion as an impudent grin stretched across his face.

I shrugged. He talked an innovative plot and I tried to imagine him making headway toward his speculative future. For two more days during his twelve-to-four watch, O'Bannion conversed with the former whore, but failed to elicit either a commitment or address. She accepted his scrawled address but he suspected that she might deep-six it.

As we neared San Francisco the weather turned damp, cold and uncomfortable. Someone asserted that our thinned tropical blood was reacting to the drop in temperature. Anyway, the brisk weather change prompted the whores to stay in their staterooms. Most of us desisted from roaming the ship unless compelled by duty.

Six long days after leaving Hawaii, San Francisco's majestic Golden Gate Bridge loomed. Austere Alcatraz, half-hidden by a thick mist caught our attention as we sailed through San Francisco's expansive bay.

Longshoremen secured our ship as a navy band blasted a rousing martial musical welcome. We disembarked and filed onto trucks. We almost, not quite, felt like returning heroes as we sped toward Treasure Island.

In the well-worn barracks we stowed our sparse gear. After squaring away our recently acquired khakis, we were paid in cash and permitted to go ashore.

Drinking establishments on Market Street welcomed us. Most of us were too excited and tense to get in trouble, so everyone made it back to the barracks in time.

None wanted to chance missing our ride to San Diego, our next destination. We were scheduled to be on our way to that familiar town in the morning.

After revile blew and breakfast was consumed, two civilians followed by a colonel and attaché walked up and down our ranks scrutinizing us. The disgruntled civilians scrutinized each nervous Marine before shaking their heads.

We were finally ordered to board trucks and were transported to the train depot. Later it was learned that rape and robbery had been committed by two males attired in Marine khaki. The perpetrators were never caught. They could have come from another ship or camp.

Fifteen hours of restless train riding were endured before we arrived in San Diego. We disembarked from the train and mounted trucks for our final ride to Miramar.

Miramar was the familiar orderly camp we had left fifteen months ago. Barracks were reserved for us. Haircuts and physicals came next. Afterwards we showered and slept.

In the morning we were issued brand new greens and accessories. We became temporary transients destined to be transferred to other facilities. We were informed that orders regarding our next destination would be forthcoming. However, first on the agenda was a thirty-day furlough, that's all we were interested in.

Aware that our first official stateside liberty was in the offing, Titmus, O'Bannion and I, along with others, ironed field scarves, khaki shirts and our spanking new greens. We polished belt buckles and spit-shined our new cordovan shoes.

Our hats were jauntily cocked as we passed through the guarded gate on our way to town. O'Bannion and I were sort of self-conscious about wearing our 4th Marine Air Wing patches but Titmus was indifferent. It was he who had prodded us into having them stitched on in the first place. "Wear it like the Fourth Marine Air wing is the best damn outfit in the Corps. Nobody gives a shit, anyway."

Titmus planned to surprise Millie and insisted that O'Bannion and I come along. We shared a bit of his tenseness, after all, he was our buddy and mentor. The bus quickly reached North San Diego and the three of us stepped off. We walked two blocks and turned into a quiet side street lined with pepper trees. Titmus scrutinized the address on a wrinkled envelope. "She's gonna be surprised."

"I'll bet," agreed O'Bannion.

"Maybe you should have phoned," I suggested.

"Nah," muttered Titmus.

"You got no romance in you," scowled O'Bannion

"You know a lot about romance!" I snapped.

"You couldn't get laid in a whore house!" shouted O'Bannion.

"Knock off the stupid bullshit!" growled Titmus. We went silent.

"What's the address?" said O'Bannion.

"Eight One Three Six," read Titmus.

"Across the street," I said.

"That's it!" said Titmus and pointed to a scrawled address on the mailbox in front of a modest tract house.

A weathered First Class Bos'n's Mate facing the door was checking his address book. The guy was in his middle thirties. Two hash marks and a row of ribbons disclosed that he'd been around.

Short and wide with a bent nose below scarred eyebrows announced that the guy had been on the receiving end of more than a few knuckles. He strode toward the white trimmed door.

Titmus hailed him. "Hey, where you going!"

The sailor checked his little black book. "Here, Mac, I got this address memorized."

Titmus unfolded his envelope. "My fiancée lives here."

The bos'n's mate looked wary. "Oh, yeah, mine does too."

Titmus shuffled. "Not here, Boats!"

"Millie?"

Titmus stuttered. "Millie!"

The bos'n's lip curled. A line from a Robert Service ballad came to me. *"There wasn't a breath in that land of death."*

"She and me are engaged," rasped Titmus with meaningful inflection.

"You're full of shit!" wheezed the bos'n and waved a letter inches from Titmus' nose.

Titmus recognized the scrawl. "Get that out of my face and make way while you still can," snarled Titmus.

"Hear this, Jarhead! I don't want to mess up Millie's yard so get your ass back to your bar or I'll...." Titmus threw an overhand right that barely missed. They were toe to toe until the sailor began boxing. Titmus continued to lunge forward while the swabbie jabbed and moved away.

They were about to get serious when a screeching '39 green Nash convertible pulled to a stop and a female driver stumbled out hollering, "Earl!" Before he could react she screeched, "Timothy!" Both combatants ceased sparring.

She darted to Titmus and wrapped her arms about him and planted a kiss. Before he could react she turned and shouted, "Timothy!" and proceeded to envelop and smooch the bos'n. "My two favorite people! What a lovely surprise! Didn't know you knew each other. In fact I thought one or both of you were dead."

The lady carried a few extra pounds but had nice legs. Before further ado a stubby soldier wearing thick spectacles emerged from the other side of the car. As he strutted, proud as a peacock, toward our perplexed group he seemed a touch uneasy.

"Meet Hilton. Hilton, dear, here they are, my two best friends, Earl Titmus and Timmy Drombowski. I've told him all about you two."

"Yes," said Hilton, "Millie talks quite a bit about you two."

"Watherbee, my husband."

"Nice to make your acquaintance," mumbled Drombowski.

"Likewise," said Titmus. Both suitors were disquieted and their hands limp as Hilton heartily shook them.

"And your friends," pouted Millie.

"Howdy," I said.

"Nice to meetcha," said O'Bannion.

Only Millie smiled. "Well, come on in the house and toast the launching of our happy union."

"Like to, but I gotta get back to the ship. There's a guy covering for me and I swore I'd relieve him on time," stuttered Drombowski.

"Aww," said Millie.

"We're due back too," sighed Titmus. "I'll keep in touch, you can bet on that."

"Do more than that. We're gonna have a big bash. I expect both of you to be there," scolded Millie.

"We sure do," stammered Watherbee.

Drombowski seemed bewildered as he departed sporting a mirthless grin. We trailed Titmus as he split in the opposite direction. We made no comments as Titmus hailed a cab and we piled in. "Second and Broadway!" said Titmus.

Titmus was really down and didn't say a word until after I paid the fare.

"Jesus!"

"Dames are hard to figure," said O'Bannion thinking he was uttering a deep philosophical axiom. Titmus gave him an intimidating look. I kept quiet.

We made way down crowded Broadway. In spite of Titmus' short confrontation, his cordovan shoes still gleamed and buckle glistened. His hashmarks and the fruit salad on his chest looked imposing. A small bruise did mar his face but didn't distract from his squared away appearance.

In a town where uniform recognition, good or bad wasn't easy to come by, Titmus was a conspicuous figure among Marine fore and aft caps and bobbing sailor hats.

As we worked our way through the crowd on Third Street, Titmus' grim countenance was contagious. A corporal wearing the Third Division patch strode by. His pink face and hashmarkless sleeve caught Titmus' scornful glance. "The Old Corps is shot to hell."

We shouldered our way through a mob of swabjockies carousing in Patrick's Bar and plopped into a corner booth occupied by two sailors. Titmus sat across from them while O'Bannion and I slid in alongside. Short haircuts and shiny blue uniforms announced the swabbies as recently out of boot camp. They were engrossed with each other.

A colored foursome played lively jazz numbers while their lithesome vocalist twisted and twirled as she bellowed out a sad song. Titmus ordered a shot with a beer chaser from the grumpy waitress. O'Bannion and I settled for San Diego's notorious ABC Beer.

The congested mob generated body heat causing rivulets of gleaming sweat to pour from gyrating dancers. One of the fresh-faced sailors spotted the ribbons on Titmus. "You been around, Mate."

Titmus grimaced.

"I almost joined the Marines," said the other.

"Be glad you didn't," grunted Titmus.

Another disenchanted waitress elbowed in. "A round of straight shots, beer chasers and include these two." He pointed at the swabbies and slipped her four dollars. "Don't take long." She didn't.

Titmus raised his glass, "To the bygone Fourth, a first class fighting regiment." We raised glasses and sipped while he downed his shot. One of the sailors ordered a round. We tried to keep up with Titmus.

One swabbie reached under his jumper and came up with a pint of bourbon. Five of us sampled and coughed. Smoke got thicker and noises louder. It didn't take long for us to get wasted, even drunk Titmus was slurring. He didn't expound but we knew he was mulling about Millie.

A gunner's mate steered by a drunken woman old enough to be his grandmother lurched against our table. O'Bannion shoved him into the crowd.

"You think I'll tell my kids how I fought the war? Pickin' up coconut fronds and digging shithouses! That's if I ever have kids," said O'Bannion.

"Well, I'll skip the part about swabbing decks, cleaning heads and chipping paint," I said.

"At least you can tell them you wasn't a chickenshit officer or ear-banging noncom."

"Forget Millie." advised O'Bannion.

"I will."

"I wish I had a girl,' I said, "even an ex-girl would be okay."

"Hah!" spat Titmus.

"I hate the navy!" echoed one of the sailors.

"Let's drink to that!" said the other.

"The Corps is even more chickenshit!" A shadow of a threat was reflected in Titmus' sudden proclamation.

The sailor caught the inflection and tried to appease. "I wouldn't want to be a jarhead."

"What'd you say?" Titmus leaned forward and squinted.

"I was agreeing with you," said the sailor.

"Nobody bad mouths the Corps except Marines," growled Titmus.

"I didn't mean nothin'," whined the bewildered sailor.

His buddy fired an overhand right that caught Titmus on the forehead. O'Bannion and the sailor grappled. Contentious customers around them commenced flailing. Ladies entered the fray scratching and screaming. It was too crowded to effectively punch or pummel.

Club wielding shore patrolmen had been standing by outside to quell the establishment's customary outbursts. They charged into Patrick's swinging wildly. Reinforcements quickly arrived to relentlessly batter stubborn skulls, ours included. Numerous patrons, we three among them, were subdued.

We were shoved into a paddy wagon and shoulder to shoulder alongside three swabbies, the animosity tendencies were stifled. Our forced stances kept us from falling as we sped toward the San Diego City Jail.

We were crudely pulled from the wagon and shoved in front of a stern gray-haired sergeant's desk. After scrutinizing each I.D. the weathered guy, possible an ex-jarhead, lamented, "The old Corps is shot to hell."

We were shoved into a huge holding cell crammed with wallowing, wretching uniformed prisoners. All of them were guilty of varied misdeeds.

CHAPTER FORTY-TWO

In the morning my head pained and I had trouble focusing. I lifted up on elbows and squinted around. The damp, crowded cell reeked of piss, puke and perspiration. Titmus sat with one eye half closed and his spine sloped against the wall. A streak of dried blood crossed his cheek and he looked beat. Next to him slumped O'Bannion looking much worse.

The cell door swung open and two raggedy-assed civilian trustees shuffled in, one black the other white. A portly guard stood by while they wheeled in two trays laden with plates of lumpy oatmeal. "Come get your San Diego jailhouse feast, soldiers!" growled the white guy as he set trays on the deck.

The black guy grinned and shook his head as a middle-aged wino in dirty garb snatched a tray and commenced gobbling. Not one uniformed prisoner touched the unsavory looking concoctions.

Fifteen minutes later the guard snarled, "Last chance to chow down!" Since there weren't any takers, the trustees carted away the weird looking cuisine.

We sat among our fellow moping inmates who continued to sound off about unjustified imprisonments. Some blamed Marines, some blamed swabjockeys, some blamed the police and others blamed all three. After the griping sessions simmered, wards tried to nap, but groans, moans and belching blasts kept most of us awake.

The two trustees returned at noon wheeling in trays loaded with spam and stale bread. Other than the beat-up bum, no one was even slightly interested.

Representatives from various military outfits periodically arrived to bail out miscreants and escort them back to ships and bases. Our names were finally called and we three were led from the cell to face stern-faced Technical Sergeant Murphy from Camp Miramar.

"Morning, Sarge," said Titmus.

Murphy flourished a wad of papers an inch under Titmus' nose. "You fuck-ups are charged with drunk, disorderly, inciting a riot and resisting arrest. There's enough shit listed here to hang the three of you."

"We were defending the honor of the Corps," said Titmus.

"Yeah!" said the sergeant. "I've heard that bullshit before!"

It might have been my imagination but his tone sounded a touch supportive.

On the ride back to Miramar I worried as O'Bannion asked, "Can this affect our furlough?"

Murphy grunted, "The captain ain't going to blow a chance to get rid of you three."

"They wouldn't cancel our leave?" I whispered.

"Hell no!" said O'Bannion sounding less than assured.

"They can do anything they damn please to do!" snapped Murphy.

"I got to quit hanging with you trouble-making boots!" grunted Titmus.

The sentry at the gate recognized Murphy and waved us through. We screeched to a stop in front of our barracks. "Clean up! And look presentable, you got office hours before the old man."

"Shit!" said Titmus.

"Prayin' and a little earbanging won't hurt," said Murphy. "The captain ain't in a good mood."

News regarding the melee in Patrick's had preceded us and we were bombarded. "Did the Marines do alright?"

"Heard some SPs got flattened?"

"A few!"

"How many did it take to subdue Titmus?"

"Who had time to count."

"Wow!"

"We held our own," I boasted.

"We didn't embarrass ourselves," assured Titmus.

The three of us were hung over. Still, bullshitting about our exploit invigorated us a bit, that is, until Murphy ordered us to follow him.

He led us to the captain's office and glowered while we four stood rigidly in front of Captain Schmidt's desk. Schmidt was in charge of transient troops. His Prussian haircut and weathered face looked far from hospitable. The old mustang was in his sixties. He had earned his commission during the banana campaigns. When the war broke out he had been called back. At one time, he probably had been a fuck-up too. Anyway, he wasn't an empathetic guy.

"You fuck-ups got something to say for yourselves?"

He deemed some interest as Titmus related his version of our Patrick's encounter. After Titmus' colorful rendition he ranted a bit about the stigma to the Corps when disorderly drunken Marines resisted arrest and destroyed property. However, he seemed somewhat ameliorated when Titmus invoked, "We had little choice, sir, the Corps honor was at stake, sir."

"You got more bullshit to snow me with?"

"No, sir!" said Titmus.

"Them swabbies were bum-rapping Marines," added O'Bannion.

"That they were, sir," added Titmus.

I tried to look sincere as I nodded assent.

Stifling a twisted grin Captain Schmidt grunted, "This episode is gonna cost each of you a stripe."

"Aye, aye, sir!" we chorused hoping he wouldn't add a cash or furlough cancellation penalty.

"Dismissed!"

We about-faced and marched out with Murphy close behind. As we shuffled away, "Lucky bullshitters," muttered Murphy.

We felt lucky. After all, we could have gotten brig time, fines, restriction, furlough cancellation or more.

"That Nazi looking mustang looks like a prick but he ain't so bad after all," grunted Titmus. We nodded in agreement.

Admiration and touches of envy were evident in our barracks. Mates called us the miracle kiss-ass Marines. O'Bannion and I sighed with relief but Titmus stayed in a dour mood. "Cheer up, Earl, you still got one stripe," said O'Bannion.

"You'll get the other one back," I added.

"I don't give a shit about stripes. As soon as this fuckin' war is over, I'm getting out of this fucked-up outfit."

A skivvie-clad listener with a boot haircut pulled a half-pint of Three Feathers from his seabag. "Let's drink to that."

He swigged and handed it to Titmus who uprighted the bottle and passed it on. Three Feathers was far from mellow but the host, O'Bannion and I were the only imbibers who coughed.

The bottle host boasted that he was SS (selective service). We three weren't enamored with Marine Corps draftees. After all, hadn't a crusty old gunny on Guadalcanal silenced bitching Marines by roaring, "Button your yaps, nobody forced you fleabags to become Marines!"

As the war progressed Marine ranks continued to be depleted. Most eighteen- year-old in the Corps had volunteered to become Marines. Others, against their wishes, were compelled to join.

Since we were well aware that many draftees had been forced to become Marines, we didn't chide this guy. Then again, it was his bottle.

Before we commenced bitching, several boisterous characters recently out of boot camp drifted in. A sinewy character with a Philippine monkey perched on his shoulder led them. The monkey's owner was three sheets to the wind as were his mates. They toted two half full bottles of booze which they charitably passed around. They were quickly emptied.

The monkey suddenly leaped from his master's shoulder and grasped to an overhead beam. He swung from one crossed buttress to another. The inebriated audience applauded.

Titmus warbled an off–tune rendition of our theme song.

Come all you gents in Ground Defense
Take shovel and pick in hand
Come get a healthy grip on them
And we'll dig into the sand.

After choruses were sung, others lustily joined in. The revelry exhausted me and I passed out.

When aroused at dawn by the reveille's shocking blare I felt far from chipper as I staggered outside. In the blazing sun we formed two shaky ranks and strove to look alive.

Captain Schmidt stood stolidly before us as Sergeant Murphy bruskly called names and handed out furlough orders. We were warned not to bring dishonor on the Corps by acting like drunken hooligans during our furlough. Several more stern admonitions were issued by the captain before we were dismissed.

With pockets full of cash, Titmus, O'Bannion, and I shouldered our gear and stomped out through the base gate.

We three piled into the next cab. Titmus directed the driver to take us to the depot. Titmus' train to Wyoming was due to depart in two hours. O'Bannion was heading for Boston on a train due to pull out thirty minutes later. My transportation to Los Angeles would leave fifteen minutes after O'Bannion's departure.

"Time for one farewell drink!" sighed Titmus. We checked our seabags at the depot and followed him into a nearby saloon. If Titmus was lost in the Gobi Desert he'd find a tavern. The emaciated old barkeep placed three schooners before us. O'Bannion raised his glass. "To Bones Donigal, that odd bastard, hope he's happy."

We clinked glasses and drank. "One for Arnie," I toasted. We gulped another.

"And one for Cassidy!" toasted O'Bannion.

"He deserted us," I said.

"Smart guy," said Titmus.

I couldn't argue with that.

"Anyhow, let's not forget Jacob Cruz, he was one helluva Marine," said Titmus.

We drank. "Someday I'm going back to see Tulipa and my little boy." I said. Neither Titmus nor O'Bannion commented but they drank anyway.

Titmus stood. "I can't stay here jawin' with you people, I gotta catch a train."

"Hold on!" said O'Bannion. "Let's down one more for good ole' Taps."

"For sure!" I seconded.

O'Bannion splurged for that last round and we escorted Titmus to his railroad car.

"See you sometime," Titmus burped and stepped onto the platform. I focused on the wisp of red thread remaining where his stripe used to be.

Before boarding he apprised the two of us. "For half-assed Marines you two ain't bad." Then he shuffled into the car and slumped by a window. As the train rumbled off we waved. I'm not sure he saw us because he didn't gesture back.

"O'Bannion, did Titmus compliment us?"

He didn't have a chance to answer because at that moment a sweet looking chick sashayed by. "See that?" he sighed.

"Did I!"

O'Bannon stared wistfully at her before saying, "Farewell drink?"

"One won't hurt," I sighed and we staggered back to the saloon.